Delectable Syn

L J Carroll

This is for my husband who has pushed me to create filthy romance stories and who was always with me every step of the way.

Contents

Delectable Syn

His torment is hidden behind a smoldering, dimpled smile.

His favourite words *"You've been a good little whore."* rasped out making them want more.

His hotel room confesses a multitude of sins.

His entire body screams one time only.

Blake Synclair is everything every woman wants without ever knowing the real him.

Ava Asherton is the curvy girl that has been blinded by hero worship and over the last nine years her feelings have changed, morphed into love.

A love that Blake doesn't want or deserve.

It's just a shame that he wants to drown in her innocence and taste her purity making it impossible to stay away from the one girl he shouldn't be pursuing.

The one girl that could shatter his carefully constructed life.

His best friend's little sister.

Prologue

The harsh breath whooshed out a moment before the crystal cut glass tumbler pressed against his sinful lips. The amber liquid flowing into his mouth, the woodsy, smokey taste pouring over his tongue and the burn delicious as it slithered down his throat.

It was the time of night he craved.

His dark gaze watched the woman before him as she inched the deep purple lace panties back up over her slender hips. He could still see her juices gathered on her thighs. His eyes tracked further still, over the flatness of her stomach, red welts blooming against the fake tanned skin. Her fake tits with a slight hint of a bruise forming from his bite. Her neck held the imprint of his fingers. It was a beautiful sight.

All the red marks inflicted by him. His lips twitched into a smirk.

An image of her blonde hair wrapped around his fist as he'd pulled hard, her cherry red lips sealed around his cock as he'd used her hair as leverage for the brutal thrusts into her throat. Sounds she'd made. Her gagging and choking sounds caused a deep, low chuckle to escape his lips. Those sounds would be etched in his memory until next time.

Her blue eyes timidly looked at him and a flash of hurt skittered across her face, her shaking hand delicately touching her abused throat. He caught the wince of pain as he took another swallow of his whiskey.

"So, Blake." her voice was hoarse. He closed his eyes briefly as his nostrils flared. He knew what was coming. It was always the same. "When will…" he held a hand up to silence her.

"Gina -" he started and another flash of hurt reached her eyes.

"Georgia." she corrected, clasping her purple lace bra in place.

"Whatever!" he snapped. "You've been a good little whore," he smirked as she flinched at him, calling her a *whore*. "But it's a one time thing." he shrugged indifferently. "We won't be seeing each other again." he watched her bottom lip quiver and another low chuckle escaped.

"Really?" her arms wrapped around her waist, making her ribcage more prominent. He could see every rib indent against her flesh, making his lips twist into a look of disgust. "After I let you…" her voice trailed off as she rubbed against her sore throat.

"One. Time. Only." his words were slow as his hand gripped tightly against the glass tumbler, his anger flaring. "Out!" he barked the last word, which had her jumping and flinching all at once.

Blake watched her gather the little black dress, which left

nothing to the imagination, her black stiletto heels and hurried out of the hotel room. The soft click of the door closing had his shoulders softening ever so slightly, his fingers pinching the bridge of his nose and his eyes closed.

He was alone, and now the true torture began. The guilt that always accompanied him in these early hours of the morning infected his veins, no matter how many hours he'd spent elbows deep in his sadist cocoon.

His pulse spiked as images of *her* long dark waves blowing in the evening breeze, *her* sparkling green eyes filled with love and adoration, *her* pouting lips curved into a shy smile. He squeezed his eyes shut, but that only intensified the images of his beautiful woman. The woman who trusted him loved him.

"What have I done?" he whispered, tipping the whiskey down his throat. The taste is now bitter on his tongue. Images of *her* laughing, wrapping *her* arms around him, kissing him, screaming his name all flashed through his mind in quick succession. "Fuck!" he roared, the glass tumbler shattered against the opposite wall.

He was overcome by the pain of the images of *her,* his anger replaced by such pain, that he doubled over. Dragging heavy breaths through his nose and hissing them out through his gritted teeth. His heart pounding against his sternum, pain lacerating his chest. His shoulders tense as red hot pain seared across his back, sweat slicking over his skin.

He tried concentrating on breathing deeply.

One breath.

Two breaths.

Three breaths.

Four breaths.

Five breaths.

Six breaths.

Seven breaths.

Eight breaths.

Nine breaths.

Ten breaths.

The pain slowly subsided. His heart beats slowed back to a normal rhythm. His shoulders slumped, leaving him feeling deflated and worn out. Stumbling across the room on numb legs, his hand catching against the chair to steady his balance before he quickly dressed.

Pushing his hair from his forehead, smoothing the light blue dress shirt down the hard planes of his chest, buttoning the dress pants before stuffing his feet into the deep brown leather brogue shoes. His shaking fingers knotting the laces before grabbing his phone, car keys and wallet.

Taking one look in the large mirror. His eyes were almost black, his dark hair was back into his usual style, his clothes were like his armour, and his posture was that of his privileged upbringing. His spine was rigid, his head held high and his hands shoved into his pockets until the tremors left. He stared long and hard at himself until the feeling of control washed over him.

His dark eyes scanning the mess of the hotel room, making him shake his head once before yanking the door open. Making a mental note to let the concierge know he'd smashed the glass and a painting and the room was in absolute chaos. His father owned the hotel, and that room was permanently reserved for Blake, so he shouldn't be overly bothered. But the moment his madness ended, he knew the staff deserved to know what they were walking into. He didn't want someone hurting themselves on the glass he'd left littered across the floor.

His pure focus as he stepped into the waiting elevator was to get the fuck out of here as quickly as possible. Get back home where he belonged with *her.*

But he knew that by next weekend he would be doing it all again. With the same type of woman, the same kind of sex, the same images in his fucking head, the same guilt and the same breathing techniques. His weekend affairs had slowly spun out of control and there was nothing he could do about it except hold on for the ride.

Chapter One

Ava Asherton curled up on the sofa, her legs tucked beneath her, ready to watch her favourite movie, 365 Days, which was buffering on the screen. It was her typical Friday night escape. A night where she could unwind from the week of work and a night she usually had the house to herself.

The house she had always called home, she shared with James, her brother, who was almost twelve years older than her. She was grateful that after his divorce he'd moved back home, was grateful that he was a constant presence in the home since they'd lost their parents. But Friday nights were usually the night when he went out drinking with his best friend, and tonight should be no different. Except James hadn't dressed for a night out, opting for sweatpants and a t-shirt; this gave her pause. A pause because she knew that James and his best friend would be at the house.

The best friend she was hopelessly in love with.

The best friend that always ruffled her hair and called her *squirt.*

Closing her eyes as she dragged a breath in, she wondered if she had time to change out of her worn pyjamas, put a little make-up on and pull her hair down before *he* arrived. The decision, Ava stood pulling the pale green t-shirt over her rounded stomach, trying to stretch it to make it hang looser, but as she took one tentative step towards the hallway, she heard the front door open.

"James!" *he* shouted, closing the door behind him. Ava stood stock still, her pulse quickening and her palms becoming clammy as she watched his lips pull into a smile that always made her weak in the knees. It lit up his entire face, transforming the sharp, chiselled features into something softer. His rich dark chocolate eyes sparkled in the light as he drew a deep breath in.

"Kitchen!" the booming voice echoed around the foyer, making Ava jump slightly.

Ava stood silently just outside of the kitchen, trying to hide behind the door frame as she listened. Something she always did when *he* was around. Something she couldn't stop herself even if she tried, and it was something that made her feel like a child. Despite being almost twenty-one. Why, because Blake Synclair had captured her heart the day he'd folded his muscular arms around her, rocking her as he whispered comforting words in her ear as she'd been told her parents weren't coming home. She remembered the feel of his hard body against hers, the warm scent of fresh, zesty, bergamot and spicy pepper wrapping around her, making her feel safe, the brush of his lips against her forehead, the feel of his thumbs wiping her tears away.

That had been eight, almost nine years ago. Sometimes when she looks at him with his cold, indifferent mask firmly in place, she wondered if she imagined the entire exchange. Wondered if in her time of grief, when she'd shattered into a million pieces that she'd conjured a nice memory to make it bearable.

"Nah." James shook his head as he straightened, passing a bottle of beer to him. "Fights about to start," he continued, flicking his eyes to the screen in the kitchen. Blake tilted his head to the side as he watched James sit at the dining table.

"Aren't we going into the living room?" Blake's voice was low, controlled as he folded himself in the seat next to him.

"Nah, Ava's watching a movie." James rolled his eyes. "You know how she gets." he smiled as he shook his head.

"And how do I get?" Ava whispered, her heart galloping in her chest as Blake turned towards her.

She watched as his eyes trailed over the wide flare of her hips, the rounded breasts straining against the tight pale green t-shirt, over the slender column of her throat and further still over her rounded cheeks, stopping on her green eyes. Ava's stomach roiled as she felt every inch of his gaze over her.

She could almost hear his thoughts.

Why is she so fat?

Doesn't she know how to exercise?

Bile rose in her throat and tears stung her eyes as she tried pulling on the t-shirt, tried stretching it away from her fat body. She watched his eyebrows furrow slightly and her cheeks turned crimson.

"Weepy, Squirt." James smiled at Ava. She pulled a breath in and squeezed her eyes closed against the thoughts in her head before rolling her eyes at the nickname she hated. "Fuck, dude." James made a gagging sound as Blake cut his eyes to his best friend. "Did you douse yourself in cheap perfume?" James's hand wafting in front of his face as if trying to dislodge the smell.

"Just fucked it." Blake smirked; James shook his head sadly, taking a swig of beer. She watched him as he turned back to her, not missing the ugly twist of her pouty lips, nor did he miss the slight shake of her hands still tugging on the t-shirt. Raising one eyebrow at Ava. "Something you want, Squirt?" he watched with a smirk as her face burned a deeper shade of crimson, watched her tongue slide across her lips before she turned on her heel.

She felt his eyes on her fat ass as she left the kitchen. Her thick thighs rubbing slightly in the boy shorts she wore, and she'd never been so embarrassed.

Ava's stomach lurched as she folded herself onto the sofa, tugging the t-shirt over her stomach. Her pulse thrumming as she looked back at the movie. His deep voice ringing in her ears, his question simple but had a multitude of answers which in Ava's head all revolved around him. The bitter laugh that escaped her parted lips made her wince. Who was she kidding? She was nothing like the women he dated. The women he dated always made her feel as fat and ugly as she was with their snide comments that only deflated her more, only made her want to eat more, and only made her want to crumble into a mass of tears.

I bet she eats chocolate and cakes all day.

No wonder she's never had a boyfriend.

She's a virgin because who the fuck would want to fuck that?

The ugly voices in her head spewed their opinions until bile rose in her throat and tears blurred her vision. She hated the way she looked and hated that no matter how much she dieted, her weight never changed. She wished she was more like the women Blake dated, the tall, skinny as fuck blondes he constantly paraded around with. Maybe if she could lose a few stone, he might just look at her a little different, might think of her more than James's chubby sister. Swiping angrily at the tears off of her cheeks and letting out a long sigh.

"You see, weepy." James's voice startled her. Her fingers quickly tugging on the t-shirt as she saw Blake with his muscular arms crossed over his well-defined chest. His dark eyes watching her. "We're going out for last orders." James continued, turning on his heel and grabbing the set of house keys.

She watched Blake glance at the television, watched him raise one eyebrow before turning back to her. She didn't need to look at the screen to know the main character was getting a blowjob. A rather forceful one which turned her on at the sheer thought of someone being a little rough with her. His face betrayed his unspoken opinion, making her face burn hotter and brighter than the sun.

You're too young to be watching this movie.

"Night Ava." Blake's deep voice washed over her in a delicate shiver, raising goosebumps along her exposed skin.

"Night." she whispered, trying to hide the breathlessness which always takes over whenever he's around. She quickly averted her gaze as she saw his lips twitch into a smirk that always made her pussy clench.

Saturday morning had dawned and whilst Ava preferred to stay in bed until mid-morning, she knew that Blake had stayed the night. She'd heard their riotous laughter boom around the house in the early hours of the morning and she'd found it difficult to go back to sleep. It wasn't often that Blake stayed at their home, but when he did, it sent Ava into a tailspin. Dirty thoughts pulsed through her mind and her anxiety flared. She knew her lust for Blake was pointless, but she couldn't control herself. That one memory flashing through her mind at seeing him in a different light. That one memory that made him seem like he cared about her. And that one memory she cherished– even if she wasn't certain if it was real or a figment of her imagination.

Steam filled the bathroom, along with the promised heat of the shower. When the warm water hit her bare back, she felt her shoulders relax, and the water eased the tension from her. But of course, she knew the main reason she was so tense. The thought of seeing him this morning made her heart skip a beat, and she couldn't help the fantasy that bubbled to the surface. *His dark eyes staring into hers, his calloused fingers brushing against her throat, his muscular arms flexing with every touch.*

Her stomach clenched, and her nipples hardened at the mental picture. *The scent of him, fresh, zesty bergamot and spicy pepper that wrapped around her.* Her fingers trailed over the soft flesh of her stomach. *His lips twitching into his sexy smirk as he inched closer.* Her hand continued through the slight curls between her thighs. *His lips were warm and soft, capturing hers in a searing kiss.* She circled once over her engorged clit. *The heat of his body, the light touches trailing down her throat, over her pulse.* Sighing aloud, Ava's fingers crept lower, parting her folds. *The dark brooding eyes watching as she sunk to her knees.* She pumped two fingers into her tight pussy, careful not to break her hyman. *Ava's lips wrapping around his cock, his hands gripping her head.* Her fingers moved faster, the heel of her hand bumping the throbbing bundle of nerves. *Breath hitching as he fucks her mouth relentlessly.* Her fingers were a blur as she moved back to circling her clit. Heat built quickly and furiously as her breathing quickened into soft pants, her thighs shaking and core clenching.

"Oh god, *Blake*." Ava moaned aloud as her climax hit.

"Ava." the husky voice of Blake on the other side of the bathroom door had her almost screaming in shock and her face flaming red.

How long has he been standing outside the door?

Did he hear?

The slight clearing of his throat was audible above the sound of water splashing against the cubicle and her wildly beating heart.

Oh god, he heard!

"Yeah?" her voice was shaking after the quick climax. She squeezed her eyes closed at the breathless quality of her voice. "Fuck!" she hissed to herself as mortification swelled within her.

"Are you going to be long?" he asked and she could just picture that smirk etched onto his face, or was he just as embarrassed as she was? She wasn't certain how she could even face him after this.

"No, almost finished." she called back, tipping her head under the water, hoping the flaming in her face would disappear.

"Thought you already finished." he chuckled from the other side of the door. *Oh, dear god he heard everything!* She scrambled for her shampoo before dolloping a good amount into her shaking hand. "Please don't be long," he continued with that same chuckle as he tapped on the door once to punctuate his words.

The sounds of sizzling bacon filled her ears and the scent of the full English breakfast she was cooking made her mouth water. It was a Saturday morning tradition that she had shared with James since their parents died and as she got older, James let her do the cooking whilst he stayed in bed a little longer. Probably because of his weekly hangover on a Saturday.

She was hoping that Blake wouldn't eat breakfast with them, hoping that he would slip out and go home. She couldn't believe he'd heard her this morning. And Ava could see perfectly in her mind exactly what his face would have looked like. He would have had that signature smirk firmly in place, his dark eyes would have been narrowed slightly and the laugh that would have fallen from his lips as he'd walked away knowing what she'd done and that he'd probably tell the story of the little fat girl with a crush, masturbating to thoughts of him in the shower - it made her feel queasy.

"Smells delicious." Blake commented as she tracked his purposeful strides through the kitchen, grabbing the coffee she'd already made from beneath her lashes. "Feeling better after your shower?" his lips tipped up in a knowing smile. Her pulse stuttering, her breath whooshing out, leaving her breathless and the heat crawling up her neck to settle in her cheeks. She didn't know what to say, didn't know how to answer as she quickly plated the breakfast with shaking hands before sliding the plate across the counter without looking at him.

"Here." Ava whispered as she busied herself with plating her food and leaving James's to warm on the hot plate.

Ava hoped that Blake would let the incident go and hoped that James would quickly join them–this was the first time she ever wanted James to interrupt her time with Blake. And as she sat opposite him at the dining table, her cutlery clanging together in her shaking hands, she knew that it would be just the two of them.

Taking a deep breath as she gathered some food on the fork, she felt his eyes on her, but she couldn't bring herself to meet his gaze. Instead, she settled for shoving the food in her mouth. She loved food, and it was the main reason she was so fat. The pleasure she got from the variety of flavours. She loved the way it made her feel, too. Which didn't help the self loathing once she'd eaten. Since she was a teenager, she had constantly been on a diet that did absolutely nothing; she was constantly trying to avoid food until her stomach cramped painfully, but then she'd give in and gorge on anything and everything.

"Do you always do that?" Blake's deep rumble of a voice startled she snapped her eyes to his. His eyes narrowed, his brows were furrowed and his jaw clenching.

"Er, do what?" Ava's voice was barely a whisper as she held her fork suspended before her. Her heart rate increasing as she saw him grind his teeth together.

"Make those noises." he pointed towards her fork. "When you eat," he continued, eyes boring into hers, which looked darker than normal.

Ava's face flamed even more as the realisation dawned on her. She was making her food noises, the noises she only made when she was enjoying her meal. The noises her mum used to smile at, from across the dining table and the noises her dad used to comment on about it being a good meal. But the way Blake was looking at her made her feel disgusted with herself. Disgusted that the fat pig enjoyed her food, that she moaned. The fat pig who made sex noises when eating. Lowering her eyes to the table as tears stung the back of her eyes.

"N-no," she stuttered the lie out in a whisper. Placing her fork on the side of her plate as her stomach roiled.

"Good." he bit out, taking a sip of coffee as the silence stretched out. "I never said stop eating," he almost growled, the words making her jump. "Just stop with the noises." his tone held no room for argument.

Ava's hands were shaking and her mind was in complete destruction mode as she picked up her cutlery and began eating again. The sounds of metal against pot filled the room before she heard the deep sigh boarding on a groan.

"You're doing it again." Blake complained in a harsh voice, his eyes blazing. It was a look she'd never seen before and she realised that he was mad at her. His knuckles were white against his tawny skin as his fists rested on the table. Tendons protruding on his powerful forearms and the muscle in his jaw was ticking wildly.

"S-sorry," she mumbled as he leaned across the table, his fingers gripping her chin tightly before tipping her head back until their eyes met.

"It's fucking distracting, Ava." he practically growled in her face before he sucked in a lungful of air and let go of her, falling heavily back into his seat. His hand scrubbing down his face and over the dark stubble. "Just stop with the noises, please," he breathed out, collecting his plate and cup and clearing up after himself.

Ava sat with her mouth slightly agape. Her heart hammering at the contact and butterflies stirring in her stomach.

What the hell just happened?

She thought as she watched his perfect, muscular ass clench and release with every step he took away from her, away from the kitchen until she was left in silence.

Chapter Two

All day, Ava couldn't get Blake out of her thoughts. Couldn't stop reliving the moment he gripped her chin, tipping her head back until she looked into his eyes that seemed almost black as his pupils dilated to an alarming size. She didn't understand why he was so angry with her and it had done nothing but make her overthink all day.

Quickly shoving her legs into a pair of form-fitting high waisted jeans, a plain V-neck white t-shirt and her favourite pair of red six-inch heels. She thought the heels made her ass perkier and added a little sway to the generous hips. But she knew nothing could disguise her unflattering figure.

Ava decided to keep the messy bun as the warm summer evening would inevitably make her hair frizzy. Applying a quick coat of mascara and a swipe of pale pink lipstick, she was grabbing her handbag, phone, phone, and keys.

The low thrum of voices in the local pub had her palms sweating ever so slightly as her green eyes scanned the large room for her friends. Praying she wasn't the first one to arrive, it was something she hated with a passion. Sat alone like a pathetic, fat loser.

She saw numerous aged regulars, sat in their usual seats, drinking the usual drinks. A group of construction men still dressed in their dirty work clothes, riotous laughter with pints in hand, and then she saw the flash of red hair. Breathing a sigh of relief, Ava strode across the pub with an air of confidence only her heels would provide until she felt someone watching her. Her steps faltered, her hand squeezed the handle of her handbag until her knuckles were white and a fine sheen of sweat bloomed at the back of her neck. She absolutely hated people staring, could almost hear the whispered words about her weight. A large, warm hand cupped her elbow, making her jump and almost trip over her heels.

"Hey, pretty lady." the slurred words and the scent of stale beer wafting off of one of the dirty construction workers almost made her want to turn and run. His dirty blonde hair, scraggly dirty beard and cold beady blue eyes had her straightening her spine and her heart pounding in her chest.

"Dickhead!" Katie, one of her best friends, shouted above the thrum of voices, her neck craned back as she looked at the dirty man still gripping Ava's elbow. "Yeah, you fuck off and leave my friend alone!" she continued, punctuating each word with a jab of her delicate finger into his chest.

"Would you prefer me to take you home, firecracker?" the drunkenness of his words, getting stronger as he swayed a little on his feet, making him dig his fingers into the bone of Ava's elbow. Without a second thought, Katie reared back her arm and sucker punched him right in the gut.

"No, dickhead!" Katie snarled. Ava couldn't help the small laugh that bubbled from her mouth as she watched him double over, letting her go instantly. "Come on, Nathan's already got the drinks." she continued, grabbing her hand and leading her through the pub as if she hadn't just punched a guy.

"Katie!" Ava exclaimed as she tried to keep up weaving through the tables and people. "I can't believe you did that!" she continued until she saw Nathan narrow his blue eyes and shake his head.

"Don't, it's no use." Nathan chuckled, still shaking his head. "She's already one bottle of wine in and you know how she gets."

"Oh!" Ava's lips were in an o shape as she sat down at the table, plopping her bag beside her. "I see; any reason for that Katie?" Ava raised one eyebrow as she eyed her friend, taking a long sip of the white wine.

"In my defence." Katie raised both of her hands in surrender. "He had it coming." she continued with a shrug of her shoulders.

Neither Nathan nor Ava were surprised at their mutual friend. After all she was the baby of a large family of boys who taught her how to fight from a young age and when she'd had a little too much to drink Katie either picked a fight with a man or a man to fuck and there was no in between.

The conversation turned to each of their working weeks. From how Katie's manager keeps making her work the late shift to Nathan having a crush on the new receptionist and then to Ava, who's finished work for the school summer holidays. Ava glanced at the door opening, her wineglass halfway to her mouth as she saw Blake stride in. The salmon coloured polo shirt and dark wash jeans with his muscular, tanned arms on full display. She couldn't help licking her lips at the delicious sight.

A tall skinny blonde trailing behind him, barely dressed with false eyelashes, lips and tan and Ava would bet her last pound that her hair colour and tits were fake too. Sighing, her shoulders slumping as he placed his arm around her as they waited to be served at the bar.

Gulping the entire contents of her drink before quickly topping it back up, her friends looking at her until they both looked over and saw the same person. She hated when she saw him with other women, hated that he had a particular taste in women–something she could never be and whilst that thought should make her see that nothing would ever happen between them and that she should move on. Ava found that she couldn't quite give up on her hopes.

"Back on his weekly rounds." Nathan chuckled, shaking his head, turning back to Ava, Ava, his hand squeezing her shoulder.

"Seems like it," Ava mumbled, tipping half of the glass of wine down her throat.

"Well," Katie began, clapping her hands together once. "It's not like he'll give her an orgasm." she shouted over the voices. A dull silence surrounded them for the longest time. Both Katie and Nathan knew of Ava's feelings for Blake. Katie was a great distraction–*sometimes*–when it came to Blake flaunting a date.

"Oh god!" Ava groaned as she downed the entire glass of wine. In her peripheral vision she saw Blake's head snap towards them and it wasn't a surprise; after all, Katie wasn't being quiet at all. Half of the pub heard her.

"What, it's true!" Katie was a little indignant. "There's more meat on a Greyhound than on *that*." she actually fucking pointed at the leggy blonde. "No man can find that comfortable." Katie turned her eyes to Nathan, who held his hands up.

"Don't get me involved." he shook his head.

"Don't tell me you find that attractive?" Katie shouted, tipping the rest of her wine down her throat.

"Why don't you ask your cousin what he thinks?" Nathan tipped his bottle towards Blake. "He's the one who brought her."

"He's a man-whore." Katie grumbled as she swayed in her seat. "Fuck's anything that moves."

"I'm off to the ladies." Ava muttered as she stood, swayed slightly. Her hand steadying on the back of her chair before she righted herself.

Her hand gently pressed against the wall of the long corridor, her feet tripping over themselves as her head spun from the alcohol she'd consumed. A large arm hooked around her waist and spinning her until she was resting against the corridor wall. Large hands slapped the wall on either side of her head. A startled squeak left her parted lips as her eyes landed on his dark, brooding eyes. His scent wrapped around her, his heat engulfed her, stealing her breath.

"Blake." she whispered, her eyes fluttering at the unexpected closeness. Taking a breath of his intoxicating scent that had her stomach clenching.

"You need to go home, Ava." his voice was low, his eyes narrowed. She furrowed her brow as she looked at him before shaking her head in defiance. His nostrils flared slightly.

"No." her voice was almost breathless as he inched closer to her. His body heat seeping into her thin t-shirt. Her nipples hardening at his closeness. His jaw muscle ticking, making the dark stubble dance across his jaw, almost mesmerising her.

"You need to sober up." his teeth clenched together, his eyes narrowed. Still, she shook her head. "It's been nine years." his lips moved to the shell of her ear. "Since you sat in my lap and shattered. Nine years since I spent the entire night whispering words of comfort in your ear. Nine years since I tried to make you feel anything but the pain of losing people you loved," he whispered, his hand balling into a tight fist beside her head. "Nine fucking years, Ava, and you have never missed the anniversary of your parents' death." his voice turned harsh as he pulled back, pinning her with a glacial stare, making her stomach drop.

"I don't want to." Ava admitted in the smallest of whispers, her teeth grazing her bottom lip. She turned her head away, her heart hammering and tears pricking at her eyes.

"Why?" Blake asked, his hand clenching and relaxing, but she didn't answer. "Ava." her name sounded like a warning, his fingers gripping her chin and tilting her head until they were once again staring at each other. She swallowed thickly, trying to stop the onslaught of tears that threatened and her breaths were sharp pants as she tried to calm herself.

"I-I..." she broke off as she swallowed the sob which tried to escape. "Want to forget." she sucked in a sharp breath. Blake's eyes softened, hand cupping her cheek as a delicate blush spread across her.

"You should never want to forget them," he sighed, his thumb wiping a stray tear from her cheek. "Today should be a celebration of your memories." his lips tipped up in a smile that had her stomach flip-flopping.

"It's hard," she murmured, closing her eyes. She felt his warm lips press against her forehead and her lungs puffed out the air which had lodged in her throat.

"I know, baby girl," he whispered, pulling back from her. "I know." he nodded once. "Let me take you home." Blake's hand left her cheek as he stood to his full, imposing height.

A flash of a memory surged to life. A memory she now knew was real and not a figment of her imagination. He'd called her *that* the night her parents died and he hadn't forgotten how he'd comforted her, hadn't forgotten just how broken she had been that night. A tiny flare of hope bloomed within her.

"I don't want to ruin your *date*." she almost hissed the last word, moving her hand in hopes of covering her stomach as his eyes tracked the movement, the back of her knuckles grazed lightly against a hard lump. Her face flamed as she realised *what* she'd touched. "S-sorry," she stuttered as he scowled.

"Be careful." his words were a harsh bite as he turned on his heel, sucking in a deep breath. Ava was still leaning against the wall, missing the heat and scent of him. "On second thoughts, make your own way home." he threw over his shoulder before she watched him walk away without a backward glance.

"Baby girl." Ava breathed out, her arms wrapping around herself.

A shiver racing down her spine, still feeling the touch of his lips against her forehead. She could still feel the heat against the back of her knuckles where she'd grazed against his erection. A very large erection. Her heart thumped hard in her chest, readying for galloping a mile a minute; but then she remembered the harshness of his voice, the coldness of his stare, and her face crumpled.

"Why are you so mad at me?" she whispered, pushing the door to the toilets open and finding a cubicle. "What have I done wrong?" she continued as she finished using the bathroom.

Washing her hands in the sink, her gaze focused on her reflection. Her eyes looked like a dying ember as they slowly went flat. Her face, a blushing mess with mascara smudges beneath her red-rimmed eyes and her lips were now devoid of lipstick. Thoughts of Blake circling around in her mind but were quickly overshadowed by the thoughts of her parents.

Blake was right!

She knew that she should be at home with James, knew that they should be swapping stories from the good times as a family.

Even if she didn't really want to.

It wasn't that she'd stopped grieving; in a way, she knew that you never really stopped, but that the days, weeks, months and years became easier to cope with. Ava was frightened to share stories of her parents with anyone, including James, because the pain it caused after all this time became unbearable for her.

Closing her eyes, her wet hands braced against the sink as she took a deep breath before straightening and drying her hands.

Chapter Three

Blake stood with his hands shoved deep into his pants pockets as he waited for—whatever her name was—to get out of the car. She'd told him her name weeks ago, when they first started talking, but he couldn't remember for the life in him what that was and he didn't really care to ask again either.

All he could smell was Ava's perfume, the light and sweet floral scent. It was the same scent he enjoyed when he visited James's home. The same scent he had wrongly assumed was from a scented candle that Ava loved to burn around the house. All he could feel was the light, delicate brush against his cock.

His hard cock throbbed in the confines of his pants, making him grind his teeth together.

Fuck!

He didn't want to think about the reason why he got so hard when she was pressed against the wall. Didn't want to think about the reason why he'd put his hand on her and certainly didn't want to think about why he'd called her *baby girl.*

She wasn't his type, end of discussion.

The hotel parking lot was busier than usual as he glanced around, trying not to let his agitation show.

"Oh, this is a fancy place." her voice was like nails on a chalkboard. Blake cut his eyes to her. Her smile was a small twitch of her lips and he realised that she couldn't move them much more due to the cosmetic work she'd had done. Not at all like the shy smiles he got all the time from.....

Why do I care so much now that she can't fucking smile properly?

Why do I care about shy smiles from Ava?

Sighing with a slight shake to his head, trying to dislodge the thoughts of his best friend's little sister out of his mind.

He didn't care how much work they'd had done, didn't care how much lip fillers, cheek fillers, plastic surgery any of the women had done. All he cared about was that they were a willing participant for his sexual pleasure.

"Come." he snapped without a glance as he strode across the parking lot to the main entrance. The usual doorman waiting. His uniform always pressed with military precision. His grey hair slicked back neatly and his trimmed beard hiding the downturn of his lips that he always gave Blake, every-fucking-week.

"Good evening, Doctor Synclair." his voice was welcoming and aged with a certain air of sophistication.

"Patrick." Blake greeted with a slight nod, without breaking stride.

"Ooh, you're a doctor." she cooed, the moment her ridiculously high heels caught up. "Want to play doctors and nurses, Blake." she continued. He clenched his jaw and dragged a calming breath in through his nose.

"Let's not talk," he ground out as they stepped into the elevator. He couldn't stand her voice, and the less she talked, the better. He preferred the low, sultry voice that always seemed a little breathless whenever they spoke.

Fuck!

Swiping his key card into the control panel the moment the doors had closed, ensured that they wouldn't be disturbed by other guests and also marked the penthouse—*his*—suite to light up.

He saw in his peripheral vision her hand, that looked more like a claw with the long red nails reach out to him. Heaving a breath, Blake moved out of her reach. He hated when they touched him. It was too intimate for his liking. She took a step towards him, but he pinned her with a hard stare, keeping her away from him in the confines of the elevator. The moment the doors opened, he launched himself out, like a caged animal being let out for the first time.

What the fuck is wrong with me?

"Someone's impatient." she tried to purr the words as he opened the hotel room door. But failed miserably.

"Hmm." he hummed, walking into the suite and checking his phone. He'd sent a text to James, letting him know that Ava would be coming home early and was pleased to know that she'd got home safely.

"What's got you smiling, handsome?" he didn't realise that he was smiling, nor did he move out of the way quick enough before her claws were on him. His back went straight, his lungs seized momentarily, pocketing his phone as his hands gripped her wrists tightly, pulling her hands away from him.

"You don't touch me." his voice was low, dangerous. "It's my only rule." his eyes were narrowed as he watched her mouth open into an 'O' shape. "Do you understand?" his grip tightened until she nodded in acceptance as he took a breath and that was when her cheap perfume invaded his senses, cloying and clogging the back of his throat. His anger surged through him like a wildfire. "Get a shower and wash that shit perfume off," he barked, letting go of her with a slight push, making her step away from him.

He watched as embarrassment flashed in her eyes as heat

swept across her barely concealed chest. He didn't care; that stench needed to go. It was overpowering the light and sweet floral scent from his shirt. No sooner had the thought swept through his mind; he dismissed it with a shake of his head.

Why the fuck am I thinking about perfume?

Blake heard the shower start, the water spraying against the glass doors as he poured himself a shot of whiskey. Slumping into the chair, his eyes trained on the archway which separated the living area and the bedroom. The glass had just reached his lips when his mind wandered back, the delicate moan that fell from Ava's lips with every bite she took at breakfast this morning. He hadn't enjoyed a meal like that in a long time. He growled low in his throat as his cock throbbed painfully this time.

"No!" the word was a rumble through his chest. Tipping the contents of his glass down his throat in one gulp. The burn evaporating the memory of Ava eating breakfast. "What the fuck!" he couldn't do this right now. Couldn't think of his best friend's sister.

She was not his type!

"So Blake." he ground his teeth together at the sound of her voice. "Where do you want me?" he looked over the blonde who was swaying her non-existent hips as she walked completely naked towards him.

Her tits were large but didn't move, and if he looked closely enough, he could still see the scars beneath from the surgery. Her sides were straight, her thighs were too thin, her ass was too flat. She had no shape. No curves. He knew before she got any closer that her hair would feel like straw from the bleach. Her skin was covered in fake tan trying to hide the scars and acne from having too many surgeries and wearing too much make-up.

Scrubbing a hand down his face, he knew he needed to stop assessing her, knew he needed to fuck her the way he wanted and leave. It was what he always did, every single week. Except tonight, he couldn't stop critically assessing the woman before him. He needed to get his head back in the game, needed to stop thinking of the little five foot three inch curvy as fuck, sultry voiced, sweet smelling girl.

And to him, she was a girl. He was thirty-three years old, and she was what—eighteen—*no, that wasn't right*. He tipped his head back slightly as he mulled over the age. Twenty, *that's how old she was*. How could he forget? She was twelve when her parents died. *Fucking twelve.* She didn't deserve that. She was too sweet to be dealt that hand in her life.

Stop thinking about Ava!

Placing the glass tumbler on the coffee table, he stared directly at *nails on a chalkboard*. Banishing all thoughts of his best friend's little sister. A woman who wasn't his type. He preferred the sluts—like the one before him—all willing, all fake and all for one fucking night. Not the sweet, innocent and pure girl that was his best friend's little sister.

"You be a good little whore and crawl to me." his lips twitched as he saw her steps falter for a fraction of a second before she sunk to her knees.

Watched as her back bowed and dipped with each movement and watched as the indents from her spine were visible against her skin. He usually loved to watch women crawl to him, but tonight his cock, which had been raging hard since the pub, pub, had slowly begun to deflate at the sight before him.

Closing his eyes for the briefest of moments and instantly regretting it.

The sight behind his closed lids was of a gentle, sweet blush covering apple cheeks, pouty lips partly open as her breath hitched in the back of her throat. Her curvy frame bowed against the wall and her sweet floral scent wrapping around him. Snapping his eyes open, his cock had roared to life again with his zip biting painfully against his throbbing erection. His hands balled into fists as he dragged a deep breath in before hissing it out from between clenched teeth.

"Stand." he barked the command which had the slut before him complying. His hand shot out and seized her non-existent hip, pulling her roughly until she was standing between his parted legs. "Thank fuck, I can no longer smell that perfume," he muttered to himself as he tried to lose himself in the willing woman.

The moment his hands splayed across her stomach, his gut clenched, but he ignored it. Moving his hands higher, his thumbs bumped over every rib, and bile rose in his throat. He hated the feeling of bones beneath his fingers without the slightest bit of pressure. Hated the way they felt and reminded him too much of work. His cock deflated extremely quickly as he continued to swallow back the bile which was threatening to come out.

"You okay there, handsome?" that fucking voice again had him grinding his teeth. "You look a little pale," she continued, her claws reaching out, making his muscles lock into place before she remembered his rule and let them fall away, hanging loosely at her sides.

"No." his voice was low as he swallowed thickly. "You need to leave," he continued, pushing her back and standing to his full six foot three-inch height. But she didn't move, only cocked her head to the side.

"I can make you feel better, Blake." she took a step closer, trying to sway those non-existent hips, hips, but he side-stepped her.

"I said." Blake dragged in a breath. "Fucking leave." he bit out the words, grabbing the empty tumbler before refiling it. "Now!" he bellowed, which had her jumping.

He watched her disappear through the archway, trying to shake her flat ass. Shaking his head, he gulped the whiskey in one.

Images swirled in his head. He pinched the bridge of his nose and tilted his head back, back, sighing long and hard, anger bubbling within him. Anger he wouldn't be able to control.

"You need to get out of my fucking head," he snarled aloud, trying to dispel the images that plagued him.

"Okay, handsome I'm going." nails on a chalkboard spoke as she reappeared fully dressed – as fully dressed – as she arrived. "Call me when you feel better." her lips twitched slightly.

"I don't fucking think so," he snapped, closing his eyes against the hurt flashing in her eyes. But his words stung her enough that she quickly left.

Alone, he slumped back in the chair. His eyes unfocused and his hands clenched into fists against his thighs. He could feel something slithering through him as the images began repeating themselves on a loop inside his head.

Her images were only fuelling the already raging anger; it wouldn't take much to tip him over the edge. The pleading look in *her* eyes had his heart pounding. The image changed and the affectionate look he loved to see was long gone and replaced with revulsion. The sight had tears gathering in his eyes.

"Get out of my fucking head!" He snarled, closing his eyes.

The image that assaulted him stole his breath. Long brown hair cascading in soft waves, framing a sweet innocent face. Pouty lips curved into a shy smile, apple cheeks blushing. Long natural eyelashes framing green eyes. A white dress criminally covering perfect curves, flaring out at the waist and hanging in pleats to the knee and red heels, contrasting against the purest look he'd ever seen. Snapping his eyes open on a growl, he fumbled with his phone and scrolled until he found who he was looking for.

Chapter Four

The moonlight filtered through her bedroom curtains, illuminating a small patch of her dressing table. Ava wasn't certain how long she had laid in bed – awake. She had sobered up very quickly after she left Katie and Nathan at the pub. James had been scrolling through looking for something to watch when she'd slumped beside him, kicking her heels off and snatching up a couple of the sweets James had in a bowl on the sofa.

They'd ended up doing exactly what Blake had told her and, with James initiating the conversation, she'd wondered if he'd already had the same talk. They'd laughed and cried and looked at the last holiday photo album before either of them made a move to go to bed and Ava had been laying in the dark wide awake ever since.

She was trying to process everything that had happened over the last couple of days with Blake. He'd never been like that with her before, never made her feel anything less of normal and had never made fun of her when she ate. But she knew that over the last few months she'd become a little bigger, not that she thought was overly noticeable, especially to friends, and she did consider Blake a friend.

Of course, she wanted to be more than friends and of course she needed to come to the realisation that it would never happen. But every time she thought of letting it all go and leave Blake with his perfect life of womanising, something happened to make that spark of hope surge forth.

It was cruel.

And she was sure that she was reading too much into it all!

Sighing in frustration into the silence of her bedroom, pushing her dark hair away from her face, her phone lit up the nightstand and the gentle buzz against the wood had her aimlessly patting for the phone.

"Oh, shit!" Ava whispered into the silence as Blake's name flashed on screen. He's calling her at two in the morning. Quickly swiping her finger across the screen and placing the phone to her ear. "Hi." she breathed out, her heart thrumming and pulse ticking wildly.

"You!" his usual husky baritone was that of a snarl, which made her flinch. "Need to stop fucking with me," he continued; she could hear the anger in his voice and it was aimed at her.

"I-I..." she began to stutter, her hands began to shake, her stomach roiled.

"Don't you play little miss innocent." his voice was getting harder, colder. "That's all you're doing, playing, and you need to fucking stop." his breathing was becoming laboured down the line.

"Blake, I don't understand." her voice was a mere whisper as she tried to stop the quiver in her voice. The bitter laugh that greeted her had tears welling in her eyes.

"Of course you do!" he hissed out, which made him sound like he was in pain. Her brows furrowed. "Those sexy little fucking moans when eating....." her faced flamed at his words. "The shy little smiles..... the innocent little blush permanently on those cheeks...... that breathy fucking voice...." he was panting hard down the phone before she heard him suck in a hard, laboured breath. Panic welled within her; he was in pain and probably alone.

"Where are you?" she asked, throwing the covers back and swatting the stray tears away. She hated the thought of him being in pain alone; nobody deserved that. Even if that person wasn't very happy with her right now, she couldn't leave him alone.

"Oh, you'd fucking like that," he panted heavily. "Stay the fuck away from me," he spat, disconnecting the call.

Ava slumped back on the bed, her mouth open and her eyes wide as she stared at her phone.

"What the hell was that about?" she asked aloud, her teeth clamping her bottom lip as she chewed.

She knew that he'd been mad with her at the pub, even more so after she accidentality grazed his erection, but that was it. He came and found her; he kissed her forehead, and he called her a pet name. Except he'd mentioned nothing of what happened in the pub. Everything he'd ranted down the phone was how she was around him, with the exception of the noises when eating – she'd always done that.

So what had changed?

That was the question she couldn't answer, and after tonight's phone call, she highly doubted that Blake would answer the question. Not that she had time to think about that; no, she needed to find him. Needed to help him.

Jumping off of the bed, she ordered an Uber and quickly redressed into the clothes she'd worn earlier before stuffing her feet into a pair of converse pumps. Grabbing her handbag, phone, and keys before she left the house.

The Synclair Hotel was every bit as fancy as any prestigious hotel, and it was her only hope. She didn't know where Blake lived and this was the only place she had overheard James and Blake talk about, especially if he had a date.

Bounding up to an ageing man, with a neatly trimmed grey beard and slick back grey hair, she hoped he'd help. Plastering on a smile as she held her handbag over her stomach, a shield she liked to hide behind.

"Good Evening, miss," the ageing man greeted with a warm smile.

"I'm hoping you can help; is Blake Synclair here?" she tried to sound confident, but it was laced with panic. The doorman blinked at her; his eyes quickly assessed her, making her feel self conscious. "He's a friend and I need to speak with him urgently." she smiled tightly as she gripped her handbag to her stomach.

"What's your name?" the ageing man asked.

"Ava." she mumbled, her shoulders slumping. If he rings up to Blake, he'll tell him not to let her in.

"Pardon? I didn't quite catch that, miss." his lips pulled in a smile as he tilted his head.

"Ava Asherton." she repeated louder. His eyes widened for a fraction of a second before he schooled his features.

"James's sister?" he asked, sweeping his arm towards the doors. She nodded. "Follow me; he's in the penthouse." he ushered her into the elevator, swiped a card until the penthouse button lit up and left her alone without another word.

Ava blew out the breath she didn't realise she was holding as the elevator smoothly rose towards the penthouse. Her nerves were getting the better of her as she chewed on her fingernail and her foot was tapping restlessly against the floor. Her heart was thumping and her stomach was clenching as the tone of his voice replayed through her mind. He sounded like he was in pain and that didn't sit well with her. She worried about why he was in pain, worried that something bad had happened to him, and she worried that she was going to be too late to help him.

The moment the elevator dinged, her lungs seized in her chest. Sucking in a breath as she tried to calm down, the doors opened. The small corridor housed only one door. A hard, white wooden door that was slightly ajar. Panic swept through her as her limbs tried to lock into place, tried to stop her from moving and the rational part of her mind urged her to call for help.

Her feet thundered against the floor, her hands clammy and shaking as she pushed the door open. The room was in pitch darkness; the scent of Blake and alcohol filled the air. Her heat rate increased tenfold as she took a step inside. Her eyes were trying to adjust to the darkness, her hand fumbling for a light switch as she tried to keep the worst of her panic at bay.

A soft glow illuminated a small area from the first switch she found and the sight that greeted her knocked the breath from her lungs. Curled into a tight ball was the shaking body of Blake. His bare back was slick with sweat that glistened in the dim light. She could hear his harsh, shallow breaths. Her feet, no longer rooted to the spot, were thundering across the wide expanse of the room, her eyes only focused on Blake.

"Blake." her voice was low as she knelt beside him. His face contorted in pain as his muscular arms wrapped around him. "What's wrong?" she continued, her shaking hand brushing the hair away from his forehead. Sweat coated her palm and the searing heat of his skin almost burnt her. "I'll be right back." she whispered.

The moment she was on her feet, her eyes darted around the opulent room. Her stomach roiling as the panic tried to send the contents of her stomach back out, but she couldn't be sick, couldn't fail him. He needed her, and she had absolutely no idea what to do. Spying the elaborate archway that dominated half of the wall, she briefly wondered how she'd missed it.

The large bed dominated the space, the deep green of the pristine bed covers held an inviting appeal. Shaking the thought from her head as she found the open bathroom door. Dousing a white fluffy towel in ice cold water. Wringing out the excess until it was damp and cold. Her mind went blank as she began to work on autopilot. Her feet carrying her faster until she was once again knelt beside his shaking body.

"Okay, just breathe." she murmured, gently placing the damp, cold towel against his forehead. A deep groan rumbled through his chest. "Shhh, it's okay." Ava cooed, pressing the damp towel carefully against his face and watching as he scrunched his features.

"Go away." he grumbled, swatting her hand away. She moved the damp towel across the nape of his neck. Goosebumps skittered down his arms, but his eyes remained closed and his face still scrunched up. "Leave." she knew it was supposed to sound harsh, but he only managed a low, feeble sound.

"Blake." she tried again, but he shook his head., a deep groan rumbling through his chest. "Can you stand?" she asked, the damp towel gently moving around his neck as she tried to cool him down.

"Leave me alone, Candice." his voice was a mere whisper, his large hand gripped Ava's wrist in a bruising hold. Her gasp of shock filled the room, making his eyes snap open. The blackness engulfed the rich deep brown and his mouth twisted in a grimace.

"Can. You. Stand." she spoke slowly, transferring the damp towel to her free hand and pressing it against his forehead. She watched his brows furrow as his eyes bounced over her face as the silence stretched out before them. Her free hand never stopped gently swiping over his face and neck, and his hand still held her wrist in a gripping hold.

"Ava?" he croaked the word out as his pupils shrunk back to normal size. His harsh, shallow breaths were slowly returning to normal, deep and even. He released her wrist, his hand cupping her cheek. "Did I hurt you?" he sounded so unsure, so vulnerable, making tears gather in her eyes. The sheer vulnerability in his voice made her heart ache.

"No." she shook her head, a small smile on her lips as she tried to ease some of the doubt from him. "Scared the hell out of me, sure." she chuckled lightly. "But you haven't hurt me, Blake." his breath whooshed out of him as he closed his eyes, pulling her until their foreheads touched.

"Sorry." he whispered into the limited space between them. "I don't feel very well," he admitted, his hand dropping from her cheek, hitting the floor hard. Ava stood, holding her shaking hand out to him.

"I think the bed might be a better place for you." she smiled shyly as he took her hand. Steadying himself, he stood to his full height. Ava noticed the shake of his legs as he took a tentative step with her. "We'll take it slow, just one step at a time." she encouraged as they walked slowly across the room. Blake's hand gripped the archway and leaned heavily against it for a moment, before Ava wrapped her arm around his waist. "Use me, I've got you." she urged as he placed his weight against her and they began walking again.

The moment they reached the bed, Ava twisted her body until she was standing in front of Blake. Her hands gripped his much larger ones. Her pulse was thumping wildly in her throat and her breaths were a little fast as his dark eyes stared down at her. Heat crept up her face, settling on her cheeks when his tongue slowly ran across his lower lip. His muscles bunched and rippled on his arms as he gripped hers in an effort to keep standing.

Ava licked her lips and swallowed thickly at the delicious sight of all tawny skin. Her eyes roamed slowly across the wide expanse of his chest, down the well-cut abdominals which looked like they were carved into perfection. The light dusting of dark hair streaking down to disappear beneath the dark wash jeans along with the sexiest deep carve of muscles framing his abdomen. The low growl had her eyes snapping back to the rich dark brown, and she watched as his pupil dilated ever so slightly.

"Ava." his voice was low, dark and a rush of excitement flowed through her at the sound. "Stay." he whispered before falling back onto the bed, pulling her with him.

She couldn't help the shriek of surprise that left her as they careened towards the bed. Panic welled within her, realising that she would crush him under her weight. His arms wrapping around her, holding her to him as they bounced on the bed a few times before it settled. His feet were still planted on the floor and Ava was sprawled haphazardly across him. She could feel the wild thump of his heart as her head landed in the crook of his neck. Ava tried to wriggle, remove the full weight of her off of him, but his arms banded around her in a crushing hold.

"Blake." she whispered with another wiggle, her hand lightly tapping against his chest.

"Don't." that one word was hard as his arms tightened ever more so around her.

"But, I'm too heavy." she admitted as her face flamed at the reality. He'd forgotten that she wasn't like the women he usually had like this. No, she was too large, too heavy. He tangled his hand in her hair and the other was still wrapped around her waist as he held her to him, ensuring that she couldn't move.

Blake's breaths evened quickly, and a soft groan left his parted lips as sleep claimed him. Closing her eyes, she inhaled his scent, a mix of his cologne and a musk that was all him and intoxicating.

A smile playing on her lips as she burrowed herself deeper into his body until her breathing evened out and sleep claimed her.

Chapter Five

Ava stood with her hands on her hips, her green eyes scanning the piles of discarded clothes in a heap almost covering the hardwood floor. Her chest rose and fell in quick succession and a fine sheen of sweat beaded her brow. It was only an hour ago that she'd wanted to find something to wear to dinner tonight, something that made her look womanly and something that made her feel desirable. But as she took stock of the mountain of clothes she'd discarded as either too small, not desirable or womanly, frustration was etched into the set of her face.

"Why bother." she spoke aloud to herself, pushing a few stray hairs out of her eyes. "Its just dinner with James." she continued, scooping up the mountain of clothes and dumping them on her bed. "Katie and Nathan." she huffed out a breath as she began putting the clothes back on their hangers.

"Happy Birthday, Squirt!" James's voice boomed into the room, making her jump, her hand flying to her chest as her heart tried to beat out of the cavity.

"Jesus!" Ava breathed as she swung around to face her brother. His tall, broad frame dominated the open doorway as he strode in. Holding a deep green gift bag with white tissue paper spilling from the top. "James, you didn't have to." she smiled as she took the gift bag.

"It's not everyday you turn twenty-one." he wrapped his arms around her in a tight hug, kissing the top of her head. "I hope you like it." his words were softer as he released her and stood back.

Ava cocked her head to the side, a smile on her face as she opened the gift bag. White tissue paper flying onto the floor as excitement filled her and her eyes landed on a cherry apple red clutch handbag that would match her red stiletto heels perfectly.

"Oh god, it's beautiful!" Ava smiled brightly as she felt the soft leather against her fingers. "It's perfect." she hugged James again, giving him a quick squeeze.

"I'm glad you like it." his hand rubbed the back of his neck. "Katie, helped me pick it out," he admitted, heat crawling up his neck. "She said you had some shoes that would go with it." he shrugged as if it was all brand new to him but Ava nodded.

"I do, and I'll wear them tonight." she scooped the tissue paper back up and put it back inside the bag.

"I'll leave you to whatever." he brushed his fingers through his hair. "We'll leave at seven, Squirt." were his parting words as he gently closed her bedroom door.

The moment she was alone once again, she couldn't stop her mind from wandering back. Back to the night, she went rushing to help Blake. The night in his hotel room where she'd found him in a heap, shaking and vulnerable. The night where she had seen a different side to him. The night where he'd held her close. The night she foolishly thought that she could be more to Blake. The night where her heart swelled and opened even more for the man she had been in love with for nine years.

Sighing into the empty room as she put the last dress on the hanger and stuffed it back inside the wardrobe she couldn't help the slither of self consciousness to ease its way into her mind, couldn't help the hard thump of her pulse as the memory of last weekend when she woke up alone, cold in the bed to the sound of the maid vacuuming the living area. Blake hadn't left so much as a note or text message, message; and she hadn't seen him since. A sad smile tugged at her lips and her eyes misted over as she gathered her underwear and towels before trudging to the bathroom for a shower.

Staring at her reflection in the full-length mirror, assessing the way her long dark hair hung in waves she had painstakingly styled, the light make-up she'd opted for was a swipe of mascara and a nude lip gloss to the plain white tea dress. The wide straps hid most of her shoulders, the bodice tightly encased her breasts, pushing them towards the low square neckline; at the waist, the skirt flared in pleats to her knee and she knew it made her look like a child playing dress up. But the red heels she had decided to wear made her feel a little daring. They were six-inch stiletto heels, which added much needed height to her short stature. Grabbing the matching red clutch handbag that was her birthday gift, she took a deep breath and left the safety of her bedroom.

The large glass fronted restaurant was empty as Ava looked through the window. The staff stood dressed in all black; the counter had bottles of champagne in ice buckets and sparkling crystal cut champagne flutes beside them under the muted lighting. Her eyebrows furrowed in confusion at the lack of patrons, it was always booked out months in advance.

"I don't think they're open yet." Ava commented as she turned to James, trying not to fidget.

"Hmm." he hummed as he placed his hand on her back, leading her towards the restaurant door. "Blake, shut down the place for your birthday." James admitted, just as the door was swung open by a member of staff.

"What?" Ava raised her voice as incredulity seeped out in that one word; as she stopped dead, her wide eyes turning to James.

"Shh." James turned slightly, moving closer. "We wanted to make this a special night; Ava and Blake's family owns this place." he shrugged as he stood back, his hand on her back urging her forward until she was stood inside.

"Happy birthday, Ava Synclair." the maître d' smiled through the greeting. Her pulse spiked at the name used. Her eyes closed briefly, sucking in a breath.

"I don't think so," James grumbled, his eyebrows furrowed in a scowl.

"Asherton." Ava whispered, licking over her lips as heat settled in her cheeks at the slip up. "Ava Asherton." she corrected. The maître d's eyes went wide before he bowed.

"Apologies, Ms Ava." he apologised, offering her a glass of champagne. Ava nodded, taking a glass. "I'll show you to the table." he continued.

Ava had her eyes trained on the floor, careful to not trip over her own feet, let alone a stray chair. The low ambient music filling the silence and drowning out the low murmurs from the staff whose eyes she could feel tracking her movements.

"Happy Birthday, Ava!" Katie and Nathan shouted together, snapping her head up, a wide smile gracing her lips as she was wrapped in a hug. "You look fucking lovely." Katie beamed, making Ava blush. "He'll never know what he missed out on." Katie whispered into her ear so only she could hear.

Ava hadn't confided in Katie about what had happened with Blake last week, but she was her personal cheerleader where he was concerned, and her feelings for him.

"You scrub up well." Nathan agreed with his boyish smile as he gave her a quick squeeze of her shoulder.

"Thanks." Ava muttered with a roll of her eyes as they all took their seats.

The moment she placed her glass on the table, she felt eyes on her. Raising them until she was staring directly into narrowed, rich, dark brown eyes.

"Birthday girl." his husky baritone washed over her in a delicate shiver. She licked over her lips as he clenched his jaw until the muscle ticked before she averted her eyes. "I hope you enjoy the evening." he continued, picking the menu up.

It wasn't until the eye contact had been broken that she noticed the beautiful blonde woman sat next to Blake. Her blonde hair was swept away from her face in an elaborate up-do, highlighting her slender face. Her eyes were a crystal blue framed with long dark lashes, her plump red lips were pulled into a sneer as she stared at Ava.

"Er, I'm Ava." she introduced herself, swallowing thickly as she extended her hand across the table. The disdain on the woman's face had Ava pulling her hand back quickly.

"I don't think that *thing*." Katie pointed at the blonde. "Is real!" Katie winked at Ava.

"Katie!" James's voice was admonishing, but the smile said otherwise. "Play nice, she could be family soon." James chuckled, picking his menu back up.

"If I didn't know any better, I'd say Katie was already on her way to being drunk." Nathan whispered in her ear with a chuckle. Making Ava nod in agreement.

Ava didn't need to look at the menu; she already knew what she wanted to eat and her mouth was salivating at the sheer thought. She could almost taste the exquisite white truffle and mushroom pasta, and she couldn't wait. Her only concern was the noises she may make and god help her, but she didn't want to embarrass herself tonight.

Grasping the flute between her fingers, she quickly tossed the contents down her throat. The bubbles dancing across her tongue, the alcohol burning her throat and making her a little light-headed.

"If I make any noises." Ava whispered in Nathan's ear, a slight shudder passing through his body. She knew Nathan didn't like being affectionate, he didn't like people getting too close. "Please, will you let me know?" she asked, her face flaming as Nathan cocked his head slightly before nodding. "Thanks."

Ava watched her friends and brother laughing and joking around the table as they ate the delicious food. She couldn't focus on what they were talking about; she was too busy watching Blake smile. The same smile that made her weak in the knees, but it was aimed at his date. A woman she could never compete with. She felt the sting of tears behind her eyes; her stomach roiled as she realised that last week was a mistake. Her heart started pounding, her mind spitting venom at her.

He probably woke up with her fat body laid across him and it made him sick to his stomach.

She was pushing her food around on the plate, trying to blink back the tears and swallow down the bile that tried to escape. Sweat trickled down her back and her vision blurred. Her thoughts spiralling out of control. Her insecurities gripped her hard, and she felt the colour drain from her face as her stomach gave a harsh lurch. Her hands shaking as she placed one against her mouth and quietly removing herself from the table without anyone noticing – *as usual* – she discretely made her way to the bathroom.

The moment she was enclosed in the stall, she fell to her knees and vomited everything in her stomach into the pristine white toilet bowl. The room was filled with sounds of liquid splashing into the bowl; her heaving around sobs that broke free as she shattered in the confines of the toilet stall.

Sweat gathered across her forehead, her neck and trickled

down her breasts and back as she rested against the toilet stall door. Her eyes squeezed shut, arms wrapped around herself as tears tracked down her cheeks. Swallowing back the sobs that desperately wanted to escape again. Her heart felt like it'd been ripped out and left in shreds, which was stupid; she knew that. She knew that she meant nothing to Blake, but it always boiled to that little slither of hope she left burning within her. But tonight, he'd doused that flame and left her in a broken mess.

She didn't know how long she'd been sitting there, didn't know if anyone even knew she was missing, but one thing she did know – she just wanted to go home to wallow in her self pity.

"Squirt?" James knocked gently on the stall door. "Are you okay?" he asked, worry evident in his tone.

"No." she sobbed the word out, unable to hold it back. James shook the door, but it was locked. "I want to go home." she continued in a long tortured sob.

"Okay, just come out." James's tone was almost pleading. She nodded and remembered that he couldn't see her. Standing on shaking legs, she smoothed her dress down before flushing the toilet and opening the door. "Ava, come here." he pulled her into him, his arms wrapping around her protectively. "What happened?" she swallowed the next wave of sobs as she shook her head.

"I don't feel well." she whispered, pulling away, swiping the tears and mascara from her cheeks. "Can we go home?" she asked, dabbing cold water on her face, trying to cool herself down.

"Sure, I'll let the others know." James looked at her with concern but didn't say anything as he placed the car keys in her shaking hand. "I'll meet you in the car." Ava nodded as she took a deep breath to steady herself.

Chapter Six

Ava sat in the confines of the car James was driving. His knuckles were turning white from the harsh grip as she watched the passing scenery.

"I know you won't tell me what happened tonight, Ava." James's voice cut through the tense silence, a hard sigh escaping his lips. "But can you please let me know if someone hurt you?" he cut his eyes to her before turning back towards to the road.

"No." she murmured, wrapping her arms around her stomach. "Nobody hurt me." she lied around a thick swallow. "I don't think the food agreed with me." she continued, refusing to look at James instead she watched as he made a turn before their home came into view.

"Okay." James breathed out as he pulled to a stop in the driveway of their home. Turning in the seat to face her, his arm resting on the back of her seat. "I care a lot for you Squirt." he smiled warmly. "And it breaks my heart to see you so upset." he gave her knee a quick squeeze before existing the car.

"James!" Ava called as she walked behind him. "Thanks for tonight." she smiled as he looked down at her before opening the door.

"Here." he held a small, square box wrapped in sage green – her favourite colour – wrapping paper. "Blake asked me to give it to you and hoped you felt better." his eyebrows knitted together as she tried to school her features.

"Thanks." she nodded, taking the present. "I'm off to bed." she didn't turn to look at James, choosing to focus on making it to her bedroom without crying again.

Firmly closing the door behind her and leaning against it, she carefully opened the present and couldn't contain the gasp as she saw in gold font *Chisholm Hunter.* Tears pricked her eyes as she opened the red leather box that had nestled in the black velvet a white gold diamond cluster pendant. Her fingertips lightly tracing the pendant with a small smile on her lips before she placed it carefully on her dressing table.

The moonlight filtered through her bedroom curtains, illuminating a small patch of her dressing table. Ava wasn't certain how long she had laid in bed – awake. Her mind torturing her with thoughts of Blake and the present. He'd never bought her such a beautiful present before. On her previous birthday's he'd bought her personalised stationary for her job, books and when she'd tried new hobbies, he'd bought her things for that particular hobby. But jewellery never.

Grabbing her phone from the nightstand, she squinted against the harsh light of the screen, debating for only a fraction of a second before typing out two text messages in quick succession. After all, manners cost nothing, it's what her parents had taught her.

Ava – *Thank you for the beautiful necklace, Blake.*

Ava – *Katie, sorry it's late, coffee tomorrow @ 10am? Xx*

Her phone buzzed against the bedcovers, the screen shining brightly in the darkness. Her heart stuttered in her chest as *his* name flashed on the screen.

Blake – *I hope you feel better. Glad you liked the gift. Sweet dreams, baby girl x*

Ava's hands were shaking as she re-read the message. In this exact moment under the cover of darkness, re-reading Blake's message as she remembered that he'd said some hurtful things to her, left her alone in his hotel room after she'd helped him and then brought a date to her birthday meal.

Ava – *Please don't call me that, Blake.*

The moment Ava hit send on the text message, her heart began beating harshly and her hands continued to shake as hurt lanced through her. She saw the three dots appearing almost instantly before they disappeared, she dropped the phone beside her.

Blake's name flashed on screen as her phone buzzed loudly against the bedcovers. Sighing as she swiped her finger across the screen and placing the phone to her ear. "Blake." she breathed into the phone nervously.

"Hi." the husky baritone of his voice filled her head. "How're feeling?" he asked.

"Not great." she admitted, licking over her lips. "I don't think the food agreed with me." she heard his sigh and a rustle of fabrics.

"Don't lie to me, Ava." his voice sounded thicker before he cleared his throat.

"I'm not!" she whispered before sighing. "Okay, fine, the food was nice."

"You didn't make those noises," he pointed out. "I don't think you liked it that much." he chuckled and her face flamed.

"I-I..." she stuttered, sucking in a calming breath. "You'd have liked that, wouldn't you? The fat girl making sex noises whilst she ate." her voice was a bitter breath in the quiet of the room.

"Those aren't your sex noises." he cleared his throat, more

fabric moving. "I've heard them in surround sound." her heart rate kicked up a notch as his voice dropped lower, huskier than normal.

"Haven't you got a date to impress?" she was exasperated and embarrassed. She needed this conversation to end.

"No, I left her at the restaurant." he was quiet for a moment. "I know I hurt you, Ava." the moment those words were out, all the anger and hurt began flooding her system, overwhelming her at an alarming rate until the alcohol within her snapped her brain and mouth filter.

"Yeah!" she snapped, squeezing her eyes closed as she concentrated on lowering her voice. "After you called me to tell me that I was playing games with you." she sucked in a breath as anger and hurt collided within her. "I don't even know what you're talking about, you laid my insecurities out and spat them in my face." she heard his sharp intake of breath, but she didn't care. "But you know what?!" her voice raised several octaves as her anger surged forth battling the hurt within her. "I knew you were in pain. I knew you needed help and I couldn't stand the thought of you being alone and hurting." she took several deep breaths and lowered her voice, she didn't want James to hear the conversation. "When I found you, I thought something bad had happened to you, I helped you and what did you do, left without so much as a word, a text *nothing*." her breaths were harsh and her heart was drumming so fast it made her a little lightheaded.

"Ava." his voice was a warning that she batted away.

"No, Blake, you need to listen to me." she bit out, her hands shaking as she tried to grip the bedcovers with her free hand. "I'm done with you." she winced at her blunder but continued in hopes that he didn't realise what she'd said. "Don't call me *Candice,* I'm not one of your sluts and don't you fucking dare call me *baby girl* ever again." she didn't wait for him to say anything else as she disconnected the call.

Ava stared at the blank screen for long moments, silent tears tracked down her cheeks and her breaths were panting at the effort to keep the sobs from escaping. She knew without a shadow of a doubt that she had effectively cut all ties with Blake in her fit of anger, her heart too raw, and now she knew that she'd have to live with the consequences even if it hurt. Because in the end Blake Synclair will never change, will never think of others except himself and would have never seen her as more than his best friend's chubby little sister.

The bitter laugh that escaped her lips echoed around the room and in that moment, under the cover of darkness, was her clarity. She had severed her ties with the man she had been hopelessly in love with.

The hum of voices, the clattering of cups and the whir and hiss of the coffee machine were like music to Ava's ears as she stood in the queue of customers. Tucking a stray piece of hair that had escaped her messy bun behind her ear, she debated on whether to try a new coffee, debated on whether she wanted to risk her taste buds being offended when slender arms reached around her shoulders from behind, a floral scent filling her nostrils as a bright, wide smile broke out.

"Morning, Ava." Katie's delicate voice was bright.

"Katie! Morning." Ava beamed.

"Thank god it's you; I've done that move to a further three other people." Katie laughed, shrugging as Ava cut her eyes to hers. "Whatcha ordering?" she quizzed as she let her go and stood beside her.

"Probably the usual, I can't offend my taste buds." she laughed to herself, quietly as Katie mocked surprise, her hand flying to her chest.

"Really! I'm shocked Ava, truly shocked." she exclaimed playfully. "So what had you texting me in the middle of the night?" Katie asked bluntly.

"Coffee, first." Ava advised as she stepped up to the front of the queue to order both of their usual drinks of hazelnut lattes.

Drinks in hand, they settled for a table near the back of the coffee shop. Ava wrapped both hands around the cup, her shoulders slumping slightly as she looked at Katie. Despite being Blake's cousin, she couldn't be any more different from the dark, brooding, sinful man. Her dyed fire red hair had been straightened perfectly, her big doe, blue eyes twinkled with mischief constantly and the smattering of freckles across her nose and cheeks that she tried to hide under make-up gave her the almost cartoon character vibe. Her figure was something Ava had always been envious of. From her tight, toned stomach, perfect rounded ass and small breasts made every single outfit she wore look perfect and every single man they encountered always turned to stare at her.

"Feeling better?" she asked around the rim of her coffee mug.

"Yeah, it must have been the food." Ava lied, Katie narrowed her eyes slightly.

"Or the blonde." Katie pointed out. "Either way, that cousin of mine." she left the thought as her eyes strayed to her chest. "Ooh, is that Chisholm Hunter's?" Katie asked as she reached across the table, her fingers delicately lifted the diamond cluster pendant from her chest. "This is beautiful, diamond cut too." Katie continued before she let go and sat back in her seat. Ava felt her cheeks tint with heat and her pulse spike in her throat for a fraction of a second before she willed her body to relax.

"Yeah, it's nice." Ava smiled slightly, and Katie laughed, shaking her head.

"It's more than nice, Ava." she chuckled. "It's a fourteen hundred pound necklace." Ava's eyes bulged at Katie's words, her fingers flying to the pendant.

"No, it can't be that much." Ava shook her head. "You must be mistaken." she continued, but Katie cocked her head to the side, her eyes narrowing slightly.

"You know I spend all of my waking moments in that store and I would know a piece of jewellery that I sell." the conviction in her voice had Ava furrowing her brow.

"It was a present."

"From James?" she asked quizzically as Ava shook her head no.

"Blake." she whispered. She watched Katie's eyes widen and her mouth open slightly. "Just for my birthday." she quickly added.

"Uh-huh." Katie nodded, took a sip of the latte and locked eyes with her. "How did he give you the present?" she asked, her voice serious, which confused Ava.

"Left it with James." Ava admitted, taking a sip of her drink. "It's just a birthday present." she huffed. Memories of the phone call replaying in her mind.

"Uh-huh." Katie smirked as Ava shook her head. "You know men only buy women jewellery for two reasons." Katie held up two fingers. "One, because she's his mother and he wants to make her happy." she put one finger down. "And two, the most important one, he's in love." Katie put the last finger down and Ava couldn't contain the burst of laughter that sprung from her lips, making Katie cock an eyebrow at her.

"Well, I can tell you one thing." Ava said, calming down the laughter. "I'm neither of those to Blake." it was a sobering reality. "I mean come on!" Ava exclaimed, throwing her hands in the air when Katie continued to smirk at her from across the table. "He heard me get off in the shower with his name flying out of my mouth, he told me to stop making *those* noises when I eat, he forced me to go home from the pub, he called me in the middle of the night to shout at me for being me and me being me, I helped him and he left." she rushed out on a long breath. "Then to top it all off he closed his family's restaurant, brought a date and then he's bought me a necklace, called me again last night and – and..." tears welled in her eyes, despite her best efforts to keep them at bay. "I told me a few truths and well, I think it's safe to say we won't be speaking again." the words were spat from her lips, frustration evident in her tone.

"Well, fuck me sideways!" Katie exclaimed. "That's a lot of information to take in so early in the morning." her eyebrows hit her hairline. "I am sorry that my cousin is a dick sometimes." she continued, her face pinching in seriousness.

"It doesn't matter, and Blake certainly doesn't matter." she huffed bitterly, taking another sip of her coffee. The sweet and nutty flavour delighting her taste buds.

"Right, okay." Katie hedged at the sheer bitterness in her tone. "So, you're turning your back on him after how long? And just like that?" Katie snapped her fingers to emphasise her point. A sceptical look on her face.

"Yup!" Ava nodded once, a steely determination making her back straighter and her shoulders set.

"Okay then." Katie clapped her hands once, a smile tugging her lips. "Let's find you a man to dirty you up!" Ava could see the challenge in her friend's eyes, daring her to back down and daring her to take back everything she had said.

"Fine, but it'll be hard." Ava grumbled as she finished her coffee. "You know men don't look at me like that," she admitted, shame tingeing her tone.

"And that's your problem." Katie pointed a long, slender finger at her. "You need more confidence. You're gorgeous, you have a killer figure any woman in their right minds would want and you have this certain quality that drive men wild." the last of Katie's words were cut off by the riotous laughter that bubbled out of Ava's mouth.

"And what would that be, do tell because at this moment in time, Katie, you're full of shit." Ava laughed and shook her head.

"Innocent!" Katie exclaimed. "That's what drives men wild when they're around you, but you never notice because of Blake." Katie seemed triumphant in her explantation, but Ava was doubtful. "Look, I'll even show you what I mean and all it will take is one night out, just us girls."

"I highly doubt the local pub will be the right place." Ava pointed out, making Katie laugh.

"Oh no, sweetie." the wicked gleam in Katie's eyes had Ava regretting the conversation. "We're going clubbing. Tonight."

"What?" Ava asked. "I thought you were working tomorrow?"

"Nope, I took the weekend off." Katie smirked again, holding her arms across her chest. "No turning back now, Ava."

Chapter Seven

The loud, thumping bass of the music vibrated through Ava's body. The strobe lights spinning and twirling across the expanse of the crowded dance floor. Bodies undulating together and the thick scent of alcohol added to the atmosphere of the best nightclub in town.

"Stop fidgeting." Katie scolded in an overly loud voice. But Ava couldn't help tugging on the very short, very clingy black dress which she had been wrestled into by her best friend. "Ava!" Katie clasped her hand tightly. "You look fucking stunning; just stop fidgeting." Katie huffed as they weaved between groups of people.

"So you say!" Ava grumbled. "You have the figure for this outfit." which was the truth.

"But it looks so much better on you." Katie admitted the moment they reached the bar. Ava blew out a breath, knowing that she wouldn't win this fight. Ever since they were teenagers, she'd made it her mission to boost Ava's confidence about her figure and always called her Marilyn Monroe, which always resulted in Ava rolling her eyes. Katie slid a small shot of pink liquid towards her. "Bottoms up!"

Ava had lost count of how much she'd drunk. She wasn't certain if she was on her second or tenth shot of Tequila Rose and she certainly wasn't certain if this was the first or fourth bottle of wine she was clutching against her chest like her life depended on it as she wobbled towards an empty booth.

"See that guy?" Katie asked, pointing towards a tall, gangly man with dirty blonde hair and beady eyes.

"Y-yeah?" Ava hiccuped, scrunching her face slightly.

"He's been watching you since we arrived." Katie smiled, like it was the best news she could ever deliver to her. "You should go and introduce yourself."

"No!" Ava vehemently shook her head, making her stomach roil and the room spin. "He's not right, no brown eyes, no dark hair." Ava slurred her words, making Katie laugh.

"Let me get this straight." Katie began. "You want a man who has dark brown eyes and dark hair?" Ava was nodding at every word Katie spoke. "You want him to be tall, full of himself?" Ava continued nodding. "But not Blake?" Katie gave Ava a pointed look.

"Oh, definitely not h-him." Ava hiccuped again, gulping more wine. "He's the worst!" Ava exclaimed. "All pretty and shit!" Katie burst out laughing. "What he is!" Ava grumbled, the room sinning on its axis, making her feel a little sick.

"Oh, I've no doubt that my cousin is everything that you say he is." Katie agreed, taking her phone out. Scrunching her face a little, her fingers moving quickly across the screen.

"Is that the m-man?" Ava hiccuped around another gulp of wine. "Your conquest?"

"What? No!" she shook her head. "Maybe someone for Plan B." she smirked as she put her phone away. Ava threw the entire glass of wine down her throat and quickly refilled her glass from the almost empty bottle. The room was spinning wildly, and she began giggling at nothing in particular. "Come on!" Katie shouted over the music as she pulled Ava to her feet. "Let's dance!" she continued. Ava swayed on her feet slightly from the alcohol before she stumbled onto the dance floor.

Bodies clashed and undulated with the beat of the music and

Ava let the music take over her mind and body as she slowly swayed her hips. Her delicate hands glided over the curves of her body, making her feel sexy as the alcohol mixed with her touches in a heady combination. Katie winked at her a mere second before turning away, but before Ava could do or say anything, a large body clashed against hers which stopped her dead in her tracks. A hard chest pressed against her back, large hands gripped her hips. Warm breath against her ear. *His* scent, bergamot and spicy pepper, cloaking her.

But it wasn't him; she knew that. The drunken haze which had captured her wholly made her a little more daring, and her brain cells seemed to have scattered. It was the only explanation as she ground her ass against the mystery man's crotch.

"Hmm, so good." she moaned, resting her head against his chest, eyes closed and her hips undulating once again, her ass ground against him.

"How much have you had to drink?" he quizzed; the deep, gruff voice sent shivers down her spine. His fingers gripping her hips tighter made her grind against him, a low throaty moan escaped her parted lips. "I'm taking you home." he continued without waiting for an answer before she was spinning slightly. His grip on her upper arm felt brutal as he forced her to keep up with his powerful strides through the nightclub.

The moment the cool summer night breeze hit her overheated flesh, her head spun and her stomach lurched as she stumbled over her own feet, but the brutal grip on her arm had stopped her from falling.

"Let me go." Ava's words slurred before she hiccuped. "I don't want to go h-home." another hiccup before her green eyes landed on dark, brooding eyes making her stumble in the high heels. "Blake." she ground out.

"You're not going home." Blake bit out before stopping directly in front of a sleek, black sports car. Almost ripping the car door from its hinges and bundling her in the passenger seat.

The moment the door slammed shut and his scent enveloped her senses, Ava's head spun trying to wrap around what had actually happened. One minute she was dancing with Katie and the next Blake was there, surrounding her. The hardness of his body, the scent of him, his hands on her and she....

Oh god!

She ground her ass against his crotch.

The purr of the engine brought Ava from her thoughts, and she looked at his perfect profile. Licking over her dry lips, she watched his jaw clench, making the stubble move as the muscle pulsed almost like a ticking time bomb.

"Why are you mad?" she whispered into the silence of the car. Her hand reaching across to touch his jaw. The soft scrape of his stubble tingling her fingertips, but the low vibration she felt had her pulling her hand away.

"I'm not mad." his voice almost growled, his hands gripped the steering wheel tighter, his knuckles turning white. "I'm fucking furious." he continued cutting his dark gaze to hers for a fraction of a second before he turned back to concentrate on the road. Ava smiled sloppily, ignoring the hard stare and the warning in his tone.

Ava's green eyes grew wide as she was pulled from the car. She tried to straighten, tried not to wobble on her heels. Her hand flying out to rest against the car whilst she tried to stop the world from spinning. The moment she focused enough to see the building before her.

"Holy shit!" she whispered, tipping her head back as she looked over the imposing building. But that was a mistake; her

LJ CARROLL

balance wavered, and she stumbled backwards, almost falling.

"Fucking hell, Ava!" Blake growled a second before her stomach collided with the wide expanse of his shoulder.

"H-hey!" she hiccuped. Her arms dangling over her head. She tried to wiggle, but his arms tightened around her legs.

"Doctor Synclair." a warm voice greeted with the hint of a chuckle.

"Patrick." his husky voice bit out a little tersely. Her eyes latched onto the hard muscle of his ass cheeks, clenching and releasing with each powerful stride he took.

"Yummy!" she mumbled, licking over her lips. The need to sink her teeth into his ass was overwhelming, but she couldn't make purchase. Every step he took, she tried craning her neck, mouth open, ready to bite down, but she couldn't get close enough.

The loud ding vibrated her skull, making her wince. The stomach dropping movement of being lifted higher into the sky without ever leaving the wide expanse of a shoulder. She tried again, craning her neck, mouth open and teeth at the ready to bite down on the perfect ass, but then they were moving again and she couldn't get close enough.

Frustrated, her hand slapped the ass she wanted to bite, hard enough her palm stung. Blake stopped dead in his tracks. She felt like she was flying until her back landed on a soft mattress with a humph and a wild giggle bubbled out of her throat.

"Did you slap my ass?" he quizzed, those dark eyes staring directly into hers. Pure liquid heat flowed through her body at an alarming rate. Her heart pounded in her chest, her breaths were shallow and her nipples were poking through the thin material of her dress.

"What if I did?" she narrowed her eyes slightly, pushing her

56

hair off of her face and trying her hardest not to let her fingers trail over her sensitive flesh.

Blake was a blur of movement in her intoxicated state as her wrists were seized, pushed into the soft blankets above her head. A delicious thick thigh between her legs and his sinfully handsome face inches from hers. A whimper fell from her parted lips as she arched against him. Wanting desperately to feel the hardness of his body against hers.

"Is this what you want, hmm?" he asked, the hardness of his voice heightening the desire that was sweeping through. His free hand gripped her hip roughly, forcing her into the mattress, but she bucked against his hold. "Is this what you've been looking for all night?" his thigh pressed harshly against her weeping pussy and a low moan filled the room. "Wanting to be treated as a common whore." the hard steel of his voice hit her like ice water. Instantly stilling her writhing body.

"W-what? No!" she couldn't hide the hurt in her voice.

"Then why are you acting like one?" he asked, his voice cold, but his eyes were glacial. Her heart continued to beat wildly in her chest and despite the words spoken, her body wasn't listening. Her pussy clenched as liquid seeped from her core and her nipples became harder. Her tongue darted out to lick across her lips and her thighs shook slightly. "Don't make me ask again, Ava." he warned.

"Because of those women." she mumbled breathlessly, squeezing her eyes shut as she tried to curb the hot lava of desire that was trying to take control of her body.

"Women?" he asked, furrowing his brow. "What women?" his nose bumped against hers as his grip on her wrists and hip tightened.

"Oh god!" Ava squeezed her eyes shut again as she dragged a deep breath in; the more she tried to control her body, the more he tightened his grip and the more she wanted to feel his roughness. Experience every-fucking-hard-inch of him. She was mindless to her desire for him, mindless to try to control herself and certainly her mouth decided to work independently from the rest of her. "The ones you date." she whispered so low, she hoped he hadn't heard.

Heat flooded her cheeks as she realised he'd heard exactly what she'd said. Those dark eyes of his roamed over every inch of her face. His nostrils flared slightly and his eyes darkened before he slammed his lips against hers. They were hard and demanding against her softer ones; goosebumps erupted over every inch of her skin at the feel of him dominating her. Hard groans ripped from her throat. His tongue was a solid muscle as he thrust it between her parted lips, sweeping, tasting, owning every inch of her mouth.

Blake moved further into her body, pulling her pelvis to his. The thick column of his erection tenting his dress pants rubbed against her wet panties. A whimper escaped as his teeth bit down on her lower lip, the pain instant, but was soothed away with a sweep of his tongue before he ripped his mouth from hers. Their harsh breaths mingling together. Their chests heaving with every breath. The pure decadent friction on her clit as she continued to rub against his hardened length, but it wasn't enough; she needed more.

"Please, Blake." she moaned, arching her back until her nipples scrapped against his chest.

"What?" his gruff voice had her stomach clenching.

"Make me yours." she begged, thrusting her hips against him.

"No." he growled, tearing himself away from her. Coldness washed over her body at the sudden loss of his heat. Her eyes snapped open and stared at him. She watched him roughly dig his fingers into his dark hair, tip his head back and drag in a deep breath before those impossibly dark eyes landed on her. "Get some sleep." he ground out before turning on his heel.

The slam of the door made her jump and tears prick her eyes as he left her alone. She didn't understand. Didn't understand what she'd done wrong. Didn't understand why he'd kissed her so demanding, bordering on brutal, but left her. Then it hit her through the alcohol fog.

"He doesn't like me." she whispered to herself. Ava couldn't stop the sob which tore from her throat, nor could she stop the flow of tears was wetting her cheeks.

Blake was the only man she had ever fallen head over heels for. He was the only man she had thrown herself at. He was the only man she was saving herself for. And he didn't want her. That was her last thoughts as she cried herself to sleep.

Chapter Eight

Blake's head banged against the closed hotel room door. His hands clenched into tight fists, harsh breaths had his chest rising and falling in rapid succession. Squeezing his eyes shut against the heart wrenching sobs in the room behind him.

"Fuck!" he hissed, fists banging once on the door behind him. "I hurt her!" he whispered, his eyes snapping open as his pulse spiked. "I fucking hurt her." his words were tortured as he muttered them aloud into the empty hall.

You haven't hurt her, sweetheart. The soft, sweet voice drifted into his mind. Pressing the heels of his hands against his eyes. The guilt sweeping through him, poisoning him.

"Go away." he muttered, willing *her* voice from his head. His heart began to pound. Images colliding together, all dark wavy hair, curvy as fuck, shy smiles and green eyes.

He couldn't do this now.

The last time he let the images take root, he'd fallen so hard not even his breathing techniques had worked.

But she came for you.

He could still hear the sobs.

He could still feel her luscious body pressed against his. Her perfect lips against his and he could still smell her perfume on him, cloaking him in warmth and that's what he needed to concentrate on – anything to get *her* out of his fucking head, at least until he went home.

"Fucking hell, Ava." he snarled aloud. The sound of the elevator opening had Blake stiffening, his arms dropping to his sides as his dark eyes turned. "Patrick." his voice was cold, hard.

"Doctor Synclair." the doorman smiled as he walked slowly towards him, removing his hat. "I hope you don't mind, but I thought you might need some help with Ms Asherton."

"She's sleeping, thank you." Blake lied, still hearing the sobs through the door. Patrick tilted his head to the side.

"Very well." he nodded once, with a look that told Blake he knew it was a lie. "Would you have a drink with me?" he asked. Blake furrowed his brow. "You look like you need one." Blake nodded once. He couldn't stand hearing the sobs any longer.

The hotel bar was already closed, much to Blake's pleasure. He couldn't stand the thought of having to make small talk with the waitresses who always made a beeline for him. Grabbing a bottle of whiskey and two crystal cut tumblers, he sunk into one of the wingback chairs opposite Patrick.

"Here." Blake handed a filled glass to Patrick. Taking a sip of his own, relishing the burn in his throat.

"Blake." Patrick sighed. "I've known you since you were a little boy." he continued taking a sip of his drink. "I know Candice hurt you, George too." Blake's gaze hardened as he stared at the ageing man.

"What's your point, Patrick?" Blake's voice was hard, his fisted hand resting against his thigh.

"My point, Blake." Patrick took a big gulp of whiskey before pinning him with a pointed look. "You need to go home and stop coming here with a different woman." with that, he drained his glass. "Leave Ms Asherton alone." His lips thinned into a hard line. "Goodnight, Doctor Synclair." Patrick tipped his hat towards him before leaving the bar.

Blake drained his own glass. Tipping his head back, closed eyes. Her words spinning in his head.

"When I found you, I thought something bad had happened to you; I helped you and what did you do, left without so much as a word, a text nothing."

"I'm done with you. Don't call me Candice, I'm not one of your sluts and don't you fucking dare call me baby girl ever again."

"Make me yours."

"What have you fucking done to me, baby girl?" he whispered, swallowing thickly. Scrubbing a hand down his face before picking the glasses and bottle up to deposit them back behind the bar, and headed back to his room. Hoping that Ava was asleep when he got there.

Stood at the large window, his arms folded over his bare chest. The sunlight streaming in as he looked out over the city. Tall high-rise buildings, cars and people milling about like little specs from his view. He'd been stood staring out of the same window since the sun rose, his head an absolute fucking mess.

He'd fucked up.

Royally fucked up.

"Seriously, what the actual fuck!" Ava shouted.

Blake chuckled and shook his head. It was rare that he'd ever heard such vulgar language from her. It was comical and he could just picture her face as she took in the room. Realisation dawning on her face, her nose scrunching, her lips parting and that fucking chest of hers rising and falling, breasts straining against the fabric.

"Blake." she gasped. His cock twitched in his sweatpants, that breathy little voice.

Fuck!

He could feel her eyes on him. Felt them roaming over his back, almost as if she was eye-fucking him. His stomach twisted painfully, making him tense a moment before he turned around. Lust swept through him at the sight. Her hair a little dishevelled, the tight black dress clung to every-fucking-curve she possessed, those pouty lips slightly parted and her eyes furrowed against the sunlight.

"How're feeling?" his voice was gruff as he tried to quell the lustful thoughts.

"Like shit." she deadpanned.

"Hmm." he shook his head. "Sit down." the hard tone of his voice made her jump slightly before he gestured towards the small dining table he'd set up. Littered with silver domed breakfast plates. He watched as her eyes leisurely raked over his bare chest, watched her pink little tongue swipe across her lips as the delectable blush settled in her cheeks. She was definitely eye-fucking him and that did something he couldn't even begin to think of. "Eat, Ava." he commanded as he sat directly opposite her.

He was losing his patience, and he knew it.

"Why are you even here?" the confusion in her voice was evident. Watching her loading her folk with the perfectly crispy bacon. Those fucking sounds went straight to his cock.

"How much did you drink last night?" the moment she registered his words, her eyes snapped to his. She opened and closed her mouth a few times, speechless. "Don't remember me picking you up at the club?" he asked, taking a bite of toast.

"Err..." she started, emotions quickly flashing across her face too quick for him to read. "Sorry." she ventured; he wasn't certain if she was being genuine about not knowing what happened or if she didn't want to speak about how he hurt her last night.

"You should be; I had to call James at one o'clock this morning, telling him you were staying here." his tone was harsh as he continued eating breakfast. "It didn't go very well." he bit out.

He'd spent over ten minutes explaining that she was safe – lie he knew – but didn't want to tell his best friend what he'd done to his little sister – no, he'd take that to the motherfucking grave. One moment's lapse in his control, one moment's lapse had almost brought the worst to the surface, and he couldn't let that happen. *Not with her.*

"Oh." he saw confusion settle on her face. "Why didn't you take me home?" her voice was low as she asked, making him sigh.

"Because I wanted to make sure you didn't have alcohol poisoning." he lied, his eyes staring directly at her over the rim of his coffee cup that was poised at his lips.

"Why though?" she continued to ask.

Fuck sake, Ava.

"Because I'm a doctor, Ava, and know the warning signs." the harshness in his tone didn't belong to him. "James doesn't know what he's looking for, but I do." he continued, finishing his coffee. "Once you've eaten, I'll take you home." again his harsh tone, and he hated himself for it.

I nearly fucked you last night!

I didn't want to stop!

It was sheer fucking willpower that I pulled away!

Have you got bruises?

Will you discover them in the shower and know what I did? Know what kind of person I am.

Fuck, Ava!

I don't think I'll be able to stop next time!

There can't ever be a fucking next time, baby girl!

But he already knew that last thought was a lie.

Chapter Nine

It had been almost four weeks since her disastrous night out and the aftermath that followed wasn't one for the weak-hearted. Blake had the good sense to stay in his car. James was a raging bull when she walked through the front door. He'd been pacing for god knows how long, his face a twisted mask of anger and worry. She still didn't understand his reaction; after all, she was with his best friend.

James had asked her repeatedly if Blake had made her feel uncomfortable, if he'd been anything but a gentleman to her, and she knew what James meant. Her big brother wanted to know if his best friend had fucked her and whilst her heart skipped a beat at the mere thought and there were holes in her memory from that night, she knew nothing had happened.

It had been almost four weeks since she'd last seen Blake, and it was the longest she had ever gone without seeing him. After she'd dealt with James's tantrum about her spending the night at Blake's hotel, she'd sent him a text message to thank him for letting her stay and for the breakfast and she'd waited almost an hour, before she realised he wasn't going to text her back. Which should have been fine; after all, she was the one who'd cut ties with him. But then he'd come for her and looked after her, which only jumbled her thoughts. Her feelings, that was something she didn't think would ever change. Despite what had happened between them, despite that she wasn't his type and despite him not liking her very much as a friend. She still was hopelessly in love with him.

Blowing out a breath, Ava slid the long maxi-dress she had

bought for the Asherton barbecue over her head, careful not to smudge her make-up, which she had spent longer than she'd care to admit doing. The dress fit her like a glove and the deep brown colour complimented her green eyes – well that's what Katie had told her – the long double gold plated necklace caressed the tops of her breasts which were on display in the low cut of the dress. She wasn't certain if the gold-coloured sandals may have been too much, but again Katie had insisted that she wore them with this dress. Smiling to herself as she braided her long, dark hair into a fish-tail braid.

Ava had just finished combing out the curls she'd framed her face with when she heard Katie's laughter, followed by James's low voice, through her open window. Quickly glancing out of her bedroom window, which looked out onto the manicured lawn at the back of the house, she smiled. James was barbecuing, Katie was standing with a glass of wine, talking and laughing with James. A few of the younger neighbours which they'd invited were scattered into groups talking, sharing alcoholic drinks and laughing. But no sign of Blake. That realisation made her stomach drop. She was really hoping to see him, which she instantly chastised herself for; after all, wasn't it her who cut ties with him – the unobtainable.

Trying to shake the thought of him out of her mind, Ava quickly descended the stairs, picking a glass of wine from the kitchen before she slowed her pace and walked through the double glass doors and directly into a hard body. The wine sloshed in the glass, little droplets spilling onto a dark green t-shirt.

"Oh god, I'm so sorry." Ava exclaimed, her free hand landing on the wet marks. Her fingers rubbing against muscles which rippled with every brush.

"It's okay, don't worry about it." at the sound of the calm, deep voice which held a hint of laughter had her craning her neck slightly until she looked at the man before her. All light brown hair and blue eyes.

"Nathan, hey!" she exclaimed, a small smile on her lips as her fingers continued to brush the wetness on his top. "Did you finally get that date?" she asked, taking a sip of wine.

"Err, no." his eyes furrowed slightly as he looked over her shoulder. His hand covering hers against his chest to stop her movements.

"Ava!" the loud yell of her name had her jumping and spinning on her heel to be greeted by Katie, throwing her arms in the air before they wrapped around her, almost choking her. Laughing, Ava wrestled her out of the choke hold.

"How much have you had to drink?" Ava chuckled as she sipped her wine. Katie smiled at her.

"Not enough!" she exclaimed in exaggerated horror. "Hey Nathan." she greeted before her face paled, eyes narrowed and her lips thinned into a harsh line. Her focus behind Ava. "You've got to be fucking kidding me." she whispered angrily, making Ava turn and her mouth dropped open as her heart stuttered in her chest before thundering until she heard the blood whooshing through her ears.

Blake striding with purpose towards the table, which had been laid out with various alcohol beverages. The pale blue t-shirt fit his tall, hard, muscular body with just enough pull against the fabric with every bunch and ripple those muscles made. His jeans clung to his tapered waist and perfect ass and his hair was sexily tousled, with his aviator sunglasses hiding the dark, intense brown eyes she loved so much. But what made tears prick her eyes and her lungs to feel constricted was the tall, skinny as fuck blonde woman dressed in what can only be described as lingerie – all lace, thin lining beneath the pale pink dress which looked like a second skin. Her white heels accentuated her long, lean legs.

"I'm gonna fucking kill him." Katie seethed, but before she could move an inch, Ava wrestled her hand from Nathan's and gripped her hand, keeping her in place.

"Katie, what's wrong with you?" Ava asked. "It's not as if this is new. Not as if he never brings a date." Ava sighed dejectedly, feeling every bit as worthless and ugly as she always felt when this happened.

"Well." Nathan cleared his throat awkwardly, Ava glancing at him briefly. "I should...." he didn't finish his sentence when Ava nodded and he walked in the opposite direction. Her focus slithering back to Blake and his little slut.

"No, Ava, it's not right!" Katie exclaimed a little too loudly, causing the little slut to look in their direction, a fake smile planted on her lips.

"Lower your voice." Ava hissed, as she watched the little slut lean closer to Blake, her lips brushing against his ear.

"No!" Katie was trying to get out of Ava's death grip. "After what he did...." Katie's eyes widened and her words trailed off before she took a gulp of wine and refused to meet Ava's eyes.

"Katie, what do you mean?" Ava whispered, almost afraid to ask. But Katie shook her head, plastered a smile onto her face and looked at her.

"We need more wine." she countered, refusing to answer Ava's question before stealing her glass and sauntered towards Blake and the little slut.

Ava couldn't do anything but watch in abject horror as Katie pushed the little slut away and said something until Blake looked directly at Katie through his aviators and that's when it happened. Katie reared back, her arm swung in a perfect arc until her palm collided with Blake's cheek.

"Oof!" the calm, deep voice of Nathan was so close it made Ava jump. "That's got to have hurt." he laughed a little before offering her an unopened bottle of beer. "Thought you might need this -" he gestured towards Katie. "It's going to be fun." he chuckled.

"Yeah!" Ava turned from her best friend who was now jabbing a finger in his well-defined chest and her lips moving at a rapid pace and looked at Nathan. "I don't know how much she's already drunk." Ava admitted, her eyes turning back as she saw James striding towards the altercation.

"Would you like to grab something to eat?" Nathan asked, rubbing the back of his neck. "With me?" he clarified with a small smile tugging at his lips.

"Why are you being weird?" Ava asked, tilting her head slightly. Nathan blushed slightly and cleared his throat.

"I'm just asking if you want to grab a bite to eat." he muttered, taking a sip of beer from the bottle.

"Yeah." she nodded. She watched James fling Katie onto his shoulder and march into the house, kicking and banging her small fists against his back along the way. "Oh, someone's in trouble." Ava shook her head. "I think that'll be all the drama for this party." she continued with a slight chuckle, trying her damnedest not to steal another glance in Blake's direction.

"She can handle herself." Nathan laughed, handing her a plate with a hot dog on as he picked another for himself.

Ava and Nathan walked towards an empty picnic table, each carrying their food and drinks. She glanced at Nathan from the corner of her eye to find him with a slight blush on his cheeks and a small smile playing on his lips. She'd never seen him like this before. Awkward and cute. The boy-next-door. She sat opposite him; her facing the rest of the garden and the party whilst Nathan was sat looking directly at her.

"Hmm." Ava hummed in agreement, picking the hot dog up with both hands. "I can't believe the receptionist turned you down. Her loss." her smile was genuine as she looked at him. Nathan was a great friend and always made nights out better with his sense of humour.

Licking over her lips, she brought the hot dog closer to her mouth, her eyes watching her movements to ensure that the ketchup and mustard didn't drip onto her dress. The moment she opened her mouth, inching the hot dog closer, she felt eyes on her. Quickly averting her gaze, she looked at Nathan, who was happily biting into his own, but over his shoulder she saw Blake staring in her direction. His jaw clenched tightly.

"Yeah, her loss." Nathan's voice filtered through her haze, but she couldn't form words. It was like Blake's intense stare had sucked all functions from her.

Gulping at the intense stare, Ava tried to avert her gaze from Blake. Tried to look anywhere but at him and the little slut hanging off of his arm, but she couldn't. His long fingers clenched against her hip and pulling her slightly closer to his body, making Ava shake her head and the sadness in her eyes to intensify when her stomach grumbled. Tampering down the building sadness which was practically consuming her, she licked over her lips again and stretched her lips wide before they closed around the hot dog.

"So, Ava." Nathan cleared his throat. "Do you want to have a movie night?" he asked, taking a long pull from the bottle of beer.

"Yeah." Ava nodded as she swallowed her bite of food. "We haven't had one in ages. I'll see when Katie's free, too." she offered,
"Mmm. Or it could be just us?" Nathan smiled cheekily and

heat tinged her cheeks. "You know, hanging out." Nathan clarified with his eyes twinkling in the sunlight.

"Oh, umm…" Ava took a sip of the beer, her eyes landing on Blake, who was still staring at her. "That…" she gulped around an invisible lump in her throat. She felt open, exposed when she felt the intense stare from across the garden. But it didn't stop the fact he was here with his little slut.

"Ava, I get it okay." he cut off her words as he glanced over his shoulder. "If you want Katie there too, it's okay." he continued in a rush of words before standing abruptly, picking his plate and bottle up.

Ava should let him leave, she should do a lot of things, but the moment she spies Blake and his little slut rounding the corner of her home, all logic and common sense leave her.

"Yes!" she blurted out, her heart thudding against her chest. Her palms slick with sweat and her stomach rioting with nausea as she watched the little slut arch against the wall, pushing her perfect tits into Blake's chest. Blinking the tears back quickly, she tore her eyes away from them at the same moment Nathan turned to look at her. A wide smile taking over his mouth.

"Yeah?" his calm voice was filled with excitement and his eyes were bright.

"Movie night, just us." she clarified with a small, forced smile.

"Great, Tomorrow?" Ava nodded, still forcing the smile. His cheeks tinted a deeper red from the heat of the sun. "I'll see you tomorrow." he beamed, nodding, before turning on his heel.

Ava sat and watched Nathan walk away with a spring in his step. She was just about to follow him when her traitorous eyes strayed back to Blake and his little slut. But the moment her brain kicked into gear at what she was seeing – little slut pressed against the side of the house, his hand gripping her hip and his other hand pinning her wrists above her head – images flooded her mind.

Images swirling and clashing together like a kaleidoscope.

His hand pinning her wrists to his bed, his other pinning her hip to his bed, and their lips fused together. Ava writhing beneath him, his hard cock still clothed, rubbing against her wet panties, igniting pleasure against her clit.

Her breaths were whooshing out of her parted lips as she recalled in vivid clarity everything. The way he tasted when his tongue dominated her mouth, they way his kiss was brutal, passionate, the way her body lit up at the feel of his perfect body against hers and of her begging for him to make her his and him walking away.

"Oh, fuck!" she whispered, blinking her eyes rapidly, trying to dispel the images of what could have been a perfect night.

Chapter Ten

It was ten o'clock at night before the last person left the garden party and Ava was snuggled beneath the blankets, the flickering glow of the television lighting up her bedroom. Katie laid on her stomach at the bottom of her bed, her feet raised in the air and crossed at the ankles and Ava had a feeling that they were both pretending to watch television.

Katie had been unusually quiet with a faraway look in her eyes and whilst Ava had tried talking to her, to make sure she was okay after her altercation with Blake and then James but she was refusing to talk. Instead, she opted to watch an old sitcom. Katie turned onto her side and propping her head in her hand. Her eyes cast towards the bed covers and sighing loudly.

"I kissed James." the words tumbled from Katie's lips in a rush, her cheeks darkening in the dim light. Ava opened and closed her mouth a few times, her eyes widening as the words sunk in. "I'm sorry but, it just sort of happened." she whispered, risking a glance from beneath her lashes. "Twice." she finished.

"Oh. My. God." Ava breathed out, shock taking over her normal brain to mouth functions.

"I know, I know." Katie mumbled. "I'm a terrible friend." she began picking at a stray piece of cotton on the bed.

"No, you're not." Ava assured her, sitting up a little more in bed. "I have a crush on your cousin and you kissed my brother. I would say we're two of a kind." Ava laughed lightly, making Katie's head snap up.

"You're not mad?" she asked, biting down on her bottom lip. Ava shook her head no, a small smile playing at the corners of her lips. She was happy for James. Happy that he was putting himself back out there. After his divorce, he swore off women, and she saw just how unhappy that made him.

"I think you should see where it takes you." Ava's voice was filled with happiness. "James has had it rough since his divorce and you, well, I'm not certain if there are any men left that you haven't already dated." Ava chuckled at Katie's mock shocked face. "I'm just saying that it could be good for both of you."

"I wasn't expecting it to be that easy." Katie admitted, a small smile on her lips. "He is pretty great and I would like to see where it takes us." the blush on Katie's cheeks deepened at her honesty. Katie threw herself back on the bed, a dreamy look taking over her face. "I won't give you all the gory details but, I hope I can still talk to you about our relationship?"

"Of course you can, after all I keep whining about your cousin, you might as well get your own back." Ava laughed briefly, her teeth scraping along her lower lip. "I kissed Blake too." Ava admitted, a blush staining her cheeks. "You see, we're the same." the moment the words were out of her mouth, Katie stopped moving and the room was thick with tension.

"Fuck!" Katie gasped, her eyes saucer wide. "You remember?" but her question had Ava's brow furrowing.

"What do you mean, Katie?" Ava's voice turned serious. "How do you know?" she probed. "Who told you what happened?" she couldn't help fire off the questions.

"Blake." she answered, her shoulders slumping slightly in defeat. "He wanted to know if you said anything to me and well I didn't know anything, so he told me what happened." she shrugged half heartedly.

"Okay." Ava said slowly, blowing out a breath. "Why didn't you tell me?" she asked, her pulse spiking out of fear of what her best friend was going to say next.

"Because he was scared that he'd hurt you." Katie jutted her chin out, eyes fixed firmly on Ava. "he heard you crying." Katie pinned her with a stare. "And I was scared because it was me who let him know where you were and that you needed him." she finished.

"Why would you even do that!" Ava exclaimed, throwing her hands up. Exasperation and anger coiling together.

"Because you love him!" Katie shouted back, and it was as if Ava had been slapped across the face with her true feelings. "You were so down that night over what he'd said to you that you were drinking yourself stupid and yeah, I wanted him to see first hand at what he was capable of doing to women." she continued, rising from the bed she began pacing. "I wanted him to see what he'd done to you without even realising it." Katie stopped at the foot of the bed, her breathing harsh with her rant. "But most of all, I wanted him to know how you felt about him and the only way you have the confidence to go for what you want is when you have alcohol flooding your veins." Katie's voice had turned low. "But he fucked up, not you, Ava. That was all Blake."

"What do you mean, he fucked up?" Ava asked, trying to process everything her best friend was saying and trying to piece all the puzzle together.

"Because in true Blake fashion, he treated you like all the other women he parades around with." Katie heaved a breath, but Ava was shaking her head, confusion evident on her face. "Dominating you, making you want him." Ava held up a hand to silence her friend.

"That wasn't him fucking up, Katie." Ava's voice was so low

and her heart was pounding against her chest. She'd enjoyed that part of him, it made her feel wanted. Not that she was going to admit to that, though.

"For fuck's sake, Ava." Katie blared, wringing her hands in a choking motion towards her. "I know that, but he left you high and dry when things turned heated, too heated for him to handle."

"I still don't..." Ava started, then realisation dawned and her eyes grew wide. "You mean he doesn't sleep with the women he dates?" Ava watched Katie take long, deep breaths, like she was trying to calm herself.

"I could kill you sometimes, sweetie." Katie's voice was sickly sweet as she clasped Ava's cheeks between her hands, their faces inches from each other. "Listen and listen good, because I'm only going to say this once." Katie's voice was deathly low, their noses bumping against each other. "They. Are. Only. Good. For. Fucking." she punctuated each word with a slight shake of Ava's head.

"I-I....." Ava tried speaking between squished cheeks, but she didn't understand.

"And yet, you still don't understand, do you?" Katie asked, sounding exasperated with the whole conversation. Ava shook her head no. "He bought you a fourteen hundred pound necklace, he shut down the restaurant." Katie spoke like she was speaking to a child. "He was trying to wine and dine you on your special birthday because you are more to him than someone to fuck." Katie released Ava's cheeks and stepped away from her.

"So why did he bring a date on my birthday and today?" Ava asked, feeling like she was the dumbest girl in the world.

"Because he wanted to make you jealous, Ava." Katie flopped back down on the bed, looking exhausted. "He's a real dick sometimes." Katie grumbled. "It was why I had to say something to him today, give him a piece of my mind and also tell that little slut dear old cousin was impotent." they both sniggered in unison. "See, this is what it's like to be fucked up by a Synclair." Katie admitted and Ava threw her head in her hands.

"If that's true." she began, her words muffled by her hands. "Then I've fucked up." she continued, still buried beneath her hands.

"Oh, what now!" Katie's words came out on an exhausted sigh.

"I told him I was done with him." Ava mumbled.

"Good!" Katie laughed, making Ava remove her hands and look at her like she had two heads. "About time he had a taste of his own medicine."

They both talked into the early hours of the morning and now Ava was alone, the summer sun filtering through the curtains. Her arm thrown across her face in an attempt to stop herself from being blinded before she groaned and reached for her phone. The numbers blinking back at her told her it was already noon, and she really did need to make a move. Throwing her phone on the bed and the bedcovers back before padding across the room towards the bathroom for a much needed shower.

Ava had spent a few hours cleaning up after the garden party, doing laundry and making lunch for herself. Her mind had been whirling with everything that had happened yesterday, from Blake to Nathan to Katie and James and back to Blake and it was exhausting to say the least. Her head was pounding, threatening a headache, her heart was working overtime beating out thunderous beats every time she thought of *him.* She had been hoping that doing the menial jobs around the house would help clear her mind, would help her stop thinking about everything, but it had the opposite effect.

Sighing to herself as she straightened the graphic t-shirt back over her stomach she threw a bag of popcorn in the microwave and set the timer before padding into the living room and opening the movie guide, looking over all the titles before settling for an action movie. They were Nathan's favourite, and she knew he'd be arriving shortly. She left it paused as the loud banging on the front door caused her to jump.

The moment she threw the door open, she felt all the air in her lungs rush out, her pulse spiked, her stomach clenched a second before butterflies erupted.

"Blake." she breathed out before squeezing her eyes shut briefly and dragging in a deep breath. "James isn't here." she continued, sounding more normal even if her body was going into full meltdown at the sheer sight of him.

His dark hair tousled in that way which makes him look fucking sexy, his stubbled jaw tight, those dark brown eyes staring directly at her and then there was his biceps straining the fabric of the white polo shirt, his tawny skin on display on those toned, powerful forearms. It made her mouth water at the sight. Licking over her lips as her gaze swept over him, she was just about to open her mouth when the loud beeping from the microwave jolted her back to the present. She quickly turned on her heel and left him standing in the doorway.

Ava had just opened the microwave door when she heard Blake close the door before his footsteps clapped against the hardwood floor. Trying not to think about his imposing presence, she quickly retrieved the bag of popcorn. The heat of the steam escaping the bag searing her fingers.

"Ow, ow, ow, ow, ow, ow." she chanted walking as quickly as she could towards the bowl and dropping the bag. "Fuck, that was hot!" she wheezed out.

"Let me take a look." his gruff voice cut through the silence and set her heart once again thundering against her chest.

Ava turned and gasped at how close he was. Her green eyes tracking his large hand, cradling hers before bringing it closer. Those dark brown eyes scanning over each finger, inspecting her with a sheer intensity that her breaths grew slow, languid and her eyes fluttered closed as cool breath blew across the overheated fingertips for a long moment.

"There's no damage." he confirmed as her eyes once again locked on his, a small smile tugging his lips. "Just a little hot." the way he spoke sent a wave of liquid heat through her veins. "I can make it better, baby girl."

Without another word, his lips gently pressed to each pad of her finger. Soft but with a certain hardness which had her core clenching with need and her nipples harden beneath her top. Those dark eyes turning a deeper shade as he stared at her through every-fucking-press of those lips. Her breaths came out in short pants as he reached the last one before he let go of her hand and stood to his full height.

Dark eyes staring into green ones for long, drawn out minutes that seemed to last an eternity. His large hand gently cupped her cheek, his thumb stroking over her cheekbone as he moved slowly, tantalisingly, to the back of her neck. His gorgeous, chiselled face inching closer. Her breaths stopped, stuck in her throat, and his sinful lips inched closer. His eyes flicking to hers and then back to her lips, making his intent crystal clear. Her breasts grazed his hardened chest; a groan vibrated through him at the slight contact, inching closer. The anticipation was killing her. Every nerve ending felt like a live wire, every pulse in her body was throbbing with need. Her lungs were burning from the harshness of her panting breaths and her fingers had a death grip on the edge of the counter.

"Ava!" the loud bellow from the hallway had her jumping.

"James." Blake sighed, his forehead gently leaning against hers and his shoulders sagging slightly. But he didn't move, his hand still at her nape and his forehead resting against hers until the sound of his heavy footfalls closed in on the kitchen and he straightened, plastering a smile to his face a second before he turned. "Afternoon."

"Hey." James's voice was shocked, but his eyes were bouncing between them. Ava quickly averted her gaze and focused on depositing the popcorn into the bowl. James cleared his throat, "Wasn't expecting you here." James continued, making Blake laugh a low, throaty chuckle that sent shock waves of pleasure through Ava's body.

"Forgot about the match?" Blake quizzed. Ava was still rooted to the spot, her back to them. "Come on, I'll drive." he continued.

"Yeah, I did." James admitted. "After wrestling Katie from you yesterday and just dropping her off this morning..." Ava smiled slightly at James' rambling. "What did you do anyway?" he asked, taking a step towards the hallway.

"Nothing much, you know what Katie's like." Blake chuckled lightly. His hand pressed to the small of Ava's back, making her tense slightly until his breath fanned over her neck. "Next time, baby girl." he whispered into her ear, making her gasp at the contact and promise laced within his words.

"Nathan's here!" James called from the hallway as Blake stiffened next to her, his eyes boring into the side of her face. She couldn't look at him. "We'll be back late; stay safe." James continued as Blake stepped away from her. The absence of his body heat made her shiver.

"Okay." her voice was wobbly as she called out, wincing at the way it sounded. "See you later." she continued, hoping that Blake didn't realise how much she was affected by him.

Plastering a smile to her face, she saw Nathan stood in the hallway. A smile on his face as he held up multiple bags of chocolate.

"Hey!" the calmness of his voice washed over her, his blue eyes sparkling before he wrapped his arms around her in a brief hug.

"Hey, since when did you become a hugger?" she laughed pulling away, the bowl of popcorn secured in her hand. She watched Nathan's mouth turn down slightly before she turned toward the living room. "Come on, movies ready and waiting." she flopped on the sofa.

Nathan sat down next to her, concentrating on opening the bags of chocolates as she pressed play on the remote. The bowl of popcorn resting in her lap. Nathan moved slightly, his leg bumping into hers, and she stiffened slightly.

"Sorry." he muttered, moving into a comfortable position. His arm was thrown casually across the back of the sofa. "You picked my fave." he whispered as the opening credits began, a smile playing on his lips.

"Yeah, I figured you'd prefer it over a romance movie." she chuckled lightly.

"I wouldn't have minded." he admitted sheepishly.

Ava furrowed her brow as she turned to look at one of her best friend's. Thoughts swirling in her head as she thought about how strange he'd been acting yesterday and again today. She knew that he wasn't interested in her in any capacity other than a friend; she wasn't his type. Nathan and Blake both had a soft spot for thin blondes. Every woman she'd ever seen Nathan with was exactly the same. She briefly wondered if it was because of the receptionist he'd been trying to bed but hadn't managed it that was making him act strangely.

Deciding to let it go, she concentrated on watching the movie. People being blown up and shot at seemed like a nice distraction from everything to do with Nathan. She'd just popped a chocolate into her mouth when Nathan's arm dropped off of the back of the sofa and onto her shoulders. His fingertips grazing her bare skin, making her stiffen in response.

"Get. The. Fuck. Off. Of. Her." the low, deadly growl of a voice had Ava's heart hammering against her chest and her breath rushing out of her lungs.

Chapter Eleven

Nathan turned his head towards the voice, smiled and stood to his full height, which was six inches short of *his* impressive height.

"Blake." Ava's voice was breathy as she looked into the intense darkness of his eyes.

"Come here, Ava." the low growled demand had her stomach flip-flopping. The anger radiating off of him was palpable and his jaw muscle was ticking wildly. Blake was staring directly at Nathan. "Don't make me ask you again." he warned, which only made liquid heat race through her veins.

Ava stood on shaking legs and moved towards the overly tall, muscular man that had stolen her heart. Blake's large hand gripped her upper arm and pulled her to his side.

"I don't want to see you near Ava again." Blake's words were laced with fury. Ava's eyes bounced between him and Nathan. She watched as Nathan smiled, all white teeth, and shrugged.

"I can't help it if she wants to see me." Nathan's warm, calm voice held a slight hint of a challenge which had Blake taking a step towards him.

"Blake, no." Ava rushed out, her palm slapping against his hard abs, which quivered under her touch. "Go home, Nathan." her words were low, but they were enough. He released the grip on her arm, only to wrap his arm around her waist. His fingers flexing against her hip, which sent goosebumps erupting down her thigh.

Nathan pushed his hand through his hair as he strode towards them, his expression stormy as he stared at Blake. His blue eyes tracking to where his fingers were flexing against her hip. His shoulder colliding with Blake's as he pushed past. Blake tensed slightly.

"Bye, Ava." Nathan called out with a chuckle in his voice at the way Blake tensed at the contact. "We should do this again." he continued, pulling the front door open. The low, deadly rumble that vibrated through Blake's chest at his words made Ava gulp around the sudden lump in her throat.

The moment the door banged shut behind Nathan, she was spun until her head rested against the hallway wall. Deep brown eyes stared at her, stealing her breath. His large hands slapped against the wall on either side of her head, their mouths a breath apart.

"You make me so fucking crazy. I can't stay away from you any longer." his voice was low, his breath fanning across her lips. "Tell me, baby girl, would you rather have that boy than me?" he asked, his eyes blazing fire in their depths as he inched his face closer. His sinful lips a breath away from hers.

"N-no." Ava stuttered out on a whisper. "It's not like that, Blake." she continued.

"Tell me what it's like, Ava." the command in his tone wasn't lost on her. Her heart was beating hard against her chest. Her breasts were grazing his chest with every breath she took and her eyes were wide, pupils dilated. Desire was coursing through her veins.

"You hurt me." she breathed out as sadness tinged her tone. "And I wanted to hurt you." she admitted in a rushed whisper. His eyes flared, his muscles tense.

"When?" the demanding, harsh tone almost sucked the breath

from her lungs. She shook her head slightly in the limited space. "Tell me, baby girl." sighing, his shoulders sagged slightly and his brow furrowed in regret. It was then she remembered her conversation with Katie, from the night at the club. She didn't want him to think it was that night.

"At the restaurant and the barbecue." she admitted. His eyes snapped to hers. "With your dates." she continued. Fire reignited in his eyes.

"The barbecue where you made me so fucking jealous with that boy, I couldn't think straight." each word was controlled and a direct contradiction as to the way he was looking at her. All-consuming fire blazing in his eyes, his jaw tense, the muscle ticking rapidly. "When you practically deep throated that hot dog." he sucked in a deep breath. "Baby girl, you drove me to madness." his hand moved slowly from the wall to her cheek, his thumb grazing her cheekbone almost as if he was memorising her. "I wanted nothing more than to throw you over my shoulder and take you to my hotel." his hand continued moving slowly to the back of her neck. "Wanted nothing more than to feel your lips on mine." he whispered as he closed the smallest of gaps between them.

Gently pressing his sinful lips to hers in the lightest briefest of touches before he pulled back. His eyes searching hers for long moments. His tongue licking across her bottom lip. Her eyes fluttered closed, her heart stuttered once, twice before it began a tortious beat until it was all she could hear.

Blake pressed his lips to hers with more pressure, unmoving, almost like a challenge. Her hands strayed from her sides and with shaking fingers she touched his chest in a featherlight touch, making him shudder. Trailing her fingertips to his abdomen, his muscles dancing under her fingers, and a small, quiet moan escaped her.

Ava tentatively curled her tongue against his lip, the tip

breaching his mouth, sliding against his teeth. His fingers curled around her nape tighter as he angled her head slightly and then his lips moved against hers in a slow, deliberate dance. The heat of his body was so close to hers, his hand blazing at her nape, and the quiet groan of satisfaction from him consumed her.

Arching her back, her hardened nipples that were poking against her tank top scraped against his solid chest encased in the white polo shirt, sending a little tremor through her body, drawing a moan from the back of her throat. Her tongue tentatively touched his before she swirled it around the tip of his tongue. Blake shuddered against her, his deep groan vibrated through his chest.

"Innocent and pure." he breathed out against her mouth, a smile tugging his lips. His eyes were heavy with desire. "So fucking pure." he whispered, making her shiver. His lips ghosted over her jaw, slowly, tantalisingly until they brushed against her ear. A low moan escaped her lips as shivers skittered over her body. "Have dinner with me." he whispered a second before his teeth nipped her earlobe, making her gasp. A rush of wetness escaped her core and the wild pulse between her thighs was beating stronger.

"Where's James?" Ava whispered.

"I left him at the match." his lips brushing against her ear. "Work emergency." he clarified. "Have dinner with me."

"Okay." she whispered, sucking in a deep breath as Blake stood to his full height, releasing the nape of her neck.

"Good girl." he smirked, gripping her hand in his as she shoved her feet back into her flip-flops beside the door before they left her home.

The large detached home was almost imposing, nestled in the middle of the other six homes. Trees lined the street, framing the impressive homes and sprawling manicured lawns. Ava glimpsed at the others and they were all the same, including the outlandish supercars and expensive SUVs, matching Blake's sleek black sports car. It was a far cry from her humble semi-detached home on the other side of town.

"This isn't the hotel." Ava pointed out as her eyes tracked across the imposing building.

"You seem surprised." his eyebrow arched. "Did you think I lived in the hotel?" he asked around a small, deep chuckle that sent Ava's pulse skyrocketing.

"Yeah." her mouth felt dry as his hand encased hers, leading her towards the front door.

The moment she stepped through the front door into the entryway, his intoxicating scent wrapped around her. Her eyes widened as she looked at the large double stairway that was framed in glass and the dark hardwood floors were warm beneath her feet and the pale blue walls made it feel light, almost airy.

"Your home's lovely." she whispered into the quietness. Blake's fingers flexed against the back of her hand, the warmth of his skin against hers felt reassuring as he led her towards the kitchen. His eyes softened as he looked at her, a smile playing on his lips.

"Thanks." he let go of her hand, she watched his purposeful strides across the expanse of the kitchen and began pulling out plates from the cupboards. The scent of the Thai takeaway they'd picked up making her stomach grumble.

"Hmm." she hummed, looking around the all white and black granite kitchen. White granite tiles covered every inch of the walls, black granite worktops and black kitchen cupboards and units. It was minimalistic and manly, which suited Blake.

"Can I trust you with a glass of wine?" his gravelly voice held a hint of laughter, but he pinned her with a stare.

"I'm sure I can handle a glass or two." she smiled as she took a seat at the black granite dining table. Her fingers smoothing over the grey leather place-mat.

Ava smiled as she watched him move around the kitchen, warming the plates quickly, plating the food, laying the table and depositing a large glass of white wine in front of her. Her eyes widened as she saw the glass, which resembled a fish bowl.

"Maybe just one glass, baby girl." he smiled before turning and collecting the plates and his own glass of wine.

Ava expected him to sit directly opposite her, like he had done when they'd had breakfast – twice. She hadn't expected him to sit beside her, his thick thigh pressing against hers. The soft scrape of his jeans against her bare thigh resulted in goosebumps prickling her skin. Her spine straightened, trying to flatten the slight roundness of her stomach, as her fingers grasped the folk. The burst of garlic, black pepper, and chilli exploded across her taste buds. The Pad Gratiem Prik Thai was amazing.

"Oh god." she moaned, chewing quickly. "This is amazing." turning her head, smiling as Blake looked at her for a moment, scooping some food onto his fork.

"Try this." his voice was low, holding the fork to her lips. Their eyes locked as she parted her lips and he carefully eased it into her mouth. His pupils dilated when her lips closed. The feel of the cool metal sliding against her lips as his hand pulled back slowly caused her eyes to flutter.

"Hmm." she hummed happily as she chewed. She watched his brow furrow for a moment, his eyes flicking from her eyes to her mouth, making her quickly swallow the food before she choked around the sudden lump lodged in her throat from the look in his eyes.

"Where's that moan, baby girl." he whispered, inching closer until they were a breath apart. Her heart hammered against her chest, her breath hitched in her throat, and her eyes fluttered closed. His tongue licked the corner of her mouth, a shudder took over her and a delicate, soft moan escaped her parted lips. "There it is." the corners of his mouth turned up in a devilish smile that had her stomach clenching and heat pooling in her core as he pulled away.

Ava's hands shook as she gripped the glass of wine between both hands and brought it to her lips, tipping the wine into her mouth. Blake's long finger gently touched the side of her neck, slowly trailing over her throbbing pulse, making her gasp at the touch.

A splash of wine flowed from her parted lips and tracked down her chin and over the column of her throat. Blake quickly seized the glass from her, placing it back on the table. His large hand cupped the back of her head, his chest pressing against her arm as her head moved to the side. Blake's sinful tongue licked up the column of her throat, removing the track of wine in his wake.

"Blake." she groaned his name, her eyes closed as his tongue reached her lips. Swiping along the plump flesh once, removing the remnants of wine.

"Incredible." he breathed against her lips. "Wine has never tasted so good." his pupils were blown wide when he sat back and the predatory gleam she saw in their depths heightened her desire.

Ava spent the rest of the meal with shaking hands, pounding heart and was so lost inside her head she didn't taste anything else. Her mind was full of Blake, his hands and lips on her. His tongue doing delicious things to her. The desire she saw in the depths of his eyes and his words. He'd said that she was innocent and pure, but she'd seen the desire burning in his eyes and realised it wasn't an insult. Her heart swelled with the realisation that Blake found her desirable.

"What's got you smiling, baby girl." Blake whispered into her ear. His large hand splayed across her stomach, making her tense before she tried to clench her stomach muscles.

"The food." she lied quietly. "It was delicious." it was almost difficult for her to talk whilst she was trying to keep her stomach sucked in.

"Hmm, well I do love the sounds you make when you eat." his lips brushed against her ear, his hand applying just a little more pressure against her stomach. Her blush was instantly heating her cheeks and her insecurities of her figure were turning ugly inside her head. "I love seeing you wearing this." his other hand delicately grazed over the pendant he'd gifted her. "Come with me." he stepped back and held his hand out for her to take.

"Where are we going?" she asked, a little unsure as she placed her hand in his. She felt the waistband of her shorts dig in slightly against her stomach. Squeezing her eyes shut for a brief moment as she tried to repel the ugliness of her body. Tried to stop the tormenting voice inside her head, reminding her that she was nothing like the women he paraded around with.

Was that why we got a take away?

Why he'd made me stay in the car?

Is he ashamed to be seen with me?

She couldn't stop the questions that were suddenly plaguing

her, nor could she stop her mouth tuning into a pinched frown as she stood next to him. Their reflection from the glass bi-folding doors was a harsh reality. Blake was well over six feet, broad shouldered, muscular and devilishly handsome with his chiselled jaw, tousled hair and deep, memorising eyes and Ava. Well, she was short, a little under five foot three, her breasts were more than a handful, her stomach wasn't flat or toned, her hips flared and she had a fat ass. The reflection she saw made her feel ugly and tears suddenly pricked her eyes.

"I want to watch the stars with you, baby girl." his voice was low as he pulled open the door with one hand. The summer evening air was warm against her skin as he tugged her into the garden.

"Okay." her voice was thick as she tried to stop the tears that were threatening to fall. His dark eyes snapped to her and his brow furrowed.

"What's wrong?" his voice softened as his thumb smoothed away a stray tear from her cheek. She shook her head, gulping down the sob that was threatening to escape. She didn't want to ruin tonight, she didn't want him, of all people, to see her like this, but she couldn't help it. The insecurities she'd had since her teens had resurfaced like a bulldozer. Her breathing was coming a little faster, her hands were shaking, and she was desperately clinging to the last bit of her restraint. "Ava, speak to me." he wrapped his arms around her, pulling her into his chest. She could feel his heart beat a little faster. "Have I done something wrong?" he asked when she didn't speak. Burrowing her face into his polo shirt, inhaling his intoxicating scent, probably for the last time.

"I-I don't know why I'm here." her voice was muffled against his chest. "I-I'm nothing like those women that you like." if she hadn't had felt his entire frame tense, she wouldn't have known that he'd heard her, her voice was that low and muffled.

"No, you're not like them." his voice was hard and his words vibrated in his chest. He moved away from her, his hands moving to her shoulders as he held her at arm's length. His head bent until he was looking directly into her watery green eyes. "You are different." his voice was rough, she watched his throat bob on a swallow and his hands cupped her cheeks. "I never want you to be like them, baby girl." he continued, brushing his lips lightly across hers before pulling back.

"Why?" she whispered the question that would likely cause her pain, but she needed to know.

"Because, I want to drown in your purity." he whispered, a smirk tugging his lips. "You scream it with every touch, every move and every-fucking-time my lips touch yours I feel it, taste it." he continued, inching closer. "Feel your innocence, taste your purity." his tongue swiped across the seam of her lips and she parted them on a tortured gasp which he quickly swallowed. Moving his sinful mouth against hers. Heat bloomed in her chest, her pussy clenched with need as his tongue swirled with hers in a delicious tangle. Their breaths were harsh as he pulled away. "And I need to drown in you, Ava." he whispered, staring directly into her eyes with a blazing intensity her legs wobbled.

"But..." her bottom lip quivered from the emotion swirling within her. The doubt of his beautiful words.

"No, buts Ava." he cut her off, his lips curled at the corners. "I want to watch the stars with you." he continued, tugging her onto the grass.

Ava laid with her head cradled in the crook of his shoulder, her side pressed into the warm grass and his large, muscular arm curled around her. His hand splayed across her stomach and his thumb slowly moving back and forth over the exposed skin. The night sky was a beautiful deep blue with flecks of twinkling stars, the moon bright and shining above. It was one of Ava's favourite things to do in the summer evenings and she couldn't stop the smile from spreading across her face.

"It's beautiful tonight." she whispered, her eyes tracking the stars as they twinkled.

"Hmm, but not as beautiful as you." Blake whispered so low she wasn't certain if she heard him correctly. A delicate shiver raced down her spine at the feel of his biceps flexing against her. "Come here, baby girl." Blake pulled her closer to his body until she was laid almost on top of him. Her hand resting against the warmth of his chest.

"I've got to go soon, Blake." she murmured, her hand lightly brushing against his polo shirt. She felt the vibration against her hand of him humming in acknowledgment. Ava just wanted five more minutes wrapped in Blake before she moved. Closing her eyes as she inhaled his intoxicating scent, a smile playing on her lips as she burrowed herself deeper into his body until her breathing evened out and sleep claimed her.

Chapter Twelve

Cool air breezed gently over her heated flesh, the cheery chirp of a bird shattered the silence, a warm hand caressed down her side, another flexed against her hip. The weight of a hard, masculine body felt delicious against hers and Ava's eyes fluttered open at the feel of soft, firm lips touching hers. Deep, rich pools of chocolate gazed back at her, making her pulse spike.

"Good morning." his voice was like velvet in the morning. His hair hung over his forehead, messily. Her small smile belied the desire that was slowly sweeping through her at the sheer sight and feel of him.

"Morning." she breathed out. Her hand cupping his cheek, the scrape of his stubble against her palm sent a wave of goosebumps skittering up her arm. Inching closer, she pressed her lips to his before pulling back. "What time is it?" she didn't really want to know, nor did she want to leave the peaceful cocoon they were in.

"Time for me to get you home." he murmured against her lips, stealing another kiss. "James will be up shortly." he continued resting his forehead against hers.

"Oh, that early." Ava scrunched her face up slightly at the ungodly hour, making Blake chuckle, a slow deep rumble. "Hmm, I like that sound." she admitted with a sigh, wriggling beneath him to free her other hand that was trapped between their bodies.

"You're going to be the death of me, baby girl." his voice held a tortured edge to it which had her brow furrowing until she felt the thick, long column of his erection nestled between her thighs. Her cheeks heated, her nerve endings surged to life, and her clit began to throb from the contact.

Ava tentatively swiped her tongue across the seam of his lips once, a groan escaped him before her lips were on his. Moving together in a slow, deliberate dance. Her hand smoothed over his cheek, stubble scraping against her palm, and the other moved over his side in a slow caress. Their tongues met with small, delicate touches. Ava arched into him as his thumb lightly brushed the side of her breast, moaning low in the back of her throat. The clothed tip of his cock pressed against her throbbing clit as a rush of wetness seeped into her panties. The answering growl that vibrated with pure need from him, she knew he felt how wet she was.

"If I don't stop, it's going to be too late." Blake's voice was hard from his harsh breaths as he pulled his lips from hers.

"T-that's okay." Ava stuttered between panting breaths. "I don't mind if you don't stop." she continued, a smile curling her lips as she stared into the intense brown eyes. She watched his pupils dilate and his throat bob in a hard swallow.

"Fuck!" he hissed, pressing his lips once more to hers. "I can't fuck you." his voice sounded pained. Her heart stuttered in her chest and her breath caught in her throat as his words took root, dousing the flaming embers of passion that was consuming her body. His forehead rested against hers for a brief moment. "You need to be worshipped, baby girl." Blake eased his weight off of her body and hope surged within her at his words. "And I can't worship you in the garden." his lips curved into a smile as he stood and held his hands out to her.

"Okay." Ava grumbled as he pulled her to her feet. "I'm gonna need a spare pair of panties at this rate." it wasn't until he tilted his head back and laughed that Ava realised that she said her thoughts out loud.

"Trust me, you'll always need a spare pair." he chuckled lightly, before moving his lips to her ear. "I just might rip them off." his whispered words sent a course of heat directly to her clit which throbbed to the beat of her heart.

After she had buckled herself into the sleek sports car, Blake still dressed in his now creased polo shirt and jeans in the driver's seat, she couldn't wipe the smile off of her face. She'd had the best night of her life and she couldn't wait to repeat it. Everything about the night before flickered through her brain. The way he looked at her; so full of heat, the way his chest vibrated when he growled, the way he'd fed her, the way his tongue danced over her skin and being in his arms watching the stars.

Blake Sinclair really knew how to make her feel special and give her one of the best nights and she knew why so many women flocked to him.

Once he'd backed out of the driveway, his large hand settled on her bare thigh with his thumb, rubbing small circles against her flesh. Ava let out a contented sigh as she relaxed into the leather seat.

"That's the best date I've ever had." Ava admitted, blushing as she looked at his profile from beneath her long lashes.

"And how many dates have you had, baby girl." the deep rumble of his voice as he slowly turned those liquid pools of chocolate to her had her blushing a deeper shade of red. "How many boys am I going to have to hurt?" he continued, a seriousness in his voice which made her swallow hard.

"None, Blake." she licked over her lips, shaking her head. "You're the only one." she continued, placing her hand over his hand on her thigh, squeezing gently.

"Good." he dipped his head once. "I'm not sharing you with anyone." his voice held a possessive edge that had her stomach flip-flopping.

The sleek sports car eased into the space across the driveway of her home as the clock ticked over to six am. Exactly half an hour before James would be waking up. Ava sucked a deep breath in and slowly blew it out, her eyes closing. Blake's hand gently squeezed her bare thigh once. His fingers curling around the sensitive flesh on the inside of her thigh, making her breath stutter in her chest.

"You're perfect, baby girl." he whispered as he leaned over the centre console, meeting her in the middle. "Stay with me tonight?" he asked.

"Okay." she whispered, her eyes staring at his lips.

"I'll pick you up before James comes home." he breathed out before his lips touched hers in a chaste kiss. "Pack a spare pair of panties." he smirked as she flushed in embarrassment.

"Okay, I've got to go." she said it more like she was reminding herself, stealing a quick kiss before she unclipped her seatbelt. "God, I don't want to." she admitted, her teeth clamped into her bottom lip. Blake pulled her lip from her teeth, swiping his tongue along the indent. His lips touched hers in a sweep of flesh against flesh.

"See you tonight." he smiled as he pulled away and sat back in his seat.

"See you later, Blake." Ava smiled before she climbed out of the car.

The house was in darkness as Ava opened the door quietly, turning to watch Blake's car pull away from the curb before she slipped in and closed the door behind her. Blowing out a breath, she didn't realise she was holding as the lock clicked into place. The sound seemed to boom around the entryway, making her wince.

"Shh." she hissed at the door. Her heart stalled, her breath seized as she listened for any signs of movement upstairs. Adrenaline surged through her body as she carefully manoeuvred her way up the stairs, careful not to step on the creaking floorboards. Ava had never once in her life sneaked into the house, but she knew James was a relatively heavy sleeper.

The moment she reached her bedroom door, relief flooded her body. Her shoulders relaxed and her breathing became less harsh. Her head rested against her bedroom door, her eyes closed. Taking a few deep breaths before checking the time on her phone. She had three minutes before James' alarm went off to get changed into her pyjamas and set the coffee machine.

"It's doable." she whispered, springing away from the door and in a rush, threw on her nightclothes.

Pulling her hair out of the ponytail she had sported yesterday, combing her fingers through the long waves as she walked with heavier footsteps across her bedroom and just as she pulled her bedroom door open, James's alarm filled the second floor with an unrelenting shrill tone which always made her wince.

Ava stood with a steaming cup of coffee in hand, her eyes staring into the garden, watching the birds swoop towards the bird feeders. A wide smile on her face as she thought about waking up in Blake's garden with the sound of birds chirping and his glorious body pressed against hers. She hadn't forgotten what had happened between them over the last couple of months and she also knew that she was playing with fire. It was just a matter of when was she going to get burnt by Blake.

"What's got you smiling, squirt?" James asked, grabbing his own coffee.

"Just watching the birds." she answered, trying to hide her flushing cheeks with her hair.

"Hmm." James took a sip of coffee as he stood beside her. His towering frame dressed in his oil covered overalls and large boots, the scent of the garage stronger than the scent of fresh coffee. "Thought it might have something to do with you sneaking in this morning." his voice was low as he bumped her with his hip.

"Umm...." sweat broke out across the back of her neck, her pulse thumped painfully at her throat and her tongue felt like a lead weight in her mouth.

Fuck!

"I know you're not a kid anymore, squirt." James sighed, rubbing the back of his neck with his free hand. "I just worry about you, you know." he took a sip of coffee. "I know what men are like and I don't want you to get hurt." he laughed, shaking his head. Ava was rooted to the spot, her stomach churning as she knew he was thinking about his own heartbreak. "I don't want you to make the same mistakes I did and fall for the wrong person." the words were harsh. Clearing his throat and taking a sip of coffee. "A man who doesn't deserve you, a man who will only *fu-cuddle* and move on to the...."

"Oh god, really!" Ava groaned, cutting him off as she tipped her head back. "You trying to give me the *talk?*" she continued, filled with sheer embarrassment at the conversation. James cut his eyes to her, a smile playing on his lips.

"Embarrassed?" James chuckled as her face turned flaming red. "Might make you think twice before sneaking in again, I've got a lot more where this has come from." her brows furrowed at his words, causing James to roll his eyes. "As I said, you're not a kid anymore, if you're going to stay out all night just let me know, so I don't worry and call Katie at midnight." he pinned her with a pointed stare. "And for the love of everything that is holy, if you are going to..." he gulped audibly. "*Cuddle* use protection." he finished with a twist of his lips like the words tasted bitter.

"Awe, James." she began in a light tone. A lightness she didn't feel. "You afraid of becoming an uncle?" she laughed, shaking her head at his groan. "Don't worry, I haven't *cuddled* with anyone." she clarified, draining the rest of her coffee.

"Right." he nodded once, finishing his coffee and turning away from the view of the garden.

"I have a date tonight." Ava rushed out. Taking a deep breath. "I won't be home for tea." her teeth clamped onto her bottom lip as James turned his green eyes on her, his eyebrows raised. "And probably will be sleeping out." she swallowed thickly, licking over her lips.

"Two nights in a row; do I get to know who the guy is?" James asked as he stared at her. She tried to school her features, tried not to let her eyes widen, tried not to let the panic she felt at his question show. Blood whooshed in her ears as every pulse in her body beat frantically. Her brain trying to think of anyone other than Blake. She floundered for long moments as her brain kicked into gear.

"It's still early days yet." she squeaked, as her lungs constricted and stars danced in her eyes. She felt faint.

"Oh, he's not married, is he?" James's eyebrows hit his hairline; Ava shook her head no. "Okay, squirt, I understand you don't want to tell me just yet. Have fun, just don't *cuddle*." James's parting words that he threw over his shoulder had her sucking in large gulps of air, trying to regain her composure. Her hands were on her knees, gulping air like her life depended on it.

She hated lying to James, and she wasn't very good at it either.

Ava stood rooted to the spot, staring out of the living room window as she watched in rapt fascination Blake unfold himself from the car, straighten the cuffs of his dress shirt and walk around the vehicle until that perfect, plump ass of his rested against the passenger door. She licked her lips at the delectable sight until he folded his arms across his chest and the way his muscles bunched and strained had her stomach clenching with need. Ava's steps faltered as she grabbed her handbag and overnight bag.

The moment the cool summer breeze that had ghosted over her this morning met her heated face carrying the zesty bergamot and spicy pepper scent, she took a deep breath. All Ava could hear was the whooshing of blood pounding through her ears as she tried to keep her panic at bay, tried not to let her overwhelming insecurities take over. Her steps were slow as she tried to take deep breaths to calm herself with every step she took, but the moment those rich pools of chocolate landed on her and the wolfish grin spread across his face, her pulse skyrocketed and her stomach flip-flopped.

"Baby girl." the deep timbre of his voice sent a shock of liquid heat through her veins. Blake pushed off the car. His eyes remained fixed on Ava's until he was standing in front of her. His large hand cupping her cheek, his thumb ghosting over her bottom lip. "God, you're beautiful." he whispered before pressing his lips to hers momentarily.

"Hi." Ava breathed out, a smile on her lips. "You look handsome, as always." her voice was shy as she spoke words she'd only thought in his presence.

"Innocent and pure." he whispered against her ear. His hand

trailing from her cheek, over her collarbone and down her side until he took the bags from her hand. "Let's get you home." and those words sent everything into overdrive.

Chapter Thirteen

Blake Synclair was a sight to behold.

Reclined back into the corner of the plush deep blue sofa. One muscular arm braced across the back of the sofa and the other resting against a thick thigh. Her pulse stuttered. His chest is bare. Her eyes fluttered as her pupils dilated. All tawny skin and hard cut muscles. Her nipples hardened. The dark hair from his navel travelling down beneath the low slung sweatpants. Her pussy clenched.

Ava gulped at the sight.

Stood before him, her hair in a messy bun dressed in a pale green satin nightdress with white lace trim across the low neckline that clung to the fatness of her body. She knew it was a little small on her. Knew that she shouldn't have bothered buying it a few months past, but she'd fallen in love with it and promised herself that she'd lose a few pounds so it fit better. But like all the other times, she hadn't managed to lose any weight despite watching her calorie intake.

Blowing out a breath, trying to calm her nerves as her green eyes continued to roam over every perfect inch of him until she reached his chiselled face. His sinful lips were pulled into a smirk as he watched her assessing him. She watched his eyes skim over every inch of her, watched his eyes darken and his hand clench against his thigh and Ava couldn't help lick over her bottom lip.

"Come." his voice was a mere growl as he crooked his finger at her. Ava's legs wobbled slightly as she took a step forward, his intense gaze watching every move. Sucking in a deep breath as she stood directly in front of him and she could feel the heat from his body. "Turn." he commanded. She was lost to his command, and she turned slowly until her back faced him. Her heart was playing a thunderous beat as she waited with bated breath. "Sit." swallowing thickly as her stomach clenched at his demanding tone.

Slowly bending forward, the edge of her nightdress whispering over the back of her thighs as she curved, knees bent. The growl that permitted the air had her pausing. She felt his knuckle graze against the back of her thigh, leaving goosebumps in their wake. A gasp left her parted lips, and a shudder flowed through her body as his hand sensually moved over her ass cheek, across the bottom of her back, before curling around her hip. His fingers flexed once before his grip tightened and he gently tugged her onto his lap.

The feel of his defined chest against her, his hand inching from her hip across her stomach, making her flinch as he pulled her closer to him. Her breathing was becoming laboured as she nestled into him. His hard cock strained against the material of his sweatpants nestled between her ass cheeks.

Oh, fucking hell!

It's huge!

"What's wrong?" Blake's voice pulled her out of her thoughts, her head resting against his chest. "You've been quiet since I picked you up." his arm tightened against her stomach, she flinched again. "You didn't make those sounds I like when you eat." his lips touched her temple.

Ava wrung her fingers lightly before picking the hem of her nightdress. Her heart still thundering in her chest, her breathing was almost pants as she concentrated on the hard muscle throbbing against her. Licking over her lips and squeezing her eyes shut momentarily, trying to form the right words.

"I got caught." her voice was low, her eyes still closed. "Sneaking in this morning." her tongue felt heavy in her mouth and Blake removed his arm from around her. She was scared he was going to push her away. "He asked me where I'd been." she rushed out, she heard the ice from the glass tumbler tinkle that was sitting beside them.

"What did you tell him?" Blake's deep rumble vibrated down her spine.

"That I'd had a date." she answered in a stuttered breath, her eyes still squeezed shut.

"I see." his index finger traced the side of her neck. Liquid slithered against her heated flesh. Ava hissed at the coldness. "Did you tell him who you were with?" he asked in a controlled voice. His finger leaving her skin, ice tinkling in the silence.

"No." she breathed out as more liquid slithered against her neck. Shivering from the coldness, her nipples hardened further.

"Why?" he whispered against her ear. His finger trailing more cold liquid. Ava arched against him. The warmth from his tongue licking some of the liquid from her skin.

"Oh god!" she moaned as more liquid trailed over her collarbone. The slow rivulet dancing across her skin to the swell of her breast.

"Answer me." he demanded as both hands gripped her hips tightly.

"I-I don't -" her words were cut off on a yelp as Blake quickly turned her until she was straddling his hips. His eyes were dark, blazing pure fury.

"Wrong." one hand gripped the back of her neck, the other picked up the glass tumbler. Her eyes were wide, his jaw tense and the muscle pulsing hard against his jaw. He tipped the entire contents of the glass down his throat before scooping an ice cube from the glass, holding it between his perfect white teeth.

Blake inched closer, the blazing fury in his eyes becoming more intense and his grip was almost punishing as he tugged on her neck, arching her spine to the perfect curve which had her breasts thrust forward. Ava gasped and shivered as ice and warm lips touched the swell of her breast. Cold liquid run beneath her nightdress, over her nipple and pulling it into a tight, hard point.

He moved slowly across her flesh. Ice gliding. Droplets dripping down her chest. His warm lips chasing away the chill. Her thighs began to quiver, a heavy seated throb pulsed and her pussy clenched as liquid seeped from her core. Blake bucked his hips, the engorged clothed tip of his cock brushed her bare entrance. A further rush of liquid from her pussy. Deep moans were pulled from her throat as pure, decadent pleasure rolled through her like a tidal wave. More cold liquid trailed down her other breast, over her nipple until they were both tight, hard points. Another buck of his hips, another brush of his cock nudging her throbbing clit. Another gush of liquid from her core.

The intense heat from his hand skimmed over her side, his thumb trailing across the underside of her breast. The ice and warm lips tracked up her throat, achingly slow. Her breaths were sheer pants as his lips reached hers, brushing the small nub that was left of the ice cube against her lips a moment before the cry of pleasure ripped from her throat with the hard pinch of her nipple.

"Your pussy's gushing all over my cock, baby girl." his deep voice and wicked, dirty words sent another wave of pleasure through her, pushing more wetness from her. Her cheeks were flaming, and she was breathless.

"P-please." Ava begged around a throaty groan as she felt the head of his cock nudge against her entrance.

"Please, what?" his hand on her neck gripped tighter, the other had a brutal hold on her hip. "What do you want?"

"You." Ava moaned as she tried desperately to grind her hips against him. But the hold he had ensured she couldn't.

"I'm right here." the low baritone of his words sent another wave of shivers down her spine.

"Please." Ava panted the word out, her eyes squeezed shut. "Blake, make me..." she trailed off, her mind was a mess of scattered thoughts, as her body hung on the precipice of a climax.

"The madness." his lips moved to her ear, brushing against them. "The torture." he whispered, teeth nipping her earlobe. A throaty moan left her parted lips. "The insanity." his lips trailed down her neck. Her back arched further. "The pain." his teeth bit down above her collarbone. Ava cried out. "The feeling it will never end." a whimper escaped as liquid heat seeped from her core, soaking his sweatpants. "That's how you make me feel." his tongue swiped over the sting on her flesh. "You drive me to insanity." his hand moved from her hip, gathering the edge of her nightdress. Satin whispering over her quivering thigh. "When I feel I'm not good enough for you to tell the truth." his fingers brushed against the slickness on her inner thigh.

"I-I'm sorry." Ava stuttered out, her eyes snapping to his. "Blake!" she cried out as he trailed one lone finger up through her folds, circling her engorged clit once, which wasn't enough to send her over the edge.

"Hmm." his groan was exquisite as he licked her juices from his finger. "Innocent and pure." he breathed out, sucking the rest of his finger through his sinful lips. "That's what you taste like. I could eat you for days." Ava threw her head back on a moan at his words.

"Yes!" she whimpered and Blake chuckled darkly, making her snap her eyes to his. The blazing fury was laced with unadulterated desire.

"This is your punishment." his tone was harsh, making Ava's eyes widen. "For lying, for not owning me." his lips tipped up in a cruel smirk. "You're my innocence, my purity."

"B-But..." Ava gulped air into her burning lungs. "James – I had no choice." she almost cried out.

"You." his hand covered her throat, his fingers flexing against her flesh. Her pulse beating harshly against his hand. "Should have told James." he pulled her closer until they were a breath apart. "That you'd been with me." his voice was low, hard. A hint of fear slithered through her body. "That's what my good girl should have done." his lips crashed to hers.

A brutal twist of hard lips against softer ones. His tongue was a solid muscle as he thrust it between her parted lips, sweeping, tasting, owning every inch of her mouth. His hands shoved the satin fabric of her nightdress until it bunched beneath her heavy breasts. Ava felt a searing heat of silky hard muscle against the exposed flesh of her stomach. His deep, guttural growl vibrated through his entire body and she felt it all the way to her toes. His exposed cock sliding over her stomach, smearing copious amounts of pre-cum on her skin. His lips bruised hers. The air was filled with lustrous moans and groans. His teeth nipped harshly and his hips bucked, his cock swelled. Ava felt the hot jets of cum splatter against her stomach as a primal roar filled the room. Ava collapsed against his sweat dampened chest breathing harshly, her body shaking and her nerve endings zinging and pulsing with pure need.

"That's what you do to me." Blake's arms wrapped around her shaking body. "Madness, torture, pure fucking insanity." His hand rubbing soothing circles across her back. "Only you baby girl." his lips pressed to her temple as he scooped her up, her thighs wrapping around his waist and her arms around his neck. "Let's get you cleaned up." he murmured against her hair as they left the living room.

The bedroom was cloaked in darkness. No light from the midnight sky penetrated the dark, heavy curtains. Blake's signature scent wrapped around Ava as she laid on her side, her knees tucked into her stomach and making sure to keep her breathing deep and even. She was glad that she'd brought a spare pair of shorts and a tank top, after her nightdress had been saturated. Her body ached something fierce as she came down from the stimulation she'd received and the orgasm she'd been denied.

She was trying to process what had happened, trying to process the different side of Blake that she'd witnessed.

He'd been so attentive during their dinner, so warm and open as they talked about their days. He'd listened intently as she spoke of her monotonous day; being off of work left her to read and do chores. Nothing extremely exciting, but he'd smiled nonetheless and made her feel seen, valued.

He'd cleaned a drawer out in his walk-in closet for her to unpack her clothes, he'd shown her how to use the jacuzzi bath and six headed walk-in shower and he'd also given her the privacy to change her clothes. Something she hadn't thought about, nor the dynamics of spending the night in his home. But Blake had; he'd thought of everything and she couldn't have been more grateful.

Then he'd changed when she mentioned about being caught. At first, he was driving her crazy with the cold liquid and the heat of his tongue as he listened to her explain what had happened. But the moment she admitted not mentioning names, he changed. She saw a darkness in him that she realised lurked just beneath the surface and it scared her.

Until she was mindless with pleasure.

Until she was begging him – once again – to make her his and once again, again, he denied her. To the point of pain. In the small hours of the night, she understood his words. Understood the madness, the torture, the pain and feeling like it would never end. She understood exactly what he'd said, and she was living through it.

Once he'd delivered her punishment and cum all over her. Which almost had her climaxing alone. She saw the blazing fury ebb away, replaced with those rich pools of chocolate she loved so much.

She'd been embarrassed as he'd carried her to the bathroom, knowing she wasn't the lightest of women. Embarrassed as her juices flowed down her thighs as he'd sat her on the countertop covered in his cum. Embarrassed that her stomach wobbled. So much so that she'd refused for him to wash her. She'd snatched the damp washcloth from his hand, slid off the counter, and turned her back to him whilst she cleaned herself.

She'd watched him in the reflection of the mirror from beneath her lashes. Watched as his eyebrows drew together, his shoulders slump and his lips part in a sigh before he'd walked away from her. It was at that moment when tears had filled her eyes.

Tears that she refused to let fall because she felt like a child.

A silly, little, virginal girl.

She had a lot of insecurities about herself and even more when it came to Blake and him wanting to spend time with her. But with everything she had seen wrapped in the beautiful, sinful package that was Blake Synclair, she wanted it.

Wanted the entire package. She wanted to be his innocence, his purity.

She also wanted to be the one to drive him to madness. To bring the darkness to the surface. Which made her feel like there was something wrong with her. Because despite being scared, scared of the unknown, she wanted to drown in his darkness as much as he wanted to drown in her innocence and purity.

She just didn't know how to survive the entire package.

Chapter Fourteen

Ava woke alone in Blake's bed and despite the warmth of the summer, she'd never felt colder. It was strange waking alone in his room. She'd expected for him to wake her the same as yesterday, with light kisses and touches. A small smile graced her lips at the memory.

Stretching the kinks out, groaning with the sting of pain from her muscles. Pain from being suspended in an all-consuming burning ball of ecstasy with no release. She'd never felt anything like that before, never left herself so needful for an orgasm. No, every time she had explored her body, it was always a rush to the finish line. But with Blake, he left her with no respite from the burning need.

Sighing as she smoothed her tank top down, ensuring that her stomach was covered before she made her way through his beautiful home. As she padded through the halls, she noted that there were no personal pictures on the walls, all were devoid of anything, with the exception of a few mirrors. His bedroom was the same. All smoky greys, the walls, the plush furnishings and still no personal pictures. The only thing she had seen was his watch that he'd left on the bedside cabinet. Everything else had its place, all neatly tucked away from prying eyes.

It was a complete contrast to her bedroom. She had pictures from family holidays, birthdays and nights out in multiple frames scattered around her room. Her dressing table was littered with make-up, perfume, skincare products, hairdryer, straighteners, brushes, jewellery. At the thought of jewellery, her hand skimmed over the pendant. A warm smile and fuzzy feeling took over her for a moment until she walked into the kitchen and was greeted by the delicious sight of Blake.

"Good morning." his rich voice washed over her as she pried her greedy gaze away from his bare torso. "Sit." he gestured to the dining table that was laid out with fresh fruit, cereal, orange juice and coffee. Licking over her lips as she sat down.

"You really know how to treat a girl." Ava smiled as she looked at the bowl in front of her, already filled with fruit for her. His eyes snared her from above the rim of his coffee cup, making her pulse spike.

"I want to hear those sounds, baby girl." he smirked as her cheeks heated, taking a sip of the coffee.

"Okay." she squeaked, popping a piece of fresh pineapple into her mouth. The acidic, sweet juice filled her mouth and she couldn't help the small moan.

"Good girl." his eyes never left hers. "We need to discuss James." he began, his jaw clenching momentarily.

"I'm sor-" Ava began, but Blake held his hand up to silence her.

"You eat." his tone was a sheer command that had heat lighting up her veins. "I understand why you didn't tell him the *truth*." he practically spat the word. "I don't like it, but I understand." he sighed, taking a sip of coffee. "James is my best friend, we've been through a lot together." Ava's eyebrows rose as her interest spiked. "Yeah." he chuckled lightly. "I know you don't want to hurt him, neither do I." Ava watched as his chest expanded on a deep inhale, a strawberry paused mid-way to her mouth. "Ava." the growl which came from him had her core clenching and her eyes snapping to his.

"Yeah?" she swallowed thickly.

"You keep eye-fucking me and we're not going to get very far."

his warning sent a delicious thrill zinging through her.

"What if..." her voice was timid and her blush deepened.

"Don't." he warned. His thumb rubbing across his lower lip, his eyes intent on her. "Keep eating." he watched as she placed the strawberry between her lips, her teeth clamping around the tip, groaning as her teeth sunk in. Juice tricked over her lower lip. Ava's hand moved. "Leave it." the demand was biting, his pupils dilated and her pussy clenched as liquid seeped from her.

"I-I don't think I can eat when you look at me like that." Ava admitted shyly. The low throaty chuckle had her nipples hardening.

"Do you want me to feed you, baby girl?" the corner of his mouth tipped up, his thumb still rubbing across his lower lip.

Oh, dear god!

Yes!

Her mind screamed at her to accept, but she didn't know how far Blake would take it. Didn't know if she'd still be left unsatisfied and she certainly didn't know if her body could handle the all-consuming burning ball of ecstasy with no release, again. Shaking her head, she popped the rest of the strawberry in her mouth and chewed slowly.

"With James." Blake sighed. "It's not going to be easy." brushing his hair back off of his forehead. "We can either tell him the truth." Ava's eyes went wide and a squeak of protest left her lips, but Blake held his hand up, silencing her. "Or we can continue with the lie you've already told him." his tone turned hard and his eyes had a cold edge to them.

Ava shoved more fruit into her mouth and chewed extremely slowly with Blake's penetrating gaze on her whilst she mulled over what he'd said. She knew that she didn't want to lie to James. He'd always been her rock. Even more so after the death of their parents. He'd always been there for her when she needed him the most. He'd never judged her. Never spoke angrily to her. He'd always protected her.

She thought back to when she'd panicked and told him that she'd had a date, he hadn't judged her but she could tell that he immediately thought it was with someone forbidden and she'd seen the way his hand had tightened around his coffee cup as that thought had taken root. That was why she'd lied.

Ava didn't want to be the reason James and Blake's friendship failed. Because despite everything, she knew that if it hadn't had been for Blake, James wouldn't have survived his marriage falling apart. Blake had been his rock during that dark year.

She also told James a partial truth, it was early days with Blake and she didn't know what was going to happen. She also didn't know what Blake really thought of her, nor did she know what exactly to call what was happening between them. She was confused, and she was also scared of finding out the truth. Scared if it wasn't what she wanted to hear.

Was she just a passing curiosity, a fat girl to fuck instead of the usual skinny blondes?

"Have you made your decision?" Blake's voice pulled her from her thoughts. Her eyes refocusing on his as she swallowed around the sudden lump in her throat.

"No." her voice was low as she licked over her lips, sucking in a breath. "I don't know what you want from me, I don't know what's happening between us." her voice shook with unshed tears. Blake's jaw tensed. "What would you call this thing between us?" her tongue felt like a lead weight in her mouth. Blake scrubbed a hand down his face.

"Baby girl, you're fucking killing me." he admitted on a long groan. His eyes unfocused momentarily, his fingers sinking into his hair. "Are you prepared for what's to come when he learns the truth?" Blake asked, resting his elbows on the table.

"I don't know." she admitted as she finished her coffee. Not missing the fact he hasn't answered her question. "James has always been there for me and I feel like this might hurt him. Although it will be better than him thinking I'm seeing a married man." Ava chuckled lightly, but Blake's eyes turned cold.

"Hmm." Blake hummed, pushing away from the table. "Go get changed, I'll take you home." he put his back to her as he filled the dishwasher.

When Blake had driven her home this morning he hadn't spoken much and every time she had risked a glance, he had an almost haunted look in his eyes. He'd given her a quick kiss on the cheek – not lips – cheek before she left the confines of the car without making plans and she didn't really know what to think about that.

Ava wanted to speak to Katie about this thing with Blake. But with her having *whatever* with James, she couldn't risk anyone knowing. Katie was her best friend, but even Ava knew she could hardly keep a secret.

And this was the biggest secret she couldn't afford to get to James.

The low thrum of voices in the local pub had her palms sweating ever so slightly as her green eyes scanned the large room for Katie. She saw numerous aged regulars, sat in their usual seats, drinking the usual drinks. A group of construction men still dressed in their dirty work clothes, riotous laughter with pints in hand and then she saw the flash of fire red hair. Breathing a sigh of relief, Ava strode across the pub, weaving through the tables and plopping down opposite Katie.

"Finally." she grumbled, pouring Ava a glass of wine. "The

bottle has been chilling for-ev-er." Katie dragged the word out with a smile.

"I know, sorry." Ava took a sip of the wine, relishing the fruity flavour across her taste buds. "I lost track of time." she admitted sheepishly.

"Uh-huh. Time." Katie smirked, raising her eyebrows. "So, where have you been?" she asked with a glint in her eye. The glint that made Ava straighten ever so slightly as she gathered the courage to lie to her best friend.

Ava had spent time forming a story in her mind, explaining that she'd met up with a few colleagues from work and the new teacher had asked her out on a date, they'd had their first date the following day. Closely followed by another and that he made her feel special. It was the best she could come up with when her mind was full of Blake and her gut was full of guilt over the lie.

Katie listened to Ava's explanation, both of them draining the glass of wine before having a refill and once she was done, Ava relaxed back into the seat. Her fingers clasping the stem of the wineglass. Katie took a sip of hers, nodding mostly to herself before pinning her with a stare.

"That's absolutely lovely, he sounds like a nice guy." Katie smiled, taking another sip and Ava breathed a sigh of relief. "Now, are you going to tell me the truth?" she asked, hurt flashing across her face.

"W-what do you mean?" Ava stuttered out as she felt heat creep up her neck.

"The truth, Ava." Katie's voice was lower than normal. "I can smell him all over you." she continued, tipping her glass towards her. Ava gulped a mouthful of wine.

"Who?" Ava couldn't believe she had just spent the last half an hour pouring her heart into the lie she'd practised, only to have Katie see right through it. But surely she didn't.

"Blake." Katie smirked as Ava's eyes widened. "He's my cousin, Ava. I spend a lot of time with him and know his aftershave." Katie shrugged as pure panic filled every fibre in Ava's body.

"You can't tell James." Ava rushed out. "It'll kill him." Ava knocked back half of her glass.

"Oh, relax." Katie waved her hand as if batting her concerns away. "I'm not going to tell him anything, just don't lie to me." Katie's tone was full of sadness at her words. "I've been your rock whilst you've been pining over him."

"I haven't been pining." Ava cut in and Katie raised a lone brow. "Okay, maybe." Ava smiled as she took another sip of her wine.

"I'm happy something has finally happened." Katie tipped the rest of the glass down her throat. "Just don't let him be a dick to you, Ava." she blew out a breath and shook her head. "I know what he's like, and I don't want him to hurt you." sincerity shone in her eyes and words, but Ava held her hand up.

"Why is everyone so concerned about Blake hurting me?" she felt better once the words had tumbled from her lips. It was the question that had been plaguing her since James quizzed her after her night staying at his hotel, all them weeks ago.

"Because he's a womanising asshole." Katie's voice was laced with contempt. "Once he gets fed up, he moves on. Just don't give him the satisfaction of leaving you." at her words, Ava's face crumpled and doubt crept in clouding her thoughts. "Oh, no you don't!" Katie snapped, making Ava jump.

"What!" Ava snapped back. "So, I'm going to get my heart broken?" she continued, draining the contents of her glass.

They hadn't seen the side of him that he'd shown her. The side that made her feel cherished. The side that had her wrapped in his embrace all night. The side that made her breakfast. The side that was in utter turmoil over the lie. The only side Katie and James had seen was the womaniser.

The unobtainable bachelor.

"No." Katie blew a raspberry as she pushed her hair away from her eyes. "All I'm saying to you is, be careful and look for the warning signs." Ava furrowed her brow, and Katie shook her head. "Watch for him losing interest. It always starts with him not wanting to take you anywhere." Katie poured more wine into both glasses and at her words, tears gathered in Ava's eyes. "What's that look for?" Katie asked, her tone softening.

"He doesn't take me anywhere now." she mumbled around her glass, and Katie's eyebrows hit her hairline.

"Okay." Katie reached a hand across the table to grip her shaking one. "How many times have you had sex?"

"Katie!" Ava exclaimed, her head whipping around, praying nobody was listening.

"What! It's a valid question." her voice raised an octave. Ava shook her head, taking a sip of wine. "How many orgasms has he given you? Ten? Fifteen? Thirty?" with every word her eyebrows rose more.

"Oh god!" Ava groaned, rolling her eyes. But Katie sat with a knowing smirk on her face, waiting for an answer. "None."

"None!" Katie's voice was even louder, causing some of the locals to glance towards them, making Ava sink down in her seat. "This is Blake we're talking about….Blake Synclair?" Ava nodded and her cheeks flamed at the disbelieving look Katie was wearing. "What the fuck have you been doing?"

"Talking…"

"We're fucking talking!" Katie shouted. "Really Ava, you've

done nothing but talk?" Katie folded her arms across her chest, the disbelieving look still on her face.

"Fine!" Ava huffed. "We talk, we slept under the stars, we kiss a lot and he makes me dinner and breakfast." Ava leaned across the table. "But apart from that, absolutely nothing." Ava's voice was low and unsure when Katie's mouth dropped open, speechless.

"Fuck!" Katie dragged the word out, pushing her hair out of her eyes. "At the hotel?" her head cocked to the side and Ava swallowed a gulp of wine.

"His home." she admitted with a small smile.

"It's worse than I thought." Katie murmured, her eyes averting Ava's as she concentrated on the nearly empty bottle of wine.

"What?" Ava asked, confusion evident in her tone. She didn't know what had made her friend act so strangely, nor did she understand the emotions flashing across her face.

"Promise me, Ava." Katie leaned across the table, gripping both of her hands. "Promise me you won't let anyone find out." her voice was urgent but Ava was in full-blown panic mode at the urgency in her friend's tone. Her eyes were blown wide, her pulse thumping wildly, her stomach churning and her hands shaking inside Katie's.

"What can't I let out?" Ava asked as she tried to settle the panic inside.

"You can't let anyone know." Katie's voice was a sheer whisper. "Don't let him know how you feel." Katie's eyes were wide, matching Ava's.

"Oh." Ava couldn't think straight, she had to keep this a secret from James that she already knew but not to let anyone know. That seemed strange, but she knew that where Blake was concerned, Katie was probably the best person to listen to.

"Yeah." Katie nodded, her stare intent and full of warning. "He'll still be a dick *sometimes*." Katie chuckled. "But promise to take care of him."

"I'll take care of him, Katie." Ava agreed, her heart and head in complete and utter shock.

Chapter Fifteen

Blake shrugged the crisp white shirt onto his shoulders, his fingers gliding over each button, fastening them as he stared at his reflection. His hair pushed off of his forehead, tousled the way he liked it. His jaw had the right amount of stubble without it being classed as a beard. His usual tawny skin was a little paler than normal. Squeezing his eyes closed briefly, he tucked the shirt into his dark blue slacks. Sucking in a deep breath as he fastened the black leather belt. The slight tremors in his hands were slowly ebbing away, making it easier for him to begin fastening the cufflinks.

Ava's questions still bouncing around his head two days later.

"I don't know what you want from me; I don't know what's happening between us."

"You and me both, baby girl." he muttered to himself, unable to look himself in the eye through the mirror.

He didn't want to see what lurked beneath him.

"What would you call this thing between us?"

"I don't fucking know!" he blared, shoving his hands into his pants pockets.

Turning away from the mirror, his eyes tracked over the utter destruction of the hotel room. The deep green bed covers were heaped in a pile at the foot of the bed. The table lamp lay broken on the floor. Discarded clothes littered the floor. The boudoir chair was overturned. The waste bin had multiple wrappers overflowing. Squeezing his eyes shut as he swallowed thickly at the sight.

With his back to the archway and the deathly silence of the room, he heard the main door open and close. His back stiffened, muscles locked into place, and his lungs constricted. The heavy perfume hit him first, the heels click-clacking against the floor thundered in his ears. The tremor in his hands increased, his breath whooshed from his burning lungs. A small hand touched his arm, the long pink nails curving over his forearm. He couldn't turn his head, could hardly swallow around the lump in his throat; his legs had locked into place.

He couldn't move a single muscle.

What have I fucking done?

That one sentence overshadowed everything that was whirling around in his head. White noise filled his ears, black spots appeared at the edge of his vision as the memories from the night before flickered to light in full streaming colour.

Chapter Sixteen

It had been almost a week since she'd last seen or spoken with Blake.

Almost a week of Blake ignoring her calls and text messages.

Almost a week since she had spoken with Katie.

And almost a whole fucking week that she had been going out of her mind.

She was laid on the sofa in deathly silence as she tried and failed to read. The e-reader was laid across her stomach, her eyes unfocused and her breath coming in deep waves as she tried to decipher everything that had happened.

Blake, where did she even begin with him? She felt like not telling James the truth had damaged what little affection they had shared. But she'd never been in this situation before and, having not spoken with Blake about the implications, she wasn't certain if she should have admitted the truth. But he'd seemed hurt that she hadn't told the truth, consequences be damned. And when he'd dropped her off at home, it was like he couldn't get rid of her quick enough and the kiss on the cheek felt like an afterthought. She'd seen the haunted look on his face, saw the demons he was battling surge forth in his tortured eyes, which looked almost black on that morning.

Katie's words had kept her up at all hours of the night over the last week.

"You can't let anyone know."

"But promise to take care of him."

Katie's words had done nothing but make her a little paranoid. But that didn't stop the flare of hope that maybe she could be the endgame for Blake. That he'd love her the way she did him.

And her promise.

"I'll take care of him, Katie."

But after a week of no contact, she wasn't certain how to take care of him, wasn't certain how to keep her promise. And she certainly wanted to take care of him. Wanted to help him ease the demons inside him.

Then she wondered if the way he'd been with her, touching her the way he did, the way he drove her almost blind with pleasure, if he was like that with his other dates. The prettier, skinnier, blonde bombshells that always looked perfect at the side of him. The thought had a deep ache settling in her chest, making her rub against her sternum to try to dislodge the pain.

"What if I was only a passing curiosity?" she muttered to herself, her thumb nail clamped between her teeth, chewing as she mulled over the possibilities. "What if he's made a clean break without telling me?" she continued, chewing on her thumbnail as nervousness streamed through her veins.

"Whose made a clean break?" James's voice from beside her made her jump. Snapping her eyes to him, covered in oil and grease and so close, she wondered how she hadn't noticed. "The mystery man, that why you've been upset this week?" James sunk into the chair, his hands supporting his chin, with his elbows digging into his thighs.

"I don't know." Ava half shrugged, sitting up on the sofa. Pulling her legs beneath her, the forgotten e-reader pushed to the side. "I don't know what's happened." she confessed, her bottom lip quivering.

"Sometimes." James sighed, scrubbing his hands down his face. "Sometimes, you won't find out what's happened, except *cuddle* with the wrong person." he continued, his voice softer than she'd heard it in a long time, tears gathered in her eyes as the ache in her chest grew stronger, more painful.

"But why do you do that?" her voice was a mere whisper as she asked the question. "Why can't men change?" she continued, her arms wrapping around herself in an effort to hold the hurt inside.

"Hey, not all men are the same." he stopped talking, placing the heel of his hands against his eyes. Dragging a hard breath in before his green eyes landed on her and his breath hissing from between clenched teeth. "Who were you seeing, Ava?" his voice was hard and his face serious. Her pulse spiked at his question.

"Why can't I be good enough, James." she ignored his question as the tears she'd been trying to hold back tumbled down her cheeks. "Why is it always the same women who gets the guy?" she practically sobbed the words out. "Why are you all such bastards?
"Hey, shh." James cooed, his arms wrapping around her, pulling her into his side as his hand soothed down her back. The smell of oil and grease from the garage was almost clogging. "You are good enough, Squirt." he began, gently rocking her. "You just haven't met the right guy, but you will." he continued, trying to soothe her.

But Ava knew she could only be soothed by one person.

The person who was ignoring her.

It had been a couple of hours and Ava had finally stopped crying and James had stopped looking at her from the corner of his eye every time she moved. She heard James talking quietly on the phone, cancelling his plans, which made her feel bad. She didn't know who he was speaking with and she didn't think that she really wanted to know. Because if he was speaking with Blake, then he was definitely ignoring her and she didn't know how to cope with that realisation.

The loud knock that pounded on the front door had Ava tensing, her heart trying to beat out of her chest and her breaths seized in her lungs all at once. Her wide eyes turned to James, a look of pure dread on her face as she felt her complexion pale.

"I'll get it." James sighed, placing his drink on the coffee table. "You stay here." he continued as he walked across the living room.

Ava listened with bated breath, trying to determine who was at the door. The need to run weighed heavily on her limbs. Her stomach clenched, sending a stream of bile into her throat as the living room door opened. A mop of dark hair behind James had her swallowing back the bile and the breath she was holding whooshing out of parted lips.

"Nathan?" Ava's voice was hesitant as she tried to see behind James's wide frame.

"Hey." his boyish smile lit up his whole face as he stepped around her brother to sit beside her on the sofa.

"I'll leave you guys alone." James hesitated until Ava nodded that it was okay. Smiling tightly, James closed the door behind him.

"Nath-"

"Sor-" They both started speaking at the same time. Nathan's hand gripped Ava's shaking one, his blue eyes staring intently. "I'm really sorry Ava." he began, his fingers digging into her hand painfully.

"It's okay, Nathan." Ava tried to wrestle her hand from his grip without success. "You're hurting me." she whispered, tears stinging the backs of her eyes. But he didn't let go.

"I shouldn't have touched you." his voice earnest, his eyes pleading. "It's just – I've always wanted...."

The living room door burst open successfully, cutting off Nathan's words. The large hulking frame vibrating with rage and a look of murder in his eyes. Stalking towards the sofa, his eyes narrowing at the way Ava's hand was gripped by Nathan's. Ava's eyes were wide and Nathan gulped audibly.

"You little shit!" James seethed, his hands fisted in Nathan's shirt pulling him to his feet.

The moment Nathan's feet hit the floor, James's fist collided with his nose. Blood spraying, bones cracking. Nathan yelping in pain and Ava was sitting with her mouth hanging open and her eyes wide as fucking saucers, unable to move.

Another punch. Another yelp. Another grunt. More blood. More bones cracking.

"Put your hands on her again and I'll fucking kill you!" James blared as his fist collided with Nathan's jaw.

"James!" Ava shouted, not daring to try to get in the middle of the scuffle. But she needed to do something before James made good on his threat and killed Nathan. "James! It wasn't Nathan!" she shouted.

"What?" his voice harsh, his breaths hasher and his arm suspended in mid-air, ready to make another sickening thud against Nathan. His pupils were blown wide, his eyes narrowed, and his mouth twisted with anger.

"All Nathan did was put his arm around me." Ava admitted, wincing when she saw his face. Already bruising and swelling down one side. "It wasn't Nathan who hurt me." she clarified, lowering her eyes to her lap.

"Get the fuck out!" James seethed, pushing Nathan away. She watched him trip over his feet, trying to scramble away. "He put his hands on you, Squirt." James was breathing deeply, trying to dispel the rage, all-consuming anger as his fists slowly uncurled. "Nobody should ever put their hands on you if you don't want them to." he continued, wiping the blood from his hands down the front of his t-shirt.

"I know." Ava whispered, swallowing thickly at the sight of blood smeared across his t-shirt. "Best go get cleaned up." she pitched a half smile.

"Yeah." James grunted, putting his back to her. "If I find out who hurt you, Ava, it'll be worse than tonight." his voice was hard, his words a warning which made Ava gulp.

Don't worry, James, you'll never find out.

Ava thought the words she was too scared to voice aloud.

Chapter Seventeen

The sterile stench of his office burnt his nostrils, sat in the high-backed black leather chair, the computer bleeping loudly, signalling his next patient had arrived as his dark brown eyes roved over the patient file. His lips tipping into a smile as he stood, his hands smoothing down his shirt.

The waiting room was full, low voices talking, waiting patients either keeping children under control or looking on their phones. His purposeful strides eating up the tiled floor, his eyes scanning the waiting room. Voices dimmed, eyes turning their focus to him. His pulse spiked as a bead of sweat appeared on the back of his neck and then he saw her. The tightly curled grey hair, her frail frame hunched into the plastic chair and her watery amber eyes landing on him.

"Good morning, Mrs Templeton." His deep voice was warm, his eyes soft as he held a hand out to her. "Come with me, young lady." he continued, helping her up.

"Oh, Doctor Sinclair." she laughed, her arthritic hand patting his. "You know how to make me feel special." she smiled as they slowly walked across the waiting room.

"Anything for you." he smiled, making the effort to slow his strides. At eighty-six years of age, Mrs Templeton had been his patient for over six years. "Here, sit down." he slowly helped her sit in the uncomfortable plastic chair in his office.

"I've made you a cake." she announced, pulling an oblong shaped cake from her bag wrapped in brown grease-proof paper and cling-film.

"Lemon drizzle?" he licked his lips as she nodded. "You're going to make me fat." he chuckled, placing the cake on his desk.

"There's nothing wrong with a bit of weight." her tone was serious. "My Edgar was like you until we married." she chuckled at the memory. "Then he started putting weight on, my fault I kept baking and cooking all day, every day." she patted his hand again, a warm smile on her face. "Have you found someone to look after you?" she asked.

Blake wasn't shocked by the question, it was the same one she asked every time they spoke and the cake was the same she made every time she visited. It was delicious, moist, full of flavour, and melted on his tongue. The thought of Ava enjoying the cake, making those sounds, flashed through his head. A stab of pain and guilt went through his chest at the mere thought of her.

"Mrs Templeton." Blake's voice held a little uncertainty, the thought had been pulsing in his head for days, weeks even and he needed to know. "Do you think your hearts big enough to love two people?"

"Dear." she clasped his hand feebly in both of hers. Her eyes holding his. "When Edgar died, I didn't think my heart would ever heal." she tried to tighten her grip. "It didn't really, just got easier. Easier to breathe, easier to cope with each passing day." tears filled her eyes at the memory. "I can tell you this, Doctor Synclair. I did manage to fall in love again, but it wasn't the same as it was with Edgar. He was my shining star in the dark sky and once you find that shining star, you'll know which one to choose." she patted his hand. "I hope that helps, for what it's worth." Blake swallowed the lump in his throat.

"Yes, it did, thank you." he gave her a gentle squeeze. "Now, I've got your results in from the tests a few weeks ago." his tone and demeanor changed, the doctor within him taking over.

"How long have I got left?" she asked, a worried smile on her face.

"Many years to come, Maureen." Blake chuckled with a slight shake of his head. "Your cholesterol is a little high."

"It's been a little high for the last twenty years." she laughed. "Nothing will change that now at my age."

"Hmm." he shook his head, but wasn't surprised with her answer. Every time he checked to make sure it hadn't changed, she always said the same thing, and he knew she won't accept any medication for it either. "There was a cause for concern, though, with one of the tests." he took a deep breath, this was the part he hated about his job. "There were a lot of triglycerides in your blood and I need to start you on some new medication." he continued, the prescription already waiting on his desk.

"Another bloody tablet." she huffed with a shake of her head. "I'm going to be rattling when I walk, young man." she admonished.

"I know, I know but Maureen, we need to keep your arteries open, help the blood flow through and keep the risk of blood clots and strokes down to a bare minimum, do we not?" he asked, tilting his head to the side. A smile twitching his lips as he saw the slight nod of her head. "Besides, what's one more tablet if it helps me to see you more often?" he watched her eyes light up, which warmed him.

"Very well, you drive a hard bargain." her lips curved slightly, handing over the prescription.

"That I do." he smiled. "Please take the first tablet today and rest." he held up a hand to stop her from interrupting him. "I know you go see Edgar, that's fine, but don't stay out too long and please rest when you get home." he looked at her sternly, his lips twitching into a smile.

"Yes, okay, but if I'm rattling next time, we'll have to stop some tablets."

"Hmm, well I'll see you in two weeks for a checkup." he stood, gently helping her to her feet. "Come on, young lady." he smiled warmly as her arthritic hand gripped his arm. "I'll take you to the chemist."

The moment he slumped back into the black leather chair, he scrubbed a hand down his face. Breathing out a loud sigh, ignoring all the text messages he'd received over the last two weeks. He couldn't bring himself to read them as he typed out a text message.

Blake – *Ava, we need to talk. My place, tonight 7pm.*

Chapter Eighteen

Ava sat on the plush sofa, smoothing the deep brown skirt over her thighs. Her heart was thumping with trepidation. She'd clasped her hands together in her lap to stop them from shaking. She was shocked when she'd received his message earlier in the day. She had been certain that he didn't want to speak to her again after radio silence for two weeks. It had taken her almost an hour deciding on if it was the smartest thing for her to see Blake again.

It hadn't helped that she'd only seen Katie once, during the last two weeks, and the look of pity in her eyes had broken Ava all over again. It had cemented Ava's thoughts that whatever Blake and her had, it was over before it even really began. And it was that thought which pushed Ava to accept the invitation to talk, pushed her into wanting to see him one last time and pushed her to want answers. Answers to what she had done wrong and answers to why she wasn't good enough.

She could hear Blake's steady breaths in the silence of his living room. Blake was sitting opposite her in a large plush chair, his knees spread slightly and his hands resting on this thick, muscular thighs. The tension in the room was almost clogging, almost intolerable.

"So, um, you wanted to..." she faltered, her words stuck in her throat.

Apprehension clawing its way to the surface. Her hands began to shake, her fingers clutched the bottom of her tank top aimlessly, pulling and stretching it away from her stomach.

She could feel his eyes on her, tracking her jerky movements, but she found herself lowering her gaze. Concentrating on the pull and stretch of the fabric.

"Ava." Blake cleared his throat. His voice hard as steel crawled over her with a violence she hadn't expected. "I'm sorry we haven't spoken in a while." Her eyes snapped to his, her pulse stuttered in her throat. She watched his throat bob in a hard swallow.

Her stomach twisted painfully, her chest ached with pure, twisted fear. The glacial look in his eyes didn't belong there and yet, she knew that the perfectly sinful man before her was just that.

Sinful. Delectable. Heartbreaker.

As shameful as it was to admit, he'd shown her a side she had craved for years. The tender side, the lustful side, and she'd wanted more. Greedy to the core in more ways than one. She wanted everything that he was willing to give to her. She wanted to be everything he needed her to be. She wanted to protect him from the demons she saw lurking beneath. She wanted to simply love him for who he was.

But as the days turned into weeks, she lost more and more hope. Hope that she could be all of those things with him. Hope that he somehow wanted those things from her. But he didn't and his silence had made her realise that, as painful as it was. He'd held her heart in a vice for two weeks, slowly twisting, slowly releasing the blood, slowly dulling her heartbeat until she felt numb from the pain in her chest. That was the heartbreak, she knew that, she'd seen it in James when his marriage fell apart. She just didn't realise how painful it actually was.

But she needed answers from him, needed to stop swallowing her words, she needed to let them take over despite the consequences.

"What did I do wrong?" she rushed out like it was one big word before she sucked in a deep breath, her stomach twisted violently and her skin a little clammy as she watched those impossibly dark eyes of his stare directly at her.

No emotion, his sinful lips in a hard line.

The tension ricocheted up another notch.

"What makes you think that you did anything wrong?" he asked, pronouncing each word carefully. Not moving a muscle as he stared at her. Her bottom lip quivered before she clamped it between her teeth. She'd had enough of the tears over the last two weeks, and she didn't want to give him the satisfaction of seeing her fall apart again. The ache in her chest was back with a vengeance. "Why don't you think I did something wrong?" he asked, leaning forward slightly, his forearms resting against his thighs. His eyes never leaving hers and that was when she saw the flicker of pain in his eyes, just a flash before is disappeared.

"I-I'm not good en-." she gulped around the lump in her throat. Almost drawing blood from her bottom lip as she sunk her teeth in further, when he cleared his throat again.

"I'm not a good man, Ava." his voice was hard, his eyes flat and devoid of all emotion. A mask she'd never seen before. A mask that didn't fit him. A mask she wanted to be gone. "I've done things that I'm not proud of – *fuck!*" he hissed, scrubbing a hand down his face before covering it with his hands. She watched his chest expand and deflate with his deep breaths.

The silence was stifling and deafening all at the same time, giving her insecurities time to surface, spit their spiteful words at her. But she had to focus, had to listen to what the man she had been in love with for years had to say. Except he was still breathing deeply, his face still buried in his hands, and then she saw the slight tremor skittering down his forearms. His muscles twitching, his tawny skin shivering.

The words tumbling through her mind that had bile rising in the back of her throat, tears stinging the backs of her eyes as the coldest, bone chilling feeling took over her body.

Why am I not good enough for you?

What could I have done differently?

How many blondes have warmed your bed?

You said you didn't want me to be like the blondes, but you went running back, anyway.

"How many blondes have warmed your bed, Blake?" she winced as she heard the brute coldness of her tone. She watched him tense and his breath leave him harshly.

Her stomach twisted again, she tried keeping her breaths even but the more she tried to breathe the more bile tried to rise up her throat. The nauseating truth was there for her to see. The truth she wanted to pretend hadn't happened. The truth she wanted to protect herself from. But she couldn't, in the harsh silence of the room, it was there.

Standing on shaking legs, her body racked with the pain of the truth. Silent tears tracking down her cheeks that she couldn't stop, even if she tried. She'd been in his clutches for too long. She needed to get away from her sinful, deceitful, delectable fucking heartbreaker. That was the thought that pushed her to stumble across the room as if her legs were numb.

"Stop!" he barked. But she didn't. Didn't stop, didn't turn even as she heard him stand. The rustle of fabric in the silence. She continued, one step at a time. "Ava, stop!" the command in his tone wasn't lost on her.

And in that moment,ripping the bottom of her top in a death

grip as her breaths whooshed from her.

"What, Blake." the coldness was still there in her voice. She'd tried to wrap that feeling around her heart, but failed miserably. "You going to give me a number?" the taunt in her words wasn't like her. Hell, she didn't even know where this side had come from, but she needed to cling to it desperately if she was going to survive walking away.

"Yeah." his voice was soft, his body heat seeping into her back. His large hands gripping her waist, sucking all the breath from her lungs. "Turn around." she shook her head no at his request. "Ava." the warning tone was back, his fingers flexed before his grip hardened.

"Go to hell, Blake." she spat, slapping his hands away from her. But before she could take a step, his words stopped her.

Dead. In. Her. Tracks.

"I'm already there." the words were so low, she wasn't certain she'd heard correctly. Turning slowly to face him, sucking in a breath at the tortured pain etched onto his face. "I'm already there." he repeated, reaching for her, but she stepped out of his reach. She watched him bow his head slightly, a hard breath leaving him. And just like that, the coldness seeped out of her in a rush that had her shuddering.

"I don't understand." her voice was gentle, taking a step towards him. And another until her palm collided with his chest. The ripple of a shiver that coursed through him tingled against her palm.

"This." he began, laying his hand gently over hers on his chest. "I don't let anyone touch me, but you." she blinked up at him as he sucked in a stuttered breath. "Nobody has ever been in this home, but you." he breathed out and Ava felt his heart racing, colliding against his ribcage. "You are the only one to drive me to pure insanity." his eyes bore into hers. His lips tipped into a slight smile at his admission.

"I-I....what are you trying to say, Blake?" she asked, her heart beating in time with his. Her stomach no longer twisting but fluttering at his words. Words she hoped weren't a lie.

"I want to show you, if you'll let me." his face hardened for a fraction of a second as he stared at her. She watched him prepare himself for her refusal. And she should, but there had always been something about him that made her want to be with him, love him and protect him that made her fucking stupid for this man.

"Okay." she nodded. "Show me." she continued. Blake nodded once, laced their fingers together and tugged her towards the front door. "Where are we going?" she asked, following blindly.

"The hotel." he never broke stride as the cool summer night air licked at her exposed skin before she was bundled inside his Aston Martin.

Chapter Nineteen

The hotel room door clicked into place behind Ava, the twist of the lock pierced the silence of the room. Her apprehension clicking back into place before the room is illuminated in a warm glow of light. Her breath catches in a gasp, her hand flies to her mouth and her eyes widen.

She wasn't certain what she was expecting to witness in the hotel room. Wasn't certain what Blake's intent was. Wasn't certain what her intent was. But as she looked around the room in abject horror, she needed answers.

The living area was littered with empty whiskey bottles, broken glass littered the floor, the smashed television hanging haphazardly from the wall, paintings slashed and torn. Spots of dried blood adorned the walls. Sofas overturned, dining table and chairs splintered. Lamps trashed and scattered across the expanse of the room.

She could feel Blake stand behind her. Could feel the tension rolling off of him in waves as she took in the living area and yet, he didn't speak. Only stood, looming and imposing.

Ava took a careful step around the chaos, following the trail of destruction through the archway. Her eyes grew ever wider as she looked over every inch of the room. The deep green bedding was a crumpled heap at the base of the bed. Table lamps broken on the floor. Clothes ripped and littered the floor. The boudoir chair overturned. More paintings slashed and torn. More spots of dried blood clung to the walls. More broken glass. Another television smashed and clinging to the wall in desperation.

Ava took another step, glass crunching underfoot. Her breaths were hard as she tried to control the overwhelming fear that was trying to take root. Chains hanging from a wall, paddles of different sizes, spikes, gags, ropes, blindfolds all littered one wall, usually hidden behind doors that were now hanging from their hinges. The waste bin overflowing with brand new packets of condoms.

She was speechless.

"Zero blondes have graced the hotel room since the night you told me that you were done with me." Blake's voice shattered the silence, his hands resting against her hips.

She didn't move, didn't bat his hands away.

"What?" Ava breathed out, unable to understand what he was saying. "But you've had dates since then." her voice was still breathy as she continued to look at the chaos before her.

"Hmm." he hummed, moving until his front collided with her back. His scent cloaked her, warmed her. "I have and I left every-fucking-one of them at the side of the road." he whispered in her ear, a shiver skittering down her spine.

"But..." she gestured towards the chaos. "What's this, Blake, if not after one of your dates?" she asked, her eyebrows furrowing. His teeth nipped her earlobe, making her moan, before his lips touched the shell of her ear.

"This is my hell." he whispered. "This is the insanity that you drive me to, the destruction I inflicted because...." his lips brushed her ear with every word. Shudders wrack her body, her nipples harden at the contact. "This was me trying to fight against what you do to me and this...fuck." his hands splayed across her stomach, making her flinch. "This is everything that makes me the worst person. Everything that makes you too good for me." his arms held her to him in a brutal hold.

"What do you mean, the worst person?" Ava asked in a whisper, her heart thudding hard at more than just his words. The feel of his hard body against hers, held possessively in his tight embrace, had her pussy clenching with sheer, liquid need.

"Only in this room." he took a breath, his muscles flexing against her as he squeezed her tighter. "Is where I inflict pain onto the blondes you've seen me with." his breath leaves him harshly. Ava feels the tremors in his arms, feels the light sheen of sweat against her from him. "Where I crave their pain, crave their suffering, and crave their humiliation." she heard him swallow thickly. "All of this is why I've been trying to fight you out of my head. This is everything why I shouldn't be with you and this is why I'm desperately drawn to your innocence, your purity." his lips pressed against her neck. "Why I need to drown in you Ava and only you." his whispered words were laced with sincerity and vulnerability which wrapped around her heart.

"Is that why you left me alone that night?" she asked, squirming in his arms. "Let me see you." she whispered, his hold on her loosened and in a heartbeat, she was spun until she was facing him. His chocolate eyes were darker as he looked at her. His lips turned down.

"It was the hardest thing I had to do that night." he admitted, his hand cupping her cheek. "Leaving you alone in that bed, leaving my shining, pure, innocent light half broken." his thumb caressed her skin. "Hearing your sobs terrified me." his eyes shone with unshed tears. "I thought I'd hurt you and I couldn't forgive myself." he admitted on a hard swallow, his voice cracking. "That's why I stayed away for so long, I didn't trust myself with you." Ava moved closer, his heat once again seeping into her.

"And now?" she asked, their lips a breath apart. Her eyes

fluttering and her heart seizing as she waited for his answer.

"I'm ready to worship you, if you'll let me." he whispered. Ava didn't hesitate to nod, a smile gracing her lips. Tears of joy shining in her eyes as he breathed a sigh. His shoulders relaxing as the tension eased.

Blake moved his hand to the back of her neck, his fingers tangling in her long, brown hair as he angled her head. His lips capturing hers in a searing kiss. His tongue sweeping across the seam of her lips before exploring her mouth in long, languid strokes. Ava moaned into the kiss, her hand cupping his stubbled cheek, trying to pull him closer, making him groan deep in the back of his throat.

"We need to stop." he husked out, breathing harshly as he pulled back. His hand was still tangled in her hair, still holding her to him.

"W-why?" she breathed out heavily, her eyebrows furrowing, making him smile.

"Because you're worth more than this room." the admission in his words sent a jolt through her.

A jolt that made her heart swell for this man that she couldn't ignore. A jolt of pure love that she would cling to and chase away his demons.

The usual doorman waiting. His uniform always pressed with military precision. His grey hair slicked back neatly and his trimmed beard, hiding the small smile as he looked at Blake and Ava hand in hand, leaving the hotel.

"Good evening, Doctor Synclair, Ms Asherton." his eyes were shining bright in the light of the hotel. His voice aged with an air of sophistication. Ava smiled in greeting.

"Patrick." Blake greeted with a slight nod. "Please, could you let housekeeping know, they can toss everything out of the room, they have my full permission." Blake continued with a dip of his head.

Ava noticed the surprised look flash across Patrick's face before he had time to keep his features neutral.

"Of course, Doctor Synclair." Patrick nodded. "I'll see to it, it would be my pleasure." he winked at Ava as Blake turned on his heel.

Once they were back in Blake's car, his hand resting on her thigh. The street lights flickering through the windows and the scenery passing by. Ava sunk into the leather seat, she turned slightly to look at Blake's profile. The light highlighting the contours of his face.

"Patrick seems nice." Ava broke the silence and watched him nod.

"We've known each other since I was little." Ava was shocked that he'd divulged this information. "I used to spend a lot of time here growing up." he turned briefly with a smile. "He's a good man." he sighed, a shadow crossing his face.

"Hmm, he seems it and he also seems to care about you too." Ava placed her hand on his, resting on her thigh.

"Would you like to stay the night at my house?" Blake asked, his fingers applying a little pressure against her thigh.

"Hmm, and just what would we be doing?" the purr in her voice caught her and Blake off guard as he did a double take.

"Fuck!" he breathed out, increasing the speed of the car. "Anything you want, baby girl." he husked out, squeezing her thigh.

A thought sprung to mind. A thought that made her stomach flutter and her pussy clench with anticipation.

Would Blake be rough with me?

She'd seen enough movies and read enough books to understand the kind of pleasure people got from that kind of sexual relationship. She just wasn't certain really just how depraved Blake really could – or rather – would be with her.

"Okay, I'll stay." she agreed, giggling as he growled into the car. A deep rumbling growl that had her nerve endings coming alive.

Chapter Twenty

The moment they pulled up outside his home, Blake squeezed her thigh until she looked at him. Shadowed in the darkness of the car, her pulse spiked, her breath hitched in the back of her throat at the delicious smile etched onto his face.

"Ava, what would you like to do?" his tone was serious. Her face flamed at the question, making him chuckle.

That was a question she wasn't expecting. She just assumed that Blake would take the lead once they were back. Instead, he was asking her and she wasn't really sure how to answer the question. She wanted to experience everything that Blake had to offer her. Wanted desperately for Blake to be the man to take her virginity. After all, she'd been saving all of herself for this man. He'd already been her first kiss, and that had been amazing. The indecision weighed on her. Her heart was thumping a disastrous rhythm with the anticipation of what it would be like, but she couldn't stop the ugly thoughts about her body from sounding off inside her head.

"Ava, get ready for bed." Blake's voice was calm as he patted her thigh. "I've got a quick call to make and then I'll join you, okay?" he asked, turning the ignition off.

"Sure, okay." she nodded, trying to banish the ugly thoughts from her mind.

She had completely forgotten about her clothes that she'd left a few weeks ago, that had been washed, ironed and put away. That was probably why she'd forgotten them the last time she was here. Shaking her head, she pulled the pale green satin nightdress from the drawer and quickly dressed for bed.

Remembering what happened the last time she wore this nightdress had a deep blush seeping into her skin. His words, his touches, the ice, his warm lips, the thick hot erection, him rubbing against her flesh until he erupted.

Everything inside of her lit up at the memory of the pleasure that she had felt without climaxing, and she knew in that instant that she wanted him to do those things to her again.

Blowing out a breath, she snuggled into the most comfortable bed she'd ever slept in. The plush bedding tucked under her arms, as she waited for Blake and anticipation swept through her.

Ava blushed, smiling as he walked in, closing the door behind him without a single word spoken. She watched in rapt fascination as Blake started unbuttoning his shirt. Watched his biceps bunch and flex with each movement of his deft fingers. A slow burn of arousal began in the pit of her stomach.

"Eye fucking me, baby girl." Blake's husky voice sent a delectable shiver over her. Her nipples hardening.

"Hmm." she licked over her lips, her eyes slowly tracking his movements. Watching as he pulled the shirt from his body, making her groan. The thick, hard cut muscles flexing with the movement. "Yummy." she whispered, mostly to herself, but she caught the smirk before he hung his head.

"Torture." he groaned, turning on his heel and the panic which rose in Ava was so quick it knocked her breathless.

Why was he leaving?

"Have I done something wrong?" she asked, her voice timid. She watched Blake pause mid-stride, watched his back expand on a large inhale of breath before he turned to look at her.

"No, you haven't." his voice was soft as he walked closer to the bed. "It's just difficult." she watched his throat bob on a hard swallow. "When you keep eye-fucking me." the corners of his mouth curved ever so slightly but Ava furrowed her brow.

"If there's something wrong with me. Just admit it." her tone was fearful and borderline bitter as she covered her flaming face with both hands.

"What?" his tone was incredulous. "There's nothing wrong with you." his hand smoothed over her calf above the bedcovers.

"Then why won't you undress in front of me?" her voice was muffled by her hands. "Why won't you touch me?" Large hands gripped her wrists, gently tugging until she was looking into those impossibly dark eyes.

"Because you flinch every time I touch you." his words were a mere whisper. "Because I don't want to push you into something that you'll regret." the sincerity in his voice and eyes were enough to reduce her to a blubbering mess. But she wouldn't cry. She heaved a deep breath and then slowly let it go.

"I won't regret it with you, Blake." she answered honestly, but he shook his head as if he didn't believe her.

"If you won't regret anything with me, why do you flinch when I touch you?" his stare was intense and his grip on her wrists tightened as she tried to yank them free. "No, Ava. Answer the question, instead of hiding from me." his tone was sharp with a certain desperate plea laced in that tone.

"I don't flinch." Ava tried to avert her eyes from his intense stare.

"Don't flinch?" Blake released her wrists and ripped the bed covers off of the bed. His breath caught in his throat as his pupils dilated at the pale green satin nightdress encasing her body. Closing his eyes briefly, he sucked in a breath, his hand going directly to her stomach. He watched and felt the flinch. "See, this is what I'm talking about." he continued, removing his hand dejectedly.

"I-I..." she trailed off as her cheeks flamed in shame and disgust.

Disgusted in how she looked, even after she had tried to lose weight, exercise, calorie count, and yet nothing had changed. She still had the same figure, still had the same little wobble on her stomach, still had the fat ass. Shame of how others saw her and what they would whisper if she was seen with Blake. But worse than that would be, if Blake finally realised that she wasn't good enough. She couldn't stand the thought of Blake thinking that, despite what he'd said to her. Despite him wanting to worship her, he hadn't seen her without any clothes on.

"Now that I've proven my point." Blake ran his hand through his hair. "Will you tell me why you flinch if you want me to touch you?" his tone was almost glum.

Ava closed her eyes against the unguarded look in his eyes. Hurting at the mere sight of it. Her heart was racing, her stomach was twisting, and she was becoming clammy. She really didn't want to express her reasons and really didn't want the ugly words whirling around in her mind to take over her thoughts.

But as she opened her eyes again and saw the sorrow within the depths of his deep chocolate eyes, saw the worry etched on his handsome face, she remembered everything. She remembered him calling her beautiful, remembered him wanting to feed her, remembered him telling her that he loved the sounds that she made, remembered their private conversations. And she realised that if she wanted to let go and take a leap of faith, she had to admit one of her biggest fears out loud to the man she loved.

Pulling herself up on her elbows, she looked directly into those deep pools of brown and took a deep breath.

It's now or never.

"Because I'm fat." she rushed out in one long breath. She watched his eyes widen, but rushed on before he could say anything. "Because I'm not like the skinny, beautiful women you are normally with." her chest heaved at the long rush of words and tears gathered in her eyes as she laid the truth out.

"Ava." Blake sat on the bed, turning to face her. "I want to get one thing straight with you." his eyes hardened as he pinned her with a pointed stare. "Call yourself *fat*." he spat the word, his mouth twisting. "Again and we're going to have a real fucking problem." he watched Ava open her mouth in utter shock.

"But you also keep saying it's torture." her voice was quiet and her brows were furrowed slightly as the corners of his mouth twitched.

"Pure torture." he murmured. "Pure fucking torture." his lips turning into a sexy as sin smile. "Because of how fucking sexy you are, Ava." he almost groaned the entire sentence. Ava's breath hitched, and her eyes widened at his words. "Because every time I'm around you, all I want to do is strip you naked and run my hands and tongue over your entire body." he stood, looming over her as his eyes roamed over every inch of her body, heat and hunger in his gaze. Igniting a fire within Ava that she knew would become all-consuming. "Because I want to do nothing more than to bathe in your innocence." his fingertips trailed lightly over her thigh, raising goosebumps. "Because I want to do nothing more than taste your purity."

his voice turned rough as he bent to press his lips to her satin covered stomach.

Ava really tried not to flinch or recoil and she really tried to believe the words he was saying so profoundly, but she still had that doubt, still held the disgust. Blake's brows dipped low as he looked at the crestfallen look on Ava's face.

"You doubt my words, baby girl?" his voice was low and hurt. He hung his head for a moment, raking his fingers through his hair before turning back to her. "Come with me." he didn't wait for a response, didn't wait for her to move before he lifted her off of the bed.

"Blake!" Ava yelled, startled. "I'm too heavy." she tried to wriggle, but he pinned her with a stare.

"Are we going to have a problem?" his words were low, his eyebrows raised in a challenge. Ava gulped and shook her head no. "If I can't carry you, I'm not man enough to have you." he continued, striding purposefully across the expanse of the bedroom.

Kicking the bathroom door open, he stopped in front of the full-length mirror, carefully placing Ava back on her own two feet facing him. His large hand gently cupped her cheek as his eyes softened and a small smile played on his lips. Running his thumb across her lower lip in a featherlight touch.

Ava's heart was thumping hard, her green eyes snared in his deep browns, her lips parting slightly as she inched closer. Leaning into his touch. When he looked at her like this, she felt beautiful. When he touched her like this, her thoughts scattered in a million different ways.

"Bla-" Ava's voice was a mere whisper, but he cut off her words. His lips pressing against hers. Ava's tongue tentatively touched his, making him groan low in the back of his throat before he pulled back.

"I want to show you what I see." he murmured softly, his hands on her shoulders before he turned Ava to face the mirror. "When I look at you." he continued, gathering her hair in his hand and slowly whispering it over her right shoulder. The soft tendrils tickling her chest. His eyes held hers through the mirror, her back to his front. "Your eyes hold a myriad of emotions in the deep green that sparkle with your happiness and the deep blue ring you have around your iris change colour with your mood." his voice was soft. "Your pouty lips are perfect for kissing." he runs his finger delicately over her lower lip, making her breath falter. "Your mouth and the sounds they make when you eat makes me want to constantly feed you just so I can hear them." his lips tipped into a smile. "Your neck, so sensitive, I love running my lips over the delicate skin. Love hearing your breath hitch in the back of your throat when I do." Blake murmured, pressing a delicate kiss to her collarbone. "Your shoulders." he hooked his fingers over the delicate straps of her nightdress, slowly moving them to her arms. "Perfect for biting." his lips tipped in a wicked grin before his teeth nipped her.

"Oh, Blake." Ava whispered, her voice shaking at the tenderness in his eyes.

"Shhh." he soothed. "Your arms, I love how they feel wrapped around me." his hands feathered over her skin, raising goosebumps. "Your hands, I love how they touch me so delicately." he moved the straps of her nightdress off of her hands, exposing her breasts and he sucked in a sharp breath at the sight. "More than a handful." Ava squeezed her eyes shut as his hands cupped her breasts, her breath stuttering in her throat. "Open your eyes." he whispered, his lips brushing against the shell of her ear.

"I can't." she admitted, her voice faltering as her fears mounted.

"You can, I want you to look directly into mine." he whispered, his thumbs caressing the sides of her breasts soothingly until she slowly opened them. "Good girl." he smiled. "These are exquisite." his hands added a little pressure. "Your nipples, I love how they harden when I touch you and I can't wait to lick and suck them like my life depends on it." her breath whooshed out of her. His hands left her breasts, gathering the satin nightdress and slowly inching it down her body until it pooled at her hips. His fingers stopping it from going any further. Her breathing was shallow, her pulse beating wildly against her throat, and tremors running through her body. "Your stomach, Ava." his voice was soft as he held her eyes through the mirror.

Ava was almost hyperventilating, she wanted nothing more than to hide, wanted nothing more than to leave because she was certain he was going to crush her self-esteem even further.

"Isn't flat nor toned but is utterly womanly and I love running my hands across it." his smile was tender. "It will one day keep a baby safe until it's ready to come into the world." she watched his throat bob on a hard swallow. Her heart swelled at his words, and she felt a slight bit of confidence. "Your hips, they were made for gripping and the way they sway when you walk, hypnotise me every fucking time." his voice became a little rough and his fingers a little tighter before he let go of the satin nightdress and watched it drop to the floor, pooling around her feet. "Your ass, fuck!" he hissed out as both hands needed the pliant flesh. "I can't wait to sink my teeth into these fleshy globes." he punctuated his words with a fierce grip. Ava moaned as she arched into his touch, heat gathering in her core.

"Your pussy." his voice was like liquid velvet. "Always so wet, so pure it drives me to madness. Your scent makes me so fucking hard it's almost painful." his fingers pushed against the inside of her thighs and the moment he felt her wetness, he couldn't contain the growl that escaped. "I can't wait to lick the juices from your thighs, can't wait to have them wrapped around my head as I devour your perfect pussy." his voice was rough, his cock hard as it pushed against her ass.

"Jesus." she whispered breathlessly as tears gathered in her eyes.

"Ava." his lips pressed against her temple in a fleeting touch. "You are nothing like the other women I have fucked." he saw the hurt flash through her eyes, saw the tears begin to fall, but he ignored it. "But to me you are perfect, beautiful, innocent and pure." he smiled as he slowly turned her to face him, his hands on her hips. "So, baby girl, now you know the way I see you." his hands cupped her cheeks, his thumbs brushing the tears that were tracking down her face.

Blake had laid out all of her insecurities to the point she felt bare. He'd uncovered her body, the one thing she had been ashamed of and said the most beautiful of words. Ava knew they were more than mere words to get her into his bed, she knew from the way he spoke almost raw with emotion and the looks in his eyes that he meant every single word. She felt like he'd cracked her wide open for the world to see. For her to finally see herself in a new light, a new way for her to view herself.

She'd been in love with the unobtainable man for nine years, but at this moment in time she felt head over heels, hopelessly and irrevocably in love with Blake Synclair.

"Blake, I..." she trailed off, her bottom lip quivering. "You make me feel beautiful." she whispered, pressing her lips to his. A fleeting brush before she pulled back. "Can I see all of you?" she asked, her cheeks blushing furiously. She watched his pupils dilate, his lips part and his chest expanded in a harsh breath.

"You want to eye-fuck all of me, baby girl?" the roughness in his voice had her nerve endings surging to life, her stomach clenched and her pussy contracted. Her tongue darted out, swiping across her lower lip as she nodded. "I'm all yours." his lips curved as his hands dropped to his sides.

With shaking hands, Ava slowly unsnapped the button of his dress pants. Taking a deep breath, her fingers gripped the zip and inched it down. Her knuckles grazed over the sizeable bulge, making her movement falter as he groaned low in the back of his throat.

Blake tracked her every movement as she pushed his pants over his hips and letting them pool at his feet. The shocked gasp that left Ava's lips made him chuckle and her wide eyes snapped to his momentarily, her teeth sinking into her bottom lip. Uncertainty shone in her eyes before she looked back down.

"Oh...I." she licked over her lips and inched his underwear down until it landed on the floor. "I don't think that will fit." she admitted, unable to look away. His large cock looked rock hard, but she'd felt the silkiness of the skin when he'd cum on her stomach. She wasn't prepared for the thick banded veins, bulbous tip that had a clear liquid gathered there. She watched it twitch before the engorged head expanded on a deep throb. Her pussy clenched and wetness pooled between her thighs.

"I'll take it slow with you, baby girl." his hand reached for hers, lacing their fingers together. "Get you nice and wet before easing into that delicious pussy of yours." he continued. Ava shuddered at his words.

Ava reached out a shaking finger, mesmerised by the moisture gathering on the head. Blake let out a harsh breath, making Ava pull her finger back. Looking up through her lashes, he stared back at her with almost black eyes.

"Can I touch you?" she watched as he bit his lip and gave a curt nod of the head.

Taking a deep breath, Ava touched the glistening head gently. Her fingertip circled once, tearing a low groan from his lips. Gathering the moisture on her finger, she pulled back, her finger glistening. Blake held his breath as he watched her tongue swipe the moisture from her finger. His cock throbbed hard and more moisture leaked out as he heard that moan, he loved hearing so much.

"Fuck!" he hissed out. Ava panicked, her eyes blown wide as she stared at him. "Pure torture." he groaned, stepping out of his discarded pants and boxer shorts before scooping her up in his arms. "Let's get into bed, baby girl." his lips touched her temple as he strode out of the bathroom.

Chapter Twenty-One

Ava laid in the middle of the large bed, her knees pulled up and her feet flat on the mattress. The covers still lay in a heap at the foot of the bed. She watched with wide eyes and short, sharp panting breaths as his hands touched her knees. Slowly sliding down her thighs, the muscles quivering under his touch, goosebumps raising in his wake.

"Open your legs." his voice was a raw husk, and it set fire to Ava's blood. Through hooded eyes, he watched her legs slowly part. Watched her chest and neck flush with heat. "Good girl." his thighs pressed against the back of hers, hooking her calves on his hips as he settled above her, the majority of his weight on his forearms.

The moment she felt the heat from his hard cock resting against her stomach, she gulped around the lump in her throat. Her heart hammering against her ribcage, her wide eyes focused on his almost black eyes. The hard throb in her core had juices pooling. With shaking hands, Ava's fingertips glided over his collarbone, relishing in the shudder from Blake. She continued down towards his chest, marvelling in the way his skin was soft over thick, hard muscle.

Blake inched closer until their mouths were a breath apart. Ava tentatively curled her tongue against his lip, the tip breaching his mouth the moment his lips parted, sliding against his teeth. Their lips met, the spark igniting the deep-seated desire. Blake's lips moved against hers slowly, deliberately. The heat of his body so close to hers, the quiet groan of satisfaction from him consumed her.

Arching her back, her hardened nipples scraped against his solid chest, sending a little tremor through her body, drawing a moan from the back of her throat. Her tongue tentatively touched his before she swirled it around the tip of his tongue. Blake shuddered against her, his deep groan vibrated through his chest.

Blake trailed his lips up her jaw, nipping her earlobe, making her gasp at the sudden sting. More moisture gathered at her core. Exposing the length of her neck, his tongue travelled the column, circling around her wild pulse. Ava arched and moaned at the exquisiteness of his tongue. Every nerve ending was firing jolts of pleasure through her body. Blake dipped his tongue into the indent of her collarbone, pulling another moan from her. His teeth sunk into her shoulder on a groan, Ava hissed as the pain bloomed over her.

"Jesus, Blake." she gasped, shocked at the hard bite.

"Hmm." he groaned against her flesh. His tongue tracing the outline of his bite. "Delicious." he breathed, pinning her with the intensity of his stare as he pushed onto his knees.

Blake's large hands landed on her hips, his fingers flexing against her. Ava's hungry gaze bounced over every inch of his delectable body. His hair fell onto his forehead. His hands teasingly inched over her curves, his thumbs brushing the underside of her breasts. She watched his chest expand and deflate, watched his eyes close and his head tip back. For a long moment, he stayed still with his thumbs moving back and forth under her breasts.

"Blake." Ava's voice cut through the silence of the room with sheer need laced in that one word. His eyes snapped to hers with an almost feral look simmering in their depths. Ava's breath rushed from her lips as he bent forward, his cock sliding over her stomach and his hands cupping her breasts.

"If you want me to stop." his words were rough as he stared at her. "Just say *hurt* and I'll stop." tears gathered in her eyes at the pain which flashed through his for the briefest of moments before it was gone.

"I won't want you to stop, Blake." her voice shook with emotion, visions of the hotel room flashing through her mind as her hand cupped his cheek. Her thumb scraping over the stubble. He sucked in a deep breath, his eyes squeezed shut momentarily, and she wondered just how hard he struggled. The thought flittered away the instant his tongue flicked her nipple.

Ava arched against him in a long, drawn-out moan. His tongue circling the hardened peak. Teeth lightly grazing, making her shudder. Heat pooling between her thighs. Her hands cradling his head as he moved to the other. Circling, flicking, teeth grazing before sucking the peak into his mouth hard. Ava bucked beneath him, moaned loudly at the intense pleasure which radiated from her nipple directly to her throbbing clit.

His fingers rolled the other nipple gently, slowly as his tongue circled and flicked the other pulling moans from her pleasure filled body. Blake bit down on her breast and pinched her nipple at the same time. Ava cried out at the pain, her fingers gripping his hair tightly, making him groan and wetness seep from his tip. He moved across to her other breast, licking and sucking on the overly sensitive nipple. More liquid seeped from her core, her thighs shaking and her body arching against his.

Seizing her hips in his large hands, his grip almost bruising, he placed her ass on his thighs. Ava's chest was heaving, breaths panting almost to the point of burning pain. She'd never felt this much pleasure before, it was almost as if her body couldn't contain it. Sparks zinged from every nerve ending, her back arched and her fingers gripped the sheet beneath her as he swept a finger through her folds, gathering some of the wetness and circling her engorged clit once.

"I love how wet you are." he husked out, his finger trailing back through her folds. He delighted in watching her shudder. "So responsive." his voice dipped another octave lower, his finger swirling around her entrance excruciatingly slowly. Ava's hips undulated against his touch, making him chuckle. "So needy." he murmured, removing his finger making Ava whimper. "Want my fingers, baby girl?" he whispered, his eyes boring into hers.

"Yes." she whimpered, arching, begging with her body.

"Hmm." he hummed as two fingers thrust inside her, grazing her hymen. Ava cried out, and her hips bucked. "Innocent." he groaned, as her pussy quivered around his fingers, trying to draw them in deeper. He pulled them out, sweeping around her entrance before thrusting them back in, harder pulling a deep moan from her. "Relax." he breathed, curling his fingers inside of her, brushing against a spot that sent an instant deep throb through her core.

The muscles in her stomach tightened, the pads of his fingers pressing, releasing, rubbing against the sweetest of spots inside of her that she didn't know existed. Moans poured from her lips Her hips undulated with each press, each rub as a deep pressure began to build inside of her. Blake's fingers never stopped pressing, releasing, rubbing over and over. A ball of decadent pleasure was building faster, bigger than anything she'd ever experienced before. Her hips moving of their own accord, her mouth open with moan after lustrous moan, her head thrashing from side to side, her fingers numb from the death grip on the sheets beneath her, wetness pouring from her in waves, and then it happened. Something deep inside her swelled tightly, the ball expanded, and she exploded on a loud scream.

"Fuck!" Blake hissed as he watched her release shoot from her, splashing against the base of his cock. His hand and forearm covered in her cum, the scent was decadent and he wanted to bathe in the purity of her.

Ava's body was throbbing, her muscles quivering and her heart a ferocious thunder. Every nerve ending sent pulses of pleasure through her body as she tried to come down from her climax, to no avail. Just as one spark zinged and faded, another surged to life in one glorious wave.

She felt the large, bulbous head of Blake's cock at her entrance, making her shudder as he eased the tip inside. His hands, wet with her release, gripped her thighs and pushed them open further. She was trying to catch her breath when Blake snapped his hips forward in one long, brutal thrust. Her hymen gave way, ripping a startled, pain filled hiss from her. Her fingernails dug into his muscular back in a death grip, making him groan as he stilled inside her.

"You're so tight." Blake moaned the words in a husky caress, squeezing his eyes shut momentarily. Inching his hands across her body slowly, his palms grazing over her nipples, eliciting a moan and shudder from her.

Ava uncurled her fingers from his back on a long, shuddering breath as the pain ebbed away, the overly full feeling in her core had her pussy clenching and releasing repeatedly making Blake moan and hiss as he slowly pulled out until just the tip remained inside. Ava tensed, locking her thighs as she waited for him to plunge back in, waiting for the pain.

"Relax." Blake whispered as he slowly eased back in to the hilt. His forearms resting on the bed, caging her. Their lips a breath apart. "I need you to relax, baby girl." he murmured.

Their eyes locked, a myriad of emotions swirling, their breaths mingling in the limited space between them. Hearts thumping erratically against one another. Ava's eyes fluttered closed as

162

his lips brushed hers and, with every caress of their lips, Blake languidly rocked against her.

The slow torture of his movements, the feel of his thick cock scraping every quivering part within her had pleasure building in the deepest part of her. The slow burn of exquisite pleasure reigniting every nerve ending until they were sizzling in an electrified current, weaving over her hypersensitive body. Her hips undulated to meet his, slow and deep. Her pussy contracted, juices gathered and her moans of pleasure were continuous, which he swallowed with every sweep of his tongue inside of her mouth.

"More." she breathed out against his lips on an exquisite arch of her body. "I need more." she whimpered.

Blake reared back, gripping her hips, and drove his cock into her on a hard thrust that sent shock waves of intense pleasure through her. Before she could take a breath, he pulled back and slammed into her harder, deeper and she cried out in ecstasy. His thrusts were hard, deep, and fast. The room was filled with combined moans and groans of pleasure, the sounds of their bodies meeting in wet slaps of skin against skin. Her body was careening towards a bigger explosion. White hot waves overtook her, muscles clenched tightly, her head thrown back and her hands gripped the sheets beneath her as the dam broke and her orgasm crested in arc after decadent arc of pleasure.

"Blake!" she screamed as her pussy gripped onto his cock tightly. Liquid rushed from her in hot splashes against his pelvis.

"Mine!" Blake growled low and deadly in the back of his throat and with one last thrust, he buried himself as deep as he could and let go.

The moment she felt him cum, the hot, molten liquid fill her, another wave of pleasure hit, another climax tore through her.

Grinding against him as she rode out every pulse, every wave and every twitch of her climax until her limbs went slack, her breathing laboured and her mind was senseless. Blake collapsed against her, holding the majority of his weight on his forearms, his forehead resting against hers and their harsh breaths filling the room.

Ava caressed Blake's back in long, slow movements as their bodies began to relax. His lips touched hers in a slow, deliberate kiss as he pulled out of her in one quick motion. Tearing his mouth from hers, his arm hooking around her and taking her with him as he flopped on to the bed. Ava tucked into his side.

"Did I..." Blake's voice was low as he thickly swallowed. "Hurt you?" Ava craned her neck to look at him, but his other arm was flung over his eyes, making her heart ache.

"No, you didn't." she whispered, her fingers trailing over his chest.

"Don't lie to me, Ava." his tone was harsh as he gripped her chin, tipping her head back until her eyes met his. The anguish and shame she saw swirling in his eyes had tears pricking hers, and she needed to soothe that pain he harboured.

"Blake, you took my virginity." she watched his throat bob on a thick swallow, his eyes pinching in the corners. "Of course it's going to be painful." she continued, her hand splayed across his chest. "And I wouldn't change a thing." a small smile curved her lips.

"Promise?" he whispered, hand cupping her cheek. Ava nodded, swallowing around the lump in her throat. His lips pressed against her forehead, his eyes closed making her shiver. "You cold, baby girl?" he asked, jostling the bed as he gripped the covers and with one fluid pull, they were snuggled beneath the blankets as they drifted off to sleep.

Chapter Twenty-Two

The hot water cascaded over Ava's body, soothing her aching muscles and the stinging ache between her thighs. Tipping her head back, water washing over her face, she couldn't help her mind wandering back to last night.

The way Blake had made her feel so much pleasure, the way he'd caressed her body, which kept her in a constant state of arousal and the way his voice had dipped several octaves. She could spend an absolute lifetime in Blake's arms.

She thought about him giving her a safe word – *hurt* – which broke her heart. The visions of the hotel room flashing again through her mind. His declaration of wanting to inflict pain, suffering and humiliation. A shiver coursed through her body. She saw the anguish and shame in his eyes when he thought he'd hurt her. Ava felt like Blake needed a word to remind himself – to save her and that was heartbreaking.

Ava knew that wasn't all there was to him. She knew he had a compassionate side. The side that tucked her close to his body to keep her warm, the side that made her food, the side that spoke such beautiful words and the side which made her feel cherished.

Blowing out a frustrated breath, wiping the water from her eyes as the thoughts continued to whirl inside her head. Thoughts of how she could make him see what kind of man he really was. A man separate from the brutality he claimed to crave.

"Ava." Blake's deep baritone startled her as he stepped into the shower cubicle. Cold air raising goosebumps on her wet flesh.

"Jesus!" Ava gasped, her hand on her chest, trying to dampen her racing heart. "You're going to give me a heart attack." she continued.

"Hmm." he grunted, pulling her back to his front and wrapping his arms around her. "Should I be worried that I woke up alone?" he continued, resting his chin atop of her head.

That one question had her face flaming bright red, and she was thankful that he couldn't see. She'd been mortified when she'd awoken this morning. Their combined juices and blood had coated the inside of her thighs and the bedsheets had big wet stains which she knew were from her. She didn't want Blake waking up with her in that state. So.....impure.

"N-no." she whispered, licking over her lips. Blake sighed, his arms tightening around her. His body still flush with her back, his cock large and throbbing against the base of her spine. "I was a bit of mess and needed a shower." she murmured sheepishly.

"I was looking forward to waking up with you naked and dirty." the huskiness of his voice sent a shiver down her spine and goosebumps raised along her arms. "Please don't leave me alone." his voice was so low she wasn't certain if she'd heard him correctly over the rushing water of the shower.

But she felt the shift in his entire body. Felt him tense ever so slightly, his muscles hardening. She felt a suppressed shudder, and she felt the harsh expel of air like a cold blast against the top of her head.

Vulnerable.

That was the first word that came to mind and for the second time this morning, she wondered how she could get him to see how beautiful he was on the inside.

"I won't leave you." she whispered around the sudden lump in her throat. His arms tightened ever so slightly, indicating that he'd heard her. Blake dipped his head, his lips to her ear.

"I don't think I could cope if you left." the hurt was evident in every word spoken. Ava tried prying his arms from around her, tried to turn to face him, but Blake tightened his hold. "Don't, baby girl." his lips pressed beneath her ear.

"Who hurt you." she couldn't stop the words from rushing out of her mouth.

The silence was deafening as they stood unmoving under the water's spray. Her heart thumping harshly against her ribcage. She felt his harsh breaths against her flesh as he hesitated, seconds suspended between them before he cleared his throat. Her breath seized in her lungs in anticipation.

"Let's get washed." he husked out. "You're starting to prune." he continued with one last press of his lips to her temple and then he was releasing her.

Ava blinked away the tears that had gathered in her eyes as she watched Blake reach for the body wash and sponge without making eye contact. She watched in complete silence as he soaped the sponge before meticulously washing every inch of her body without any sexual touches, fleeting glances or lingering kisses and Ava had never felt as despondent in her life.

By the time Blake emerged from the bathroom, Ava had thrown on a pair of yoga pants and a long t-shirt. Her hair was wet, clinging to the back of the t-shirt as she stripped the bed. In her peripheral vision she watched him stride to the walk-in closet in nothing but a towel wrapped around his waist, making her pulse stutter at the magnificent sight of him. But he didn't look at her, didn't speak to her.

Ava had just finished smoothing the clean sheets across the bed when she stopped dead in tracks, her tongue stuck to the roof of her mouth. Blake sauntered in with dark grey sweatpants hung low on his hips and absolutely nothing else.

Fucking gorgeous!

"Eye-fucking, Ava." Blake smirked as he neared the bed, making her blush. "Hmm, gives your nickname a whole new meaning." he murmured roughly, his hand smoothed over the clean bedsheet. Ava's eyebrows pinched together. The change in him was almost enough to give her whiplash.

"Nickname?" the confusion evident in her voice. Her pulse began to throb, her stomach clenched as she continued to rake her gaze over his tawny flesh.

"Squirt." he clarified, his fingers clasped her chin and tipped her head back until their eyes met. Her skin felt like it was on fire as she blushed furiously.

"Oh god, that's dirty." she groaned, embarrassed. Blake inched closer, his sinful lips tipping up into the sexy grin that made her knees weak.

"It's sexy." Blake growled in her ear. "Damn fucking sexy that you let go that hard." his lips brushed against the shell of her ear, raising goosebumps down her arms. "I can't wait to see if you'll squirt with only my mouth on you." he admitted and Ava gulped.

"I didn't even know I could do *that*." her mouth twisted before she grabbed the discarded bedsheets, making him chuckle.

"Now I know why you need all them spare panties." he chuckled as she tried to hide her face. "Leave them in the hamper, the cleaner will take care of them."

"Cleaner?" she questioned, cocking her head to the side. "I'm not letting them see this mess." she squeaked with a death grip on the dirty sheets. Blake's eyes softened as he looked at her.

"You wanting to take care of the laundry, says a lot about you." he smiled, holding his hand out for her to take. "I'll show you where the washing machine is kept." he continued as she placed her free hand inside his.

Ava had mastered the high-tech washing machine and left the sheets to wash, whilst Blake made brunch. Sat at the dining table, she watched him move around the kitchen, at ease and she loved the way he took care of her and she loved being in his home, in his personal space. He was unguarded in his home and she absolutely adored seeing his different sides.

She hadn't really tasted the brunch Blake had made. She was lost in thought over last night and his words and again this morning, and she knew that it wasn't all to do with what he did in the hotel room. She felt like something else had happened to him, and she wondered if he'd ever open up to her.

"Would you'd like a piece of lemon drizzle cake." he chuckled at the look of confusion on her face. As he set a steaming latte in front of her. "It's home made." he quirked an eyebrow as she licked over her lips. "And I'd like to tell you about the young lady who made it for me." he watched her teeth capture her bottom lip, uncertainty shining in her eyes. "For me, please?"

"Okay, I'd like that." she nodded once.

"Here." he smiled as he placed the cake on the dining table. Opting to sit opposite her with his own coffee. "I want your honest opinion on the cake." he pinned her with a stare.

Ava smiled, taking a bite of the cake. The fluffiness filled her mouth, the zesty, sweet flavours burst in sheer perfection across her tongue.

"There it is." Blake's tone turned deeper, his eyes watching her, making her blush and chew quickly.

"Oh god, this is amazing." she admitted once she'd finished chewing. "Who made this?" she asked, taking a sip of her latte.

"Well, there's this lovely young lady." Blake's tone was light, his smile bright, and Ava was a little jealous. The envious nature of her dark thoughts tried to tumble through his words, but she focused on him. "She's my favourite patient." he took a sip of his coffee. "I met her six years ago, when I started at the practice." he took a bite of his own piece of cake.

"Oh, so you've known her a long time, then?" Ava couldn't help the envious tint to her tone, making him smirk across the table. One lone eyebrow raised at her.

"Yes, I have." he nodded, his smirk still in place. "She has some health issues, but considering that she's eighty-six, she's not doing too bad."

Ava almost choked on her piece of cake, a stray crumb tickling the back of her throat. Coughing, trying to dislodge it before taking a gulp of the latte. Her eyes wide as Blake laughed at her reaction.

"Eighty-six, did you say?" she wheezed out. Her eyes watering from coughing.

"Jealous, baby girl?" Blake asked, a chuckle in his tone. Her cheeks flamed bright red as she refused to answer. "Anyway, Maureen has been making me this cake for the last five and a half years. When I saw her yesterday, all I could think about was you trying it and being a little nervous in case you didn't like it." he took a sip of coffee, his eyes watching her over the rim of his cup.

"Well, it's amazing." Ava agreed. "Why were you nervous?" she asked, tilting her head slightly.

"It's just Maureen." he cleared his throat, his eyes softening further. "Makes me feel special when she brings me my favourite cake and that it was also her husbands favourite too." Ava watched as a delicate blush crept up his neck to settle in his cheeks and she softened even further at the sight. "It just, I don't know." he shrugged. "Fills me with joy, I guess." he cleared his throat again and Ava realised that he's not used to opening up so much, which made her smile.

"Well, thank you for sharing." she took the last sip of her latte. "What health issues does Maureen have?"

"Usual for her age." Blake nodded, gathering the empty plates and cups. "High cholesterol, arthritis, unsteady on her feet, brittle bone and yesterday." he turned his back to her as he loaded the dishwasher, making Ava frown. "Yesterday, I had to give her more medication to help with the possibility of her developing blood clots which could end up with her having a stroke." he finished, hands braced on the granite counter, head bowed.

"Awe, sweetheart." Ava cooed, making her way towards him. She noticed him tense, every muscle going rigid, before she laid her hand on his back. "Will you see her more often?" she asked, rubbing her hand gently across his back, noticing the muscles relaxing before tensing again.

"Yeah." his voice sounded hoarse. "Umm, why did you..." he broke off, shaking his head.

"Why did I what?" Ava asked, her teeth clamping on her lip as her pulse spiked. She didn't know what she'd done, but the way Blake was tensed and not moving made her feel like she'd done something wrong.

"Why did you call me *that*?" he almost hissed the word out, but his voice was too hoarse.

Ava's mind rushed through everything she had said until realisation dawned on her. *Fuck!*

"I'm sorry." She breathed out, removing her hand from him. "It's just -" her words were cut off when Blake's arm shot out, his fingers curling around her waist as he stood to his full height. Pulling her towards the warmth of his body.

"It's just, what?" he asked, voice gentle. His dark eyes blinking slowly as he looked at her.

"It's something mum always said to dad when anything bad had happened." Ava shrugged, feigning nonchalance.

"I...." she watched him swallow thickly before he crushed his lips to hers in a brutal clash of lips and tongues. Stealing her breath and making her weak in the knees. Long, harsh strokes of his tongue lashed against hers, pulling moans from her. His fingers tangling in her hair, pulling her backwards, gaining deeper access into her mouth. Deep groans vibrated through his chest before he pulled away. "Say it again." his panting breaths fanned over her lips, his eyes seeming lighter.

"Sweetheart." she breathed out, unable to look away from the wonder in his gaze.

"Perfect." he whispered back, his lips curving into a beautiful smile. "I like that, baby girl." he admitted, wrapping his arms around her, his lips pressing to her forehead. "I wish you could stay tonight." he whispered.

"Yeah." Ava whispered back, her hands lightly tracing along the band of his sweatpants. Her lips pressed against his nipple, making him suck in a sharp breath.

"Hmm. I wish I hadn't agreed to meet James." Ava looked at him through her lashes. "Pub, that's where we'll be." he smiled, lips brushing the corner of her mouth.

"Oh, so will you be coming back to ours?" she couldn't help the question nor the thoughts running through her head. "Maybe you could sneak into-" the growl from the back of his throat broke off her words. His hands fisted in her hair, pulling her head back until they were a breath apart.

"Going to give me another show in the bathroom?" his voice was a sheer husk, his eyes molten. "Next time, I want to watch you cum all over your fingers moaning my *fucking* name, baby girl." he nipped her bottom lip, tearing a gasp from her.

"Okay." she breathed out, the deepest blush taking over her face. "Only if you'll do the same for me." her words were barely audible, but the way his pupils dilated and his nostrils flared she knew he'd heard her.

"Pure fucking torture." he groaned, nipping her lip again. "I'll see you tonight." he kissed her lightly, swatting her ass, which made her yelp at the sudden contact.

"Bye, Blake." she smiled as he released her, but before she could launch herself back at him, he folded his arms over his chest.

"Bye, Ava." he grunted as she slowly backed out of the kitchen.

Chapter Twenty-Three

The local pub wasn't overly busy for a Saturday night. The usual bar hogs were dotted around, mostly widowed, aged men, some were divorced and others were single. All above fifty years old and all of them needed to take more care of themselves.

Blake liked this local for one reason, there weren't many single women that came in. The memory of having Ava pressed up against the wall. All breathy and pouting lips. He didn't know where he'd got the strength from that night not to fuck her against the wall, but he knew that next time the opportunity presented itself, that's exactly what he would do.

The thought of someone watching him fuck her to a squirting climax had his heart rate increasing and blood surging to his cock. The fun he could have with his pure and innocent Ava.

"What got you smirking?" James's voice pulled him out of his thoughts. His eyes refocusing on his best friend. "Another conquest?" he quizzed, looking over his shoulder to see only the regulars.

"No." Blake took a gulp from the pint in front of him. "What's wrong?" he asked, licking the foam from his lips.

He'd known James since they were kids. They'd been through hell and back over the years, quite a few fist fights between them too. But Blake knew that when his eyes pinched in the corners and he refused to look him in the eye, something was plaguing James. It was his only tell that something was bothering him. Blake watched James's hand go to the back of his neck, rubbing slightly before pulling on his neck.

"Look, I don't know how to say it." James began, taking a generous gulp of his pint. "Shit!" he licked the foam from his lips, eyes pinching even more. "I'm dating Katie." he rushed out, which reminded him of Ava. When she had something she needed to say, it was always blurted out. Blake knew that it was before they lost their nerve.

"And?" Blake shrugged, it didn't matter to him who Katie was dating. But judging by the astonished look on James's face, he thought otherwise.

"What do you mean, *and*?" James asked, tilting his head to the side.

"I mean, she's a grown woman who can make her own decisions." Blake smirked, his thumb grazing across his lower lip. "Besides, you should be worried about those brothers of hers. You know they're feral." he couldn't help the dark chuckle that escaped as James's throat bobbed on a hard swallow.

"Hmm." James twisted the glass for a moment. "You really aren't bothered?" he asked, eyebrows hitting his hairline. Blake shook his head no. "Shit! I thought you would have been. I mean, I know how I would feel if it was you and Ava." James admitted, taking a gulp of his drink. Blake schooled his features, ensuring the mask of indifference was firmly in place.

"You know she's not my type." Blake lied, placing his hand on his thigh as he tried to control the tremor that had started. "The blondes are much more my-"

"Bullshit!" James cut him off, making him raise one eyebrow. "Don't give me that look, we both know that Candi-"

"Don't say her fucking name." Blake snarled, the hand on his thigh shaking. His other had a death grip around the glass to stop the shake from being noticed.

"Then don't lie, fucker." James laughed, taking another gulp of his drink.

Blake's pulse was pounding in his throat, the collar of his polo shirt felt like it was choking him. He concentrated on not spilling his drink as he raised it to his lips, gulping half of the drink in one as he willed himself to calm the fuck down. For long moments they just sat in silence, as he tried to get his head into a safe place, tried to stop the onset of a panic attack and tried to stop the guilt from wracking his body. He couldn't let anyone see him like that.

Ava saw you like that.

Ava soothed the pain that was ravaging your body.

He didn't need this, couldn't deal with this. Not tonight. Not any night. Taking a deep breath, he stared at James, who was moving his lips, but he hadn't heard a word he'd said. He was getting too lost in his head.

".....and you know it's just that hero worship." James took a sip of his drink as Blake blinked a few times, trying to understand what he was saying, to no avail. "It's hard to explain, but fuck if it isn't terrifying." he chuckled, a slightly pained look on his face. Blake continued to blink slowly, his brain failing to understand the conversation that he hadn't been listening to. "It's bad enough I already punched that kid for touching her and I'm glad he's stayed away." James continued, and Blake decided he was talking about Katie.

"Well, fuckers should know not to touch what's yours." Blake laughed, finishing his drink. But the look on James's face had him pausing. "Wait, you're talking about Katie?"

"Ava." James shook his head. "Want another?" he tipped his empty glass in Blake's direction.

"Yeah." he nodded, his eyebrows furrowing and a slow build of anger began to surge within him as he repeated James's words in his head. Before he could think better of it, his phone was out.

Blake – *Who the fuck touched you?*

Ava – *You?*

Growling low in his throat, his scowl deepening and his fingers flying across the screen.

Blake – *Do you want a spanking? Who touched you, I won't ask again!*

Ava – *Hmm, what would that be like?*

His perfect fucking girl!

Blood rushed directly to his cock at her words.

"Fucking hell." he hissed out as his cock brushed against the zip painfully.

Blake – *I'll show you if you don't tell me who touched you.*

Ava – *Okay :-)*

"What the fuck, baby girl." he muttered to himself, his anger being replaced by full on desire of spanking those perfect round globes. He could just picture the way they'd wobble and bloom a full, deep red.

He didn't want to think about how quickly she could calm the storm within him.

Blake – *Answer the question Ava!*

Ava – *I don't know what you're talking about. You know you're the only man to touch me. What the hell are you and James talking about?*

Blake – *You! Fuck, you make me so hard, you're getting a fucking spanking, baby girl.*

He stuffed his phone back into his jacket pocket the moment James placed two fresh pints on the table. Blake felt it vibrate in his pocket, but refused to look at it. A smile already on his lips at the little minx wanting to be spanked.

Fuck!

"I'm worried about Ava." James sighed, slumping into his chair. Blake quirked an eyebrow. "She's seeing someone." he took a sip of his drink, emotions flickering across his face.

"And you don't like the guy?" Blake asked, already knowing the answer.

"I don't even know who it is." James hissed out. "She won't tell me anything." he took another sip of his drink. Blake had to keep himself in check during this conversation, he didn't want James finding out this way about his relationship with Ava.

Fuck, he didn't even know himself what the relationship was.

"Ava's always been a good girl." he tried hard not to smirk at his own words. "I'm sure she's picked someone who's right for her." he continued, taking a generous gulp of his own drink.

"Hmm. I don't know." James's hand scrubbed down his face. "She likes you, after all." Blake froze at his words, making James chuckle. "Oh come on, we both know about the hero worship." he continued, but all that was buzzing around in his head was that James knew Ava liked him.

Has she already said something to James?

Fucking hell, Ava, what have you done?

"I don't think so." Blake muttered around the rim of his glass. It was getting harder to keep the mask of indifference in place.

"Yeah, well, let's keep it like that." James warned with a pointed look. "I think the guy she's seeing is married."

Blake's pulse stuttered, his lungs seized, and the slither of liquid lodged in his throat. Smacking his chest to dislodge the liquid as he coughed, his eyes watering slightly.

"Married?" Blake wheezed out.

"Yeah." James looked at him with his eyes narrowed slightly. "I don't like it."

"Yeah, brothers never do." Blake pointed out, taking a sip of his drink and hoping he didn't choke on it again. He didn't like the way James was looking at him.

"It's not that, he hurt her." James's voice was low and pained. Blake couldn't stop his stomach from twisting and was petrified of what was going to come next. "She was an absolute mess, and then he disappeared for a few weeks." James shook his head, another sip of his drink. "She stopped fucking eating, and all she did was cry herself to sleep. Every-fucking-night."

Blake's heart cracked at the words, the pain blooming in his chest. He knew that James was telling him what she'd been like when he wasn't man enough to accept her. When he wasn't man enough to control his demons.

"Hmm." Blake grunted, turning his eyes to his drink. Unable to stand the look on James' face.

"But then, he just contacted her out of the blue and you know what?" James asked, his voice rising slightly. "She just left, went running straight back to him like nothing had happened." he shook his head. "I'm worried, whoever it is will break her." he admitted, tipping more of his drink down his throat.

"Well, it's something she's going to have to live through. We've all done it." Blake stated. "And if he is married, you know he'll be treating her right." James's eyebrows hit his hairline. "You know all married men, keep their queens and kids tucked away from prying eyes and keep their princesses closer, treating her like she deserves." Blake shrugged as he took a gulp of his drink, his heart pounding in his chest.

"Yeah, but the fuckers never leave their wives though, do they, Blake?" the accusation in James's tone wasn't lost on him.

"No, they never leave the Queen." Blake agreed with a curt nod.

"Hmm. You going home or staying at mine?" James asked, effectively ending the conversation about Ava.

"Yours." Blake answered, both of them finishing their drinks.

Chapter Twenty-Four

In the darkened room, devoid of any light. The moon was hidden behind thick clouds Ava's pulse spiked, fluttering her eyes open, her mind heavy with sleep, an imposing dark figure stood beside her. His hand clamped over her mouth. Terror seized her, every muscle stilling as her eyes widened until the intoxicating scent mixed with alcohol filtered through her senses. Her nipples hardened and her stomach fluttered.

"You promised me a show, baby girl." Blake husked out, his lips against her ear. "And I'm here to collect." he nipped her ear, she gasped against his hand.

In one quick move he ripped her bedsheets back; the groan that left him was low, deep and almost animalistic. She'd hoped that he'd sneak into her room, which made her decide against wearing anything to bed, with the exception of the necklace he bought her.

She watched in rapt fascination his muscles bulge and flex as he flicked the button open on his jeans, the sound of the zip being pulled down filled the room before they dropped in a pool at his feet. His underwear following until she saw the large, thick cock jutting out, making her lick her lips. She wanted to taste him, wanted to run her tongue along the length. She wanted to do a lot of things with him and, as she reached out a hand, he grabbed her wrist.

"This is my show, not yours." his low warning was clear and Ava knew he didn't want her to touch him.

"W-will you tell me what to do?" she whispered quietly. His

groan set her nerve endings on fire as he stretched out at the bottom of her bed. His thighs spread slightly with his hands resting on top.

"No, I want to watch how you pleasure yourself." his husked out quietly. "I want to watch what makes you tick, what makes you squirm, and what makes you moan my fucking name." he continued, his hand wrapping around his cock.

Ava's stomach clenched and a flood of heat dripped from her pussy at his words, but she was nervous. Nervous at touching herself with him, watching. But she wanted to watch him too. Wanted to see how he made himself cum and she wanted to watch it explode.

Taking a deep, un-calming breath, raising in her wake. The pad of her finger circling her pulse, feeling it throb hard against her before she continued down to her collarbone. His breathing deepened in the quietness of the room. Her eyes watching him slowly move up his long length, a delicate moan escaped her.

Her fingers caressed the tops of her breasts, her nipples ached with anticipation. She arched her back, cupping the heavy flesh. Another moan escaped as she pinched her nipples. Her eyes watching Blake slowly move up and down his cock. She could see the liquid gathering at the tip and she wanted it in her mouth. Another pinch, harder, had her arching again, a longer moan.

"Spread your legs." Blake husked out. "Show me how wet you are." he continued, squeezing his cock. The deep groan vibrating from the back of his throat.

Ava slowly parted her legs, her feet flat on the mattress. He groaned again as she bared herself to him. Her juices were running down into the crack of her ass cheeks. Her face flamed, knowing he could see. She slowly run her fingers through the slick folds, moaning quietly as she circled around her clit. Bucking her hips as she applied more pressure before easing off and rubbing the length of her pussy. Blake's hand was moving a little faster, more liquid gathered at his tip. His chest heaved with heavy breaths and Ava couldn't take her eyes off of him as she eased a finger inside. A gasp escaped her and a deep moan left him as she pumped the finger inside of her.

"More." Blake panted, his hand squeezing around his shaft. Ava eased another inside, moaning at the pleasure of her pussy fluttering around her fingers. "Stretch yourself for me." he continued. Ava slowly pumped those two fingers inside, the room filling with wet noises and her hips bucking. "More, get yourself ready for my cock." his voice was harsh pants as she eased another finger inside, filling her, stretching her.

More juices leaked across her palm and her thrusts got faster, harder. The heel of her hand bumping against her clit. Her moans were continuous, her back arching, hips bucking. A burning deep within her was rising fast into an inferno. She tried keeping her eyes on Blake as her orgasm was building with intense quickness, but she couldn't stop her eyes from rolling into the back of her head as shivers broke out across her body, her thighs were trembling.

Her wrist was seized in a harsh grip, her fingers left her quivering pussy, and Blake loomed above her. His throbbing cock slicking up and down her folds, the head bumping her clit. His devilish smile made her moan.

"You." he whispered, his lips brushing lightly against hers. "Never moaned my name." he continued rocking his hips.

"B-b..." Ava stuttered around a moan as his cock bumped her throbbing clit. Still slicking through her folds without penetrating her.

"But nothing." his teeth nipped her lip. "You deserve to be

punished." he smirked at her gasp. His hips thrusting faster. "That's what naughty girls get." he continued.

"What kind of punish-" her words broke off on a moan as she thrust her hips to meet his.

"Naughty fucking girls." he hissed out, his hips pumping against her. "Don't get to cum." he breathed out around a long, hard groan as his cock throbbed out his release against her folds. The hot liquid seared into her skin in splashes. His quiet groans filled the space between them. "If you touch yourself, naughty girl, I'll know." he breathed out against her lips.

Ava felt the coldness seep into her naked body as Blake stood. Her heart beating rapidly and her chest heaving, she watched as he redressed. Watched the smirk tip up his lips as he refastened his pants. The heavy, pulsing feeling was racking her body as the orgasm she so desperately wanted was out of reach. She knew how she would feel in the morning and yet as she thought about defying his orders not to touch herself, she wondered if he would really know. The dark chuckle had a shudder waving across her muscles.

"That look tells me everything." he continued to chuckle as Ava's cheeks flushed. "If you touch yourself, naughty girl you will be severely punished." he warned.

All Ava could think was how severe as he slipped out of her bedroom.

The dull light of the morning filtered through the curtains, her body ached from the denial of her climax but her pulse spiked at the thought of Blake being in her home and that thought was enough to have her leaping from the bed, quickly dressing in a pair of pyjamas. Pulling her door open, she peeked out, listening for any sounds, but all she could hear was James snoring. Blowing out a breath, her bare feet padded against the hardwood floor as she avoided the creaking boards.

Stood with her back to the door as she waited for her coffee to be ready, warm muscular arms banded around her. His well-defined chest pressing against her back. The scrape of his stubble against her cheek as his lips brushed against her, tracking up her jaw until his teeth nipped her earlobe.

"Has my naughty girl learnt her lesson?" he husked out into her ear. A shiver slithered down her spine, raising goosebumps.

"Hmm." she hummed, moving her head to the side. His lips instantly pressing against her neck, his tongue licking against her slowly. "Blake." she moaned, arching her back.

"Good girl." he breathed out. "Come to my house." he asked, his tongue flicking against her earlobe before his teeth nipped her.

"I-I've got work tomorrow." Ava stuttered out as she ground her ass against his thick shaft bulging in the confines of his jeans. "But I can come for a little while." she moaned as his lips trailed down her neck.

"Hmm, I'll see you soon baby girl." he pressed another kiss against her neck before he stood to his full height.

"Soon." she nodded, a smile playing on her lips as she watched him leave.

Ava was sat nursing her coffee, still in the pyjamas and still had not had a shower. She hadn't heard much from Katie over the last few weeks, since Blake went hiding and she missed her friend. A small smile tugged at her lips as she thought about her. She knew that they were both in the same place at the moment, making new relationships with the hope that they would last. James had been happier lately too, which was because of her friend, and she could tell which days they'd been together due to his mood. Which made her happy.

She hadn't seen Nathan either, since James punched him and

if she were being honest, she missed him. He was her friend too, but then she thought about him trying it on with her and that didn't sit well with her. She didn't like him like that, never had. Which made her wonder when he started to feel like that. Sighing as she took a sip of her lukewarm coffee, thinking back to when she'd messaged him apologising for James's behaviour, but she hadn't heard anything back from him. She wasn't certain if he'd also cut Katie out, too.

Shaking her head, she threw the last of the coffee in the sink. Thinking of Nathan and Blake's messages last night, she knew that Blake now knew what had happened. She also knew that it was part of the reason why Blake punished her last night. She was just caught off guard when he messaged and didn't realise that James spoke about her. But it also made her wonder just how much her brother divulged to his friend. Did he tell him everything, like when she fell apart for the two weeks that Blake had cut all contact. It was made worse because of her relationship with Blake. Mainly because she didn't want Blake to know just how much he hurt her, knowing that it would only hurt him more and that was something that she didn't want.

She only wanted to love him.

Chapter Twenty-Five

Ava hadn't been at Blake's long before she was relaxed on the plush sofa, glass of wine in hand, listening to the soft music he'd already had playing when she arrived. She felt strange lounging in his living room whilst he wasn't here. Felt strange to make herself at home. But it was something she would like to experience more often. Taking a sip of the wine, which she nearly spilt when Blake sauntered in with a large black box emblazoned with *Bordelle* in gold font across the top.

"For you." his teeth scraped across his bottom lip as she took the box from him.

"You didn't have to." Ava smiled as she carefully opened the box.

Blake sat opposite her on the plush chair, his thighs slightly parted and reclined back. His dark eyes watched as she removed the black tissue paper. Her eyebrows furrowing slightly at what lay beneath it. Red leather straps all connected by gold circles. She tilted her head slightly, holding the piece up before her. Blake's thumb moved across his bottom lip, a wicked glint in his eyes.

"What is it?" Ava asked as she kept looking but couldn't understand what it was.

"Body harness." he husked out, Ava's eyebrows raised. "There's the wrist and ankle straps in there, too."

"Oh." Ava's pulse spiked as she looked at him. The wickedness etched onto his face, his pupils dilated and his breathing a little deeper.

She picked the wrist and ankle straps, which matched. But beneath was a beautiful white lace half cup bra and matching thong. They were beautiful.

"I like you in white and red." he admitted, his eyes tracking her movements. "Would you wear them for me next Friday?" he asked on a deep breath. "Beneath that white dress and those red fuck-me heels." his palms rubbed against his thighs briefly.

"What's happening next Friday?" she whispered, her cheeks heating as she watched his cock rise beneath the sweatpants.

"Our date, baby girl." he breathed out. "I'd like to take you on a date." she watched his throat bob on a hard swallow. "Come here."

Ava put the box aside, her heart racing and her stomach fluttering she walked towards him. Blake's grin turned wicked as he pulled her closer, his hands gripping her ass cheeks. Ava straddled his hips, pressing a chaste kiss to his lips.

"You liked the red heels, huh?" Ava's tone was teasing as she moved until her lips were against his ear. "I'll wear only them for you, *Syn*." she husked out, making him groan as he playfully swatted her ass. "Is this the spanking you promised." she asked, cheeks tinting pink. She felt his cock throb against her.

"Does my naughty girl want a spanking?" he asked on a hard swallow, his fingers flexing against her ass cheeks.

"Hmm, I want to know what it's like." Ava whispered, her teeth sinking into her lip as he groaned low in the back of his throat. His eyes looked pure black as he stared at her.

"Get this fine ass upstairs." he husked out, his fingers gripping her ass cheeks. "Strip naked and wait, like the naughty girl you are." he continued, his voice laced with liquid heat that travelled directly to her pussy and with a final slap on her ass.

Ava's pulse quickened, her breath became laboured as Blake slide her off of his lap. Her eyes widened at the significant bulge of his sweatpants, making her lick her lips before she turned on her heel.

She could feel the weight of his heated gaze on her ass as she walked through the living room, which only made her heart beat twice as fast. The moment she was in the hallway, Ava couldn't contain her excitement any longer and raced up the stairs two at a time.

The anticipation bubbling inside of her was palpable as she stood naked in his bedroom. She wasn't certain what to expect nor did she expect the rush of heat through her veins when he'd called her a naughty girl, but the voice he'd used, full of desire and pure fire, sent the tremor directly through her.

Goosebumps raised against her naked flesh, her hair whispering against her spine, her nipples already into hard peaks and her juices gathering between her thighs. Her heart pounded in her chest as she heard his footsteps outside the bedroom door. Squeezing her eyes shut as she sucked in a breath, the door opened slowly and the imposing presence behind her had her pussy throbbing with need as she opened her eyes on a long exhale.

Ava watched as Blake walked across the bedroom with purposeful strides, his impressive erection perfectly outlined in the sweatpants and his naked torso. All tawny skin, rippling muscles that were clenching and releasing with every step he took. Ava licked over her lips as she stared in rapt fascination of him settling in the middle of the bed, back against the headboard and his legs stretched out before him. He looked perfectly relaxed until those blazing black depths locked onto her green ones.

"Come here." he commanded with a wicked curve of his mouth, causing another wave of wetness to coat her thighs. On shaking legs, Ava joined him on the bed, but before she could settle beside him, Blake's hand gripped her upper arm. "Head towards my feet, ass in the air." the fire in his voice sent another wave of pleasure through her as she complied with his command.

Ava's breath quickened as she placed her knees on either side of Blake's hips, her forearms against the bed, and her breasts on his shins. She knew that he had a direct view between her legs, knew that he'd see the arousal coating her and she felt embarrassed until she heard the deep moan from the back of his throat.

His hand pressing against her back was a silent command to stay where she was. His other caressed the fleshy globe of her ass. Soothing, feather light, whispering touch across her flesh. A shiver ran down her spine.

Ava's breath whooshed from her lungs as the stinging slap against her ass cheek bloomed across her flesh, heat instantly rushing to the surface. She heard his breathing change, heard it become deeper as his hand caressed the sting away. Her head snapped back on a shocked gasp the moment his hand landed another stinging slap directly over the previous one.

"Fuck!" she hissed out between her clenched teeth as a series of stinging slaps bounced off of her flesh. The searing heat across her ass cheek centred her concentration. Another stinging slap landed directly in the centre of her ass cheeks. The vibration from the impact of his hand sent liquid rushing from her pussy and a deep moan fell from her parted lips.

"Does my naughty girl like being spanked?" he husked out, smoothing his hands across the tender flesh.

"Y-yes." she stuttered, his fingers gripping her hips in a brutal hold. "Jesus." she breathed as he blew a stream of cool air across her throbbing cheek.

"Hmm." he pulled Ava closer until her feet hit the headboard. "Such a naughty fucking girl." he chuckled as a tremor shuddered through her body. "Let's see if you taste just as naughty." his voice rough.

The moment his tongue flicked against her clit, Ava bucked on a low moan. Blake's grip tightened on her hips. His tongue licking a line directly to her opening, swirling his tongue once. Ava moaned, her fingers tangling in the bedsheets. Parting her folds with his tongue, he zig-zagged up her centre in slow, deliberate movements. His groan vibrated through her core.

Her hips undulated, his tongue circling her throbbing, engorged clit relentlessly, pulling moans of decadent pleasure from her. The tight ball was building with every flick of his tongue against her clit, juices gathering at her opening. Her thighs began to shake, her breathing was hard pants.

Blake's hand landed against her ass cheek in a stinging slap, pulling a shriek of pain from Ava. His tongue slithered down her centre, swirling around her opening and further still. Circling once around her tight, puckered asshole, Ava froze at the strange sensation.

"One day." Blake's husky voice commanded her attention. "I will eat that delectable ass of yours." he continued with a dark chuckle. "Like the naughty fucking girl that you are." Ava quivered at his words.

"Blake." Ava moaned loudly as his tongue thrust into her pussy. "Oh!" she ground her hips against his tongue. "Fuck!" she hissed, his teeth nipping her tender pussy.

Blake grazed his teeth down the length of her pussy, slowly. His fingers digging into her hips as he held her in place. Swirling his tongue around her clit before sucking it into his mouth, hard. A deep pressure building inside of her had her moaning louder.

Blake sucked her clit, his teeth grazing gently over the throbbing bundle. Juices gathering at her opening a mere moment before his tongue swept them into his mouth over and over. The ball of pure fire and heat was building faster, bigger, and it stole her breath.

Her hips moving of their own accord, her mouth open with moan after lustrous moan, her head snapped back, her fingers numb from the death grip on the sheets beneath her. Deep inside her, the liquid fire and heat swelled tightly, the ball expanded, and she exploded on a loud scream.

Blake's hips bucked against Ava's torso as her orgasm splashed against his chin and chest. The long groan of pure satisfaction poured from him as he lapped up the copious amounts of liquid. Ava rode her orgasm until she collapsed against his legs. Tremors twitching through her muscles. Her breath ragged.

Blake wound his arm around her torso and pulled until she was on her knees, straddling his hips. Her back to his chest. His lips run the length of her neck, pulling a moan from her. His other hand freeing his throbbing cock, rubbing the tip against her entrance. Ava rocked her hips gently against the tip, shuddering when it grazed her oversensitive clit, causing more liquid to seep from her core.

His arm tightened around her waist, halting her movements. His cock slowly easing into her tight opening. His jaw clenched and the low guttural moan filled the room. Inch by glorious inch, Ava was filled with Blake's cock until her ass touched his groin. She felt stretched and full to capacity, but that didn't stop her greedy pussy from pulsating. Blake's hands splayed across her stomach, slowly inching their way up until they captured her breasts.

"Ride me." He bit out, hands squeezing her breasts once. "Naughty girl." His fingers pinched her nipples hard, making her yelp and her hips grind down on him.

Ava raised up on her knees, the thick column of his cock dragging exquisitely against her inner walls. A light moan fell from her parted lips. Her heart thundering against her chest, her nerve endings firing off more pleasure through her body as she slowly sank back down.

His tongue trailed the length of her neck, his fingers circled her nipples as she rose slowly. Her pussy fluttered, his cock throbbed, and his teeth clamped down on her shoulder. The tight grip on his cock was like a vise as she sunk back down hard.

"Fuck!" Blake hissed, his hands gripping her hips. "Harder." he bit out, raising her back up and slamming his hips up to meet her descent. Their hips clashing harder, deeper and she cried out in ecstasy. "Harder!" he ground out, slamming his cock deep inside of her. Her pussy contracted, juices leaked from her as she ground down before raising back up. Blake slammed her back down, over and over.

The room was filled with combined moans and groans of pleasure, the sounds of their bodies meeting in wet slaps. Her body was careening towards another explosion. White hot waves overtook her body, her muscles clenched tightly, her head thrown forward and his teeth bit down on her neck as the dam broke and her orgasm crested in an arc of pure pleasure.

"Blake!" she screamed as her pussy gripped onto his cock tightly. Liquid rushed from her in hot splashes against his groin.

"Naughty. Fucking. Girl!" Blake bit out and punctuated each word with a slam of his hips and buried himself as deep as he could, spilling hot jets of cum inside her. The grip on her hips would leave a bruise as he stilled her movements and their harsh breaths filling the room.

Blake scooted down the bed, his arms banded around Ava's trembling body until they were laid on their sides. His lips peppering kisses down her neck, his tongue soothing the bite marks on her shoulders.

Chapter Twenty-Six

Blake squeezed his eyes shut against the marks that would defiantly bruise, tightening his arms around her as his heart thundered painfully against his ribcage, almost stealing his breath.

His thoughts tormenting him.

What have I done?

How did I lose control that much?

Fuck!

"W-"
"I'm-"

They both tried to speak at the same time, successfully cutting each other off. Blake sucked in a sharp, hard breath as Ava exhaled a long, drawn out breath.

"Wow!" she breathed into the quietness of the room. He furrowed his eyebrows as his chest constricted. "That was....Just....Wow!" she continued.

Blake gently moved onto his back, taking Ava with him. But he wasn't prepared to see her wide smile and bright eyes. He was speechless. There was no animosity, no hurtful look, no tears gathered in her eyes. Nothing but happiness.

He didn't understand. Didn't understand why she was so willing, didn't understand why she accepted everything he did to her. But one thing he did understand was his need to apologise to her. Apologise for bruising and marking her when he'd become a little too rough with her.

"I'm sorry." his voice was soft as he caressed her arm, whilst the other held her against his body. "Sorry, for nearly losing control baby girl." he continued, the anguish in his voice made it quiver.

"Blake, don't apologise." she raised up until she was looking directly into his eyes. "I want to do *that* again." she confessed, blushing profusely. His eyebrows shot up in shock at her admission.

But he knew better. Knew that he couldn't let it happen like that again. Knew that the next time he slipped, she would leave him.

"I'll do better next time." he promised, pulling her closer. His lips gently pressing against her forehead. "I promise." he whispered against her skin.

He just wasn't certain if it was a promise he could keep.

Every time he looked at her naked and wet for him, a deep-seated desire swept through him. A desire to hurt and claim her. A desire to give her pleasure through pain. Something he was battling with controlling every time they were together.

This is one of the things he was frightened of. This was one of his demons that he was trying to fight and this was one of his reasons to only pick the blondes from the SadistKink app. That was something nobody knew though until he'd shown Ava a little, told her what he craved when he was in that hotel room.

He knew he hurt them for his own pleasure, knew they received pleasure through the pain he inflicted on them, but he also knew that to be with Ava, it was something he'd need to leave behind.

He didn't want to inflict pain on her like that. Didn't want to see her tears from what he'd done to her. But that pulsating need deep within him every time he looked at her was clawing and begging to be let loose.

But he knew that he needed to do better, knew that he needed to fight the urge before she left him. And she would the moment he unleashed himself on her, she would be terrified.

He could feel his heart pounding against his chest at his thoughts and knew the moment Ava moved her head, those green eyes looking at him through those long lashes of hers, that she heard the thunderous rhythm. He needed to clear his head. Needed to focus on something else. Something other than the sadistic demon who wanted to chain her, whip her, and fucking claim her.

"Blake?" her voice was that perfect balance of breathlessness that made lust thump in his gut.

"Take a shower with me." he whispered, rising from the bed. His tight muscles uncoiled as he stood to his full height. Stretching his hand out for Ava before they padded across the expanse of his bedroom.

The room filled with billowing steam as he gently tugged her until she was under the spray of warm water. His fingers clasped her chin, tipping her head back, watching the water slither down the dark waves. Mesmerised as each droplet coated before dripping onto the shower floor. Blake ran his fingers through her hair, the soft wet strands clinging to him as if begging to be wrapped around his fist and pulled. The vision of him doing just that with her bent over, his cock buried deep within her. Pulsing wet kisses down the length of his cock. His grip tightening the more he snapped his hips into her.

"Sweetheart." Ava's voice penetrated his thoughts. He blinked down at her, his cock already half hard. "You're shivering." her hands softly touching his chest, the shudder rolling through him.

He wrapped her hair around his hand, gripping the strands and pulling slightly. The deep growl that vibrated through him was almost feral as he crashed his lips to hers. Demanding and hard. Her nails scratching down his abdomen sent a fresh wave of lust through him, groaning into her mouth. Pulling slightly harder on her hair, making her gasp into his mouth. His tongue sweeping in, taking what he wanted from her.

Moans spilling into him as he swallowed every last one. Their chest heaved with heavy breaths. His cock rock hard and pulsing against her stomach. Her delicate hands gliding down his body as he gave in to the shudders she tore from his muscles. Lips moving harshly against each other, his deep groan pouring out as she wrapped her hand around his cock. His hips snapping forward at the contact.

Ripping his mouth from hers, he stared at her. Her cheeks flushed, her lips swollen, and her hard nipples scraping against him. Their harsh breaths mingling, warm water pulsing over their bodies.

"I want you again." he admitted with a harsh breath. "I want your mouth on me." he blinked slowly as she lowered herself onto her knees. His heart rate quickened at the delectable sight. His hand still fisted in her hair, but he reminded himself that he needed to be gentle.

His eyes fluttered as her tongue darted out, flicking against his tip. He heard her low moan as she tasted him, licking over her lips. Slowly she inched closer, her breathing heavy and lips parted. It was mesmerising as he watched her slowly suck the tip of his cock through her swollen lips. The groan that left him as her tongue grazed the head of his cock echoed in the bathroom.

The wet heat enveloping his cock inch by inch was torturous and exquisite. Her lips tight around the shaft and her tongue sliding against the soft skin, a light scrape of her teeth had a surge of pleasure clenching his muscles. His cock swelling and clear liquid spilling from him onto her tongue.

He couldn't control the moans that left his mouth as he watched her take more of him inside her perfect mouth. His hand still fisted in her hair, his muscles tense from the effort of holding himself back. He wanted nothing more than to thrust into her, use her hair as leverage, but he had to hold back.

Had to be gentle with her.

The pleasure that coursed through him, tingling up his spine as he felt the vibrations of her moan against him. His cock throbbed as more liquid seeped onto her tongue. He couldn't look away from her, couldn't close his eyes as she sunk deeper onto him. The moment he reached the back of her throat and heard her breath hitch, his balls started to draw up inside his body. The tingling in his spine was full shivers as goosebumps erupted across his skin. His muscles locked in place and then her hand wrapped around the rest of his shaft, squeezing.

"Fuck!" he hissed out, the pleasure almost unbearable as he fought the urge to spill into her mouth. "More." he husked out through clenched teeth.

She placed her other hand against his thigh, slowly caressing up towards his hip. Her mouth moving slowly back up, her tongue zig-zagging, making him swell further. Her palm squeezing his shaft as her nails scraped down his thigh, giving him the perfect amount of pain as she quickly plunged down and he couldn't hold back.

A roar of exquisite pleasure ripped from his parted lips as his cock pulsed, spilling his cum into her mouth. The feel of her throat contracting heightened his pleasure. But the knowledge that she was swallowing everything that he gave her had his knees almost buckling.

Her greedy little mouth continued to suck his deflating cock before he pulled her off with a gentle tug of her hair. Every hair stood on end as he watched her tongue swipe across her lips, her eyes heavy lidded.

"Was that..." she trailed off as he let go of her hair, gripping her upper arms and pulling her back to her feet.

"Fucking perfect." he whispered, cupping her cheeks and pressing his lips to hers for a gentle brush of lips. "You took me so well, baby girl. The memory will drive me insane." he admitted, making her blush.

Once they had finished showering and still wrapped in the fluffy towels, they were laid on his bed. Her back to his front, his hand splayed across her stomach and a small smile tugging his lips. The silence was content, their combined body heat was comfortable and the way her fingertips lightly grazed the back of his hand made him feel relaxed.

He knew he was in trouble with Ava and knew he wouldn't do a damn thing about it.

Chapter Twenty-Seven

The large glass fronted restaurant seemed different from the last time she was here. Mainly because the main floor was full of patrons. Some couples enjoying a romantic meal and some groups enjoying a meal before a night out. The staff were a hive of activity, dressed in all black, gathering drinks from the bar and loading trays before weaving through tables under the muted lighting. Blake laced his fingers with hers as he guided her through the glass door.

"Good Evening, Doctor Synclair." The maître d' smiled brightly as he shook his hand.

"Francesco." Blake acknowledged with a curt nod.

"Please, come." Francesco turned and lead them through the restaurant.

Ava's eyes widened as they approached a wrought iron double staircase that was covered with deep green vines, curving around the twisted wrought iron balustrades. The loud chatter of the guests quickly becoming lower as they climbed the stairs. The dim lull of music filtered through the silence as they reached the top of the stairs, leading to a balcony that overlooked the restaurant.

"Oh, it's lovely." Ava breathed as she looked around. Francesco slowly backing away and retreating downstairs.

All little tables were generously spaced, each holding a lit candle housed in a glass dome. There was nobody else on the balcony, which made her smile. She'd waited all week to see

Blake, and she wanted to be truly alone with him. The deep green vines continued along the length of the balcony, curved around the wrought iron.

"I'm glad you like it." Blake smiled as he pulled her chair out. His lips brushing her temple as he helped ease her chair beneath the table. Which was already laid out with a bottle of white wine resting in an ice bucket.

"I do." She smiled as Blake sat opposite her. "I didn't know it had a balcony." she admitted, Blake's eyes twinkled in the dim light as he poured wine into their glasses.

"It's only ever reserved for the Synclair family." his lips twitched as she gaped at him. "Well, unless we shut the restaurant down for the evening." he continued, unable to stop the slow smile that graced his lips.

"I still can't believe you did that." Ava laughed with a shake of her head.

"Hmm, well, it was worth it." she watched his eyes dim slightly and his forehead crease. "It's a shame you didn't enjoy the night, like I'd hoped." he took a sip of the wine. "But let's focus on tonight."

"I agree." Ava smiled, raising her glass for a quick clink before she took a sip. The fruitiness burst across her tongue as the slight burn of the alcohol slithered down her throat in a delicious mix, had her taking another sip. "This is lovely." she admitted with another sip.

"It's from our vineyard." Blake cleared his throat as Ava's wide eyes stared at him. "It's in Mendoza, Argentina. I'll take you there." he continued like it wasn't a big deal.

"I'm confused." Ava's eyebrows furrowed. "I thought your family owned a hotel and this restaurant only?" he chuckled at her question.

"We do." he nodded, taking a sip of the wine. "We have hotels and restaurants in eighteen countries around the world and a vineyard which supply's the hotels and restaurants with all different wines." he clarified.

"And you're a doctor." she said slowly.

"I am and when my father retires, I will take over running Synclair Holdings, which is the main company that runs each hotel and restaurants." he admitted, a tint of pink washing over his cheeks. "I don't normally tell anyone, but you're different, Ava." his smile was unguarded and his words sprung more hope deep within her that maybe she was more to him than someone to warm his bed. Maybe he felt something similar to how she felt about him. "Pass me your hand."

Ava held her hand out, Blake's fingers brushed lightly against hers before he flipped it palm up. His lips lightly brushing her wrist, pulling a gasp from her. His tongue darting out, flicking against her pulse just once.

"Close your eyes, baby girl." he whispered, his dark eyes shining in the glow of candlelight. The moment her eyes were closed, a cold leather box was placed against her palm. "Open your eyes." he whispered.

Her eyes opened to the gold font *Chisholm Hunter,* emblazoned atop of the red leather. Her eyes flicked to Blake, who was watching her intently. Tears pricked her eyes as she opened the red leather box that had nestled in the black velvet a white gold diamond tennis bracelet.

"Blake, it's beautiful." she gasped, her fingers lightly tracing over the diamonds. "You shouldn't have." she continued, looking at Blake.

"I wanted our first date to be memorable." he admitted, taking the bracelet and securing it around her wrist.

"All I need is to be with you." she whispered, her cheeks flushing. "And it's always memorable." she watched his eyes soften at her words.

Ava watched Blake stand abruptly and in two strides he was cupping her cheeks, his thumb ghosting over her bottom lip. His eyes boring into hers as his pupils dilated before his lips gently brushed against hers. His tongue licking across her bottom lip. Her eyes fluttered closed, her heart stuttered once, twice before it began a tortious beat until it was all she could hear.

Her hands touched his chest in a featherlight touch. Trailing her fingertips to his abdomen, his muscles dancing under her fingers, and a small, quiet moan escaped her. His hand curled around the nape of her neck, tangling in her hair. His other trailed a blaze of heat down her side, his fingers curling around her hip.

Ava tentatively curled her tongue against his lip, the tip breaching his mouth. His fingers curled around her nape tighter as he angled her head slightly, and then his lips moved against hers. His fingers dug into her hip harder as he urged her to her feet without removing their lips.

The heat of his body so close to hers, his hand blazing at her nape, and the quiet groan of satisfaction from him consumed her. Arching her back, her hardened nipples that were poking against her white dress, scraped against his solid chest encased in the light blue dress shirt, sending a little tremor through her body, drawing a moan from the back of her throat. Her tongue tentatively touched his before she swirled it around the tip of his tongue. Blake shuddered against her, his deep groan vibrated through his chest.

"Innocent and pure." he breathed out against her mouth, a smile tugging his lips. His eyes heavy with desire. "And all mine." he whispered, making her shiver. His lips ghosted over her jaw, slowly, tantalisingly until they brushed against her ear. A low moan escaped her lips as shivers skittered over her body. "Are you wearing my gifts?" he whispered a second before his teeth nipped her earlobe, making her gasp. A rush of wetness escaped her core and the wild pulse between her thighs was beating stronger.

"Yes." she whispered, sucking in a deep breath. "The harness is in my handbag, though." she continued as Blake stood to his full height, releasing her.

"Good girl." he smirked. Before reclaiming his seat. "I hope you don't mind, but I ordered our meals when I told them we would be in attendance." he admitted, taking a sip of wine.

"No, not at all." she smiled at him as she tried to will her body to calm down. "I'm sure it'll be lovely."

She watched Blake nod his head a moment before two steaming plates were placed in front of them. Licking over her lips as the scent of chicken with pasta and a rich creamy sauce with steamed green vegetables.

"I want to hear them sounds, baby girl." he warned, picking up his cutlery.

The meal was delicious and she couldn't help make the sounds he always asked for. The way the flavours burst across her tongue, all savoury until she took a sip of wine and the fruity flavour mixed perfectly, creating a unique blend for her to savour. Which reminded her of the unique man sat opposite her.

The man who held her in the palm of his hand. The man who had the power to crush her, break her. The man who already had. The man who she'd forgave once he'd told her the truth. The man who was so guarded with others, so strong, but yet with her she saw the vulnerability in him. Heard it when he'd whispered, *please don't leave me alone.*

But she also knew that his demons were far from being slaughtered. She knew that she had to help him, knew that the majority was what he'd admitted in the hotel room. His craving to inflict pain, suffering and humiliation for his sexual pleasure. She'd done some research on sexual sadistic practices and, whilst some, was more than what she had thought possible. A part of her wanted to try with Blake. Wanted to experience everything he had to offer without fear. Ava just wasn't certain how to broach the subject without him shutting down, and certainly without seeing the tortured anguish on his face.

"May I have this dance, beautiful?" Blake asked, his hand outstretched and a smile on his face.

Blake pulled her into his body, her palm colliding with his chest. The heat seeping into her and his intoxicating scent engulfing her. Her heartbeat quickened as his hand spread across the base of her spine, pulling her closer until they were chest to chest.

The music that had been a dim lull increased in volume as Blake smoothly swayed them to the music. Her hand grasped in his, resting against his chest. She could feel the deep, steady beat quicken as she looked up into his eyes, a smile on her lips.

"I've wanted to do this all night." his deep voice husked out against her ear.

Delicate shivers run the length of her spine. Her nipples hardened. His lips brushed against her temple. Her skirt swished against her thighs as Blake spun them until his back was to the balcony edge. His eyes blazed as her teeth sunk into her bottom lip. Her heart swelling and hammering against her chest, the words bubbling to the surface. Words that would let him know just how she felt about him. Words that she shouldn't say, but she couldn't hold them back any longer. As the overhead lights dimmed to nothingness and they were surrounded by flickering lights, her lips parted.

"I want to be everything you ever need, sweetheart." she breathed out, and she felt his heart thump hard against their joined hands. "I want the entire sinful package, Blake." she blinked slowly, her lips curving. "I want all of you, demons and all." she heard the sharp inhale of breath.

Blake's hand smoothed down her back, over the curve of her ass until his fingers gripped the hem of her dress. Slowly inching it up, the soft fabric whispering over the backs of her thighs. The warmth from his palm against the bare flesh of her ass had her gasping aloud. His head dipped, lips pressed beneath her ear.

"When you look into my eyes, baby girl." he whispered, fingers flexing against her ass. "You're a gift to me, you're beautiful and you're all mine." he continued, his lips brushing against her. His palm blazing to the curve of her hip and curling around the thin strap of the white lace thong. The snap of the fabric had liquid heat burning through her. "I did warn you that I'd rip your panties off." he chuckled against the shudder that slithered down her body as he pulled them slowly between her thighs. The fabric grazing her swollen clit before he tucked them in his pants pocket.

"Blake!" she moaned, his teeth nipping a trail down her neck. "P-people." she gasped out, her eyes fluttering shut.

"Hmm." his teeth grazed up the length of her neck until his lips were against her ear. "I can't wait for your eyes to watch over the dining room below, whilst I sink my cock deep inside you." his breathing was heavy. "To hear you moaning my name for everyone to hear, for them to look up and see the sheer pleasure on your face a moment before you erupt all over my cock." he sucked in a sharp breath.

Blake spun them around, her back pressing against the vines on the wrought-iron railing. His hands seized her hips and in one quick motion, she was looking out over the diners below. Her dress flipped up over her ass. His fingers brushed against her pussy.

"So wet for me already." he whispered into her ear. "Does my little slut like the thought of people watching me fuck you." his dark chuckle and degrading name had her trying to stand, but the hand against her back stopped her from moving. "Hold on to the railing, slut." he husked into her ear as the blunt head of his cock nudged her soaking entrance. "I want to hear you scream." his teeth clamped onto her neck at the same time his cock thrust deep into her on a long guttural moan.

Ava shuddered and yelped as the burning, stretching engulfed her. The fullness of his cock as he dragged it slowly out, brushing against her inner walls. A light moan fell from her parted lips, his tongue soothed over the bite on her neck. His hands gripped her hips as he slammed into her, ripping a scream from her throat. Her pussy contracted, juices leaked from her before he slammed back in with a severity that had her tightening her grip of the balcony. Blake slammed into her over and over again. Pulling screams from her every time he bottomed out inside her.

The room was filled with combined moans and groans of pleasure, the sounds of their bodies meeting. Her orgasm was quickly building from every thrust of his thick, large cock. Her muscles clenched tightly, her head thrown back, and his teeth bit down on her neck as the dam broke and her orgasm crested.

"Blake!" she screamed as her pussy gripped onto his cock tightly. Liquid rushed from her in hot splashes against his groin.

"My. Fucking. Slut." Blake bit out and punctuated each word

with a slam of his hips and buried himself as deep as he could, spilling hot jets of cum inside her. The grip on her hips would leave a bruise again, as he stilled her movements and their harsh breaths filling the room. His lips peppering kisses down her neck, his tongue soothing the bite marks on her shoulders. "Look below, baby girl." he whispered against her neck.

"Oh!" she gasped as her eyes looked out over the diners, every one of them enjoying their meals and conversations. She looked over her shoulder at Blake. "How?"

"Were in a soundproof glass box." he hissed, pulling out of her and re-buttoning his pants before he smoothed Ava's dress down over her. "Look over there." he pointed to the right-hand wall where there was a steel frame and she followed his finger as it ran along the ceiling to the other wall. "Glass that seems to be suspended in mid-air, but it does curve beneath the balcony, cocooning us into a private box." he explained, showing her the entirety of the glass box with a wicked smile on his face. "Even if my little slut does like being watched." he slapped a hand against her ass cheek.

"Hmm, it was exciting." she blushed profusely at her admission, which only made Blake's eyes ever darker as a growl vibrated through his chest at her words.

"Fuck, Ava." he groaned, his arm wrapping around her waist, pulling her into his side. "Keep talking like that and we won't make it home before I'm fucking you again." he admitted, pressing his lips to the top of her head.

"Hmm, there's an off-" her words were cut off on a yelp with a stinging slap against her ass.

"Perfect, little slut." he breathed out, guiding her across the balcony. "I need to get you into that harness." he ground out, quickening his pace, making Ava giggle.

Chapter Twenty-Eight

The moment the door closed behind them, Blake's arm wrapped around her waist, pulling her back to his front roughly. His stubble scraping against her jaw as his lips moved against her flesh. Her pulse thudded against her throat, her stomach clenching, and their combined juices coated her thighs.

"I want to try something." Blake whispered in her ear. "But I need to know, if you trust me." he continued. She could feel his chest expand against her back, could feel him hold his breath the moment the words were out. Her mind raced and her body heated with the possibilities.

"I trust you." she whispered, arching her back as his teeth grazed against her neck.

"Upstairs, wear only the harness." he husked out. "I'll be there shortly." he continued, his fingers running the zip of her dress down until it was hanging off of her shoulders before he stepped back.

Ava gripped the dress as she walked through his home, her breathing becoming more laboured with the thoughts whirling through her mind until she was standing in his bedroom. Anticipation flooded her body, she quickly discarded the dress and bra before quickly shimming into the harness.

Red leather straps curled around her thighs, five straps curved against her hips. Three straps wrapped around her waist with one long strap down the centre of her breasts before a further two straps encircled her throat. Every strap was entwined and held together with gold metal circles.

Goosebumps raised against her naked flesh, her hair whispering against her spine, her nipples already into hard peaks and their juices gathering between her thighs. Her heart pounded in her chest as she heard his footsteps outside the bedroom door. She sucked in a breath, the door opened slowly and the imposing presence behind her had her pussy throbbing with need as she opened her eyes on a long exhale.

"I'm going to blindfold you." he whispered, lips brushing against her ear.

"Okay." Ava breathed out, her heart stuttering in her chest as he brought the red leather blindfold in front of her.

"You remember the safe word?" he asked, plunging her into darkness. The leather cool against her eyes and securing it in place.

Her breathing quickened, she could hear the almost desperation in her breaths. The crisp fabric of his shirt scraped against her back, the buttons cold on her heated flesh. The fresh, zesty bergamot and spicy pepper of his aftershave became stronger, her arousal was mixed with his decadent scent.

"Hurt." she whispered, knowing that she wouldn't utter the word regardless of what he did to her tonight.

"Good girl." his hands lightly caressed down her arms. Goosebumps erupting down her flesh until his hands tightened around her wrists. "Two steps forward." he continued. The warmth of his pants touched the back of her thighs, urging her forward until her knees touched the cold bedding, making her shiver. "Lay down, body flat against the mattress and ass in the air." his voice had lowered, spikes of pleasure from his gruff tone raced through her.

Shivering against the cold bedding, her nipples puckered, her stomach clenched and the warmth from his hands slowly, tantalisingly whispered across her back. His fingers tracing the red leather straps.

"These loops." his voice was rough as his finger pulled on the loop at her neck. "Are twenty-four carat gold." he unhooked his finger, snapping the leather strap against her flesh.

A light moan escaped her lips as her back arched. The sound of a clip latching into place had her breathing deeper. The gentle tug against her throat made her head bend, exposing her throat. The feel of cool leather down her back, swishing against the base of her spine, made her think of a leash.

His hands grazing over every contour of her back, every indent which sent shivers racing across her flesh. She heard his breathing deepen, his hands stopping as he reached the curve of her ass. She almost cried out when he stepped away from her, his hands leaving her body.

Ava heard the distinct rustle of fabric, the light tap against plastic and deep breaths as she realised that he was removing his shirt. She knew exactly what he looked like, could see in her mind his muscles flexing and bunching with each movement. Her tongue swiped across her lips. Her pussy clenched with need and a shudder racked her body at the deep chuckle.

Hot naked flesh seared her, large hands touched hers and ragged breathing ghosted across her neck. Blake's wet tongue pressed against her thundering pulse, flicking lightly. His hard cock, seeping pre-cum, rested against her ass cheeks and her breath hitched in the back of her throat as his tongue licked up towards her ear.

"You looked absolutely beautiful tonight." he whispered, his tongue flicking her earlobe. "But bent over my bed in nothing but red leather, you're absolutely stunning." he continued, his lips pressing beneath her ear. A moan escaping her, his lips continuing down her neck. His tongue tracing along her shoulder, his teeth sinking in, and his groan of pleasure vibrated through her.

As quickly as Blake had covered her body, he was gone again. The cool air licking against her heated flesh making her shiver. Something heavy thudded against her on the mattress, making her jump and raise onto her forearms. Ava's breath hissed out of her as a stinging slap landed on her ass cheek. The pain bloomed over her before the heat from his palm warmed her flesh.

"Naughty girl." Blake tsked, his fingers flexing against the fleshy globe. "Lie back down." the command in his voice and another stinging slap on her ass startled her for a moment before she complied. "Open your legs, wide." his breathing became harsher, his hands gripped her ass cheeks and cool air whispered over her puckered hole. "Good girl." the praise in her darkness and the feel of his heated stare set her alight.

Ava felt him move behind her, felt his thighs brush against her calves. The hairs on his legs scraping against her soft skin making her tingle. Blake's warm, wet tongue licking against her heated cheek had her breath stuttering and her forehead burrowing into the mattress. Wetness seeped from her core as she trembled with anticipation of what was to come next.

Solely at his mercy.

The leather strap whipped against the top of her ass, his teeth bit down hard on her stinging cheek. Ava couldn't help her body's reaction as she reared back, throwing her head back.

"Fuck!" she shouted, the pain blooming over every nerve ending she possessed. Another whip, another bite. "Ow!" she hissed out, the pain almost overwhelming.

His groan against her flesh vibrated through her core, his

tongue easing the sting of his bite. His hands gripping her ass cheeks, the cool air over her sacred entrance was replaced by the wetness of his tongue. Circling once around her tight, puckered asshole, Ava froze at the strange sensation. She expected him to move lower, over where she needed him the most, but he didn't.

His hands gripped her firmly, stretching and exposing her. His tongue swiped slowly across her entrance, she felt the ring of muscle contract at the same time as her pussy. Blake's moan was from deep within as he probed her with the tip of his tongue. The sensation was dizzying, her breathing ragged, her stomach contracting, and a desperate moan poured from her.

"More." she whispered, blushing furiously as she tried to push back against his mouth. "Please." the desperation in her voice made him growl.

"What do you want, naughty girl?" he asked, his finger lightly tracing over her back entrance.

"You." she panted, every muscle in her body was coiled tight, pulses of pleasure thrummed through her veins.

"Hmm." his tongue swiped against her puckered hole again, she moaned loudly. "Tell me what you want." he coaxed. She felt his hand move from her cheek, felt it ghosting over her side before leaving her.

She squeezed her eyes closed behind the blindfold, she tried to stop the furious heat from deepening in her face and she tried to control her breathing but the moment she felt cold, thick liquid meet her asshole everything in her snapped. The rational part of her brain vanished, her lustful need taking over every fibre of her being as she licked over her lips.

"I want you." she began in a low whisper that quickly turned into a moan as she felt his finger ghost over her, smearing the cool thick gel that was quickly heating against her exposed hole. "To fuck me." she rushed out on a harsh breath as his finger applied more pressure. A slight sting ricocheted up her spine as she felt his finger slip past her tight ring of muscle.

"Hmm, you're taking my finger so well." he husked out. More pressure, more of his finger slipping inside her. "Tell me, would you like my cock in here." her breathless moan and her hips pushing back, pulling his finger deeper inside her ass. Her pussy clenched, juices spilling from her. "Or, would you like my cock in that greedy pussy of yours whilst I continue to finger your tight ass?" the way his voice sounded so full of desire, the feel of his harsh breath against her skin had her shuddering and her ass clenching around his finger.

"Please, Blake." she pleaded, trying to get more of him. "Fuck me." she begged shamelessly.

"I love it when you beg, naughty girl." his lips pressed against her ass cheek, his finger swirled inside of her as his other hand gripped her hip. "Stay still." he ordered. Everything stopped. She held her breath, her muscles locking into place, her heart thundering in her chest as she felt him rise up behind her. "Relax." he breathed out as she felt the blunt, wide tip of his cock against her pussy.

Blake snapped his hips forward, his balls slapping against her as his cock struck deep inside her. Her inner walls rippled against the thickness of him, trying to pull him in deeper. She felt him move the finger from her asshole at the same time as his cock dragged along her inner walls, nudging the sweetest spot inside of her until she was completely empty. Tears sprung to her eyes, the pleasure overwhelming and the absence of him startling.

"Oh god." she breathed. "Please, Blake, I need more." she begged.

Her breath left her on the longest moan possible as his cock plunged back inside her on a brutal thrust, she felt two fingers breach her ass at the same time. The fullness was intense and her muscles convulsed around him.

"Fuck, you're taking me so well." he groaned. "I'm going to fuck you hard and fast."

That was the only warning she got. His hand seized her hip in a bruising hold, his short nails digging into her flesh, the bite of pain heightening the pleasure as he slammed both his fingers and cock into her ripping a scream from her throat. Her pussy contracted, juices leaked from her before he slammed back in with a severity that had him tightening the grip on her hip. Blake slammed into her over and over again. Both cock and fingers hitting deep, her muscles contracting, her screams torn from her every time he bottomed out. Her pussy gripped onto his cock and her ass gripped onto his fingers tightly. Liquid rushed from her in hot splashes against his groin.

Blake continued to slam into her. Hips and fingers in time together and instantly stilling burying himself as deep as he could, spilling hot jets of cum inside her. Harsh breaths filling the room for long moments. His fingers left her ass and the cool air stung her sensitive flesh. His lips touched between her shoulder blades. "You did so well, baby girl." he whispered, pride lacing his tone as he pulled out of her. Their combined juices gathering on her thighs. "Let's get you cleaned up." his lips pressed lightly against her.

The moment the blindfold was removed, Ava squinted against the light and shivered against the heated look in Blake's dark eyes. The muscles in her legs wobbled as she stood before him, his fingers slowly peeling the red leather body harness from her and his eyes staring directly into hers. The moment it fell in a heap around her ankles, he scooped her up in his arms and padded across the vast expanse of his bedroom. Powerful strides ate up the floor until they reached the bathroom.

Carefully setting her down on the toilet, she winced slightly against the slight sting of pain in her backside.

Blake flicked the taps of the jacuzzi bathtub and poured soap into the water as it filled. He kept his back to her, and she watched him breathe deeply in slow, rhythmic breaths. His hands were shaking slightly, and she watched goosebumps appear on his tawny skin. Her eyebrows furrowed as she continued to watch him silently. The minutes seemed endless until he shut the taps off, still not speaking or looking at her.

Ava watched him climb into the bathtub, his dark eyes snaring her as he held his hand out for her to take. The warmth of the water against her calves eased some of the tension in her muscles. His arms snaked around her waist as he gently sunk them both into the bath. The bubbles snaking around them and the slight groan as the water enveloped him, but the hiss that escaped her lips from the sting against her abused flesh had him tensing against her back.

"I'm sorry I hurt you." his voice was so low, so dejected that tears sprung to her eyes. "I can't be fucking trusted with you." his admission had her chest aching for him. "I know I keep asking, but please forgive me, baby girl." his lips lightly pressed against her temple. She snuggled closer, her head resting against his shoulder and a small smile tugging her lips.

"I could have stopped you anytime, Blake." her voice was just as low as his, her fingers entwining with his. "But I like what you do to me." she felt every muscle in his body tense, felt his breath seize in his lungs. "I like the pleasure and the pain, and I don't want you to stop." she admitted, her cheeks flushing and her pulse spiking.

"I'm frightened of hurting you." his breath left him on a long exhale. "Frightened of you leaving and frightened that I can't control myself with you." she heard the brokenness in his voice, felt the pounding of his heart against her back.

"Sweetheart, I don't want you to control yourself." her voice took on a harder edge. "I want you Blake Synclair and that means all of you." she raised their joint hands and kissed across his knuckles.

"I need you to be my purity, baby girl." his voice shook and his fingers tightened in hers. "I need your innocence and purity." he continued, his lips brushing against her ear. "Do you understand?" he whispered.

"Yes, I understand but..." she squeezed her eyes closed for a fraction of a second, the words she wanted to say on the tip of her tongue, but she knew she couldn't say them. Taking a deep breath. "You have all of me, Blake." her voice wavered thick with emotion.

"Hmm." he hummed against her, she felt the vibration in his chest. "Let's get washed and curl up in bed."

She didn't think about the fact that he changed the subject, didn't think about him not saying anything further to her because she knew that he wouldn't say the words she desperately wanted to hear from him. But one thing she did know was that he showed her how he felt and for now, that was enough.

Chapter Twenty-Nine

Monday came by too quickly. She hated knowing that she had five full days to work and four full nights alone before she could see Blake again. It was the same every week, and it was becoming a problem for her. When she'd brought it up with him, she saw something in the depths of those intense, dark eyes. Something she couldn't decipher and something which at first caused her a slither of unease, but she had quickly tampered that down. She remembered listening to him, listening to him, explaining that his work took a lot out of him and the rest he needed. She remembered the smirk on his face and the desire filling his eyes as he'd told her that he wouldn't get any rest if they saw each other during the week, and she understood. Especially after their weekends together by Sunday night, once she was back in her own bed, exhausted she slept like the dead and realised that Blake probably did too.

Blowing out a breath of frustration, her hand curled around the steaming mug of coffee as she headed to a new classroom. Her heels click-clacking against the floor, echoing down the long corridor. She'd been assigned to a new teacher for this week, help them keep the children in line and help individuals who required additional learning help. She didn't mind being assigned to a new teacher, after all, as a teaching assistant, it was her job. But she didn't like having to learn about the children she hadn't met before, didn't like not knowing their strengths and weaknesses. Even more so after she took a course last year on safeguarding of children. Learning what signs to look out for, learning how to speak with children who were suffering and most importantly reporting her thoughts and fears for individual children.

It was this course that set Ava aside from the other teaching assistants and it was often the reason why she was sent to new teachers and new students to speak with them.

Smoothing her free hand down the black pencil skirt a moment before pushing the classroom door open and coming face to face with the new teacher. Tall, broad, dark hair and piercing blue eyes staring at her made Ava stop in the doorway.

"Good morning, Mister?" her voice was low as she tried to smile under the scrutiny of his gaze.

"Jones, Mister Jones Cain." he stepped forward, offering his large hand to her. "And you are?" his lips twitched as she felt heat crawling up her neck, their hands clasped in a firm handshake.

"Ava, your teaching assistant." she answered, snatching her hand back.

"Nice to meet you, Ava." the way he said her name made her cock her head to the side. It held a certain tone she'd only ever heard Blake use, and she didn't like it coming from the man before her.

"Likewise." she muttered, claiming the seat beside his desk. Grasping the coffee mug in both hands. "So, first day." she smiled, taking a sip of coffee.

"Yeah, I haven't lived here long." he admitted, taking the chair behind his desk and turning to face her fully. "I'm a little nervous."

"You'll do just fine." Ava smiled reassuringly.

The loud ringing of the bell pulled her from her thoughts and the awkward silence that had descended between them. Thank god for small mercies as the class of nine year old's filed in and taking their seats.

Ava sat unmoving as her eyes cast across the classroom, looking at each child until she stopped on a little boy. His hair dark and ruffled, his eyes just as dark that held a sadness which spoke to Ava, his bottom lip trembling slightly. She noticed that his small hands were shaking as he tried to clasp them together, resting them on the table.

The little boy before her reminded her of Blake, in so many ways and not just from the looks. The poor little boy looked broken, and she'd seen Blake look exactly the same when she'd gone to him in the hotel room and it broke her heart. Without a second thought, placing her cup on the edge of Jones's desk, she walked over, crouched low and placed her hand gently on his arm.

"Can I talk to you for a moment?" she kept her voice low and gentle. Her smile small as he nodded, causing his hair to fall onto his forehead before they left the classroom.

Before they had even made it into the small, comfortable room that was like a second home to Ava the boy was shaking uncontrollably, tears had welled in his dark eyes and his teeth were clamped so tight against his bottom lip, she feared that he'd draw blood.

Taking her seat in a plush chair, she watched as he threw himself onto the sofa opposite her. His small hands gripping the cushions beneath him as if his life depended on it. Ava was taken aback at just how broken the little boy before her was and it was upsetting for her to witness.

"I'm Ava, what's your name?" she kept her voice gentle, her eyes tracking his every movement.

"G-George." he stuttered, sniffling loudly.

"Awe, that's a lovely name." she smiled, leaning forward

slightly in her seat. "I bet your mum and dad are really proud to have you as their son." she started off, his dark, tearful eyes snapped to hers. His lips trembling and his frame still shaking, but she could see a hopefulness in the depths of his eyes. A look she'd seen in Blake's and in that moment, the likeness between the two was startling. But she knew Blake didn't have children, knew that he didn't even have an ex-girlfriend. Shaking her head, she concentrated on George.

"Do you know my dad?" he asked, his voice full of hope, which made Ava's brow furrow slightly.

"I can't say that I do, in all honesty." she admitted and watched as his shoulders slumped. "But why don't you tell me about him?" she asked, hoping that this could be the reason why he was so upset. She watched him take a deep stuttering breath, tears tracking down his cheeks.

"I don't know." he mumbled, his eyes cast downwards again. "I-I haven't seen him in a long time." he sniffled again, wiping his nose on the sleeve of his school jumper. "Mum said he needed time away." his little shoulders shrugged half heartedly.

"Oh, and what does dad do for work?" she asked, her stomach tightening as she watched George cave in on himself.

"H-He helps sick people." he mumbled, his feet kicking against the floor. "He used to help me, too."

Ava's mind whirled, her stomach tightened and acid tried to snake up her throat as her heart pounded against her chest. She didn't want to think about the possibility of Blake being a father, didn't want to think that she might be keeping father and son apart, but the similarities were too big to ignore.

Does Blake have a child?

Could this be the poor little boy who craves his dad, be his child?

Don't be stupid, you've known Blake your whole life and you know he isn't leading a double life.

So why can't you see each other during the week?

Is that when he goes back to his family?

Ava took a deep breath, her eyes re-focusing on George as she put all of her thoughts behind her.

"Oh, so he's a doctor." she feigned excitement into her tone. "That's such a big job to have and requires a lot of dedication." she continued, her smile small as her inner turmoil threatened to rise to the surface. "But I'm sure your dad thinks of you every day that you're apart."

"Really?" his eyes bright, head cocked to the side. She nodded, swallowing thickly. "Will he come home soon?" he asked, the hope in his voice nearly shattered Ava.

"I'm sure he will once he's finished making the sick people better." she soothed and watched as he wiped the tears from his eyes.

"I'm having a birthday party soon." he brightened more, his fingers relaxing against the cushions. "Do you think dad will come?" he asked, his shaking subsiding as his anxiety faded.

"I don't know George." she admitted, when all she wanted to do was promise him that his dad would be home for his birthday party. "But I do know that you will have so much fun, you won't have time to worry about who's celebrating with you."

"Miss Ava?" his voice turned timid again. "You can come to my party if you'd like." his smile was small, almost as if he was preparing himself for rejection.

"I'd love to." she smiled, looking at the smile which broke out across his face, revealing two dimples in his cheeks. Which almost stole her breath, she was looking at a younger version of Blake. "But I don't think you really want a teacher at your party, George." she wanted nothing more than to go to the party but she couldn't, it was against school policy and more than a little weird, especially if Blake and George were related. "Now, shall we go back to class?" she smiled, trying to hide the slight tremor in her hands.

Her working day had been hard, she'd spent all day watching George and all day finding more and more similarities between him and Blake, to the point she wondered if it would drive her insane. Which is why she found herself clutching a glass of wine in her pyjamas, curled up on the sofa when James walked in from work.

"Hey squirt." his eyebrows rose as he took in the glass of wine. "Bad day?" he queried, slumping in the chair.

"Something like that." she mumbled, her eyes glancing at her phone as if she was expecting Blake to call her. Shaking her head, she looked at her brother. Watched his forehead crease as he scrubbed a hand down his face with a sigh.

"Should you be drinking?" he asked, his eyes boring into hers as she scrunched her face up.

"Why not?" she asked, taking a sip. Enjoying the burst of fruit flavour over her tongue, instantly reminding her of the wine she had with Blake.

"Look, I know you don't want to talk about the mystery man." he sighed again, leaning forward with his forearms against his thighs. "But I think you should tell me who he is." Her heart rate kicked up a notch as she tried to hide the panic look on her face.

"It's not serious, James." she sighed, uttering the truth. "Once it's serious, you'll be the first to know." she tried to smile but the way his eyes narrowed, had her gulping around the sudden lump in her throat.

"Not serious?" the incredulity in his tone made her raise her eyebrows. "Not serious but serious enough not to use protection?" Ava sighed, she couldn't cope with this conversation today.

"Oh god, it's none of your business if I'm using protection or not!" she snapped, taking another sip of wine to try to keep her temper at bay. She knew that she and Blake hadn't used any condoms, but she didn't really understand why James was making it his business.

"So you admit that you're not using anything?" James moved to the very edge of the chair, like he was ready to pounce.

"Of course I am!" her voice raised an octave, her eyebrows hitting her hairline.

"So how come you're pregnant?" James snapped, hurt etched onto his face. Ava's eyes widened, her pulse spiked, and she felt sick.

James gently took the glass of wine from her as she began to shake slightly, her mind trying to catch up to what had just been thrown at her. Her stomach trying to expel the contents, making her drag a deep breath in and trying to dispel the wave of nausea. Images of little George filtering in her mind, of how broken he was over his absent doctor father and then everything clicked into place, calming herself down.

"I'm not pregnant, James." her voice was soft.

"I saw the test in the bathroom bin, Ava it's okay we'll get through this." his voice softened as she felt all the colour drain from her face. "But does the mystery man know?" his hand reached out, gripping hers.

"No." she whispered, he sucked in a sharp breath. Her heart swelling with how gentle he was being with her, reminding her of the dark times when they'd lost their parents. He'd make an amazing dad. She smiled, squeezing his hand. "Because I'm not pregnant, James." she sucked in a breath, still squeezing his hand. "I'm on the pill and have been for a while." she admitted, her smile growing bigger. "I'm not the only woman to use the bathroom in this house, I think you need to speak with Katie." she watched as every emotion imaginable flickered across his face in quick succession. His hand became clammy in hers as the realisation dawned on him. "You'll make an amazing dad, James, but speak with Katie." she urged, letting go of his hand.

"Fuck!" he muttered, slumping back in the chair with wide eyes, making her chuckle.

"You seemed to take the news better when you thought it was me who was pregnant." she couldn't stop the amusement from colouring her tone. "Go on, have dinner with Katie and talk about your future." she smiled encouragingly, reclaiming her glass of wine.

Chapter Thirty

Blake was reclined on the sofa, the crystal cut tumbler glass filled with whiskey clutched in his hand. His eyes staring blankly at the television, not creating the distraction like he'd hoped. His thoughts taking over his mind. He looked at his phone, no messages or missed calls. He took a sip from his drink in hopes of drowning the disappointment he had no right to feel at the no contact from Ava. After all, it was his rule not to see each other during the week. His rule to limit their contact to weekends only, but as he sat staring into the blackness of his phone screen, he couldn't remember the reason why he decided on these stupid rules.

Gulping half of the whiskey, the burn slithering down his throat as he stood abruptly and grabbing his phone. Ignoring the quizzical look, ignoring the call of his name as he strode out of the living room, and he didn't stop until the crisp, cool evening breeze slapped across his face. The grass cold against his bare feet as he stood in the back garden. His heart quickening as his phone buzzed in his hand, a smile gracing his lips until he looked at the name flashing across his screen.

"Hello mother." Blake greeted, taking a gulp of his whiskey. Knowing he's going to need it.

"Oh, honey." his mother's voice was bright but soft. "How are you?" she asked and he could just picture her laid on the chaise lounge, her grey hair elegantly coiled, making him smile.

"I'm good, mum." he sighed, another sip of whiskey. "How're you and dad?" he asked, his eyes looking out over the trees that lined the back of the garden.

"Oh you know, very well." he could hear her shuffling. "It's almost your father's birthday." her voice turned suddenly soft and his pulse thumped against his throat. "We hope that you'll make it this year for the party." she continued softly, his hand shook as he finished the whiskey. "We miss you, Blake." she admitted, which made him feel like shit.

"Yeah, I know mum." he cleared his throat, sweat beaded at the back of his neck. His heart rate kicked up another notch as he glanced over his shoulder, making sure he was alone before he spoke again. "I'll be there, mum."

"That's wonderful, honey." his mum's voice became even brighter and he could imagine the wide smile on her face. "Your father will be so pleased, too." she continued, he heard her swallow probably had a glass of wine. "And will you be bringing…"

"I will be bringing someone, mum." he swallowed around the lump in his throat, once again glancing over his shoulder. "She's called Ava." his voice dropped lower, ensuring he wasn't overheard.

"Oh, honey." his mother's voice saddened. "You're causing yourself unnecessary problems." she continued, her voice ever sadder.

"Don't worry about that." Blake ground his teeth together, his back snapping straight. "That's for me to worry about." he gritted out.

"And how exactly am I to explain to Candice's parents?" she asked and he could imagine her beckoning his father to the phone to talk some sense into him.

"Mother, don't worry about them." he couldn't help the hard, harsh tone he used. "I'll deal with them. Is Aunt Mavis attending the party?" he asked, changing the subject and glancing again over his shoulder.

"No, she isn't." his mother didn't sound pleased but let their conversation move on. "She's on holiday with her new partner." she made a crude noise, making Blake chuckle. "Gallivanting around like a teenager, she's old enough to know better." she admonished.

"Hmm, well, I'm sure she's having a lovely time." Blake looked over his shoulder again. "Mum, I've got to go, but I'll see you in a few weeks." he promised, his eyes narrowing slightly at being watched.

"Oh, okay, honey. Love you."

"Love you too, mum." he finished the call and pocketed his phone. Wiping his free hand down his face on a long, frustrated groan. "Three days, baby girl. Three fucking days." he muttered to himself, turning on his heel and striding back towards the house.

Chapter Thirty-One

Ava's eyes widened as she saw the large black box emblazoned with *Bordelle* in gold font across the top, laid on her bed. The smile on her face widened as she smelt his familiar cologne faintly. Her pulse spiked as she realised it wasn't long ago since Blake had been in her room. There was a plain white card resting against the box, turning it over, she read his note:

Ava,
I can't wait to see how stunning you will look tonight.
Everything that you need for the night is in this box.
B x

Her hands shook slightly as she removed the lid and her gasp rung out into the empty room. Laid in the black tissue paper was a red satin and lace panelled skirt with gold suspender clips, matching bodice bra, nude stockings and a red choker. Her heart rate kicked up a notch as she looked over the lingerie. Lingerie that Blake couldn't wait to see her in.

Quickly checking the time, she had an hour before he would be picking her up. Giving her some time for a quick shower and fresh make-up. Her lips curved into a wicked smile as she took the long white wool coat from the wardrobe which would cover her body and hide the lingerie beneath.

Ava licked her lips at the delectable sight of Blake stood resting against the passenger door of his Aston Martin, folding his arms across his chest and the way his muscles bunched and strained had her stomach clenching with need. Closing the door behind her. The long white wool coat fastened, stopping the cold autumn breeze from chilling her almost naked body beneath. Her overnight bag clutched in her other hand.

She watched Blake push off the car, his purposeful strides meeting her halfway up the driveway of her house, making her blush.

"Baby girl." his tone was pure desire. His large hand cupping her cheek, his thumb ghosting over her bottom lip before pressing his lips to hers momentarily.

"Hi." Ava breathed out, a smile on her lips.

The drive was short and hurried across town, the now familiar passing scenery whizzing by. Her adrenaline was slowly taking over her body as she wondered what his thoughts would be the moment she removed her coat, revealing the lingerie only. The thrill of anticipation ran through her as she turned slightly to look at his chiselled profile. She'd missed him so much this last week and was practically overwhelmed at finally spending the night with him.

"Have you eaten?" he asked with a smile as he glanced at her before turning back to the road.

"Yeah." she asked, folding her hands in her lap.

"Next time, don't eat." his hand came to rest on her thigh over her coat. "I like to feed you." he admitted, a smile never leaving his lips. "But I do have a surprise at home for you." he continued.

"Another one?" she asked, raising her eyebrows.

"Well, more for the both of us." she watched his eyes darken slightly as he looked at her, making her lick over her lips. "Did you like my gift?" he asked, gently squeezing her thigh.

"Hmm, I did." she nodded. "I'm beginning to think you only want me in lingerie." she laughed lightly with a slight shake of her head.

"Amongst being naked, yeah I do." he smirked as he turned into his driveway. "I can't wait to see you in it." his voice turned huskier.

The moment they walked through the front door, her overnight bag thudded to the floor and his hands were on her hips. The predatory gleam in his dark eyes had her stomach clenching and her heart skipping a beat. Her back hit the hallway wall, his hands slapped against the wall and his head ducked down to look directly into her eyes as her breath hitched in her throat.

"I've missed you." he admitted, his hand slowly unbuttoning her coat. His fingers grazing against her flesh with every button flicked open. "Fuck!" he gritted out as he looked at the red satin and lace lingerie.

Her coat fell to the floor, his hands seizing her wrists and holding them above her head. Her heart thumped hard against her ribs as his lips crushed against hers with a ferocity she'd never experienced before. His tongue forced its way into her mouth, swirling with hers as he swallowed all of her sounds that he ripped from her throat. Her pussy clenched against his heated thigh and her nipples were tight and hard as they scraped against the defined muscles of his chest. He ripped his lips from hers, trailing them hungrily down her throat. Her harsh breaths had her chest heaving, the heat from his lips were torturous as he reached her collarbone. Blake ripped his mouth away, his breath fanning against her swollen lips.

"I missed you too." she was breathless, her eyes were lidded with pure desire but she watched his eyes soften. His fingers flexing against her wrists.

"Turn around." the command, his tone didn't match the soft look in his eyes as he released her wrists, stepping back from her. "Hands above your head." he continued.

Ava faced the wall, her hands braced against the cold plaster with laboured breaths. His primal groan went directly to her core, wetness gathered at her entrance as his hands skimmed over her satin covered hips and further still. Her head bowed as he unclasped the suspenders, his breath hard against the back of her neck as he inched the panelled skirt over the back of her thighs. The cool air gliding over her heated flesh, goosebumps erupting as his knuckled scraped against her. Ava sucked in a harsh breath as the skirt bunched around her hips.

"Open your legs." Blake husked out and the moment she widened her stance, she felt him sit between her parted thighs. "Your pussy is already gushing, like the good little whore that you are." he growled low, hooking one of her legs over his shoulder.

The warm wetness of his tongue licked directly up the middle of her core. The loud moan tumbled from her lips as she steadied her hands against the wall at the same time his tongue flicked against her engorged clit.

"Oh God!" she moaned, her eyes glancing down. The sight of Blake's head between her thighs, the sensation of his wicked tongue exploring her meticulously, had her climax already beginning to build. Her breathing became hard pants, the muscles in her thighs began to tremble and pleasure raced over every nerve ending in her body. Throbbing and pulsing in delightful waves. "Blake." she moaned his name like she was praying.

Blake's tongue thrust inside of her wet heat, groaning against her, sent a fresh wave of moisture to leak directly onto his tongue. His fingers gripped her ass cheeks, pulling her against his mouth as he continued to thrust in and out of her. Ava's moans filled the hallway as her hips ground down against his tongue, sending another deep groan from his mouth, the vibration ricocheted through her body.

"I could eat this pussy for days." he moaned, tongue flicking against her engorged clit once, twice before his dark eyes latched onto hers. The sheer desire in them stole her breath. "But I have other plans for tonight." he circled a finger through her wetness, dipping inside the pad of his finger, grazing over the sweet spot, causing more of her juice to gather on his finger before he pulled out. His eyes never leaving hers, he reached his hand up towards her mouth. "Taste yourself." the demand in his voice had a fresh wave of pleasure slithering through her. The moment her lips parted, his finger brushed over her tongue. The sweet, slightly acidic taste of her arousal wasn't as unpleasant as she thought it would be, but it was mixed with the taste of him. "Does my little whore like the way she tastes?" the smirk deepening as her eyelids fluttered, moaning around his finger.

"Yes." she breathed out, his finger trailed over her lips, coating them with her saliva.

Blake unhooked her leg, his hands gripping her hips to steady her briefly before rising to his feet. The heat of his body against her back made her shudder as he splayed his hands across her stomach, inching upwards until he grasped her breasts through the satin and lace bra. His thumbs grazing over her nipples slightly. His lips touched her neck, a fresh wave of pleasure crested over her and with a quick yank, a loud tear and her breasts tumbled free.

"Hmm, flimsy little things." he whispered against her flesh. His tongue flicking against her rapid pulse as he ground his hard cock against her ass cheeks. "Be a good little whore and undress me." he continued with one last flick of his tongue.

Ava turned on shaking legs, her hands flying straight to his shirt. Her fingers fumbling with the small buttons, making him chuckle until her fingers curled around the edges, her knuckles grazing against his chest, making him shudder before she yanked with every ounce of strength she possessed. Buttons flew from the shirt, tinkling as they landed against the hardwood floor. Blake's eyes darkened even further, running his tongue across his lower lip as he stared down at her.

The clanking of his belt shattered the silence as it landed against the floor, quickly flicking the button of his pants, tearing his zip down before she eagerly hooked her fingers inside of his pants and boxers. Yanking them down to the floor, where he quickly kicked them to the side. His hand gripping the back of her neck, tangling in her hair as he pulled her closer. Her breath caught in her throat as their lips crashed together. His teeth nipping her bottom lip, making her gasp before his tongue delved in, swirling with hers as he swallowed all of her sounds that he ripped from her throat.

Her hands ghosting over his hips, one lightly inching over his sculpted ass, her nails sinking in as he dominated her mouth and swallowing his groan. Her other whispering through his pubic hair, lower until she cupped his balls and squeezed gently, making his cock expand and throb against her.

"Turn around." he barked, ripping his mouth from hers. "Hands together on the wall." he continued, his left hand circling both wrists, pinning them against the plaster. His other guiding his engorged cock to her entrance until the blunt tip sat just inside, letting go. He gripped her hip pulling her forcefully back, impaling herself on a scream as every single inch of his thick cock tunnelled into her, bottoming out. "hmm, you took me like a fucking pro." he husked out, the hand on her hip moving to her breast, his fingers pinching her hardened nipple making her moan. "Good little whore."

"Please, Blake." she whimpered, throwing her head back. "Fuck me!" she begged.

"I do love a good whore who likes to beg." he chuckled darkly, his hand wrapping around her throat.

Her inner walls rippled against the thickness of him, trying to pull him in deeper. She felt him drag his cock along her inner walls, nudging the sweetest spot inside of her until the tip was resting at her entrance. His hand around her throat tightened, making her gasp and her heart thunder against her chest as he slammed back in. Ava moaned loudly, his fingers flexing against her throat tightening as his thrusts became relentless, brutal, and almost punishing. Bottoming out on every stroke, her inner walls quivering, the ball of ecstasy building deep within her.

Blake's fingers tightened again, his cock throbbing inside of her. Blackness invaded the corners of her vision as she tried to gasp for air. His lips skimming against her shoulder, teeth grazing as he mercilessly pounded into her.

Their combined moans and groans of pleasure, the sounds of flesh against flesh. White hot waves overtook her body, her muscles in both her pussy clenched tightly, her vision dimmed significantly as he applied more pressure against her throat. His teeth sunk into her shoulder and her orgasm crashed into her with a ferocious force, blackness clouded her vision.

Her pussy gripped onto his cock, and liquid rushed from her in hot splashes against his groin.

"My. Fucking. Whore." Blake punctuated each word with a slam of his hips. Burying himself as deep as he could, spilling hot jets of cum inside her as he stilled his movements. His hand instantly releasing her throat. Harsh, gulping breaths filling the hallway for long moments. "Are you okay?" he asked, turning her gently to face him.

"Yeah." she croaked, her throat felt like she'd swallowed glass. "Take it you like the lingerie." she asked, a lopsided grin on her face. Blake's forehead rested against hers, his breath fanning over her face in short bursts.

"Absolutely stunning." he whispered, his hand gently cupping her cheek. "The red mark around your throat will go in a couple of hours." he continued, his thumb brushing against her cheek. "Go get changed and I'll make you some honey and lemon tea." he pressed his lips to hers gently. "It'll help with the soreness." he pulled himself away from her, unable to stop his eyes from tracking over every inch of her, making her blush.

"Okay, Syn." she smiled, grabbing her overnight bag.

The moment she walked into the living room, the pale green satin nightdress clinging to her curves, Blake growled low in the back of his throat, his eyes darkening as he stared at her.

"Fuck me, Ava." he ground out, beckoning her to sit on his lap. "We'll never get to watch this movie." he admitted, his cock snuggled against her ass cheeks. "Here." she took the steaming mug of tea, the scent of honey and lemon filling her nostrils as she took a sip, soothing her throat as she swallowed. The sweet, tart taste making her moan. "Fuck." he groaned, his arm banding around her waist, holding her close.

Ava smiled as she snuggled further against his bare chest, feeling every hard muscle against her back. A fresh wave of desire curling around her until her eyes landed on the television and scrawled across the screen *365 days: This Day.*

"Interesting choice." Ava smiled around the rim of her cup.

"I heard that the first one gave you an excellent visual on sucking cock." he whispered huskily. His lips brushing against her ear as a shiver run down her spine. "I wonder what this movie will teach you." his lips pressed to her temple briefly as they settled down to watch the movie.

Chapter Thirty-Two

The thrum of voices all colliding and vying for prominence in the pub. Bodies scattered around, some standing at the bar and some sitting around the various tables. It was busy as usual for a Saturday night, both Blake and James were sat opposite each other with their first pint in front of them.

"So," James began, taking a sip of his pint. "I found a positive pregnancy test in the bin last weekend." he continued, his eyes bouncing around the pub. Blake sat silent, blinking slowly as he processed the words spoken to him. His face a perfect mask of indifference as he took a sip of his drink, his tongue swiping away the froth from his lips.

"Ava's pregnant?" he tried to keep the fear out of his voice, despite it lacing through his veins.

"Yeah," James shook his head, another sip of his drink. But that one word had his heart thumping wildly against his chest, sweat blooming across the nape of his neck and his breaths struggling to maintain a normal pattern. "She still won't tell me who the mystery man is, by the way." he shook his head sadly. "But I thought it was Ava's too…"

"Ava's not pregnant?" he cut his friend off, clenching his jaw, his grip on the pint glass increasing. And the fucker laughed.

"Nah," James continued to laugh. "Katie is." he admitted, his eyes darting around the pub. "I'm going to be a dad." The smile that graced his lips made something inside Blake snap back into place. Something that had been absent for a long time. But the relief overshadowed the feeling, relief that Ava was not

238

pregnant.

"Congratulations." Blake raised his glass in a mock cheer, before gulping half of his. He knew he should be happy for his friend, he just couldn't muster the happiness tonight.

"Thanks, but I'm gonna need some help" James admitted, taking another sip.

"Yeah, well, my advice is move Katie in." he gave a pointed look at his best friend, a small smile at his own memories surfacing. "She's going to be horny as hell and you don't want her knocking on your door at all hours of the night." he took a long sip of his drink and watched James's eyes widen before a grin took over his face.

"Yeah?" he grinned wider, Blake nodded. "Fuck!"

"But when she hits the third trimester, talk and eat as quietly as you can and try not to breathe around her." he smirked as James furrowed his brow. "She'll rip your eyes right out," he laughed. "But when the baby is born, I'll give you some much needed training." he shook his head and instantly froze. His back snapping straight, his muscles tensing as images tried to take over again.

Dragging in some deep breaths, squeezing his eyes shut momentarily before taking a sip of his pint. James had his head cocked to the side, watching him with his mouth turned down in a frown.

"Still not getting better?" he asked, concern lacing his tone. Blake's pulse thumped wildly against his throat, slight tremors in his hands as he breathed out long and hard.

"I've met someone." Blake tried to keep his voice controlled, but failed miserably. James's eyebrows shot up to his hairline, shock evident on his face. "Yeah, I wasn't expecting it either." his hands balled into fists as he tried to subdue the tremors. "It just sort of happened."

"Oh!" James's hand scrubbed down his face before those green eyes pinned him in place. "Does Candice know?" his voice was quiet, sad even as he asked the question.

"No." Blake shook his head, guilt flooding his veins. "I'll tell her and George, soon." he admitted

"Hmm." James took a gulp of his drink. "So where did you meet the woman?" his heart beat hard in his chest, a thin sheen of sweat blooming across the back of hi neck.

"Work." he lied as his lips tipped up in a small smile as he pictured Ava. "She's special, I never expected to say that about another woman again." a small blush settled on his cheeks at his admission.

"Does she know about you know?" James asked, his eyes boring into his as Blake shook his head no. "When are you going to tell her?"

"Soon as they know, I guess that's the best thing to do." he drained the rest of his glass and checked the time on his watch. "Fuck!" Blake stood. "I'm late." shoving his phone in his pocket.

"Late?"

"She'll fucking kill me, I promised I'd be there." his words rushed out, fishing his keys from his coat.

"You going to tell them tonight?" James asked, draining his drink too.

"On George's birthday, I'm not that much of an asshole." he chuckled darkly, knowing exactly the type of person he was.

"I know you're not Blake." James smiled tightly. "Wish him happy birthday from his Uncle James." Blake nodded before rushing from the pub.

Chapter Thirty-Three

Ava stood a slight shake of her hands, clutching the small box wrapped in midnight blue wrapping paper with a small white bow on top. Her pulse spiked as the front door opened and those rich, dark eyes landed on her. His lips pulling into a smile as he stepped aside to let her into his home.

"Hey." she smiled, her eyes tracking over him. The salmon polo shirt clung to every muscle that was carved meticulously into his torso. She couldn't help licking over her lips.

"Hey." he breathed out, his hands cupping her cheeks, bringing their mouths together in a slow brush of flesh. "What have you got there?" he asked, stepping back, locking the door behind her.

"Happy Birthday, Blake." she held the present out to him. His eyes sparkling as he took the small box from her. "It's not much." she continued until he pinned her with a pointed look.

"It'll be perfect." she watched his throat bob on a hard swallow, carefully removing the wrapping paper and revealing the black leather box. Her heartbeat kicked up another notch as he opened the lid. "Ava, these are perfect." he smiled, his eyes looking over the cuff links monogrammed with his initials.

"I thought you could wear them for work." her teeth clamped her lower lip as a slow blush covered her cheeks as she watched him still looking at the cuff links. "But you don't have to." she rushed out, he snapped the box closed. His free hand winding around the nape of her neck.

"Thank you, baby girl." he whispered, his lips brushing against hers. "I'll wear them everyday." he continued. Her hands brushed his chest in a featherlight touch, making him shudder. Trailing her fingertips to his abdomen, the muscles dancing under her fingers, and a small, quiet moan escaped him. His forehead dropped to hers, his fingers flexing against the nape of her neck. His breathing a little deeper as her hardened nipples scrapped against his chest. "I need you." he admitted in a whisper.

"Can we..." Ava began in a whisper, her fingers delving under the polo shirt, earning another shudder from him. The incredible heat from his body warming her hands. "Try something new?" she continued, the moment the words were out of her mouth, his eyes snapped open, boring into hers, making her swallow.

"Tell me." dipping his head until his lips brushed against her ear. "What does my dirty girl want to try?" his voice had turned husky, making her shiver.

"Wax." she whispered, her face turning a deep shade of crimson as his breath whooshed out against her neck. She felt his heartbeat quicken against her fingers.

"Where did you hear that?" he asked, lips brushing against her neck.

"Internet." she admitted, his tongue flicked against her pulse before his teeth grazed against the same spot.

"Hmm." his lips travelled back to her ear. "You're sure about trying it?" he husked out, teeth nipping her earlobe.

"Yes, I want to try." her pulse was thumping wildly, his tongue traced the shell of her ear, turning her breathing ragged as a delicious tingle shot directly to her pussy, making it clench.

"Strip and lay on the dining table." he pulled his mouth from her, his eyes dilating and a wicked smirk on his face made her stomach flutter. Ava turned on her heel, his hand connected with her ass cheek in a stinging slap beneath her yoga pants. "Dirty girl." he continued.

The cool air licked against her thighs as she peeled the yoga pants off, her panties quickly following. The small gathering of juices slicked her thighs. Her hands trembled slightly as she flung the thin white jumper from her. Her stomach clenching as anticipation weaved through her as she dropped her bra onto the pile of discarded clothes.

The ice cold granite had her gasping and shivering the moment her ass touched the table. Goosebumps erupted across her body as she laid on her back, closing her eyes. Her nipples were hard, aching points as the cool air danced across them. Her breathing was slow but deep as she tried to keep still, tried to keep the anticipation from taking over her being.

Ava heard his footsteps in the hallway, heard the purposeful strides a moment before the kitchen door opened. She heard his sharp intake of breath followed by a deep, low growl, which had her pussy clenching with need.

"Fucking beautiful." he husked out. "Open your eyes." the slight command in his voice was overshadowed by the husk. She snapped her eyes open on a gasp. Blake stood completely naked. All tawny skin, rippling muscles and his large cock, fully erect against his abdomen. "Good girl." he praised, setting down a lit candle in a black jar with gold writing on the chair closest.

Blake's large, warm fingers encircled her ankle, lifting until his lips pressed lightly against her skin. His stubble scraping against her skin, more goosebumps erupting. His tongue flicking against the bone, his hand curving around her calf as he bent forward. The heel of her foot landed against his back, her knee resting on his wide shoulder. His lips continuing in a slow, leisurely trail toward the apex of her thighs. Her breathing became laboured when his tongue snaked out, licking her juices from the inside of her thigh. His groan vibrated through her core and her clit throbbed in response.

"You taste so fucking good." he moaned, picking her other leg up and throwing it over his shoulder. His hands gripped her ass cheeks, lifting her slightly. "Now, be a good fucking girl and cum on my tongue."

Blake's tongue flicked against her clit, Ava bucked on a low moan. Blake's grip tightened on her ass. His tongue licking a line directly to her opening, swirling his tongue once.

"Oh god." Ava groaned as she arched her back as she tried to gain more of his delectable tongue.

Parting her folds with his tongue, he zig-zagged up her centre in slow deliberate movements. His groan echoed around the kitchen. Her hips undulated, his tongue circling her throbbing, engorged clit relentlessly pulling moans of pleasure from her. The tight ball was building with every flick of his tongue against her clit, juices gathering at her opening. Her thighs began to shake, her breathing was hard pants.

Blake's tongue slithered down her centre, swirling around her opening before sucking her juices into his mouth. Ava moaned loudly as his tongue thrust into her pussy.

"Oh!" she ground her hips against his tongue. "God!" she hissed, grounding against his mouth.

Blake grazed his teeth down the length of her pussy, slowly. His fingers digging into her ass cheeks as he held her in place. Swirling his tongue around her clit before sucking it into his mouth, hard. A deep pressure building inside of her had her moaning louder. His answering groan had her juices gathering at her opening a mere moment before his tongue swept them into his mouth over and over. Her orgasm was building quickly. Her hips moving of their own accord, her mouth open with moan after lustrous moan, her head snapped back.

"Cum. Now." Blake's harsh command had the liquid fire and heat swelling tightly, her pleasure expanding a second before she exploded on a loud scream. "Good girl." he groaned as her orgasm splashed against his chin and chest.

The long groan of pure satisfaction poured from him as he lapped up the copious amounts of liquid. Ava rode her orgasm until she collapsed back against the granite table. Tremors twitching through her muscles and her breath ragged as he stood to his full height. Those big hands gently lowering her legs back to the table. A shiver wracked her body as the cold hit her quivering thighs.

"Close your eyes." his voice was low and full desire. "Good girl." he whispered as she complied.

Her senses were instantly heightened, she heard his short bursts of breath and felt the deep throb pulsing through her body. Pleasure lighting every nerve ending, sparking through her veins. She heard his bare feet move against the granite floor, felt the absence of his body heat. Her fingers tingled as she moved them slightly against the smooth, cold table. Her breathing was still harsh with her orgasm.

"Getting impatient?" his voice startled her, his breath whispering over her neck. "Pinch your nipples, dirty girl." his tongue licked up to her jaw. A deep groan mingled with her moan as she pinched her nipples, arching her back. "Fucking beautiful." his lips lightly pressed against the corner of her mouth.

"Jesus." she hissed as warm liquid drizzled across her left nipple. The liquid hardening in the cool room, curving around her nipple. A low moan escaped her parted lips as more liquid laved her right one.

"Absolutely stunning." Blake whispered in her right ear. "Red, really suits you dirty girl." he continued, his teeth nipped her lobe.

She instantly missed his body heat as she heard his feet pad against the floor. Suddenly the room fell silent, she couldn't hear anything above her own laboured breaths. Fear spiked through her, quickening her heartbeat, and sweat slicked her palms. Her muscles locked into place as she tried to strain her hearing, tried to focus on her surroundings.

"Relax." his husked words had her instantly sighing in relief. "Open your legs wider." he continued, and she realised he was standing by her feet.

Warm liquid splashed against her engorged clit, making it throb deliciously in response. A cool stream of breath breezed across her pussy a moment before something cold slithered down her folds. She felt his warm knuckles grazing against her flesh before the cold entered her alongside two large fingers. Her breath caught in her throat as her thighs clenched and her pussy pulsed against the cold. More warm liquid drizzled against her left thigh. The coldness and his fingers left her.

"Oh god." she moaned, her hips bucked, the cold returning to her flesh. Harsh, wet coldness slithered up her folds. The wet coldness stopped against her pulsating clit, warm liquid drizzled across her stomach in a slow, deliberate trail back to her breasts. Her breathing was ragged, her heart thundering and her nerves sending sparks of pleasure through her body as the liquid solidified against her.

"Open your eyes." his command had her snapping open. Watching as he removed the small nub of an ice cube, his pupils were blown wide and his nostrils were flaring. "You're so fucking wet." he groaned out. His fingers pinched her clit, the slight crinkle sound of wax being removed as she moaned and bucked her hips.

Blake's hands curved around her thighs, roughly pulling until her ass to the edge of the table. His cock thrust deep inside her in one long, hard snap of his hips. His deep groan filled the room as his eyes travelled the length of her body.

Blake's finger trailed over the hardened wax on her stomach, slowly dragging his cock out, grazing the swollen spot inside her, causing the loud moan to escape before he slammed back inside her. Her breath left her in a whoosh at the impact. Her pussy clamped down hard and her eyes fluttered closed.

"Fuck!" he hissed out, his fingers still trailing up her body. His fingers pinched her nipples, the slight crinkle sound of wax being removed as she moaned and bucked her hips.

His hand gripped her throat, fingers flexing and her throat closing. Her pussy contracted, juices leaked from her before he slammed back in with a severity that had her thighs clamping around his hips. Blake slammed into her over and over again. Her screams were a muffled, harsh breath and blackness dotted the edge of her vision every time he bottomed out inside her.

The room was filled with combined moans and groans of pleasure, the sounds of their bodies meeting. Her orgasm was quickly building from every thrust of his thick, large cock. Her muscles clenched tightly, her body arched against the table, and fireworks exploded behind her eyelids as the dam broke and her orgasm crested. Her pussy gripped onto his cock tightly. Liquid rushed from her in hot splashes against his groin.

"My. Fucking. Dirty. Girl." Blake bit out and punctuated each word with a slam of his hips and buried himself as deep as he could, spilling hot jets of cum inside her. The grip on her throat would leave a bruise, as he stilled and let go of her abused throat. Their harsh breaths filling the room.

"Happy Birthday, Syn." Ava rasped through her sore throat, a small smile playing on her lips.

Chapter Thirty-Four

Ava laid on the plush sofa, her head in Blake's lap as he absent-mindedly combed his fingers through her hair. The television was playing the final instalment of 365 days movie. She loved spending time like this with Blake, it brought back her memories from the movie nights they'd already had.

"Baby girl." Blake paused the television as she turned to look up into those deep brown eyes, a smile playing on her lips. "Would you like to go away with me for the weekend?" he asked slowly, still combing his fingers through her hair, but she saw the slight flash of fear in his eyes.

"A whole weekend?" she clarified, to which he nodded and a large smile curved her lips. "With you?" he nodded again.

"Next weekend." he clarified, his eyes pinched in the corners as he waited for her answer.

"Where are we going?" Ava tried to sit up, but Blake wouldn't let her move. Excitement flowed through her at having him all to herself, free to roam together without fear of being seen. It was one of the things she wanted the most. She watched as his eyebrows drew together and his free hand rubbed against his jaw.

"The Manor." he almost whispered, and Ava's eyebrows rose.

"The Manor as in the country hotel?" she asked, remembering seeing the images James had once shown her mum of the hotel and it had been utterly beautiful. Surrounded by forests and lakes. Ivy clung to the front half of the building, which was over five floors. She'd never been, but she could imagine how nice it was if the well-kept grounds were anything to go by.

"Hmm." he nodded but yet, he still rubbed his jaw and Ava knew that was a nervous habit. "It's not a hotel, but my family home." he admitted sheepishly.

"What?" Ava swatted his hand away as she sat up. "You lived in the Manor?" she couldn't believe it, she'd always assumed it was a hotel.

"I did, but spent the majority of my time with Aunt Mavis and Katie." he clarified, tilting his head to the side. "Does that make a difference?" he asked, rubbing his thumb across his lower lip. Ava was flabbergasted. It wasn't everyday you find out that what you once thought was a hotel is actually a house with actual people living inside.

"No." she quickly confirmed, her hands landing on his shoulders as she straddled his hips. "It's just weird to think that it was a hotel and yet it isn't. You know?" Ava was rambling, and she knew it, but she really couldn't believe the stately home was his childhood home. He raised an eyebrow as a slow smile took over his mouth. "I mean, wow!" she breathed, her shoulders slumping in a long exhale.

"You okay there, baby girl?" he chuckled as Ava's cheeks flamed. "So is that a yes to the weekend away?" his hands rested against her hips, his thumbs brushing over the exposed skin of her waistband. Ava held up a finger as she took a breath.

"To meet your parents or will they not be there?" the moment the words were out, her teeth sunk into her bottom lip. She watched as his eyes lit up the deep brown and a sliver of caramel weaved through their depths.

"My parents will be there, along with a hundred or so guests." he answered carefully. "It's dad's seventieth birthday party, and I thought you might like to go." he shrugged one shoulder as if it was no big deal, but to her, it meant everything.

Meeting the parents and family friends.

Oh, good lord!

"I mean, yeah." Ava took a breath, nodding. "I'd love to go but what kind of dress will I need?" she was quickly thinking where she could get a dress that was fit for The Manor and something that wouldn't embarrass Blake.

"Wear the white one." he was deadly serious but Ava stared at him. "The one you wore for your birthday and our date." he continued, his eyes boring into hers. "I love that dress on you and on my bedroom floor." Ava blushed at his words.

"What will you wear?" Ava asked because she knew the tea dress she wore wasn't the type to wear to a party at a stately home.

"A shirt and pants." he sighed. "Look, that dress was stunning and perfect for the party." he was trying to make her feel better, but she wasn't certain. "That dress makes me want to rip it off of you, makes me so fucking hard I can hardly concentrate." he pulled her closer, their lips almost touching. "We'll see how many dark corners I can lure you into, lift that innocent skirt up and fuck you." his voice was pure liquid heat. "Don't forget those red fuck-me heels, I definitely want you in them." his grin turned wicked, pressing his lips to hers in a chaste kiss.

"You liked them, huh?" Ava's tone was teasing as she moved until her lips were against his ear. "I'll wear only them for you, sweetheart." she husked out, making him groan as he playfully swatted her ass. "I liked that." she admitted, cheeks tinting pink. She felt his cock twitch as his pupils dilated.

"You're killing me, Ava." he groaned against her lips, his forehead resting against hers. "We need to finish the movie before you have to go home."

"Remind me again why I can't stay?" Ava asked, her eyes sad as her fingers brushed through his hair.

"Trust me, I don't want you to go either, but we've both got work tomorrow and as much as I love fucking you, I need my rest." He brushed his lips against hers in a chaste kiss before pulling back.

"I know, I just don't like it." Ava pouted.

"Hmm, neither do I." Blake groaned as she ground her hips against his stiffening cock. His fingers flexing against her hips before he tightened his hold, stopping her from moving. "Let's finish the movie." He slid her off of his lap until she was nestled beside him.

Monday morning dawned with rain pelting against her bedroom window, a typical English autumn. Groaning as she flung the bedcovers back. She hated the rain, hated being at home, hated Mondays, and hated being away from Blake.

She'd left his home on Sunday evening after they'd shared dinner, with both of them needing to be up early for work, made sense. But she found that she didn't like being away from him. They only had a few days before they had the whole weekend together, away from her brother, and she couldn't be any happier. Especially because they'd be able to explore without fear of being seen. That's one of the main things she was beginning to despise. Hiding.

Ava – *Morning Blake, miss you xx*

She typed out a text before jumping in the shower. The hot water stinging the red marks on her breasts and stomach from the wax. Smiling as she remembered Blake rubbing an ointment into her skin after carefully washing her yesterday.

Wrapped in a towel, she checked her phone.

Blake - *Miss you too, baby girl xx*

Her smile was instant as she read the text, before quickly dressing for work and throwing her hair up in a messy bun, to stop it from frizzing in the heavy rain.

The school corridor was quiet as she carried her coffee towards the classroom, but the moment her hand gripped the handle footsteps came thundering towards her.

"Miss Ava!" the small voice shouted excitedly. Turning her smile bright as she saw George running towards her, his backpack banging against him and his dark hair whipping across his forehead.

"George! Good morning." She smiled, taking a sip of her coffee.

"My dad came!" he breathed out heavily as he skidded to a stop. "He came to my birthday party!" his smile was beaming and all dimples making her chest tighten.

"That's great!" she shared his enthusiasm as she pushed that niggling feeling to the back of her mind.

"Yeah! He was late but brought me the best presents ever!" he was practically bouncing on the spot.

"What did you get, George?" she asked around the rim of her coffee cup, taking a much needed sip.

"Dad got me a Spider-Man costume." his excitement was palpable and adorable. "Also some web shooters too!" his hands flew out mimicking Spider-Man, making her smile.

"Oh no way, that's awesome!"

"I know and he's promised me we can play any game I want tonight!" he clapped his hands excitedly. "He's coming home after work and I can't wait to see him."

"Well, that's great George." the pang in Ava's chest began to throb and that niggling feeling began to resurface but she again pushed it back. "What game are you going to play?"

"Monopoly!" he shouted, throwing his hands up. "Dad's so good at it but I've been practising." he puffed his small chest out triumphantly.

"Well, when I used to play with my dad, I used to buy all the railways first and then start with the reds, yellows and finally greens." she lowered her voice conspicuously. "And I always won." she watched his dark eyes widen and his infectious dimpled smile light up his whole face.

"That's what dad always does!" he cocked his head to the side, "do you know my dad?" it was the second time he'd asked her that question and she really hoped that she was lying to the little boy.

"No, I don't know him, but he sounds amazing." she gulped around the lump in her throat.

"Yeah, he's the best!"

"I'm glad you had a lovely birthday? George, but we best get to class." she turned to open the door at the same time the bell rung.

"Morning, Ava." Jones greeted as she took her seat beside his desk.

"Morning." she placed her nearly empty mug on his desk as her phone buzzed.

Blake - *I can't wait until Friday, have dinner with me? xx*

Ava - *Can't wait xx*

Ava's day had been extremely busy, and her feet were killing her. The anticipation of seeing Blake tonight for dinner had been her main focus of the entire day, and she couldn't wait to be wrapped in his arms, their lips exploring and hands groping. A smile graced her lips as she walked to her car, quickly checking her phone. Her eyebrows drew together, the smile instantly morphing into a frown as she read the test message she'd received.

Blake – *Sorry, baby girl, something's come up at work. See you Friday xx*

Her thoughts instantly going to George's conversation from this morning, his dad going home to play Monopoly. Her chest tightened, tears gathered in her eyes before she quickly blinked them back.

Could Blake be leading a double life?

Could Blake be George's father?

Fuck!

The drive home passed by in a blur, her mind racing with thoughts of Blake leading a double life, thoughts of her being a home wrecker, mistress and thoughts of her being unable to stay away from him. Knowing herself that after all these years she'd take anything the Blake offered her. Even if it was just the weekend.

The moment she walked into her bedroom, she felt like shit. Her chest hurt, her head hurt, and her fingers were clamped around her phone as she stared vacantly at the blank screen.

"Hey squirt." James's voice startled her from the doorway.

"James!" she almost screamed. "Stop sneaking up on me!" she chastised, her heart beating out of time.

"Where's the fun in that." he laughed, shaking his head at her narrowed eyes. "Got plans for the evening?" he continued as he came to sit on her bed. Ava was still rooted to the spot in the middle of her room, her phone still gripped in her hand.

"No." she quickly blinked back the tears that were beginning to form. "Why?" she asked, tearing her gaze away from the phone.

"Just wondered." James half shrugged, his hand rubbing the back of his neck. "Where's mystery man tonight?" his green eyes watched her carefully as she licked over her trembling lip.

"Busy with work." she cocked her head to the side as she watched her brother. "Why?"

"No reason, I just find it strange that you only see each other on a weekend." he scrubbed a hand down his face. "Listen, Ava..."

"No!" she shook her head, a surge of anger washing over her. "You listen to me, James. I am sick to death of you always trying to get information from me, why can't you just be happy for me?" she asked, her eyes narrowed on him.

"Because I don't want you to get hurt!" he shouted, throwing his hands in the air. "I wouldn't have to keep asking if you just told me who it was!" he continued, jumping to his feet and stalking towards her. "We've never had secrets between us before and I don't like it, Ava." the tips of his shoes touched hers as he stared down at her.

"Okay!" she shouted back. "You don't like secrets, well, tough!" she took a step back. "I've already told you, once it's serious I will let you know!" her voice was higher, shriller with every word she shouted.

"Fuck sake, Ava!" James blared. "Just fucking tell me who it is!" he took another step forward, and she knew what he was doing. Knew he was trying to intimidate her into confessing.

"No!" Ava took another step back. "It's my life, not yours and my mistakes to make!" she stopped dead, her teeth clamping on her bottom lip as James snarled at her slip up.

"So he's fucking married?" his voice turned low, his eyes narrowed and his body trembling with rage. "I thought you were better than that, Ava." he shook his head sadly as hurt flashed in his eyes. Ava knew he was remembering catching his wife fucking another man and knew he was reliving the pain he suffered through.

"He's not married." the fight had been sucked out of her as she slumped her shoulders.

"How do you know?" he asked, taking a step away from her.

"Because, I've known him for a while." she admitted, her voice trembled slightly. *His* name on the tip of her tongue but she knew that she couldn't tell James the truth.

"It better not be that fucking kid who had his hands on you." James bit out, his hand ruffling his hair.

"Nathan?" she asked, cocking her head to the side as he nodded. "No, it isn't." she licked over her lips. "It's someone from work, that's why we don't see each other during the week." she lied, her chest aching all over again. "But I am going away this weekend with him." James raised his eyebrows in surprise.

"So it is serious then?" the hurt in his voice almost made her tell him the truth.

"No, it's just a fun weekend away." her smile was small.

"Okay, I'll leave it for now." James cleared his throat. "I just want what's best for you, squirt." he swallowed thickly. "You're all I have left and I want to protect you." he squeezed her shoulder before turning on his heel.

"Right back at you." Ava tried giving him a small smile but she couldn't. She hated lying to James, hated the way it made her feel, but she had no choice.

Chapter Thirty-Five

Ava had been snuggled into the plush interior of Blake's car, his hand resting against her thigh for the better part of an hour. The street lights flickering through the car as they passed gave Ava time to settle down. The morning had been a little overwhelming, James had been up early wanting to ensure that she set off safely. Ava trying to sneak out of the house without James noticing to eventually, settling on a lie that she needed to fill her car up before they could set off for the weekend. Luckily, it worked, and she left to drive across town to Blake's home. They decided to hide her car in the garage as a precaution, but all it had done was fry her nerves.

It didn't help that she hadn't slept much this week, was constantly thinking over everything from George being so excited to see his dad again, to the run down she'd got off last night when he'd sent a quick message to let her know what time they needed to set off. She was trying to piece everything together, trying to convince herself that Blake wasn't leading a double life, trying to convince herself that she wasn't his mistress. But all that had happened was create questions. Questions she was desperate for answers, but also frightened about what she'd learn.

"You've been quiet this morning." Blake's deep rumble filled the car, pulling Ava out of her tangled thoughts. "Everything okay?" he asked, glancing at her briefly before turning back to the road.

"Yeah, everything's okay." she lied, her fingers threaded through his, resting on her thigh. "I didn't sleep much."

she admitted, glancing as he furrowed his brow. "Nervous, I guess." she nodded, flicking her gaze to the passing scenery.

"What have you to be nervous about, baby girl?" he asked, squeezing her hand.

"Oh, I don't know." she looked at his profile with a soft smile on her face. "Meeting your parents," she laughed as he shook his head.

Finding out I'm your mistress.

"You've nothing to be nervous about where they are concerned." his tone was serious and his eyes pinched at the corners.

"So you say, but do they even know that you're bringing a date?" she asked, tilting her head.

"They know I'm bringing someone, yes." he spoke slowly, letting go of her hand and she immediately felt like he was pulling away from her. "I thought it be best to not surprise them." he continued, both hands on the steering wheel and his eyes on the road.

"Oh, well, that's good." Ava felt the absence of his hand, making her feel a little cold. She watched as the scenery slowed down, watched as the car moved over into a little off the road cut out surrounded by trees with the grey clouds blanketing them in a shroud of darkness. "Blake -" she turned, but the door shut and he was striding around the car, yanking her door open before kneeling in the dirt.

"I don't want you to be nervous." his voice low as his hands cupped her cheeks. "It's just a party." his lips brushed against hers lightly. "We'll barely see my parents this weekend." his tongue traced across her lips, slowly. Her breath hitched in the back of her throat. "So tell me, baby girl, how many orgasms do you need?" his pupils dilated, his lips moved across hers tenderly.

Blake's hand caressed her face, his thumb smoothing the delicate path across her cheek until he'd cupped the back of her neck. Pulling her closer than his lips devoured hers in a heated exchange. His other hand trailed down her neck, fingers grazing her collarbone. His tongue twining with hers, swallowing every moan he pulled from her. Ava arched into him as his hand skimmed the side of her breast, his thumb moving over her hardened nipple.

"Blake." Ava breathed out as his lips skimmed her jaw. "Someone might see." her eyes fluttered closed, his teeth nipping her earlobe.

"Hmm, they just might." he whispered into her ear. "They might just see me worshipping your delectable pussy." his hand unbuttoned her jeans. "Lift up, baby girl." he continued, yanking her jeans and panties in one until they reached her knees. "Let's see how wet you are." his tongue traced the shell of her ear. Her eyes rolled as he thrust two fingers inside of her. Her pussy rippling around his fingers, her juices coating them. "Always so ready for me." he curled his fingers inside her.

"Fuck!" Ava moaned as her hips bucked. His lips trailing the length of her neck. His fingers stroking, pressing, releasing until she felt the tightening deep within her. "Blake." she moaned louder, her thighs shaking. "Stop, I'm going to..." her hips undulated against his fingers.

"You want to cum on my finger, face or cock." he husked out, lips brushing against her ear. "Either way, you are cumming, baby girl. It's your choice."

"Oh, fuck!" Ava ground out. "Cock." she gasped, her chest heaving with panting breaths.

"You want to meet my parents with my cum dripping out of you." he whispered, removing his fingers. "You are a dirty fucking girl." he unbuttoned his pants, shoving them until his cock sprung free and they bunched around his ankles.

His large hands gripped her legs against his chest and bending forward until his cock nudged her entrance. Her juices coating the tip before he thrust deep inside, dragging exquisitely against her inner walls. A deep moan fell from her parted lips. Her heart thundering against her chest, her nerve endings firing off sparks of pleasure through her body as he reared back before slamming forward relentlessly.

"You're so fucking tight." he groaned, slamming back into her.

His pace was fast, fierce, and relentless as he pounded into her. Her pussy fluttered, his cock throbbed and his teeth clamped down on his lip. The tight grip on his cock was like a vise as he bottomed out. Her pussy contracted, juices leaked from her as she bucked against him. Blake slammed back into her over and over.

Their combined moans and groans of pleasure, the sounds of their bodies meeting in wet slaps of skin against skin, were mixed with the sounds of trees rustling, birds chirping and a lone car in the distance. Her body was careening towards an explosion. White hot waves overtook her body, her muscles clenched tightly, her head thrown back as the dam broke and her orgasm crested in arc after arc of pleasure.

"Blake!" she screamed as her pussy gripped onto his cock tightly. Liquid rushed from her in hot splashes against his groin.

"Fuck me, baby girl!" Blake bit out and punctuated each word with a slam of his hips and buried himself as deep as he could, spilling hot jets of cum inside her. His breathing ragged, his heart pounding and sweat coating his forehead. He didn't want to move, but the car was quickly getting closer. "Someone's coming, baby girl." Blake pulled out of her in a hiss.

Ava's eyes were wide, her chest heaving with panting breaths and her legs felt like jelly, but as Blake's words registered, she could hear the car getting closer. She quickly righted her clothes at the same time as Blake. Her face flushed with pleasure, quickly deepened in colour as the car slowed.

"Everything okay?" the unfamiliar, friendly voice called out.

"Yes, my girl gets travel sick." Blake called back with his lips twitching as he glanced at Ava. "We're just going to set back off." he continued, shoving his hands in his pants pockets.

"As long as everything's okay, you have a nice day now." with that, the car set off again.

"Oh god, that was close." Ava let out the breath she was holding.

"Do you feel better now?" Blake asked as she settled back. "Or do you need another orgasm?" he smirked, raising one eyebrow as he stared at her.

"I'm okay." she nodded, teeth grazing along her bottom lip. "For now." she added, fastening her seatbelt.

"Trust me," Blake's voice was rough as he leaned into the car. "When I'm done with you this weekend, you won't be able to walk straight." his smile was wicked before straightening. Ava's blood was on fire at the wicked promise of his words.

Gravel crunched under the tyres of the car, trees and shrubbery lined the curvature of the driveway. Ava's pulse quickened as The Manor came into view. The five story building looming in the distance. Ivy climbing the building, like an enchanted creature. It was even more stunning in person than the pictures she'd seen. From it sits dark wood Georgian windows, the thick wooden door and large, elaborate metal hinges set against pure Yorkshire stone.

The closer the car came to the Manor the more Ava's pulse quickened and her palms dampened as she gulped around the sudden lump in her throat.

"It's beautiful." Ava whispered as she glance at Blake. His jaw was tight and his knuckles were white on the steering wheel. "Are you okay?" she asked, concern lacing her words and marring her expression. The silence stretched out before them as Blake navigated the winding driveway and Ava wasn't certain if he was going to answer her. She reached out a hand to rest it on his forearm. "Hey, you okay?" Ava tried again as the car slowed to a stop.

"It's been a long time since I was back here." Blake muttered, almost to himself, as his grip lessened on the steering wheel. "I forgot how beautiful it was too." those liquid pools of chocolate snared her with a tilt of his perfect lips.

Ava schooled her features, trying not to show the hurt at his obvious lie. Something was bothering him, and yet he didn't want to talk to her. He wanted to lie directly to her face. Biting back the sigh which threatened to fall from her lips, she dropped her hand back into her lap and stared directly at him.

"Do you need another orgasm, Syn?" her voice was low as she raised an eyebrow at him. His lips pulled into a smouldering smile, his dimples appearing beneath the stubble.

"With you, always." his voice had lowered an octave as his hand cupped her cheek briefly. "But let's meet the parents first." he continued before stepping out of the car.

The moment Ava joined, Blake threaded their fingers together a moment before the front door opened, revealing a short, stout man in his early sixties with a dour expression etched onto his face that had Ava swallowing around the lump in her throat.

"Doctor Synclair." the man greeted with a stiff voice.

"Theodore." Blake gave a curt nod as he strode past into the home, pulling Ava behind him. "This is Ava Asherton, my guest this weekend." Blake finished with a coldness to his tone Ava hadn't heard before nor did she expect to be called a guest by the man she was hopelessly in love with. The bite of his words stung her, but she tried to smoother it down.

"Of course, Doctor Synclair." Theodore nodded before turning that dour look on her. "Welcome, Ms Asherton." he bowed slightly, taking the keys from Blake's outstretched hand. "Usual room, Doctor Synclair?"

"No." Blake refused to meet her eyes as his back stiffened. "The east wing." Theodore's eyes widened slightly before he bowed.

"Certainly, sir." was all he said before leaving them in the grand foyer and Ava briefly wondered what the exchange was about. Let alone the east *fucking* wing.

A large crystal chandelier suspended from the double height ceiling, highlighting the sweeping staircase. The hard oak wood floors were littered with area rugs in pale greens and golds matching the walls. Gold gilded frames adorned the walls with oil paintings, which made the foyer look like the stately home that it was. Ava sucked in a breath as her eyes scanned the room, her mouth opening slightly.

"Oh, wow!" Ava breathed. "I bet these walls could tell some tales." She laughed as she caught Blake's horrified expression.

"I hope not, baby girl." he shuddered. "I dread to think of what they might say." his eyes twinkled in mischief as he lowered his mouth to her ear. "I wonder what they'd say after this weekend." he whispered, his hand gripping her ass cheek before lacing their fingers together again. Ava's blush was instant along with her stomach clenching deliciously.

"Is that how you treat all *guests*, Doctor Sinclair." she couldn't help letting the hurt seep into her words.

Blake's hand tightened around hers as his breath stuttered out but he didn't make comment as he began navigating the long hallways until they reached two solid wooden doors that opened into an elaborate drawing room. All pale yellow, crushed blue velvet and gold gilded mirrors and oil paintings. The furnishings were solid oak, highly polished with thick cushions which looked as though you'd melt into them. Two pairs of dark brown eyes stared at Ava curiously as she tried to hide behind Blake.

"Mum, Dad." Blake's tone was hard and his posture stiff.

"Blake, honey." an elderly lady with grey coiffed hair stood, her thin arms stretched out away from the tailored tweed suit she wore. Blake let go of Ava's hand to embrace his mum in a tight hug. "It's good to finally have you back home." she kept her hands on his arms as she looked at him with tears in her eyes. "What's it been five years, darling don't do that again." she chided with a smile on her face.

"Marion, let the boy go." an elderly man with thick grey hair smiled, shaking his head. "You're embarrassing him, in front of this lovely young lady." he smiled, extending a hand to Ava. "I'm Winston Sinclair, it's lovely to meet you." Ava took his hand in a firm shake.

"Ava." she smiled, letting go of his hand, moving her head to the side as she saw the striking resemblance. Like father, like son had never been truer and the sudden image of George flashed in her mind, almost stealing her breath.

"Asherton." Blake clapped his dad on the shoulder, a smile on his face before he pulled him into a hug.

"Is she any relation to that nice boy, James?" Marion asked, a warm smile lighting up her face. Ava watched Blake stiffen even more than he turned towards his mum.

"Yeah." Blake cleared his throat. "This is James's sister." Blake's arm gripped her fiercely and pulled her into his side, almost possessively.

"Oh, how wonderful." Marion clapped her hands delighted. "You are such a pretty little thing." she cooed, smiling brighter than before. "It's lovely to meet you."

"Likewise." Ava smiled, still nestled against Blake's hard body. "Thank you for having me as your guest this weekend."

"Nonsense." Marion swatted her hand in front of her. "As Blake's friend, you are always welcome." Ava sucked in a sharp breath at hearing *friend,* fall from his mum's lips.

"Mum." Blake's tone was harder than steel. "Can we not." he snapped, raising his eyebrows.

"Marion." Winston warned, rubbing his hand up and down Marion's arm in a comforting gesture. "Don't speak to your mother like that." he snapped, eyes blazing a fire Ava had seen more than once in Blake's eyes. "We need a nice family weekend." the warning at Blake wasn't lost on Ava.

"Oh, honey, would you be joining us for lunch?" Marion asked tentatively.

"Not today, we've got plans." his fingers flexed against her hip. "Dinner though, mum." Ava watched worry flash in her eyes before looking at Winston.

"I don't think that would be wise." Winston's voice was a little stern, which had Ava furrowing her brows and her pulse spiking at the instant thought that they didn't really like her. "The Appleton's will be in attendance this evening."

Ava didn't think it was possible for Blake to get any stiffer, but she was wrong and she also felt an almost unbearable heat pour from his body, a moment before the hand clamped to her hip began trembling.

"It's okay, Blake." her voice was gentle as she looked up at him. "We can stay for lunch." her smile was small and encouraging as their eyes met and the torture she saw in them cracked her heart.

"No." Blake shook his head. "Not today, Sunday, before we leave." he addressed his parents before hastily pulling her from the room.

Chapter Thirty-Six

The east wing was much like the foyer and long hallways. All wooden doors, elaborate gilded frames and luxurious decorations. The last wooden door in the long hallway opened up to reveal the largest bedroom she'd ever seen in her life. All dark wood and blues with the walls adorned with Blake's accomplishments, a picture of him at his university gradation stood between his parents with the sun shining down on them. It was a far cry from the home he lived in now, with nothing on the walls, nothing personal on show for anyone to see. But here, it was like she could glimpse into Blake's past life.

Turning, her gaze swept around the room, spotting gold and silver trophies which had her head cocking to the side a moment before she stepped towards them. The need in her to read the inscriptions, but the warm grip on her wrist had her stopping in her tracks.

"I'd like to tell you something." Blake's voice was low in the quiet room as he pulled until her back collided with his front. A whoosh of air knocked from her lungs and then his arms banded around her. His stubble grazing her cheek. "This was my bedroom, growing up." he sighed before his chest expanded against her back on a deep inhale and his arms tightened around her waist. "I was stood in this very spot when I decided that I wanted to be a doctor."

Ava's pulse spiked and her mind whirled as she realised that he was sharing a part of himself with her and she couldn't stop her heart from swelling at the reality of this moment. She didn't move or breath too harshly for fear that he would stop.

"I remember the day like it was yesterday." he continued, his voice still low. "I had retreated here after being told that my grandfather had been diagnosed with esophageal cancer." he sucked in a deep breath. "I was devastated and angry that there was nothing his doctors could do. Angry that no amount of money could solve the problem." his lips lightly touched her cheek as his breath stuttered. "I was also too young to understand just how little time I'd have with him." his arms tightened ever so slightly. "I was eight years old when I decided that I wanted to be a doctor, wanted to help people and I wanted to diagnose people before it became too late."

"Were you close with your grandfather?" she whispered into the silence, praying that he'd continue.

"Yeah." he breathed out, his stubble grazing against her skin as he moved his lips to her neck, pressing lightly over her raised pulse. "He taught me a lot of things but it was his sense of humour, the kind that had be laughing so carefree and he always had a glint of mischief in his eyes that used to drive my grandmother to insanity at times." she could feel his mouth stretch in a small smile. "After he died, the anger returned, and, and I didn't know how to handle it, didn't really know what to do with myself and my parents were the exact same." he sighed, long and hard. "I went off the rails for a little while, caused fights at school, began vandalising anything I could get my hands on, until I found a little hidden gem on the estate." he turned her effortlessly in his arms until his dark gaze locked with hers. "A place I'd like to take you, to share with you." his lips tipped in a smile.

"I'd like that." she admitted, her hand pressing lightly against his chest and she delighted in the shudder that rippled his muscles across his torso.

The dark grey clouds blanketed the sky with an almost ominous presence. Blake's hand gripped hers as they walked along a rough path with tree roots weaving through the long grass. Trees surrounded them as the cold, late September air whipped against her cheeks. The silence was comfortable, but it didn't stop her mind from racing with thoughts of what he wanted to show her, thoughts of what he'd already shared with her and thoughts of what he was going to share.

The long disused path slowly opened up to a large clearing dotted with wildflowers, shrubs and trees, a natural lake which was overgrown dominated the area. The low sounds of water rippling against the reeds greeted them, as Blake slowed his pace as they neared the water's edge.

"It's lovely and peaceful here." Ava breathed out as she looked across the water, squeezing his hand. "I bet in summer with all the flowers in bloom would be absolutely breathtaking." she turned slightly to see his smile and his eyes trained on her.

"I'd like to see you bathed in the sunlight laid among the flowers." he admitted with a wicked smirk as her breath hitched in the back of her throat. "No one around to bother us, secluded here I wonder how loud I could make you scream." he pulled her to his body, his free hand instantly cupping her jaw and his thumb dancing across her flushed cheek.

Blake's rich, dark eyes stared into hers, time stretched out ahead of them until her heart was beating frantically in her chest and her breathing was laboured as her lips parted slightly. Her eyes tracked the slow swipe of his tongue across his lower lip, her hand felt his heart thud hard against her palm. His lips brushed against hers in a delicate, slow caress. Something inside of her snapped, swelled as the full staggering love she felt for this man seeped into every fibre of her being.

Ava's tongue slowly swept through his mouth, twining with his. The low moans which escaped as Blake deepened the kiss, one hand still on her jaw and the other still entwined with hers. She felt his heartbeat quicken against her palm with every delicately slow caress of their mouths together.

Blake pulled away, his forehead resting against hers. Their harsh breaths mingling in the close confines and for long moments they stood unmoving, breathing in each other until their heartbeats slowed and their breathing returned to normal.

"This right here." Blake whispered, his forehead still resting against hers and his hand still cupping her jaw. "Is where I found solace in one of the darkest times I'd ever lived through." his voice wavered and his eyes swirled with emotion. "Until I found this place, I didn't know how to quiet the anger, didn't know how to deal with the pain inside of me." he continued in the low whisper. "Now, I want to change the memories and replace them with images of you in my favourite places." the admission had tears pricking the back of her eyes and her stomach to flutter. She gently slid her hand up over his chest until she delicately cupped his cheek.

"Blake, I want to share everything with you too." she whispered as her lips curved slightly. "I love you so much it hurts." she continued in a low whisper. She watched his pupils dilate, she felt his jaw tense before he took a step back. His hands falling from her as he took another step away and when her hand fell from his cheek, she saw the wild look in his eyes. A wildness that bordered on fright.

"We need to get back." his voice was rough and hard as he spun on his heel.

Ava's shoulders slumped, her heart thumped out of time with trepidation as she watched his purposeful strides as he walked away from her. Tears filled her eyes, but she couldn't let them fall, nor could she stay in this beautiful, tranquil place. She didn't want to get lost making her way back to the manor, but she also didn't want to let Blake retreat away from her, didn't want him to get stuck inside his head and she certainly didn't want to give him time to leave her. Those were the thoughts that had her feet thundering against the long grass, eating up the distance between them quickly.

"Blake!" she called out just as her hand reached for his, stopping him in his tracks. "Don't walk away from me." her voice gentle as she entwined their fingers. She watched his back stiffen as his fingers flexed against hers in a hard squeeze.

"We're going to be late." he muttered, tugging her hand until she was standing beside him. "I want to take you for dinner." his voice was rough, but the hardness had left.

"Okay, just don't leave me." she whispered, risking a glance at his profile catching the brief nod before they navigated the hidden path towards the manor.

The small country restaurant had low ambient and Yorkshire stone walls with a large roaring open fire dousing in the room with a heat that settled into Ava's bones, erasing the cold from the confession of her feelings. Blake sat opposite her with his back to the room, the dark green jumper wrapping around his biceps deliciously. The rich darkness of his eyes reflected the orange flames from the fire as he looked at her. His elbows resting on the table and a small smile on his lips made him look calm. But Ava saw his pulse thumping in his throat, watched him swallow thickly on more than one occasion since they'd sat down together.

"This is a hidden gem." Ava spoke softly, breaking the silence that had descended since they had left the manor.

"Hmm." the small tumbler was perched against his sinful mouth as he hummed. "My grandfather owned this place." he sat the glass back on the table. "He always said that after his first date with grandmother, he knew that he'd buy it one day." Blake smiled at the memory.

"Wow." Ava's eyes widened slightly. "So the Synclair's buy places as declarations?" she purposely left *love* out of her question. Taking a sip of the white wine, her eyes watching his lips spread into a warm smile, his dimples popping out beneath the dark stubble.

"Something like that." he admitted, his voice low.

"Well, I'm glad that it's still open." her eyes scanned the room, landing on an utterly beautiful blonde woman with a scowl on her face, her green eyes watching them and she instantly felt uncomfortable.

"Yeah, it's been a long time since I was last here." his voice brought her attention back to him, but she couldn't shake the uneasiness from the stunning blonde's intense stare. "Are you okay?" he asked, his brows furrowing. She nodded, his hand gripped hers across the table. "You don't look okay, tell me what's wrong." he urged, his lips in a thin line as his eyes bore into hers.

"It's that..." she licked over her lips, her eyes landing on the stunning blonde briefly before locking eyes with Blake. "There's a woman glaring at us." she whispered.

The moment the words were out of her mouth, she felt Blake tense and her palms grew damp the moment he cast a glance over his shoulder. She watched the muscle in his jaw begin to tick rapidly and the tremor began in his hands. Ava squeezed his hand gently and their eyes collided, but what she saw in their depths was a torture she didn't understand.

Was she an ex-girlfriend?

"Let's go." Blake muttered as he stood abruptly, shoving his hands into his pockets.

"Okay." Ava breathed out as she stood, smoothing the pale pink jumper over her stomach before reaching for Blake, but he quickly sidestepped her and strode from the restaurant.

Who the hell is she?

What does she mean to Blake?

The moment she settled into the warm confines of his Aston Martin, she couldn't keep the trepidation from seeping into her bones as she watched an almost haunted look take over his eyes, watched as he retreated into his head. She'd only ever seen this look on his face once before and he'd cut all contact with her. She didn't want that to happen again, but deep inside of her, Ava knew that after this weekend he'd cut all contact with her again. She could tell by the way he pulled away from her, could tell in the hard set of his jaw and the white knuckles against the steering wheel.

"Who was that woman?" Ava shocked herself as she voiced her own question out loud in the confines of the car. The silence that followed the question was deafening and soul crushing. Her teeth clamped against her bottom lip and her fingers clasped together as she realised that he wasn't going to answer her. She looked at the dark passing scenery, spindly arms of the trees hanging over the country lane reminding her of claws in the darkness.

"A family friend." Blake gritted out into the silence, startling her. She turned to look at his profile cast in shadows, waiting for him to continue, but as the tires hit gravel and the car snaked along the driveway, she realised that he wasn't going to say anything else.

Sighing, she unclipped the seatbelt the moment the car came to an abrupt halt and threw her door open. She didn't look behind her, nor did she slow her steps as she stalked past the ageing butler who'd ceremoniously opened the door with a flourish. She didn't even acknowledge the *good evening* as she practically ran to his bedroom.

Chapter Thirty-Seven

Blake's powerful, purposeful strides ate the distance Ava had put between them. His eyes tracking the delectable, rounded ass in those skintight jeans she'd worn to torture him. That he was sure of, but he could hear the slight hitching of her breath as she raced away from him and he knew that she was on the verge of tears. Tears he had caused, again.

"Fuck!" he hissed low in the silent halls of his family home.

His hand gripped the solid balustrade which he used to propel himself up the stairs, two at time until he reached the long hallway that led to his bedroom. His eyes once again watching Ava's ass, making him groan in the back of his throat.

"Stop!" he barked the command a second before she reached for the door handle. Breathing a sigh of relief as she stopped dead in her tracks, he stalked towards her. The riot zapping through every muscle, fibre of his being. The riot of her running away from him, of her being upset because of him.

Blake's hand gripped her cold, shaking one as he pushed the door open before slamming it shut behind her. His eyes pinched and his chest tightened as she sagged against the door, trying to pull her hand from his grip without success.

"Let me go." Ava muttered, hurt lacing her words. He watched as she lowered her gaze to the floor, watched her bottom lip tremble slightly in the darkness of the room.

"No." his voice low and his fingers gripped her chin, tilting her head until he was looking directly into her watery green eyes.

"I'm never letting you go." he whispered, trailing his fingers from her chin to the back of her neck. His forehead resting against hers as he breathed in deeply, harshly. The scent of her perfume all light floral and sweet. "I need you, baby girl."

Blake leaned in a fraction of an inch, almost uncertain, before their lips touched slowly together. His large hand moved from her neck in a featherlight touch to her collarbone, raising goosebumps in their wake until he cupped her breast. Her hardened nipple beneath the jumper grazed against his thumb once, twice as a moan escaped her lips. He trailed his lips slowly along her jaw, down her throat, before clamping around her clothed nipple. Ava arched her back, a low gasp falling from her lips.

Another gasp poured from her parted lips as he applied slightly more pressure on her clothed nipple. His fingers gripping the bottom of her jumper, slowly inching it over her flesh. Her stomach rippling, his knuckles grazing the soft skin. His breath caught in his throat as he exposed her to his gaze. The moment his eyes landed on the white lace bra he groaned deep in the back of his throat.

"Lift your arms up." he rasped out. His pulse throbbing wildly as she complied. "Good girl." in on fluid movement the jumper was off, discarded on the floor.

Blake's lips brushed against her jaw, a gasp left her lips as he continued running his lips across her soft flesh until he reached her ear. Flicking his tongue against the lobe she arched into him, a low moan filled the air between them. His heart thudded hard against his ribcage, his hands threatened to tremble as they glided over the curve of her back.

Lips blazing down her throat, he flicked the clasp of her bra open and with excruciating slowness he dragged the strap down her shoulder until her breast was bare before him. The warm wetness of his tongue caused Ava to gasp, shudder and moan all at the same time as he laved her bare nipple in slow strokes. She was absolutely delicious. The taste of purity delighted his taste buds, sucking the tight nipple into his mouth. Groaning low, his tongue swirling, his mouth sucking elicited the most sinful moan from her lips. His aching cock was raging and leaking into his boxers, begging to be freed, begging to be buried deep within her but he wanted to take it slow. Draw out her pleasure and delight his taste buds only her skin could offer.

His lips brushed against hers as his left hand, just as slowly as the right, dragged the strap of her bra down her shoulder and both her breasts were bare to him. His hands blazed a slow, torturous trail of heat down her sides, over the flair of her hips until his warm palms touched her perfectly rounded ass. His lips not leaving hers as he slowly gripped the back of her thighs and lifted her in one fluid movement.

Blake gently laid her on the large bed, the cool deep blue sheets framing her pale skin. Watching her eyes darken with desire as she shamelessly tracked his rushed movements, eye-fucking him as his clothes were discarded in a heap on the floor. He loved her eye-fucking him, loved the way her pupils dilated, the way her tongue darted across her lips as if she couldn't wait to taste him. Loved the way her chest heaved as her gaze bounced over every muscle he possessed.

Pressing his lips to her stomach, his fingers snapped open the button on her jeans, the tear of the zip loud in the silent room and then he was slowly dragging them off of her. Exposing every delectable inch of her to his greedy gaze. His tongue darted out across and ran across his lips. The pure, innocent scent of her arousal made his mouth water and his chest to tighten almost painfully.

Blake gently pulled her thighs apart, hooking her legs around his waist. The heat from her pussy almost seared him, making his cock throb deep and hard in response. Brushing his lips against hers. His hands gently cupped her breasts, his thumbs grazing over her nipples. Ava's breaths were almost panting and her back arched off of the bed as the tip of his throbbing cock nudged her wet entrance.

"Eyes on me, baby girl." his voice was husky and low causing a moan to tumble from her lips as she snapped her eyes to his. "I want to see how good you take my cock into that sweet pussy of yours." his words and husky tone had her moaning again.

"Please." Ava whimpered as he sunk an inch into her tight heat. Her hips moving towards his, trying to gain more of him to no avail. She panted, grinding her hips again until he pushed another inch inside.

A hiss leaving his mouth as her pussy tried to clamp around him. Tried to pull him deeper inside of her. He loved how tight she was, how responsive she was and he loved the sounds she made as he slowly, tortiously sunk into her, inch by inch until he was deep inside of her.

Gliding his hands down her arms, feeling the goosebumps raising on her skin until he entwined their fingers together above her head. His lids were hooded as he watched hers roll, fluttering closed. Brushing their lips together, his tongue slowly swept through her mouth, twining with hers as he began a slow, tortuous decent of his hips until the tip was at her entrance again before he slowly eased back into her.

There was no rush, only slow, deep thrusts. Their lips still sealed together, languidly moving in sync with his deep thrusts. Their hearts beating in time. Two bodies writhing together.

The slow burn that had been building inside of him tingled down his spine, his balls drawing up close to his body. He felt her thighs tremble, their lips began moving quicker as her pussy clenched harshly against his cock. Milking, sucking and fucking perfect. Their thrusts turned deeper, harder as they chased their orgasms.

One more deep thrust had them both careening over the edge, white sparks danced across his closed eyelids, Ava arched her back off of the bed and the loudest moan ripped from her throat. Hot, wet splashes hit his groin and he couldn't hold back. Erupting deep inside of her trembling, shaking body. The deep guttural moan ripped from his throat as he pulsed repeatedly deep inside of her.

Resting his damp forehead against hers, a slow smile curving his lips as their harsh breaths mingled together. Slow, tingling aftershocks had his legs feeling numb. His forearms resting on either side of her head as he held his weight off of her a moment before he brushed his lips across hers in the softest of caresses.

"Don't walk away from me again." he whispered, wrapping his arms around her rolling onto his back and taking her with him. Her head resting on his chest and her thigh draped across his.

"Then don't shut me out, Blake." her voice trembled in the darkness, making him squeeze his eyes closed. The deep ache in his chest intense and absolutely terrifying him.

"I promise." he whispered back, tightening his hold on her as he tried to keep his mind quiet. Tried to keep the voices in his head at bay, tried to stop the tremor in his hands and certainly tried to stop his breathing from becoming too fast, too shallow.

Squeezing his eyes shut, dragging a deep breath in before slowly letting it out. Concentrating on Ava's deep, heavy breathing and her delicate palm against his chest lulled him to sleep.

In the deathly silent and pitch dark bedroom, Blake's arm

tightened around Ava's waist, pulling her closer to his warm body. The bed covers bunched at their waists. His lips ghosted across her neck, her delectable, plump ass pressed against his hard cock. Her breathing deep and heavy, still lost in sleep and her words were all his mind could focus on.

Words that had pulled him from slumber. Words that had caused a fine sheen of sweat to coat his forehead and the back of his neck. Words that made his heart beat out of time and words that caused terror to take root deep inside of him.

"I love you, so much it hurts."

His heart pounded painfully against his rib cage, his hand tucked between her perfect breasts. He wanted to wake up like this, with her in his arms every day. His eyes squeezed shut, his lips pressed against her pulse as his reality crashed around him.

He knew this couldn't be his reality, laid with Ava like this in the early hours of the morning. Tucked together, no matter how perfect they fit. His lips brushed against her ear, delighting in the way she shivered even in sleep.

"I can't ever let you go." he whispered, lips grazing against her neck. "I'm an addict when it comes to you baby girl, I can't get enough of you." tears welled in his eyes, his chest swelled with the deep, terrifying ache at his admission.

An admission he had no right in speaking, which was why he only did so whilst she was asleep, in his arms where she was supposed to be. But he knew soon he'd have to face his reality. Knew that the moment he did that he would lose Ava for good.

"Please don't hurt me." his words were a whispered, choked plea before he squeezed his eyes shut and tried to drift back off to sleep.

Chapter Thirty-Eight

Ava stood staring at herself in the full-length mirror of the bathroom. Her hands smoothing down a few stray hairs as her mind wandered back to yesterday. To Blake sharing a little insight into his grandfather's death and how he'd coped afterward. Then her mind wandered to where she'd messed up and confessed just what she feels for him. To his reaction which wasn't surprising but what did surprise her was his whispered words after a tense dinner.

"I'm never letting you go."

She tried not to think of the stunning blonde in the restaurant, tried not to think about the way Blake changed, the way he closed himself off. Instead, she thought about the way he'd made her feel precious, wanted as he'd stripped her and made love to her without any rush or separation between them. It was the first time he'd taken her slowly, the first time he hadn't given in to his own desires, the first time he hadn't been rough with her. Whilst she craved that side of him, last night opened up a whole new side to him and gave her a glimpse into how he felt about her without the need for words.

A small smile tugged at her lips, her pulse beating a little faster than her hazel eyes critically assessed the way she'd coiled her hair in a half dutch-braid, half loose bun at the nape of her neck with curled tendrils framing her face. Her make-up was a light coating of mascara and cherry red lips to match her shoes and clutch bag. It was the first time she'd opted for red lips, but with Blake telling her how much she suits the colour, she thought that she'd step out of her comfort zone. The white tea dress which she had worn for both her birthday meal and their first official date still fit perfectly. The wide straps covering most of her shoulders, the bodice tightly encased her breasts, pushing them towards the low square neckline, at the waist the skirt flared in pleats to her knee. The diamond cluster pendent hung delicately from her throat and the diamond tennis bracelet sparkled every time she moved her wrist.

"Hmm." Blake hummed as their eyes locked in the mirror as he leaned against the door frame. His hands shoved in his black pants pockets. His muscular arms straining against the deep blue dress shirt. The first two buttons open, exposing the tawny skin and thick neck. His pupils dilating as they slowly trailed across her body. "I think you're secretly wanting me to sneak you off into as many dark corners as I can find." his voice dropped an octave as he pushed off of the door and stalked towards her. "Wanting me to lift this innocent skirt up and fuck you raw." his eyes blazed and his voice was pure liquid. His hands skimming up her bare thighs.

"Oh god." she moaned the moment his fingertips skimmed against her greedy little pussy that was already aching for him.

"If I don't stop." he whispered, lips brushing against her ear. "We'll never make it to the party." his lips pressed lightly beneath her earlobe before he stepped back away from her. "Ready?" he smirked as heat settled in her cheeks.

"In more ways than one." she smiled, turning away from the mirror. "Keep it up and I'll need to change my panties." she grumbled, looping her arm through the crook of his elbow.

"Don't worry, I'll rip them off later." he husked out as they left the bedroom. Her pulse spiked and stomach clenched at the promise.

The moment they reached the bottom of the elaborate staircase, Ava stopped in her tracks with wide eyes. The guests before her were a mixture of ages with the majority of the men dressed in tuxedos and the ladies were all adorned with fine jewels and ballgowns. Her fingers dug into Blake's arm, her lips twisted into a frown and her eyes narrowed on his rich, dark gaze.

"Ballgowns." she hissed and watched as he furrowed his brow. "They're all wearing ballgowns, Blake." she continued, her pulse thudding hard as her palms became damp. She was underdressed for the party and could already feel eyes on her. Assessing her, whispering about her. Her lungs seized as panic began to well within her.

"So?" his voice was one of unconcern. He turned to face her, his hand lightly cupping her cheek and his lips in a warm smile. "You look absolutely, stunningly prefect." his forehead resting against hers. "And you're all fucking mine." he whispered the last words in a low growl before he stepped back.

The double wooden doors opened briefly and the music from the string quartet filled the hallway, muting the chatter from inside the room before they were closed again and plunged back into silence.

"You're not embarrassed?" she asked, sucking in a deep breath as she tried to dampen down the rapidly rising panic.

"Fuck no." his lips moved to her ear. "Why would I be embarrassed when I have the most beautiful woman on my arm." his words brought tears to her eyes. "Tell me baby girl, why I would be embarrassed when I know every man in that room will be staring at you wishing they were the one you were clinging to." he whispered and her heart stuttered in her chest at the sincerity of his words.

"But..."

"Do you need an orgasm before we enter that room?" his tone serious but the wicked curve of his mouth told her he hoped that she did.

"Ballgowns...."

"Don't give a fuck about ballgowns." he husked out. "All I care about is you and how stunningly perfect you look." his thumb gently swept across her cheekbone. "So, one, two or three orgasms?" he arched one eyebrow as his eyes bore into hers.

"Three." her tongue darted across her lips. "Throughout the night." she confirmed, making him growl low and deep in the back of his throat. "I'm okay, for now though." she giggled when he groaned in frustration.

"Teasing me, I think you'll be getting a spanking." he husked out before entwining their fingers together and striding towards the double wooden doors.

"You better, Syn." she murmured the moment the double wooden doors opened, music flowed from the opulent ballroom and she felt like she'd been transported into a period drama.

Large crystal chandeliers hung from the carved double height ceiling, the flooring was antique parquet wood that shone in the delicate light and the walls were a light yellow with deep red velvet furnishings.

Her lips parted and her eyes widened as she took in the room. There was a large stage opposite the double wooden doors they had entered through which held the string quartet, to their left held a large bar filled with various alcohols and mixers. Tables covered with deep red velvet cloths and gold framed red plush chairs covered the outer area of the ballroom. The majority of the tables were already occupied and the staff which were weaving in between the tables, gold trays filled with various drinks held aloft, all wore white shirts and black pants with bow ties.

Ava was stunned into an awed silence as she watched some guests waltzing in time to the music across the large dance floor. Other guests were mingling or chatting with their friends seated at various tables. The weight of eyes on her prickled her skin, her pulse spiked as she looked at some of the faces. Some were looking with avid curiosity etched onto their aged faces, and some were that of disdain. She felt Blake stiffen beside her, felt the fine tremor in the hand which was holding hers and as she looked at him, she saw his jaw muscle ticking and his nostrils flare on a deep inhale.

"Blake." she whispered, putting her back to the room and tugging slightly on his hand until those rich dark eyes landed on her. Again, that haunted look had taken root in his eyes and she knew of only one way to erase that look. "I'd like that orgasm now." she continued, her tongue darting across her bottom lip.

"Is that so?" his lips curved as he bent his head towards her ear. "And what exactly do you want me to do?" his words were pure whispered heat that had her pussy clenching and releasing her arousal into her panties.

"I want to cum on your..."

"Father." Blake cut her off a second before she felt a hand rest against her shoulder from behind. Her eyes widened and her cheeks flamed, her breath caught in her throat.

Oh fuck!

Did he hear?

Oh, I hope not!

"Blake, Ava." his greeting was pleasant with no hint that he'd heard her. Her shoulders slumped on an exhale as she slowly turned to face Winston Synclair. "I know you kids want to spend some time alone." his eyes twinkled with mischief and her face flamed even more. "But please come and mingle with the guests. Some are practically salivating to see you Blake." there was a certain warning in his tone that Ava didn't understand. Mainly because she was too focused on the mortification which was running rampant throughout her body.

"Hmm." Blake gave a curt nod. "We'll get a drink and find mother." Blake's tone was a little cold as he stared at his father for a long moment, almost as if they were having a silent conversation before those dark eyes landed on her. "Would you like a glass of wine?" the husk in his voice sent a shiver down her spine.

"Please." she answered gratefully before she smiled at Winston, praying that her face had returned to her normal colour. "Happy Birthday, Mister Synclair." no sooner had the words left her lips when Blake tugged gently on her hand before he walked away without waiting for a response.

Ava couldn't help but notice the continued glances as they walked towards the bar, couldn't help notice the hushed whispers. She felt like they were the entrainment for the evening and it was a feeling she didn't like. Her pulse was thumping hard and her stomach was twisting when they came to a stop, Blake putting his back to the room, effectively cutting himself off the gawking. But Ava, she was standing facing the guests, facing the curious, stunned looks and the whisperings.

"Why are people staring at us?" she whispered, tearing her gaze away from the room to settle on Blake. "It's making me nervous." she admitted, clamping her teeth on the bottom lip.

"Don't be nervous." he smiled tightly, handing her a glass of wine before grabbing a tumbler full of amber liquid. "We'll have..." Blake stiffened, his hand gripping hers tightly before he let go and turned on his heel.

Ava peered around his broad body and was met by an elegant couple. The man was tall, broad dressed in a tuxedo. His light brown hair pushed back with silver strands glinting in the light. His posture just as stiff as Blake's. His face was a stern mask of rugged skin and deep lines, making him appear older than what he probably was. The woman stood beside him was lavished in a beautiful midnight blue ballgown, diamonds hung from her ears, her throat and her wrists. Her blonde hair was in an elegant bun and her green eyes flicked between her and Blake. A twist to her lips and deep-rooted sadness in her eyes.

"Blake." the man's deep voice was laced with contempt and his eyes narrowed slightly as Blake turned towards Ava.

"Please give me a moment." his eyes held that haunted look but his voice was controlled enough to put Ava at ease as she nodded. He gave her a curt nod before turning and ushering the newcomers away from her.

As she stood alone in the ballroom, her hand shaking slightly as she drained the glass of wine in one gulp. Her stomach twisted painfully and her mind raced. All the thoughts that she'd been trying to put to the back of her mind were once again racing to the forefront, fighting for dominance.

Is Blake be leading a double life?

That thought had sweat beading along the back of her neck.

Has his double life collided together?

That thought had her stomach clenching painfully hard.

Am I Blake's mistress?

That thought had bile rising in the back of her throat.

Is Blake be George's father?

That thought had her scurrying from the room. Her eyes wild, her heart pounding and her shaking hand covering her mouth to stop the riotous vomit from escaping her mouth. Bursting through the double wooden doors, she desperately scouted for a bathroom, but she'd rarely spent time in the downstairs of the manor and wasn't certain where she'd end up.

Quickly turning on her heel, she darted for the stairs. Her chest heaving, hand still clamped against her mouth as her stomach still tried to propel its contents. Her eyes watered at the horrible burn against her throat and inside her mouth as she darted down the long hallway towards Blake's room.

Throwing herself into the room, the door banging against the wall and her feet tripping over themselves a moment before she fell to her knees and vomited everything in her stomach into the pristine white toilet bowl. The bathroom was filled with sounds of liquid splashing into the bowl, her heaving as her stomach continued to expel everything from its confines.

Sweat gathered across her forehead, her neck and trickled down her breasts and back as her forehead rested against the toilet seat. Her eyes squeezed shut, hands braced on the toilet as she sucked in deep breath, after deep breath calming the thoughts and her stomach.

Chapter Forty

In the low ambient lighting of Blake's bedroom, Ava watched in rapt fascination as he started unbuttoning his shirt. Watched his biceps bunch and flex with each movement of his deft fingers. A slow burn of arousal began in the pit of her stomach. she licked over her lips, her eyes slowly tracking his movements. Watching as he pulled the shirt from his body, making her groan. The thick, hard cut muscles flexing with the movement.

Those rich dark eyes turned to her, and she saw the fire burning in their depths as his long, powerful legs strode across the expanse of the room before he sat, leaning back in the boudoir chair covered in deep blue fabric. His thighs parting and his hands resting against the chair arms.

"Take that innocent little dress off." his voice was a low command that had Ava reaching for the zip.

Slowly sliding the dress from her shoulders, the fabric whispering against her skin, raising goosebumps. She heard him groan as her lace covered breasts were uncovered. Her stomach quivered as the dress pooled around her waist a moment before she let it drop to the ground. She watched his thumb rub across his bottom lip as he watched her bra fall to the floor.

"Keep the shoes on." he demanded, unsnapping the button of his pants. The sound of the zip inching down sent a shiver down her spine. Her eyes hooded the moment his large, thick cock sprung free. Licking over her lips, she stepped out of the dress pooled at her feet. "You be a good girl and crawl to me." he rasped out, his hand wrapping around his thick length, giving it a hard squeeze.

Ava's pulse quickened as she slowly sunk to her knees. Her hands slapped against the floor and his groan filled the room. The shuddering anticipation flooded through her as she moved towards him on all fours. Her green eyes never leaving him and with each undulation of her back and ass had him moving his hand up and down his throbbing cock.

"Stop." he barked the command as she reached the chair. "On you knees." she raised up onto her knees.

Her stomach clenching and pulse ticking wildly when Blake's hand gripped the back of her neck, pulling her closer. The glistening head of his cock touched her lips lightly as he slowly painted her with the clear fluid. His cock expanded as he breathed out deeply, applying more pressure against her lips until they parted. The groan that left him as her tongue grazed the head of his cock echoed in the room.

The salty masculine taste of him burst across her tongue as he fed her inch by tortious inch of his cock. Ava tightened her lips his thick shaft as her tongue slid against the soft skin, dipping over the veins running its length. His cock swelling and clear liquid spilling from him onto her tongue, making her moan. Sinking deeper onto him, her breath hitched as he reached the back of her throat and his cock throbbed as more liquid seeped onto her tongue before he pulled his cock free.

"You suck my cock so well." he husked out, his hands gripping her upper arms and yanking her back on her feet, the same time as he stood to his full height. "You're going to be a good girl and bend over this chair."

Ava gripped the chair arms as she draped herself over the velvet material, the lingering warmth from his body seeped into her bare flesh. Her breath whooshed from her lungs as the stinging slap against her ass cheek bloomed across her flesh, heat instantly rushing to the surface. She heard his breathing change, heard it become deeper as his hand caressed the sting away. She felt the blunt, wide tip of his cock against her pussy. Blake snapped his hips forward, his balls slapping against her as his cock struck deep inside her. Her inner walls rippled against the thickness of him, trying to pull him in deeper.

Her head snapped back on a shocked gasp the moment his hand landed another stinging slap directly over the previous one, at the same time his cock dragged along her inner walls, nudging the sweetest spot inside of her until she was completely empty.

"Syn!" she hissed out between clenched teeth as a series of stinging slaps bounced off of her flesh. The searing heat across her ass cheek centred her concentration.

He slammed his cock into her, ripping a scream from her throat. Her pussy contracted, juices leaked from her before he slammed back in with a severity that had him landing another stinging slap directly in the centre of her ass cheeks. The vibration from the impact of his hand sent liquid rushing from her pussy and a deep moan fell from her parted lips.

Blake slammed into her over and over again. His cock hitting deep, her muscles contracting, her screams torn from her every time he bottomed out. Her pussy gripped onto his cock and her ass stung with blinding heat as another slap landed against her raw flesh. Her orgasm zipped through her at lightening speed, liquid rushed from her in hot splashes against his groin.

His hands gripping her hips in a brutal hold as he continued to slam into her. On a deep, primal groan and instantly stilling burying himself as deep as he could, spilling hot jets of cum inside her, sending a flurry of pulses through her core. Harsh breaths filling the room for long moments. His fingers flexed against her hips as he pulled his deflating cock from her. The cool air stung the sensitive flesh of her ass. His lips touched between her shoulder blades before she was scooped into his arms.

"Let's get into bed." his lips touched her temple as he strode across the room.

Blake pulled the bedcovers back, gently laying her onto the cool sheets before he laid down, his arms banding around Ava's trembling body until they were laid on their sides. Her back to his front making her hiss as the coarse hairs rub against the raw flesh of her ass cheeks.

"Night, Syn." Ava breathed, snuggling deeper into his embrace.

"Night, baby girl." he whispered, pressing a soft kiss to her neck as he pulled her tighter against him.

The following morning had been spent with Blake tending to the handprints he'd left across her ass cheeks the night before with his eyebrows furrowed and sorrow in his eyes. Whilst Ava had the brightest smile on her face as the cool ointment slithered over her skin. The rough pads of his fingertips caressing her raw flesh so delicately had a fresh wave of desire coursing through her body, but she knew better than to try to coax Blake into another bout. Especially when he was battling his demons.

They'd just finishing packing their bags when Theodore appeared in the doorway of Blake's bedroom letting them know that lunch would be served in fifteen minutes which had Ava throwing on an oversized pale green t-shirt and her skintight jeans under the watchful eye of Blake.

"Pure fucking torture." he groaned, scrubbing a hand down his face. "Come, before I fuck that delectable ass of yours." he continued entwining their fingers together.

"Hmm, now you know how I feel when you were your polo shirts." Ava groused, earning an eyebrow quirk from him. "They cling to every perfect muscle you have and it makes me want to..."

"Don't." the command in his voice wasn't lost on her as they descended the stairs. "I'm not opposed to taking you back upstairs and fucking you." he ground out before stopping before a large wooden door.

"Uh-huh." Ava smiled as his blazing eyes stared at her. "Later, Syn." she giggled as the door swung open, revealing a dining room.

The walls were a light green that had small, gold gilded frames filled with family pictures place in precise locations around the room. The dining table was a deep oak and only had four solid oak chairs, making her realise that this was the family room and not for visitors or friends, which made her smile.

Marion and Winston Sinclair were already sitting, both with a glass of wine in front of them and dressed in country-casual clothes of tweed and crisp shirts, reminding Ava of a pair of avid horse riders.

"Mum, Dad." Blake greeted as he took a seat closest to his father, with Ava settling opposite Marion.

"We're so glad you could join us today." Marion smiled, her hands clasping together. "We would really like to get to know Ava some more." she continued, her dark eyes locking with hers.

"Oh, umm..." Ava's pulse spiked and her stomach fluttered as she floundered for a moment until Blake's hand landed on her thigh, squeezing comfortingly. "What would you like to know?" she asked, licking over her dry lips.

"What do you do for a living?" Winston asked, taking a sip of his wine.

"I'm a teaching assistant." she breathed out, moving in her chair as a sense of unease washed over her.

"That's not all you are, Ava." Blake's voice was low as his fingers flexed against her thigh. "Ava also is the safeguarding supervisor at a primary school." he continued, meeting his father's gaze head on.

"That's wonderful." Marion exclaimed. "What was your most recent case?" she continued, leaning further across the table with genuine interest. Ava's heart thundered against her ribcage and her palms became clammy as images of George flooded her mind.

"It's more of an ongoing case." Ava began taking a sip of the water in front of her. "There's a little boy who reminds me of Blake, actually." she sucked in a deep breath as she felt his eyes on the side of her face.

"Oh, what's the little boy's name?" Marion asked, tilting her head slightly as she flicked her gaze to her son before landing back on her.

"George." Ava whispered, swallowing around the lump in her throat as she saw the fearful look in Marion's and Winston's eyes as they looked at Blake. "He's been upset that his father has been absent, and it's caused him to have panic attacks." she didn't dare glance at Blake, instead she trained her gaze on the shrimp salad which had been silently delivered. "But it's slowly getting better, his father attended his birthday party a few weeks ago and bought him a spider-man outfit." her voice was shaking as much as her hands. "His father seems to be making more of an effort in recent weeks, which is good because boys need their fathers." she cleared her throat before picking up her cutlery.

"Yes, of course they do." Winston agreed, his voice sounded like a warning but Ava couldn't meet any of their gazes. She was petrified of what she might see.

Petrified of seeing a truth that she didn't want to. Petrified of seeing his parent's disdain for being a mistress and petrified of seeing the hurt etched onto Blake's face.

"Hmm, it's always hard on the children." Blake muttered, removing his hand from her thigh, which she instantly missed but still couldn't risk a glance at the man she loved. Instead, she opted for a nod as she ate in complete silence.

The white noise of Blake talking with his parents didn't register, they could have been talking about anything and Ava wouldn't have heard anything. She was too wrapped up in those thoughts she didn't want to think about, but was too tired to stop them from rushing to the forefront of her mind.

Is Blake be leading a double life?

Am I Blake's mistress?

Is Blake be George's father?

Does Blake's parents blame me?

The lunch passed by in a haze of thoughts and before she knew what had happened, she was bundled inside the Aston Martin and settled into the warm confines. She couldn't keep the trepidation from seeping into her bones as she watched an almost haunted look take over his eyes, watched as he retreated and without a word spoken between them, they made the long drive home.

Chapter Forty-One

It had been three days since Ava had returned from The Manor and whilst the drive back had been a long, quiet drive with Blake spending the majority of their time with that haunted look. That haunted look she hated and feared in equal parts. She had expected him to retreat, to put distance between them, but he hadn't. She had woken up every morning to a *'good morning, baby girl'* text message, which instantly put a smile on her face, and this morning hadn't been any different.

Her Wednesday had begun like all the rest, but with her being the safeguarding supervisor, she had been given a small office that was private for her talks with students and a space for her to complete reports and calls with social services.

Ava had been sitting in her new office finishing a new report on a student which needed to be emailed to social services when her desk phone rang, making her jump in the silence.

"Hello." she heard a heavy breath on the other end of the receiver and then silence. "Hello?" she asked again, her eyebrows furrowing.

"Ava?" the choked voice had her pulse instantly thudding wildly in her throat. He sounded like he was in pain, like he was struggling to breathe.

"Blake, are you okay?" she rushed out, quickly hitting send on the email she had been typing to social services. "Sweetheart, talk to me." she pleaded, cradling the desk phone between her shoulder and ear. And as she was met with more silence, worry swept through her.

"I...I..." she heard him suck in a hard, laboured breath. Panic welled within her, knowing what was happening and that she wasn't with him to ease the suffering of the panic attack which was trying to grip hold of him.

"Breathe." she tried to soothe him best she could and tried to keep the panic out of her voice, which was harder than she thought. "Come on Blake, just breathe with me." she heard him suck another deep breath in followed by a moment's silence and then he blew it out.

"Need you." he managed to gasp out around another deep breath.

"I'm right here with you, just breathe." she tried to stop her hands from shaking as she heard him struggling. "Where are you?" she asked, already grabbing her handbag from the bottom desk drawer.

"H-hospital." the moment those words registered her stomach dropped, her breaths whooshed out of her and her stomach roiled.

"I'll be right there, don't move." she rushed out, hanging up and bolting for the exit.

The drive to the hospital was spent in sheer panic, she had called the headmistress to explain that she'd had to leave with a family emergency and that she wouldn't be back for the remainder of the working day and technically it was true. Blake was hers and he needed her.

Her mind was a whirl and her heart was in her throat as she pulled into the hospital car park. Her green eyes scanning the area for a place to park when she saw Blake's Aston Martin, left haphazardly blocking two spaces. The sight didn't do much for the panic within her, but she had to focus and find a parking spot.

In one fluid movement, she was out of the car and striding across the car park towards Accident and Emergency when she saw a familiar figure hunched over and shaking. Her heart slapped against her throat as she quickened her pace until her shaking hand landed on his back.

"Blake, I'm here." she whispered and in the blink of eye, his arms banded around her like she was his lifeline. His head buried in her neck. She could hear his harsh, shallow breaths and the searing heat of his skin almost burnt her. "One breath." she whispered, pulling away from him with her hands gripping his forearms. "Come on, sweetheart, one breath." she encouraged, smiling slightly as he took a deep breath in before blowing it out.

They repeated the process a further nine times until his pupils had returned to normal.

"Ava." he whispered, trembling hands cupping her cheeks, and tears gathered in his eyes.

"Shhh, it's okay." Ava cooed. "I'm here, we're okay." she continued, but he shook his head, squeezing his eyes closed.

"M-Maureen." he whispered, his forehead resting against hers. "She's had a stroke." the sheer vulnerability in his voice made her heart ache.

"Is – is she okay?" Ava licked her lips and swallowed thickly as he tensed ever so slightly before blowing a breath out, making his shoulders slump.

"I hope so." he whispered, sounding unsure and in that moment she knew that he'd only managed to get here before the panic gripped him. "Will you come with me?" his voice was almost too low for her to hear in the limited space but as he stepped back she saw the fear etched onto his face and she knew after learning why he wanted to be a doctor, that he felt he'd failed his patient.

"Of course, I would love to meet Maureen." she smiled as he sucked in another deep breath before entwining their fingers together.

The clean hospital scent invaded her nostrils with a sharp sting, her low heels click-clacking against the tiled floor, the sounds of people coughing, machines bleeping and people rushing around almost gave her pause. Blake seemed to have a renewed sense of calmness as he strode with his usual purposeful strides, gently tugging her through the halls until they swished through grey painted double doors.

The ward they had entered was quiet and peaceful, but the hospital scent still clung to her nostrils. Her heart was beating out of time as she squeezed his hand reassuringly. A few nurses were close together around a desk talking and an attractive blonde cast an appreciative glance over Blake, which had Ava's insecurities trying to rise to the forefront.

She was trying to dampen down the insecurities, trying to be strong for Blake, but try as she might. Ava knew exactly what they looked like together and also knew what other people thought too. As if sensing her discomfort, those rich dark eyes glance at her, his eyebrows furrowed slightly before he dipped his head, lips skimming the shell of her ear.

"What's wrong, baby girl?" his voice sends a shiver down her spine and heat to tint her cheeks.

"Women." she mutters, her tongue darting across her bottom lip. "They keep looking at what's mine." she continues blowing out a frustrated and insecure breath.

"Hmm." his nose trails down her throat. "We'll just have to change that." he husks out, dropping her hand and turning fully towards her.

His hands inched up her sides and over her exposed throat before cupping her jaw, his thumbs lightly brushing over her cheeks. Her breath stuttered in her chest and her pulse throbbed as he inched closer until their mouths were a breath apart. His eyes boring into hers. His tongue licking across her bottom lip. Her eyes fluttered closed, her heart began a tortious beat until it was all she could hear.

Ava curled her tongue against his lips, the tip breaching his mouth, sliding against his teeth. He groaned low in the back of his throat as their lips moved in a slow, soft caress that stole her breath. Arching her back, her hardened nipples that were poking against her blouse, scraped against his solid chest encased in the white dress shirt, sending a little tremor through her body, drawing a moan from the back of her throat. Her tongue swirled around the tip of his tongue. Blake shuddered against her, his deep groan vibrated through his chest.

"Feel better?" he asked, his forehead resting against hers, harsh breaths mingling together.

"Yes." she smiled as his hand trailed down her body until his fingers entwined with hers. "I just might need an orgasm, though." Blake's teeth nipped her lobe.

"Just the one?" he whispered against her ear. "Don't worry, I'll have you screaming my name later." he promised before standing to his full height.

The private room wasn't overly large, and the walls were stark white. The bleeping of a machine filled her ears as she looked around before settling on Maureen Templeton. Her tightly curled grey hair was brushed away from her face. She was propped up with a multitude of pillows behind her, making her look frail and her watery amber eyes were sparkling as she saw Blake.

"Doctor Synclair, how lovely to see you." her voice sounded almost weak as she held out an arthritic hand.

"Maureen, you gave me quite the scare." he admitted, taking her hand in his and giving it a light squeeze.

"Please, this is nothing." she huffed, waving away the concern. "But if I get to you more often, I just might enjoy my stay here." she laughed lightly before peering around his large frame. "And just who is this lovely young lady?"

"Ava." she smiled, stepping around Blake with a small smile on her lips. Maureen turned to train her amber eyes on him, a smile tugging her lips.

"Is she your shining star?" Ava furrowed her brows at the question, but Blake gave a nod, a smile tugging his lips. "Well, she is just adorable." turning her gaze back to Ava. "Can you cook?"

"A little, yes." she nodded before sinking her teeth into her bottom lip, not certain where this conversation is going.

"This young man needs taking care of." Maureen's voice was matter of fact, but her eyes were soft. "He likes my lemon drizzle cake, I think you deserve the recipe." with a slight nod of her head and determination set in her tone. "Do you have those mobile devices?" she asked.

"Yes." Ava agreed, thinking she meant phone, quickly taking it from her handbag. "Why?" she asked, cocking her head to the side.

"My days could be numbered." she feebly squeezed Blake's hand in a comforting gesture without taking her watery gaze from Ava. "Despite this young man's efforts, I'm an old lady." she puffed out a laugh, shaking her head slightly. "And you dear, need to take down my recipe." with that she launched into a detailed recipe and cooking instructions for her lemon drizzle cake that Blake adores and Ava's heart swells at the thoughtfulness of his patient.

"How are you feeling, Maureen?" Blake asked, his hand still captured by hers. Ava watched how his face softened and lips tugged into an affectionate smile, which warmed her all the more. She could see just why he liked Maureen so much. She was a vibrant woman who probably didn't take things lying down, which would keep him on his toes as her doctor.

"I'm better." her voice changed and became a little softer, the spark that was there earlier seemed to almost disappear. "It's my seventh day in here and they won't let me out just yet."

"Hmm, that's for the best at the moment." Blake squeezed her hand. "The doctors here want to ensure that you are fit and well before returning home." his face became a stern mask. "Because they already know that you won't listen to them." he chuckled as she laughed lightly.

"Yes, well, sometimes you can't play by the rules, not when I need to see my Edgar." Ava noticed her eyes glass over with unshed tears before her breath shuttered. "I'll need to see him soon." her voice wavered.

"I know, but please let me take you." Blake's voice was soft, but his eyes pinned her with a stare. "You know it's not healthy to be catching the bus this time of year."

"You're too kind to me." she smiled before turning to Ava. "I hope he treats you just as good, Ava."

"He does." Ava swallowed thickly as emotion clogged her throat. "Sometimes too good." she admitted.

"Never, too good." Blake's voice turned an octave deeper as his eyes blazed at her, sending a shuddering wave across her body.

"Ah, young love." Maureen smiled before she fought a yawn.

"Maureen, I'll come by again soon." Blake leaned across, kissing her forehead and Ava thought the poor old woman may just have a heart attack. "When they decide to discharge you, let me know and I'll take you home." he stood back smiling before letting go of her hand.

"I will, young man." she beamed brighter than she had before. "I hope to see you again too, Ava."

"I'm sure you will. I hope you feel better soon."

The moment they reached the parking lot, Blake pulled her into his arms. His intoxicating scent wrapping around her with his warmth. Her pulse quickened, and her stomach fluttered as his lips pressed against the top of her head.

"Come home with me." he husked out, tightening his hold on her as he sucked in a deep breath. "I want to thank you for coming today." his words were low, but she heard the gratitude laced within every word.

"You don't need to thank me." she stepped back, her hands lightly touching his chest. Smiling as she felt the shudder ripple his muscles. "I'm always here for you, sweetheart."

"Hmm." the stunning smile that took over his lips stole her breath. "I believe I owe you an orgasm." his voice rough with need as his pupils dilated.

"How could I refuse." she licked over her lips, a smile playing on her mouth. "I'll follow you." she took a step back before rushing to her car. Need and want ignited within her, making her rub her thighs together.

Chapter Forty-Two

Blake's dark eyes blazed, his sinful mouth curved into a smouldering smile as his large hands captured Ava's hips and slowly walked her into his living room. The soft fabric of the sofa hit the back of her bare calves. Her heart thundered, stomach fluttered and her pussy throbbed. His fingers flexed against her hips, tightening ever so slightly as she slowly bent forward the edge of her pencil skirt whispering over the back of her thighs as she curved, knees bent before her ass cheeks touched the soft sofa.

Ava licked over her lips, her green eyes watching as Blake started unbuttoning his shirt. Watched his biceps bunch and flex with each movement of his deft fingers. A slow burn of arousal began in the pit of her stomach. His chest expanded on a breath as he exposed more of his rippling abdominal muscles straining against his tawny skin had her mouth watering for a taste.

"Eye fucking me, baby girl." Blake's husky voice sent a delectable shiver over her. Her nipples hardening against the lace of her bra.

"Hmm, always." she pulled her bottom lip through her teeth, her palms rubbed over her thighs the moment his shirt hit the floor.

"My turn." he rasped out, taking a seat on the coffee table. His knees landing between hers, quickly opening them. Her skirt bunched at the top of her thighs. "Unbutton your blouse." his dark eyes flicked to her breasts, his thumb running over his bottom lip as her fingers slowly undid each button until it fluttered open.

Blake's large, warm hands landed on her knees as he leant forward, pushing her thighs further apart. Wetness pooled between her thighs as his fingers gripped the side of her lace panties and inch by inch, slid them down. The cool air of the room collided with the wetness seeping from her sex, eliciting shudder through her body and a lustrous moan from her lips.

"Please." she breathed out, sucking in a shallow breath, her pulse spiking wildly in her throat as he loomed over her. His fingers curving around the back of the sofa and the other trailed from her jaw to the back of her neck.

"I don't know what I'd do without you, Ava." he whispered. The raw, unguarded look in his eyes that she saw fleetingly before he closed them made Ava's heart ache. His forehead resting against hers as he breathed in deeply. She moved her head slightly back, but his grip tightened.

Ava touched her lips to his, a fleeting touch of flesh. The second pass was more leisurely. The third she'd intended on leaving her mouth pressed to his, but Blake snaked his tongue out and swiped once across the seam of her lips. She gasped, and his sinful tongue delved into her mouth. He moved her slightly before he was exploring her, their tongues twining together and sliding their lips against each other. It was slow, sensual, full of need and it shattered Ava to her very core.

She almost cried out as he pulled his lips from hers, his dark brown eyes staring into her green ones. Again, she saw the rawness there that made her ache to touch him, ache to hold him and ache to love him.

"I don't ever want to find out." the vulnerability in his voice sent a shiver through her.

Their lips once again slid slowly together. His large hand

moved from her neck in a featherlight touch to her collarbone, raising goosebumps in their wake until he cupped her breast. Her hardened nipple grazed against his thumb once, twice as a moan escaped her lips. Blake trailed his lips slowly along her jaw, down her throat before clamping around her lace covered nipple. She arched her back as the electrified jolt from his lips tore through her as if she was naked.

Another moan poured from her parted lips as he applied slightly more pressure on her clothed nipple. His fingers hooking around the cup of her bra and with excruciating slowness, he dragged it down until her breast was bare before him. The warm wetness of his tongue caused Ava to gasp, shudder and moan all at the same time as he laved her bare nipple in slow strokes.

Blake's weight transferred as his right hand curved around the back of the sofa. His lips brushing against hers as his left hand, just as slowly as the right, dragged the cup of her bra down and both her breasts were bare to him. His hand continued to blaze a slow, torturous trail of heat down her side, over the flair of her hip until his warm palm touched her exposed thigh. His lips not leaving hers as he slowly caressed her skin.

Ava slowly, tentatively, touched the rippling, hard planes of his stomach. The heat from his bare skin almost seared her. The feel of his soft skin, pulled tight over his hard muscles, made her mouth water and her stomach clench. With her palms flat against his stomach, she slowly moved up his torso until her fingertips glided over his small nipples. She felt him shudder against her. She couldn't stop her slow, tentative touches. He felt divine.

Slowly, her fingertips grazed his nipples again before she trailed them back down the rippling muscles, until she hit the waistband of his dress pants, quickly flicking them open she pulled them and his boxers down. His large, hard length slapped against his stomach. Moaning at the sight, she trailed her finger down the impressive length. Blake's low groan seemed to vibrate through her as she wrapped her small palm around him.

Marvelling at the thickness, the velvety soft skin over the hard muscle caused more moisture to gather at her thighs. Blake continued to moan as she stroked him and moisture gathered at his tip before he trailed slow, sensual kisses along her jaw, down her throat until his warm, wet tongue laved her nipple.

She watched through hooded lids as he rained kisses down her stomach, over her hip as he slowly knelt on the hardwood floor. He blinked those long lashes at her slowly before he moved his hands down her thighs, a growl tore from his throat and Ava was transfixed at the mesmerising sight of him leaning forward, applying pressure on her thighs to spread ever wider for him until his tongue licked a possessive line directly up the centre of her pussy and curled around her clitoris.

The jolts of electricity sprung off of her in a ball of decadent pleasure and coursed through her limbs, tightening her muscles. Her fingers plunged into the thick, dark strands of his hair as his tongue swirled around her clitoris once, twice, before his teeth grazed against the sensitive bundle of nerves. Her hips bucked against his mouth a moment before his large hands gripped her hips to keep her in place.

The sheer pleasure was exquisite, her moans increased considerably as she threw her head against the back of the sofa, arching once again. A rush of liquid seeped from her and his tongue lapped faster before probing her inner folds and moans tumbled from Ava, her hand still buried in his hair as she tried to grind against his mouth. The rumble from his throat sent a delicious tremor through her as his left arm pinned her pelvis to the sofa as a long, thick finger dipped into her wet heat.

His tongue moved back to her clit as the pad of his finger pressing, releasing, rubbing against the sweetest of spots inside of her. His tongue licked faster against the bundle of nerves a slow burn began in the pit of her stomach and her grip on his hair tightened as her body arched against him.

Moans poured from her lips Her hips undulated with each press, each rub as a deep pressure began to build inside of her. His lips clamped around her clit and he sucked hard as his two fingers plunged inside her, pressing, releasing, rubbing over and over. A ball of decadent pleasure was building faster.

Her hips moving of their own accord, her mouth open with moan after lustrous moan, her head pushed into the back of the sofa, her fingers numb from the death grip on his hair, wetness pouring from her in waves, and then it happened. Deep inside, she swelled tightly, the ball expanded, and she exploded.

"Blake!" the deep moan of his name was more of a prayer as her juices splashed against his mouth and chin.

Blake pulled away from her as slight tremors rippled through her with every harsh breath she took. He kissed his way back up her body until he was once again staring into her eyes with fire blazing in their depths.

"Pure and innocent." his voice gruff with untamed desire. "I could eat you constantly." he groaned.

She felt the hot, wet silken head of his cock sweep through her wetness as she stared into Blake's almost black eyes as he eased himself into her. Their lips once again slid slowly together as he pulled his hips back, dragging his long, thick cock out of her pussy, leaving the head inside before he thrust back into her slowly.

Their eyes locked, a myriad of emotions swirling, their breaths mingling in the limited space between them. Hearts thumping erratically against one another. Ava's eyes fluttered closed as his lips brushed hers and, with every caress of their lips, Blake languidly rocked against her.

The slow torture of his movements, the feel of his thick cock scraping every quivering part within her had pleasure building in the deepest part of her. The slow burn of exquisite pleasure reigniting every nerve ending until they were sizzling in an electrified current, weaving over her hypersensitive body. Her hips undulated to meet his, slow and deep. Her pussy contracted, juices gathered and her moans of pleasure were continuous, which he swallowed with every sweep of his tongue inside of her mouth.

Blake reared back, tightening his grip on the back of the sofa he drove his cock into her on a hard thrust that sent shock waves of intense pleasure through her. He pulled back and slammed into her harder, deeper, and she cried out in ecstasy. His thrusts were hard, deep, and slow. The room was filled with combined moans and groans of pleasure, the sounds of their bodies meeting in wet slaps of skin against skin. White hot waves overtook her, muscles clenched tightly, her head thrown back and her hands gripped his ass cheeks as the dam broke and her orgasm crashed through her.

"Fuck!" she moaned as her pussy gripped onto his cock tightly. Liquid rushed from her in hot splashes against his pelvis.

"Mine, always!" Blake growled low and deadly in the back of his throat and with one last thrust, he buried himself as deep as he could and let go.

The moment she felt him cum, the hot, molten liquid fill her, another wave of pleasure hit, another climax tore through her. Grinding against him as she rode out every pulse, every wave and every twitch of her climax until her limbs went slack, her breathing laboured and her mind was senseless.

Ava caressed Blake's back in long, slow movements as their bodies began to relax. His lips touched hers in a slow, deliberate kiss as he gathered her in his arms and sunk down on the sofa. His cock, still buried inside of her, nestled against his chest.

"I have to go." Ava mumbled against his chest, trying to snuggle deeper.

"Don't you want me to feed you?" he whispered, pressing his lips to her head.

"I....yes." she stuttered, making him chuckle.

The dinner Blake prepared for them both was a delicious seared steak with a garlic sauce and roasted vegetables. She was full and sated by the time she parked in her driveway, furrowing her brows at the stunning blonde stood on her doorstep.

"Can I help you?" Ava asked as she reached the front door, almost gasping as the blonde turned to face her. It was the same blonde woman from Blake's grandfather's restaurant in the country. She watched as her red lips pulled back into a devastating smile.

"I'd like to talk to you about Blake Synclair." her voice was soft but her eyes were that of a scorned woman.

Chapter Forty-Three

The harsh breath whooshed out a moment before the crystal cut glass tumbler pressed against his sinful lips. The amber liquid flowing into his mouth, the woodsy, smokey taste pouring over his tongue and the delicious burn as it slithered down his throat was the delicious.

His dark gaze locked onto his phone, the buzzing against the coffee table bringing him out of his thoughts. Ava's name flashed across his screen, making him close his eyes for a moment as he contemplated not answering. He didn't want to speak with her, didn't think he could speak with her. Taking another sip of the whiskey before he answered.

"Ava." his tone was hard as he squeezed his eyes shut.

"Hey." her breathy voice made his chest ache. "So, I was wondering if I could come over in about an hour." her voice was full of hope and he could hear her breath quicken as the silence stretched out.

"Not tonight." his words were slow as his hand gripped tightly against the glass tumbler. "I've had a long day and I'm just heading to bed." he lied so effortlessly.

"Oh, okay." she sounded disappointed. His fingers pinched the bridge of his nose and his eyes closed. "Is Friday still okay?" the way she asked with uncertainty in her voice almost broke him.

"Friday." he confirmed, casting his dark gaze across the small living room. "I've got to go." he whispered, disconnecting the call, tipping the whiskey down his throat. The taste suddenly bitter on his tongue.

Images of her laughing, wrapping her arms around him, kissing him, screaming his name all flashed through his mind in quick succession. "Fuck!" he roared, the glass tumbler shattered against the opposite wall.

"Blake!" her soft, sweet voice was loud and clear, making him snap his head towards the one thing he didn't want to see.

Chapter Forty-Four

Ava sat drumming her fingers on the desk in her office, her mind was in pieces as she stared at the mobile number for George's mum. He'd been out of school for a week and whilst she didn't think his parents would bring him harm, she wanted to speak with his mum.

Speak with her for her own selfish reasons.

Reasons she didn't really want to admit, but she knew that she had no choice. Especially after the conversation she'd had with a stunning blonde on Wednesday night.

Blowing out a breath full of trepidation, she dialled the number, knowing that her relationship may change if the stunning blonde was telling the truth.

She waited with bated breath for the incessant ringing to end.

"Hello." the soft feminine voice brought her pulse spiking and sweat to slick her palms.

"Good afternoon, Miss Shaw." Ava took a shaky breath in as she tried to steel herself for the conversation. "It's Ava Asherton from Sunnyside primary school, I'm George's teaching assistant." she always found it easier to say that to parents rather than tell them she's the safeguarding officer for the school.

"Oh, hi." she sounded a little confused. "Is everything okay?"

"I was just calling to see how George is feeling?" her fingers continued drumming against the desk as her heart hammered and her stomach coiled and twisted.

"He's getting better...." she broke off.

"Baby." a masculine voice sounded down the line.

A voice she'd heard before.

A voice that had whispered dirty things to her.

"Sorry, Ava. It's my partner, I won't be a moment." Miss Shaw tried to muffle the conversation but Ava had heard enough to know a truth she didn't want to admit. Air whooshed from her lungs as they seized, her stomach clenched hard and her throat tightened.

"Miss Shaw." Ava croaked down the line. "I won't keep you any longer." she rushed out before hanging up.

Throwing her head in her heads, Ava took a deep breath as a numbness washed over her. The hard beat of her heart was all that she could feel. Words were tumbling through her mind. Words that she'd thought before when Blake had pulled away from her when she thought they were breaking up.

Sinful

Delectable

Deceitful

Fucking Heartbreaker

Ava never realised just how true those words were until now and there was only one thing for it.

Ava – *I'll be with you soon, sweetheart x*

She ground her teeth together as she typed out the text message. Anger whipping its way through her system making her hands shake and her heart pound.

Blake – *Can't wait to see you, I'll cook dinner xx*

His response had tears gathering in her eyes until she willed them back. Settling for the numbness to wash over her once again.

Blake's home had never felt so cold, empty, lifeless. Even the plush chair didn't feel the same. It felt hard, unyielding. The October rain splattered against the living room window, the deep grey clouds casting shadows of misery into the one place she'd loved. She couldn't help think just how fitting the weather was now that she was here, ready to face the one man she trusted.

Ava wrapped her arms around herself, breathing deeply as she tried to stop the swell of tears when his footsteps sounded in the hall. She needed to be strong for the conversation she needed to have before she would allow herself to shatter into a million pieces.

"Hey, baby girl." Blake's warm smile, the stubble hiding his dimples, almost had the tears spilling over as he walked into the room. His carved torso on full display, the sweatpants slung low on his hips. Ava ripped her gaze away from his perfection and landed on his deceitful, beautiful face.

"We need to talk." she was thankful her voice didn't waiver, didn't crack. She watched his eyebrows furrow and his lips turn down before he sat on the coffee table directly in front of her.

"What's wrong?" he asked, his voice soft and his eyes worried. Reaching a hand out to soothe down her thigh had her flinching, making him pull back. "You're scaring me, Ava." he admitted, and those words cracked directly down the middle of her heart.

"Me, scaring you?" her voice was incredulous, her eyes wide. He sat staring at her, unblinking and unmoving. "How do you think I felt when a beautiful woman came to see me?" she asked, her voice low as her shoulders slumped.

"I don't understand what you're talking about." he admitted, his worried eyes tracking every movement she made.

"Oh, don't you." her voice was deathly low as she leaned forward, their faces so close. "Allow me to explain then, Blake." she took a breath to stop her hands from shaking. Her eyes turning cold, flat as she stared at the man she loved with everything that she had. "I want to talk about your wife." she licked over her dry lips as she watched him recoil away from her.

His face a mask of horror and pain.

"Ava." his voice cracked as he swallowed thickly.

"Don't Ava me." she warned. "Tell me Blake, where do you keep your precious little wife?" her voice hardened with every word spoken. "Tell me why you lied to me." she held a hand up to silence him. "Tell me why you thought it to be best I learnt it from your wife. Why you thought it would be best for her to show up at my home to tell me that you are fucking married!" her voice climbed higher with every word.

She watched the colour drain from his face, watched his hands begin to shake and she watched as his breaths became harsher with every word she flung at him. She knew that he was on the verge of a panic attack, but at this moment in time, she needed answers from him.

"Tell me, how many kids do you have?" she asked, her voice like steel as her eyes narrowed.

"None." he whispered.

"Don't you fucking lie to me!" Ava shouted, bouncing up from the chair. Her entire body shaking with rage, hurt and heartbreak. She watched the pain in his eyes intensify as she stood before him. Watched him lick over his bottom lip and watched tears gather in his eyes.

"One." he shoved his head in his hands. "A little boy." he continued, still hiding behind his hands. Refusing to look at her as he spoke broke a little bit more of her heart.

Her mind jumped directly to the boy in her glass who looked so much like Blake, the little boy who suffered with panic attacks just like Blake. The little boy who'd been happier since his birthday because his dad went home. Her stomach roiled, acid swishing around as it tried to slither up her throat.

"George!" Ava shouted, her hand flying to her mouth as she gulped the bitter bile back down. "Your son's name is George." she continued, the moment he looked at her, with such fear, vulnerability and horror etched onto his face and laced within the depths of his dark eyes. "He's in my class!" she screeched, she watched him wince at the high pitch. "I've comforted him during his panic attacks, I've told him countless times that his *daddy* doesn't mean to be absent from his life so much." she continued shouting. Her feet eating up the expanse of the living room. "And all the while you were fucking me!" she screamed at him, but he didn't move, didn't speak. Only sat watching her with a pain so profoundly etched onto his face it stole her breath.

But she couldn't fall for this again.

She'd done it more than once. She'd forgiven him every time

he'd been absent. Every time he'd been running around with his little sluts. Every time he'd gave her pain during sex. Every time she'd looked at him, saw the true demons and sadness in his eyes, and forgiven him. But she couldn't do it again.

This was the one thing she couldn't forgive.

"I don't want to see you again." her voice was cold, hard as she ripped the necklace from her chest and her bracelet from her wrist before storming past. His hand shot out, fingers curling around her wrist. Her other hand raised before connecting a stinging slap across his cheek. "Get the fuck off of me." she hissed out between clenched teeth. He didn't, his grip tightened. "Go back to your *wife* and *son*." she spat those words, which were enough for him to release her without a single word spoken, as she threw the tainted jewellery at him.

As she walked out of his home, she knew just how *Delectable Syn* was deceitful and a fucking heartbreaker and it hurt, more than she could have possibly ever imagined.

The moment she locked herself in the car, her head resting against the steering wheel, she gulped back the bile that was threatening to spill out of her mouth. Before dragging in a deep breath, her hands shaking as she placed them on the steering wheel.

James had tried to warn her even without knowing who she was seeing. James had tried to tell her that she'd get her heart broken and James had tried his best to stop this from happening. It was just a shame that she'd never listened. Just a shame that her misplaced feelings, adoration, hero worship had cost her a broken heart.

Her heart that Blake had stolen and claimed as his own. Her heart that felt like he'd ripped it to shreds and thrown it back inside of her chest. Her heart that she knew would never really recover from this.

"I need to get out of here." she whispered to herself as her watery, stinging eyes landed on Blake's silhouette in the living room window, watching her.

Chapter Forty-Five

His pulse spiked as images of *her* long dark waves blowing in the evening breeze, *her* sparkling green eyes filled with love and adoration, *her* pouting lips curved into a shy smile. He squeezed his eyes shut, but that only intensified the images of his beautiful woman. The woman who trusted him loved him.

"You're better than this." his eyes snapped open at the sound of her voice soft, sweet so close he could see the look of disgust in her green eyes.

"Fuck off!" he snarled.

"You need to stop with the womanising." her soft voice brought his pulse spiking.

"You did this to me!" he roared, his hands fisting in his hair.

"You're hurting me." he closed his eyes for a fraction of a second.

"You fucking hurt me!" he bellowed as thick, hot rage swept through his body.

"You need to come home." his hands clenched into fists, his muscles quivering with the pent up anger as he heard the pleading in her voice.

"You fucking...." he almost screamed at the top of his lungs. The heel of his hands pressing against his eyes as he took a deep breath. "I fucking love you!" he snarled, pouncing to his feet. Fist connecting with the wall once. "Fuck!" he roared.

The pain lancing through him in thick hot rivulets had him doubling over. Dragging heavy breaths through his nose and hissing them out through his gritted teeth. His heart pounding against his sternum, pain lacerating his chest. His shoulders tense as red hot pain seared across his back, sweat slicking over his skin.

He tried concentrating on breathing deeply.

One breath.

Two breaths.

Three breaths.

Four breaths.

Five breaths.

Six breaths.

Seven breaths.

Eight breaths.

Nine breaths.

Ten breaths.

The pain slowly subsided. His heart beats slowed back to a normal rhythm. His shoulders slumped, leaving him feeling deflated.

Chapter Forty-Six

It had been a whole week since Ava had shattered into a million pieces.

A whole week of seeing the concern on Katie's face every time they were in the same room together.

A whole week of James trying to get a name of who was responsible for her heartbreak.

And a whole fucking week where she had done nothing but be sick every time she thought of Blake, every time he called her and she sent it to voicemail and every time he sent her a text message which she quickly deleted without reading anything the deceitful heartbreaker had wrote.

After all, she knew it would all be lies from him.

Ava stood with Jones at the front of Sunnyside Primary School, watching as parents arrived to collect their children. Her green eyes scanned the playground and her breath caught in her throat as her pulse spiked and acid swished in her stomach. Every muscle locked into place, freezing her and her eyes widened.

Blake Synclair, in his crisp blue shirt peaking out of the dark wool coat he wore, made him look as delicious as he always did. He was standing with another dark-haired man that had his back to her. The gasp that left her lips at the same moment Blake trained his rich dark brown eyes on her.

"Dad!" George yelled, and she watched in abject horror at the warm smile which curved Blake's lips.

"I-I've got to go." Ava stuttered as she quickly turned on her heel and bolted back inside the school.

The tears once again surging forth like a tidal wave. The sob which broke free from her mouth sounded like a wounded animal screaming for help as she sunk into the office chair. Her shaking hands flying to her face as she sobbed her broken heart out in the quiet room of her office.

The moment she walked through the front door with her eyes swollen and red from crying, she breathed a sigh of relief that the house was empty. Dropping her handbag and keys by the front door before she flopped down on the sofa.

Staring at the ceiling in the pitch dark and deathly silence, all she could hear was the dull thud of her barely beating heart. Her teeth clamped onto her quivering lower lip in hopes of stopping the next wave of tears that she was quickly blinking back.

She felt hollow inside, felt like he'd sucked everything out of her and left her empty and broken. Ava had been tormenting herself with thoughts of Blake. Tormenting herself with how he'd blinded her. Tormenting herself at how he'd managed to weave the deceit into everything that he'd told her. How he'd managed to make her believe that he loved her the way she did him.

"Hey, squirt." James greeted, turning the lights on in the living room as she jumped, raising her head to look at him covered in oil and grease. "You okay today?" he asked, his knuckles tapping against the back of the sofa.

"Yes." she croaked out the lie, turning away from her brother.

"Uh-huh." his hand rubbed the back of his neck. "Look, I know I gave you a hard time over – well, mystery man." James faltered, his eyes cast downward.

"I don't want to talk about it." her voice was low and dangerously close to breaking around a sob she was desperately trying to swallow back.

"Ava…" James groaned. "It's…." he stopped talking, placing the heel of his hands against his eyes. Dragging a hard breath in. "It's killing me seeing you like this." anger surged forth through her body, white hot and fiery as she jumped up from the sofa.

"You know what?" Ava pushed past him with a death glare. "I'll grab some clothes and make myself scarce." she shouted, her eyes narrowed. "So you don't have to see me like this!" she continued shouting as she began racing up the stairs.

In her fit of temper, the rational part of her brain didn't think about the implications of packing an overnight bag and storming out. Which was why she found herself parked in a reserved parking spot outside of Synclair Hotel.

Blake Synclair's reserved parking spot, to be more specific.

The rational part of her brain had only just kicked back in, but unless she wanted to spend the night in her car, she really didn't have any choice but to rent a room for the night. It was more preferable than going back home. Especially when James will try to talk to her again or worse, the pitiful looks Katie keeps throwing her way.

Blowing out a frustrated breath, she swings the door open, grabs her bag and that was her confidence gone. Bowing her head, she shuffled her feet slowly towards the main door, trying not to look at anyone on her way and trying to keep the tears from falling once again.

"Good evening, Ms Asherton." at the sound of her name, she snapped her eyes to the distinguished aged man with a kind smile.

"Patrick, hi." she forced a cheeriness to her voice that she didn't feel.

"Doctor Synclair isn't in residence." he tilted his head for a moment, his eyes tracking over her face before he held his hand out.

"Come with me, I don't think he'd mind you being in his room." Patrick escorted her to the elevators and swiped the key card for the penthouse suite.

"Uh, I don't have a card for his room." she flushed slightly and chewed on her bottom lip. Certain that he would make her leave.

"I have and for tonight it's all yours." he smiled, his eyes softening. "Just let me have it back before seven in the morning."

"Of course." she took the card. "Thank you, Patrick."

"Anytime, Ms Asherton." with that, the doors slid closed, and she was once again alone to wallow in her self pity.

Self pity at how naïve she had been.

Self pity at how she'd given everything to Blake and what did he do, ripped it all apart and gave her everything back broken.

Dropping her bags beside the door, her eyes scanned the pristine hotel room. It was a far cry from what she had seen the last time she had been here. The ache in her chest intensified as she closed her eyes briefly and took a deep inhale. Sad that his scent didn't fill her nostrils, sad that she didn't feel his arms around her and sad that she didn't feel his lips against her neck.

"I need a drink." she muttered to herself, shuffling across the expanse of the room towards the drinks cabinet.

Searching the drinks cabinet, she found a full bottle of whiskey, not something she usually drank but she needed the alcohol to numb her pain.

Throwing the full glass down her throat in one gulp, the burn had her coughing slightly before she refilled the glass and gulped it down in quick succession. The alcohol began to numb her, and she swayed slightly as she filled the glass for a third time.

The glass clutched in her hand, Ava stood, her eyes unfocused for a long, silent moment. Her heartbeat slow, her breaths shallow and tears gathered on her lashes. Sucking in a deep breath, she knew that she was only torturing herself, but she couldn't help it.

Pulling the door to the closet open, her pulse spiked as she saw his clothes neatly hanging from the rails. She needed to feel close to him. On a long sigh, she stripped the clothes from her body. Reaching out a shaking hand, she pulled one of his white shirts from the rail. The fabric crinkled beneath her fingers as she brought it to her nose and inhaled deeply. The wash of sadness flowed through her when his scent was missing, making her bow her head and her breath to stutter as a sob tried to spew forth into the deafening silence. A shiver tore through her body as she shrugged the shirt over her naked body, leaving the buttons undone.

Sat on the large bed, the coldness of the covers raising goosebumps with her phone in one hand and the glass of whiskey in the other, her thumb hovered over Blake's name. She didn't want to ring him, and yet she wanted to hear his voice. Felt the sheer desperate need flood her body like blood flowing through her veins.

It was bittersweet that now she was the one to walk away he was constantly calling or messaging her. Sighing into the empty room, she tipped the glass down her throat and jumped when her phone buzzed in her hand, Blake's name flashing across the screen. Through the alcohol buzz that had numbed her mind but not her traitorous body, her thumb swiped across before she placed the phone to her ear.

"Ava?" the husky rasp in his voice made her stomach clench and her heart ache.

"You need to stop calling me, Blake." she whispered, trying to not slur her words. Silent tears tracked down her cheeks as she said the words she didn't mean. All she wanted was to crawl into his lap, have his arms wrapped around her as he whispered those sinful words into her ear that set her body on fire.

"Never." he whispered painfully. "I need to talk to you." he continued, she heard rustling through the receiver.

"No." she shook her head. "I can't." her whispered words were tortured, the tears blurred the surrounding room.

"I know where you are." she took a deep breath, her eyes squeezing shut as her pulse spiked.

"Then come get me." she whispered so low that she wasn't certain he'd heard her, but the moment she heard his growl down the phone she knew that the deceitful, delectable heartbreaker was coming for her and the line went dead.

She knew why she'd said it. She wanted to see him, wanted to kiss him, wanted to make love to him, wanted him to hold her close and wanted to hear him whisper into her ear.

One last time.

Chapter Forty-Seven

The Aston Martin screeched to a halt at the back of Ava's car. His palms were clammy and his heart was thundering in his chest as relief flowed through him. His mind had been racing as he'd squeezed the accelerator to illegal limits as he'd weaved through traffic across town. Racing with the possibility that she would have left before he'd managed to get here.

Slicking his hands down his shirt, striding purposefully across the car park with the usual doorman waiting.

"Doctor Synclair." Blake held up a hand to silence him.

"I know." his voice bit out with a curt nod. "Thank you." he muttered as he passed.

The warmth of the hotel tried to wrap around him and the familiar scents tried to soothe the turmoil within, but Blake knew nothing would ease his torment until he had Ava wrapped in his arms once again. The consequences of his thoughts were clogging his mind, the selfishness of his actions was warring within him, but he didn't care.

All he cared about was Ava, back where she belonged.

With him.

His breath stuttered out as his dark gaze fell on Ava. Her dark hair spilled across her shoulders, her small hand gripped the glass tumbler, her face was a broken mask of emotion and her body was naked beneath his shirt. She looked like a broken angel.

His hands balled into fists, his chest expanded on a deep inhale, and his eyes tracked over every-fucking-curve she possessed. He couldn't help the growl that tore from his throat, couldn't help the possessiveness that whipped through him, but her words nearly broke him.

"Hurt me." she whispered, her tongue flicked across her lip and he felt every-fucking-sweep of her gaze across his body.

"No." he snarled, stalking towards the bed. "I need to talk to you." the anguish in his voice was palpable and his heart cracked again as she shook her head.

"Hurt me or leave." he watched her gulp the entire contents of the glass before she placed it on the bedside table.

Swallowing thickly, his trembling hand shoved through his hair as he sucked in a deep breath. His stomach roiled at the thought of what she wanted him to do. Acid swished and burnt his insides, which had him squeezing his eyes closed. Flashbacks from the night he'd brought her here, when she'd begged him to fuck her, when he'd denied her. His breathing shaky as he tried to calm the riot inside of him.

He didn't want to do it.

Didn't want to treat her like he did the others he brought here. He wanted her wrapped around him, wanted to have her, and wanted her to listen to what he had to say. He knew the only way she would listen was if he gave her what she wanted. Knew that once it was over and she was wrapped in his arms, she'd listen and knew that for all of his selfishness, he'd never let her go.

Before he could think about what he was doing, his hands gripped her ankles and pulled roughly until she was laid on the bed. His breathing quickened and his hands trembled slightly as he unbuttoned his shirt. The moment the fabric hit the floor, he heard her breath hitch in the back of her throat.

Blake's lips twitched as he shoved his pants and boxers to the floor, before kneeling on the bed. His hands gripping her thighs, his fingers digging into her soft flesh, wrenching them apart. His tongue darted across his lips as he looked at her pussy, open and wet for him. The scent of her arousal stoking the primal urge inside of him to take her.

"Is this what you want, hmm?" the hardness in his voice raised goosebumps along her skin as he covered her body with his. Gripping her hip roughly, forcing her into the mattress but she tried to writhe against him. "Want me to treat you like a dirty whore?" his thigh pressed harshly against her weeping pussy and a low moan filled the room. "Want to be fucked hard and fast." the hard steel of his voice was low against her ear. "Want me to hurt you, to drive you to pure fucking painful madness?" his free hand wrapped around her throat.

He felt liquid seep from her core and her nipples hardened against his chest. Her tongue darted out to lick across her lips and her thighs shook slightly.

"Yes." she breathed out.

His dark eyes roamed over every inch of her face and saw the hatred burning against the twist of her lips, saw the desire and torment in her eyes. His nostrils flared slightly and his eyes darkened before he slammed his lips against hers. They were hard and demanding against her softer ones, goosebumps erupted over every inch of his skin. Hard groans ripped from her throat. His tongue was a solid muscle as he thrust it between her parted lips, sweeping, tasting, owning every inch of her mouth.

Blake moved further into her body, pulling her pelvis to his.

The thick column of his erection rubbed against her wet folds. A whimper escaped her as his teeth bit down on her lower lip, making her hiss out in pain before he ripped his mouth from hers. Their harsh breaths mingling together. Their chests heaving with every breath. The friction on his cock as he continued to rub against her.

"Syn." she moaned, arching her back until her nipples scrapped against his chest.

"What?" he bit out.

"Fuck me." she begged, thrusting her hips against him.

His fingers tightened around her throat, he felt her try to swallow as her throat rippled against his palm. Her body arched against him as he snapped his hips forward in a brutal thrust. Her pussy clenched around his cock, her wetness was pure fire against him.

Blake trailed his lips up her jaw, nipping her earlobe, making her arch against him. Exposing the length of her neck, his tongue travelled the column, circling around her wild pulse. He dipped his tongue into the indent of her collarbone. His teeth sunk into her shoulder on a groan, the metallic taste of her blood on his tongue as he broke the skin. Ava hissed through her clenched teeth.

"You wanted the pain." his words were rough as he stared at her. Those green eyes were filled with tears and the acid in his stomach swished painfully. "Want me to stop?" he couldn't help the slight mock in his words, but as she shook her head no and he fought back the bile that raced up this throat.

His hand inched over the curve of her waist, cupping her breast tightly as he lowered his mouth and bit down on her breast and pinched her nipple at the same time. Ava's fingernails raked down his back, making him groan. He moved across to her other breast, biting and pinching her nipple. His other hand flexing around her throat as he released some of his grip.

Blake reared back, gripping her hip, and drove his cock into her on a hard thrust, groaning as she convulsed around him. She was so tight, it took everything in him not to cum. Squeezing his eyes closed, he pulled back and slammed into her harder, deeper, faster.

Bile continued to race up his throat on every slam of his hips into her that he was continuously swallowing back. Her nails cut into his skin as his brutal thrusts slammed into her.

He felt her pussy ripple and tighten on every thrust until he pulled his cock from her. Smirking as her eyes snapped to his in pure fire. Her strangled cry ripped from her throat as he denied her what she wanted.

"Welcome to the pure fucking painful madness." he snarled against her ear. "Up on all fours, dirty whore." he continued, removing himself from the bed. His cock throbbing and was leaking with need.

He couldn't do this!

She wanted this!

She hates me enough to endure this!

Fuck!

Ripping his belt free from his discarded pants, his fingers grazed over the smooth, unyielding leather that was cool to his touch. His dark eyes blazed a wicked fury he'd never felt before as he watched her perfect plump ass swap slightly from side to side. It was hypnotic.

Breathing deeply, wrapping the buckle end of the belt around his fist, he moved with a slow purpose. He heard the slight whimper of need fall from her lips that had his lips thinning into a hard line. With a harsh exhale and with his eyes squeezed shut, he lashed out. The leather whistling through the air, the loud crack against her perfect plump ass and her scream of pain had the bile rising quickly. The acid burning this throat, the ugliness of him twisting his insides and the scream of pain had sweat licking across his skin.

"More." the demand in her voice had his knees trying to buckle.

Another two whips in quick succession had the same pain filled scream ricocheting off of the walls and his stomach lurching. In this moment, he hated himself for doing as she'd asked. Hated himself for the deep red welts that bloomed across her creamy flesh, but most of all he hated the whimper of need falling from his perfect, innocent and pure Ava.

"Does the dirty whore want me to stop?" his voice was rough and laced with self hatred.

"No." she gritted out, making him shake his head with disgust.

"Tough!" he growled, jumping back onto the bed. His hand lightly touched the welts on her ass and the hiss of pain fell from her lips as she tensed ever so slightly. "You can't handle any more." he gritted out, unwrapping the belt from his hand, he was intent on discarding it.

"You need to give me the physical pain, Syn." she spat at him with her forehead resting on the bed. Wrapping the belt around her throat, he pulled gently until she was arched perfectly.

"No!" he growled low and dangerous in her ear, his fist white knuckled from the grip on the belt as if it was the grip on his sanity. "I never meant to hurt you." the pain in his voice was palpable.

"If you're not going to hurt me, then fucking leave." she spewed the words so hurtful it felt as if his chest caved in and air expelled from his lungs.

He knew that he should walk away. Knew that if he did what she asked for, he'd lose her forever, but as his cock brushed against her soaking wet pussy, he couldn't help snapping his hips and burrowing deep inside her quivering heat. The deep tortured moan that spilled from her lips had him rearing back and thrusting forward again. Another deep moan, another thrust until he couldn't stop.

Blake knew the moment the belt tightened dangerously around her throat, knew that the death grip he had on it was cutting off her air supply, but his brain had snapped. Snapped back to all the other whores he'd had in this room. All of them begged him to do just this, flirt with the edge of danger.

Squeezing his eyes shut and swallowing back the bile in his throat as her pussy convulsed around him in a brutal grip. Her body shook violently as her orgasm rushed through every fibre of her body.

"Dirty fucking whore." Blake growled deep and low in her ear, earning another brutal squeeze on his cock before he erupted deep inside of her. "And you're all fucking mine." he continued in her ear. He felt the shiver glide down her spine and he wondered briefly why she liked the depravity.

Releasing the belt from her throat and discarding it on the floor, his arms wrapped around Ava and gently lowered her to the bed. His cock still buried deep inside of her. The aftershocks of her climax sent shivers down his spine as they lay on their sides with her back pressed against his chest.

"I need you to leave." Ava croaked out on a harsh breath, but he couldn't leave.

Not like this.

"I'll never leave you, baby girl." he whispered, pressing his lips to her neck. She tried to move away from him, but he tightened his hold on her.

"Let me go, Blake." she whispered a moment before her elbow collided with his side, making his hold loosen as he sucked in a painful breath.

Her nails dug into his hands a moment before she began slapping viscously against his hold. The sharp stings of pain caught him off guard and within a blink of an eye she was standing, her beautiful green eyes full of tears were narrowed into slits.

"If you don't leave." her voice was too low, too full of hatred. "I will." that was the last straw as he jumped off the bed.

"You told me you loved me!" he roared across the expanse of the bed.

"You're married!" she screamed back as tears slithered down her reddened cheeks.

"I need you!" he blared at her, his hands pulling his hair in pure frustration.

"Get the fuck out!" the ear-splitting banshee scream had him wincing, but he wasn't leaving. "I hate you Blake Synclair!" she continued, and those words were enough for the emotion he'd tried to hide come flooding in hurtful waves and tears clung to his lashes.

Bowing his head as a silent tear fell down his face, had him re-dressing and walking away.

Blake's head banged against the closed hotel room door. His

hands clenched into tight fists, harsh breaths had his chest rising and falling in rapid succession. Squeezing his eyes shut against the heart wrenching sobs in the room behind him.

"Fuck!" he hissed, fists banging once on the door behind him. "I've lost her!" he whispered, his eyes snapping open as his pulse spiked. "I've fucking lost her." his words were tortured as he muttered them aloud into the empty hall.

Chapter Forty-Eight

Ava wrapped her arms around her shaking body, guttural sobs ripped from her sore throat and the pain she felt across her abused ass cheeks helped dull the pain in her chest. Even if it was only for a little while.

She knew that she'd pushed Blake into hurting her.

She could see the disgust etched onto his handsome face when she'd demanded it. She could see just how much it hurt him to do what she wanted. But what she hadn't expected was just how painful he could make her hurt, and certainly didn't expect just how much she enjoyed that side of him. It made her wonder just how broken she actually was. Made her wonder just how messed up her head was because of him and definitely made her realise just how much she loved him.

Blake Synclair – Sinful. Delectable. Deceitful. Heartbreaker.

Ava thought that she was strong enough for one last kiss, one last fuck, one last hug and one last night but as her body shook violently and the coldness of the room iced over her naked body, she knew that she had made a mistake. Knew that she only craved him more. Knew that she only wanted him. Knew that there would never be anyone else who could make her burn for him, make her love him the way Blake did.

Squeezing her eyes shut as the words they'd screamed at each other vibrated against her skull.

"You told me you loved me!"

"You're married!"

"I need you!"

"Get the fuck out!"

"I hate you Blake Synclair!"

Words that in the heat of the moment hurt them both, words that left a deep throb of a headache.

She knew that she couldn't forgive him for the lies. Couldn't forgive him for making her his mistress and certainly couldn't forgive herself for taking a little boy's dad away from him.

But the selfish part of her wanted to keep Blake. Wanted to forget everything that she'd learnt about him and wanted to make sure he stayed with her forever.

The problem she faced was that she knew that she'd lost him forever in the space of one night.

The morning dawned with big, thick storm clouds and splattering rain against the windows. Ava groaned and hissed in pain as she turned onto her back before she quickly flipped back onto her front. Her eyes felt swollen and scratchy from another night of crying herself to sleep.

Her dreams hadn't been much nicer and she'd tossed and turned for the majority of the night. Blake had been in her dreams, cherishing her and showing her how much she meant to him before it morphed into the stunning blonde, Nancy and her cruel words that had cast the shadow of doubt on Ava and made her delve into the deceitful lies Blake had told her. There was no respite for her mind and there certainly was no peace where he was concerned.

She knew that despite everything that she still loved him and despite her better judgement, knew that if he came to her again she wouldn't be able to stay away from him. Ava didn't want to stay away from him and in the cold light of day as her words and actions from last night flooded back in, she knew that he would definitely stay away from her.

A soft knock on the penthouse suite door had her bolting upright and her heart skipping a beat as her mind went directly to the image of Blake stood on the other side of the door. Shaking her head and blowing out a breath, she knew that wouldn't be the case and she felt stupid for even thinking that. Especially when it was her who pushed him away and told him to leave her alone.

Wrapping a thick, white towelling bathrobe around her naked body, she padded across the expanse of the suite. Her hands shook slightly as she tied the bathrobe tightly before opening the door.

"Patrick." Ava greeted with a slight furrow to her brow.

"Good morning, Ms Asherton." he politely smiled before gesturing to the partial open door. "May I come in?" her heart slapped against her throat as she nodded her head by way of acceptance. "I've brought coffee with me too." his smile was kind as he held two take-out cups in a double cardboard cup holder.

Ava sat in the chair that gave her a direct view of the rest of the suite, smiling tightly as she took the proffered cup of coffee. Her eyes tracked Patrick's movements as he sat with a rigid spine on the edge of the sofa, the coffee cup clasped in his hand.

"So, uh....does Blake want me to leave?"she asked; her voice was low and unsure as she sunk her teeth into her lower lip which was mainly to stop it from quivering.

"On the contrary, Ms Asherton." Patrick turned slightly as his eyes pinned her with a stare. "You can stay as long as you need." the relief that washed through her was palpable. "I bet you're wondering why I'm here?" he smiled before taking a sip of his coffee.

"Yeah, I am." she swallowed thickly as her stomach tried to twist with unease.

"I've known Blake since he was a little boy." Patrick began, his voice soothing. "He's a special man who isn't afraid to stand up for what he wants." Ava furrowed her brow and tilted her head slightly at his words. "He risked the fallout with his father to become a doctor and it never deterred him from his goal." he smiled but his eyes held sadness in them. "I don't know what has happened with you both and I don't want to know." he sighed before taking another sip of his coffee. "He's a good man, Ava and he always has been." he held his hand up to silence her. "He's been lost for a very long time and during that time he's made some questionable choices."

"I don't understand why you're telling me this." Ava admitted with her shoulders slumping slightly and Patrick smiled, his eyes softening as he looked at her.

"I'm telling you this because you have brought the old Blake back. The old part of him that was lost and it's nice to see someone that is willing to fight for him and to love him." he shook his head slightly as he finished his drink. "I can see that you love him, but you have to understand that this road for him isn't easy."

"What do you mean, isn't easy?" she asked clasping the coffee cup in both hands as they shake slightly. She watched Patrick look at his watch before standing.

"I've taken up enough of your time, Ms Asherton." he turned on his heel, striding across the suite until his hand curved around the doorhandle. "I hope that you don't throw everything away on a whim." those final words echoed around the suite, so much so that she didn't hear the door close.

Flopping back into the chair pulling her knees to her chest

and wrapping her arms around them, she placed her chin on her knees and let her mind fill her with the constant, heartbreaking images of Blake flood through her mind until she was once again a blubbering mess.

Chapter Thirty-Nine

Ava's legs felt shaky as she descended the stairs, her hand gripping the balustrade tightly until her feet landed on the foyer floor. She wasn't certain how long she had been upstairs and after expelling the contents of her stomach, brushing her teeth and cleaning up her make-up, her thoughts had quietened down and her stomach had settled. Blowing out a breath, straightening her shoulders, door opening until a large hand gripped her wrist and pulling with strength. Immediately plunged into darkness, a squeak tore from her throat and her heart hammered against her chest until his scent wrapped around her.

"Where've you been?" his voice was rough and the scent of whiskey on his breath washed over her lips as his hand wrapped around her throat.

"I just..." she broke off as his lips nipped and sucked the length of her neck, a moan escaping as she arched her back. "Needed a..."

"Hmm, you taste so fucking good." he husked out, his tongue trailing across her shoulder. A shudder of pleasure skittered down her spine. Her hands fisted his shirt as she arched against him. "Orgasm one, fingers, mouth or cock?"

"Mouth." she breathed out and her toes curled at the primal growl that ripped from his throat a second before his teeth sunk into her shoulder, making her cry out from the pain.

Blake's fingers slid beneath her dress, his knuckles caressing her thigh as his other flexed around her throat. Her chest heaved, heart pounded, and pussy clenched as his palm blazed to the curve of her hip. His fingers curling around the thin strap of the white lace thong. The snap of the fabric had liquid heat burning through her and a gasp escaping as another shudder then slithered down her body. The lace material was pulled slowly from between her thighs. The fabric grazing her swollen clit before he tucked them in his pants pocket.

Those dark eyes of his roamed over every inch of her face. His nostrils flared slightly and his eyes darkened further before he slammed his lips against hers. They were hard and demanding against her softer ones, goosebumps erupted over every inch of her skin at the feel of him dominating her. His fingers flexed against her and tightened ever so slightly as a moan ripped from her throat. His tongue was a solid muscle as he thrust it between her parted lips, sweeping, tasting, owning every inch of her mouth before his hand dropped from her throat.

"I need you to be quiet while I fuck this greedy little pussy." he husked out. "Can you do that, be nice and quiet like the good girl?" his hands bunched her skirt around her hips. The cool air of the darkened room making her shiver. "Or are you going to be my naughty girl, who needs to be gagged?" she saw the blazing fire in his eyes and god help her, she couldn't promise to be quiet.

"Gagged." she whispered, licking over her lips, her eyes lidded with desire.

"Hmm." His chest vibrated with the hum. "Open wide, naughty girl." he smirked as he stuffed her ripped panties inside her mouth. The fabric was rough against her tongue and the taste of her arousal danced across her taste buds. "Keep your hands pressed against the wall and your legs wide." he growled low, hooking one of her legs over his shoulder as he quickly knelt before her.

The warm wetness of his tongue licked directly up the middle of her core. Her chest vibrated with the moan, which was muffled from her panties as it tried to escape. She steadied her hands against the wall at the same time his tongue flicked against her engorged clit before his teeth grazed the pulsing bud. The sensation of his wicked tongue exploring her meticulously had her climax already beginning to build. Her breathing became hard pants, the muscles in her thighs began to tremble and pleasure raced over every nerve ending in her body.

Blake's tongue thrust inside of her wet heat, groaning against her, sent a fresh wave of moisture to leak directly onto his tongue. His fingers gripped her ass cheeks, pulling her against his mouth as he continued to thrust in and out of her. Ava's muffled moans were getting louder as her hips ground down against his tongue, sending another deep groan from his mouth, the vibration ricocheted through her body and her eyes fluttered closed.

Her pussy clenched around his tongue, and her stomach tightened as her climax neared. Ava ground down against his tongue, thrusting inside of her. His fingers gripped her ass cheeks tighter, and the pleasure was rolling through her in waves, but the moment his teeth sunk into her thigh she exploded in throbbing, hot sparks of delightful pulsing waves. Her muffled scream had Blake growling before yanking his mouth away and clamping a hand across her mouth.

"Such a naughty girl." his voice was rough but his eyes were still blazing as he removed the panties from her mouth.

The dryness was uncomfortable, Snaking her tongue into his mouth, they both groaned with the combined taste as she swirled her tongue around his, gathering as much as she could before he ripped his mouth from hers.

"Fuck!" he hissed out, breathing as hard as each other. "I could keep you locked in here for the rest of the evening." he groaned out before taking a step away from her.

The room was suddenly cast in a blinding light which had her almost choking around the fear of being caught that was lodged in her throat. The deep smirk on Blake's lips had her face flaming and stomach clenching.

"God, you frightened me to death, then." she admonished with a light slap to his chest before she realised they were in a bathroom.

"Scared my father caught us?" he chuckled, making her shake her head. "Don't worry, I won't let anyone ever see you fall apart in pleasure." his arms banded around her. His chest to her back. "That's for my fucking eyes only." he husked out into her ear before he let her go and stepped back. "Come on, let's get cleaned up and go get my naughty girl a well-deserved drink." his hand landed a stinging slap to her ass and she couldn't help the groan the flew from her lips.

"You better do that again, Syn." Ava's voice was breathless as she turned towards the mirror to clean up her make-up.

"Hmm, don't worry, I'll do that with my fingers deep inside you." he smirked as he washed his hands and face. Washing her glistening arousal from his mouth before he smoothed out the dress shirt.

The moment they walked through the double wooden doors, Ava felt like they were plunged into another party. The lighting had been dimmed considerably, the music was louder and the dance floor was almost full of couples gliding elegantly around the floor. Breathing a sigh of relief when she noticed that nobody paid them any attention as they walked towards the dance floor.

Ava's hand was seized and within an instant she was twirled into Blake's strong arms. Her startled gasp rushed out as the heat from his body surrounded her. His muscles shuddering beneath her palm against his chest.

"I couldn't resist having you in my arms for everyone to see." his words were possessive and full of heat as he swayed them in time with the music. "You're so beautiful, baby girl." he whispered, his eyes staring directly into hers and shining with warmth.

Blake's large hand blazed a searing trail of liquid heat over the contours of her spine, over the flare of her hip, and squeezing ever so gently before she was spun away from the warmth of his body. A smile broke out across her face as she was pulled back into his body. His lips pulled into a smouldering smile, his dimples appearing beneath the stubble had her pulse quickening and her pussy clenching with need.

Their mouths were a breath apart. Blake snaked his tongue out and swiped once across the seam of her lips. She gasped, and his sinfully wicked tongue delved into her mouth. His hands inched up her sides and over her exposed throat before cupping her cheeks, angling her head for better access, then his tongue was exploring the deepest, darkest parts of her mouth, twining his tongue with hers and sliding his lips against hers. He swallowed her little moans which spilled into his mouth and time seemed to stand still as he claimed her mouth on the dance floor.

"Let's grab a drink." he pulled his mouth away and their harsh breaths mingling as he dropped his forehead against hers. "Then we'll have orgasm number two." he smirked as her cheeks flamed.

Blake signalled a passing waiter as they sat at an unoccupied table with his arm resting across the back of her chair. The male waiter smiled, handing her a glass of wine before grabbing the tumbler full of amber liquid and setting it down on the table. Blake narrowed his eyes slightly as the waiter lowered the tray before scurrying away.

"I enjoyed dancing with you." Ava smiled around the rim of the wineglass before taking a sip. Blake turned towards her, his eyebrow raised and a smile playing on his lips.

"Me too." he moved closer to her. "I don't usually dance." his lips grazed her ear. "Only for someone special." he husked out before pulling back, his hand gripping the glass tumbler.

"Oh." her eyes widened as his words filtered through her brain, making her heart skip a beat. "Well, I must be seen as this is the second time we've danced together." she continued, taking a sip of her own drink.

Blake's hands gripped the chair Ava was sitting on and in one fluid yank, her chair banged against his. A startled squeak left her and her heart thudded against her chest. Without a glance, his arm curved around her, pulling until her body crashed into his side. The warmth from him seared her. His stubbled jaw scraped against her cheek as his lips trailed the length until his teeth nibbled her lobe, stealing her breath.

"Three times, we've danced together three times baby girl." he whispered, his tongue dipping into her ear making her moan. "I need you close to me." slowly inching her dress up, the soft fabric whispering over the of her thighs, his fingers nudging her legs apart.

"You can't do that here." Ava hissed as his teeth nipped beneath her ear. Her thighs quivering as she tried to keep them closed, but it was no use.

"Remember that night." he whispered, his fingers trailing slowly up her inner thigh. He groaned when his fingers became slick with her juices that slicked her thighs. "In the restaurant, when you were so wet for me." his breathing was turning heavy as he slicked through her folds. "At the thought of people watching me fuck you." he groaned low against her ear as she lightly moaned. "You screamed so loud that night." he growled as his fingers swirled around her engorged clit. "Let's see how innocent you can be." his lips pressed against her wild pulse at the same moment two fingers sank into her.

"Oh god!" she breathed out, her pussy quivering around his fingers, trying to draw them in deeper.

He pulled them out, sweeping around her entrance before thrusting them back in, harder, making her sink her teeth harshly into her bottom lip to stop her from moaning loudly. She kept her eyes trained on the dance floor.

"Good girl." he breathed, curling his fingers inside of her, brushing against the spot that always sent an instant deep throb through her core. "Keep watching all these people, while I make you cum all over my fingers." her cheeks flushed and her chest heaved.

The muscles in her stomach tightened, the pads of his fingers pressing, releasing, rubbing against the sweetest of spots inside of her. Her teeth drew blood and her nails dug into the palms of her hands as she stopped the moans from spilling free. Blake's fingers never stopped pressing, releasing, rubbing over and over. A tight ball of pleasure was building faster, bigger.

"I'm going to squirt if you don't stop." she whispered, hoping that he'd stop, but the answering growl had her hips moving of their own accord.

"Squirt all over, naughty girl." his rough voice and his teeth nipping her lobe had her careening over the edge and wetness pouring from her in waves when her orgasm hit. The deep throbbing exploded, and she knew that she'd soaked his hand. The deep growl in her ear sent a pleasurable tremble through her body. "Good girl." he whispered, removing his fingers as he pressed a kiss to her neck.

"Mrs Synclair." Ava practically shouted, quickly smoothing her skirt down beneath the table.

"Ava." Marion smiled as she took a seat opposite her. "Are you enjoying yourself?" she asked, taking a sip of the wine she had gripped in her hand.

"Hmm, yes." she flushed a deeper shade as she watched from her peripheral Blake wipe his fingers on his pants. "It's been lovely." she smiled tightly, her shaking hand gripping her own wineglass.

"Mother, you've outdone yourself." Blake's rough voice made her shiver. The glass tumbler pressed against his sinful lips before taking a generous gulp of his whiskey.

"Awe honey." her voice and smile were warm. "You have your father's charm." she shook her head. "I'm sorry we haven't spent much time together this weekend, but I'm sure you two have kept busy." Marion looked behind her briefly before turning her dark gaze back on them. "Are you still attending lunch tomorrow?" her eyes held a hint of trepidation as she finished her wine.

"Yes." Blake gave a single nod with a small smile, but Ava could tell that he wasn't overly certain of his words.

"We can't wait to have lunch with you both." Ava smiled, gripping his trembling hand that was resting against his thigh. Squeezing gently, silently letting him know that everything's okay and hoping that he doesn't have a panic attack.

"Oh well, that's settled then." Marion stood gracefully with a warm smile. "I'll see you tomorrow." with that she made her way across to the dance floor. Mister Synclair securing her before leading her into an elaborate dance.

"I'm ready for orgasm three." Ava whispered, licking over her lips as his dark eyes snared her. "I just hope this time it's with your cock."

"Is that so." he stood abruptly, pulling her with him. "Tell me naughty girl, do you want to get spanked whilst I fuck that greedy pussy?"

"Why, Syn, that's an offer I definitely want to accept." she smiled as he growled low in the back of his throat before leading them from the ballroom.

Chapter Forty-Nine

The crisp late October morning air almost stole his breath as he burrowed deeper into the dark wool coat. The sun was beginning to peek from behind grey storm clouds. The loud creak of the black metal gate pierced the deafening silence, making him wince at the noise.

Blake's pulse spiked and his palms became a little clammy as he strode down the winding path. Manicured lawns on either side with colourful flowers dotted haphazardly. He couldn't contain the smile that broke out across his face.

"Morning buddy." Blake's voice was light as he sat. "Daddy's home." the mere words were enough to make his heart swell and expand. But the silence he was met with had him sighing. "I know you're upset with me, your mum is too." his voice wavered with sadness that was beginning to seep through his body.

His dark eyes unfocused, his heart rate kicking up. He hated the silence with his little boy. Hated how much he craved to hear him talk. Craved to hear him call out to him. Craved to feel his little arms wrapping around his leg when he came home.

Home, that one word holds so much meaning, holds so many memories and yet he has three. Three homes that are for all of his different sides.

The Penthouse Suite – that's his home when his demons come alive.

The Detached House – that's his home when he wants to see Ava.

This home – holds as much of his heart as he gave to the two most precious people in his world.

His wife and son.

"I know I haven't been home much lately." he swallowed thickly, closing his eyes to see the memory of Ava filtering through. "But you see, daddy's been trying to get better. Trying to be happier, just like I promised you." tears filled his eyes, his bottom lip quivered. "And for a short time, I was really happy. The happiest I'd been in a long time." his voice broke, a silent tear slithered down his face. "I miss you and your mum so much that it hurts. The pain is unbearable, and it hurts daddy so much." more tears tracked down his face. "But...." he sucked in a stuttering breath as his words trailed off.

The click-clacking of heels against the floor thundered in his ears. The tremor in his hands began, and his breath whooshed from his lungs. A small hand touched his arm, the long pink nails curving over his forearm.

"We need to talk." the soft, delicate voice had him squeezing his eyes closed.

He knew it was coming. He knew that she wouldn't stay away much longer, not when he was home.

Blake wondered how much she'd heard before the sound of her heels had him biting his tongue. Wiping the tears from his face with shaking hands, he stood and took a deep lungful of air as he concentrated on shutting down his emotions. Shutting everything down until the mask of indifference was firmly in place.

"Daddy will be back, I promise you George." he whispered

before turning on his heel. He nodded once at her. "Not here, not in front of him." he whispered.

They walked in silence for a few moments, only the sounds of her heels click-clacking on the floor could be heard. The crisp morning air had her shivering until he wrapped his arm around her shoulders, hugging her into the side of his body to share the warmth emanating from him.

"You need to tell the truth." her voice was so low as she looked behind her briefly.

"I know." he whispered right back with a nod. "I know." he repeated and the pain he felt every time he was home cracked through every facade he could place around him.

"Tell me what I can do, Blake." her voice cracked slightly. "Tell me how we can make this right." she continued, her slender hand tapping against his stomach. A gesture she'd done for years when he needed help, when he was struggling with himself.

"I....don't know." his shoulders slumped. "I've fucked up, I know I have." he admitted as they stopped in front of his car. His eyes travelling to the small baby bump, his hand reaching out to gently press against it. "Brings back so many memories of when George was bundled safely inside, growing to be strong." his voice was so low he wasn't certain she'd heard, but the moment he looked at her, the sad smile on her face and tears gathered on her lashes he knew. Knew that she'd heard him. And he couldn't stop himself from wrapping his arms around her, pulling her close as his lips pressed against the top of her head.

"So you're just going to leave?" the hurt in her tone sliced through him as she gestured to the bags on the front passenger seat. "You're giving up?" she wiggled out of his hold, her face pinched in anger and her eyes blazing at him. "You're not going to fight?" she threw her hands in the air. "Blake, you're better than that." she fumed.

"Don't you think I know that?" he hissed, his anger surfacing like a volcano eruption, quick and fiery. "But what can I do when she won't even fucking speak to me." his hands were clenched into fists at his side. "When she won't listen to anything and everything I want to fucking say to her." his voice was rising, cutting through the tranquillity of the morning. "I hurt her, Katie." his anger evaporated as quickly as it surfaced and now all he was left with was the pain.

"Because you didn't tell her the truth!" her voice was shrill. "Because you were too scared to tell her anything, that's why you lost her." her hands were shaking with her temper. "So, I'll ask you again what are we going to do about Ava?" she tilted her head slightly, her eyes staring directly at him. "I'll sell my own fucking soul to Lucifer if I have to, just to get the pair of you in the same room long enough for you to tell the fucking truth." her fierceness made him smile.

"Always ready for a fight, Katie." he chuckled. "But I don't know how to make this right." he admitted with a long drawn-out sigh.

"First of all, tell her the truth about Candice and George." her eyebrows raised as his jaw clenched. "Then you tell her how you feel." she nodded once. "That's how you will win her back and let's be honest here, Blake." she continued, arms folding across her chest. "Ava has been in love with you for years, she won't let herself throw it all away, but you have to tell her the truth."

Blake knew Katie was right. Knew that this could have all been avoided if he'd just told her.

"But how can I explain that I love my wife, son and her without fucking it all up?" he asked, desperation in his voice.

"Don't say it like that, for starters." Katie wrinkled her nose and twisted her lips in distaste. "Let her meet them." the moment the words were out of her mouth, he froze. Every muscle seized, sweat bloomed across the back of his neck and his hands began to shake.

"What if she doesn't like them?" his voice was so low and his eyes were wide in fear. Everything inside of him hurt and pulsed with terror as he voiced one of his main fears.

"Hey, since when has Ava ever met someone she doesn't like?" she asked with a smile. "You're worrying over nothing, Blake and you know it." she patted his arm like he was a child. "Go get Ava and let her meet Candice and George." with those words she turned and walked away, leaving him stood beside his loaded car.

He had packed yesterday. Packed enough clothes to go to his parents' home for a few weeks whilst he thought everything through. But after speaking with Katie, he knew he couldn't hide from the brutal truth of his life any longer. Not if he wanted to keep Ava.

Chapter Fifty

The Aston Martin screeched to a halt, Blake's heart pounding against his chest, his breaths were coming hard and fast as adrenaline coursed through his entire being. Throwing the door open, he didn't even bother closing it. His feet eating up the pavement at an alarming rate until he was standing at the door. His shaking hand banging against the wood door.

When he'd returned home to drop his bags off, the words he longed to say to her banging as loud around his mind as his fists were on the door. Sweat beaded his brow and the back of his neck. Her promises to him, promises that she was breaking.

She'd promised to never leave him, and yet, she'd done it, anyway.

The door swung open and those green eyes he was desperate to see were staring back at him, full of sorrow. His chest ached at the devastating sight.

"You promised." Blake's voice was dangerously low, his body practically vibrating with the need to wrap his arms around her and never let her go.

"Blake, I can't..." Ava's shoulders slumped. "Why can't you leave me alone?" Blake tried to grab her, but she smacked his hands away. His breaths were becoming more laboured, his heart more erratic in their beats, and his stomach was twisting violently.

"Please, I'm begging you." Blake's fingers gripped his hair and pulled in sheer frustration as she shook her head. "You promised." Blake's voice was barely above a whisper as it trembled the words out. "Baby girl, you promised." tears filled his eyes as he stared at her. "To love every part of me and to never leave me." he sunk to his knees as he felt the weight of his words.

A single tear tracked down his cheek.

"Don't, Blake." Ava's voice wavered on the verge of tears as he looked at her.

"I know I hurt you, but please listen to me." his voice was pleading, but he watched her shake her head. "Please, let me tell you everything." his shoulders dropped, hope fled as she took a step away from him.

"No, Blake." her words were a sheer whisper. "You need to go home to your wife and son." his eyebrows knitted together, his stomach twisted as bile rose in his throat which he quickly swallowed back and he felt the colour drain from his face.

"I can't." he whispered as he watched her almost crumble before him. His arms banded around her, his forehead resting against her stomach. "Let me take you somewhere." his voice was as desperate as his actions. His arms tightening around her when she tried to once again step away from him.

"Then tell me about Nancy." she said so low he wasn't certain he'd heard correctly, had his eyes snapping to hers. "Tell me about George, Blake." her tone was harsh and her eyes were filled with dread. Blake sighed, long and hard. His arms still banded around her, afraid to let her go.

He needed to tell her everything. Lay all his cards on the table. Relive the hardest parts of his life. The thing he promised to never do. But as his heart hammered against his chest and the pain he felt at losing Ava, he knew that he'd have to tell her everything. Knew that he owed her that much. But the fear rooted deep within him that she would leave him despite telling her what haunted him made him drag in a deep breath and trust his cousin.

"Nancy is my sister in law." he murmured, standing to his full height. "Not my wife." his arms quickly banding around her again to stop her from retreating. "I need you to come with me."

"Why?" her voice wavered.

"Come with me and you'll see." he tried to encourage her, but he still felt her feet rooted to the spot. Sighing, he quickly scooped her up and bundled her inside the car, locking the doors like the possessive asshole she had created, to ensure that she couldn't escape.

They drove out of the city into the countryside. The silence in the car was deafening and his knuckles were white from his death grip on the steering wheel. As the large rolling hills came into view, he could feel the weight of her stare on the side of his face, but he couldn't look at her. Every emotion he'd ever felt was coursing through his body, etched onto his face.

He just wasn't certain how he was going to cope once they were finally face to face.

Gravel crunched under the car's tires as he slowed to park in his reserved spot. His breath leaving him on a deep exhale as he tried to centre his emotions. His fear, his anxiety before he left the warmth for the bitter afternoon cold. He heard Ava exit the car, the door slamming shut behind her.

"What are we doing here?" her voice was low and unsure.

He watched her eyebrows furrow, watched her burrow deeper into her jumper before her bloodshot eyes locked on his.

"I think it's time I told you the truth." his hand gripped hers, tugging her towards him.

The loud creak of the black metal gate pierced the deafening silence, making him wince like it always did. The noise was terrifying and haunted him in the early hours of the morning when he was alone.

Blake's pulse spiked and his palms became a little clammy as he kept his grip firm on Ava's hand. They walked slowly down the winding path. He watched from his peripheral as she took in the manicured lawns that cost him a small fortune to ensure that they were kept perfect all year round. The colourful flowers dotted haphazardly reminded him of better times.

"Do you remember when you called me and I told you I was at home." Blake started his voice low as he stopped with the stone cottage on his left and the manicured garden to his right.

"Yeah, it was the fourteenth of October." Ava murmured, taking a step back. His grip tightened on her hand and giving her a gentle tug towards him before he began walking again. "But you weren't home." the accusation was quick to rid her voice of the confusion. The moment they reached the bottom of the garden, he stopped. "I was parked outside your house that was in pitch darkness."

"I was here." his voice was low as he tried to dampen the emotions warring within him. "I lived here with my family." his voice low as he let go of her hand and taking a step behind her, wrapping his arms around her shaking body. He needed to feel her against him. Needed the comfort only she brought him. "And when I'm missing them, I come home."

"Oh, Blake!" he heard the devastation in her voice but he needed to continue.

"Ava, I'd like you to meet Candice and George." a small smile on his face as he watched the confusion etch onto her face. "My wife and son." he turned towards his most heartbreaking view. "Candice, George, this is Ava."

"Blake, I don't understand." Ava whispered as she stared before her.

"Candice and I met in our last year of high school." his small smile was sad. "I fell head over heels for her." his voice lowered even further as he spoke the truth in front of his family. "We were engaged, married and expecting George within twelve months of meeting and I wouldn't have changed it for the world." he took a deep breath. "This home was a wedding present from my parents and Candice loved it here away from the city. She'd said it was a perfect place for George to grow up and I agreed with her." his chuckle was full of hurt at his words. "That night when you called was the anniversary of their death. George was only three years old at the time and Candice was twenty-two." tears were clinging to his lashes.

"Blake, why didn't you tell me?" he heard the hurt in her voice.

"Because if I told you, I would be admitting that they're gone." a sob broke out of his lips. "And I couldn't admit that. Couldn't admit that my wife and son were gone."

Ava turned in his arms and wrapped her arms around his waist, holding him close as he shattered at the truth he'd denied for twelve years. His body shook with his sobs, pulling her closer, crushing her soft curves to his body. Clinging desperately to the comfort that she brought him.

"The weekend at my parents, I spoke with Candice's parents

Mister and Mrs Appleton and I told them about you and who you were to me." he sucked in a deep breath before blowing it out again, in an effort to calm his emotions.

"I bet that was hard." he felt her eyes on him, watching every twitch of muscle which made him smile and now, he knew that he needed to tell her the rest.

"You once told me." his voice was rough with the turbulent emotion running rampant through his body. "That you loved me." he swallowed thickly, looking directly into her tear filled green eyes. "I never said it back to you that night, because I felt guilty." his admission was hard. "Guilty for wanting to be with you, guilty for losing control with you, guilty for taking everything you ever offered me, guilty for leaving my family." his lips quivering. "But most of all, I was guilty for loving you." he took a deep breath. "I really do love you baby girl." he pressed his forehead to hers.

"I know." Ava whispered.

Chapter Fifty-One

Ava stood with Blake's arms wrapped around her, his intoxicating scent engulfing her and warmth filling her. The coldness of the day was unable to penetrate her thin jumper and she relished the heat from his body. Her eyes once again landed on the two black granite grave stones that had perfectly etched gold writing of their names, date of birth and death and it broke her heart. He'd lovingly spent twelve years looking after them and she realised that for the past few months, she had in fact been competing with ghosts. Ghosts of his past and wondered if he'd ever be able to let it go enough to be happy.

The beautiful winter flowers surrounded the graves and the view beyond the low garden wall was breathtaking and full of the countryside.

She stood in pure silence as her mind thought over every interaction she had ever had with Blake from her being little, which caused her eyebrows to furrow and her lips to thin into a line. She didn't understand how she didn't know that Blake was married or that he had a son. Until a memory lodged deep within her mind of James rushing to pack a bag and their mum shouting at him to drive carefully. Ava had never realised what had happened and with her only being nine years old at the time, her mum had never spoken about it. But she remembered that James was gone for a few months before he returned home, which hadn't lasted before he too left after his marriage.

Her heart was hammering against her chest as she let his words sink in. Let his words weave through her mind until she wondered how lucky she was to have him. How lucky she was that he'd come for her and just how lucky she was that her delectable, sinful man loved her.

But she still needed answers from him, still needed some clarity on things before she could fully accept everything that he was saying to her.

"How do you know George from school?" she asked, her eyes scanning the open fields. She heard him sigh before he turned her to face him.

"He's my first cousin." Blake's eyes were soft, and his lips were curved into a small smile. "It's Katie's eldest brother, Damien's son." she furrowed her brow, shaking her head slightly.

"I heard you call his mother baby." she couldn't keep the hurt from her voice but all he did was chuckle as he pulled his mobile phone from his pocket. She watched his finger swipe across the screen before holding it out as the ringing filled the silence.

"Blake, to what do I owe this pleasure?" Damien chuckled down the line as Ava gasped. Her hand flying to her mouth. The voice was practically identical to Blake's.

"I've got someone with me who would like to speak to you." Blake smiled at Ava, his free hand cupping her cheek.

"It better not be Sara." Damien groaned. "I can't deal with her right now." he continued.

"No, it's not George's mum." Blake chuckled, shaking his head. "It's Ava Asherton." he smiled as he looked at her, nodding encouragingly.

"Hi, Damien." she almost whispered. "I'm Katie's friend." her teeth sunk into her lower lip as she heard him breathe harshly down the line.

"I know who you are." his voice had turned a little hard. "She's knocked up by your brother."

"Hmm." Ava glanced at Blake, who shook his head.

"Stop being an asshole, Damien." Blake almost growled. "Tell her about George." the command in his voice wasn't lost on Ava and it turned her insides to molten lava.

"What about him?" Damien almost spat the question before he inhaled harshly. Monotonous beeping sounding through the line.

"About why you called him George." Blake rolled his eyes.

"Oh, that." Damien fell silent for a moment. "I don't know, it just seemed fitting that with our sons being born on the same day, six years apart, we wanted to honour your son's memory." Damien's voice was low and rough. "Why?"

"Because, Ava thought George was my son." Blake admitted, his smile falling from his lips making Ava feel like shit.

"I'm George's teaching assistant." she interjected. "And when I saw Blake at school, I just assumed..."

"Ah, Blake, you sly dog!" Damien laughed down the line. "When are you going to tell James you're fucking his little sister?" he continued, laughing.

"Bastard!" Blake chuckled as his eyebrows furrowed. "I've got to go." Blake hung up on a still laughing Damien.

"Blake..." her voice quivered with emotion. "I'm sorry for not listening to you, sorry for making you do things that you didn't, but most of all..." she sucked in a deep breath. "I'm sorry for not being there for you when you needed me." tears welled in her eyes as his hands cupped her jaw. "I love you so much." she whispered, a small smile curving her lips as tears tracked down her cheeks.

"I love you too, baby girl." he stuttered a breath, his lips pressing to her hair. "I can't stand the thought of not being with you, of not seeing you every day and of you not waking up in my arms where you belong." he breathed out a deep breath. He tipped her head back until they were looking at each other. "I never thought I could love like this again, but then you blasted through every defence I ever had. You're my gift from Candice, from George and I won't ever let you go." his lips crashed to hers as he poured every emotion he possessed into her mouth.

"Are you ready to move forward?" she asked, her voice was quiet and their breathing was harsh.

"With you, most definitely." his smile was wide. "I want everything with you, Ava." he admitted, his dark eyes penetrating hers. "I want us to live together." he spoke the last words in a hushed whisper.

"Really?" Ava couldn't help the surprise in her voice, nor could she help searching his eyes for the truth in his words.

"Really." he brushed his lips against hers. "I want to wake up with you everyday wrapped in my arms."

"That'd be nice, Blake." she admitted, licking over her lips. "I sleep better when I'm with you." her cheeks flushed at her admission.

"Me too. You chase my demons away." he breathed out. "We just need to come clean with James." he dropped his forehead against hers, his thumbs smoothing over her cheeks.

"Don't remind me." Ava groaned, not looking forward to

confession with her brother.

"I'll be right there with you as your boyfriend." he chuckled at the startled look on her face. "It'll be okay, I promise." he pressed his lips to hers once more. "Come on, let's go home."

They strolled back down the winding path, his hand gripping hers with Blake's past behind them. His car came into view and she felt lighter and happier than she had done when they'd arrived.

Now, all they needed to do was explain their relationship to her brother and that thought alone filled her with trepidation.

Chapter Fifty-Two

Ava's heart thundered in her chest, and her stomach roiled as she stood on the doorstep of her home. Her breath stuttered in her lungs and her hands became clammy. She felt all the colour drain from her face when she heard James hollering at Katie from the hallway.

"Come on, baby girl." Blake whispered into her ear, sending shivers coursing down her spine. "I'm right here with you." his lips brushed against her lobe with each word before he pressed his lips beneath her ear. His hand cupping hers reassuringly, squeezing her fingers.

"Okay." she breathed out, sucking in a deep breath before shoving the front door open.

The scent of garlic wafted in the air and the warmth of the home chased away the cold October evening. Ava's wide eyes searched the hallway before deciding to follow the scent of food to the kitchen. Pausing just inside the door, her lips stretched into a smile as James had his hand rubbing over Katie's small baby bump with adoration in his eyes. Ava stepped back and collided with Blake's hard chest.

"No, come on." Blake whispered, giving her a gentle push into the kitchen. His presence was reassuring behind her.

"James." her voice was low and unsure as she walked into the kitchen.

"Hey squirt." James smiled. "Didn't think you'd be home for tea." he cocked his head to the side, his smile faltering as Blake stepped into the room behind her.

"Hmm, well..." she twisted her fingers together. "I sort of wanted you to...uh...erm..." her green eyes fluttered towards Blake's dark eyes, seeking help. She didn't know how to tell him she was in love with his best friend.

"What Ava is trying to say." Blake stepped around her, draping his arm across her shoulders and pulling her close to his body. "I'm the mystery man." he finished, his spine going rigid, and she knew he was preparing himself for the torrent of abuse from his best friend.

"Finally!" Katie exclaimed, clapping her hands on James' shoulders before he could take a step. "Isn't this great?" Katie looked at James, her smile wide, but Ava could see her brother shaking with rage.

"You?" he spat vehemently, moving Katie's hands from his shoulders. "You're the one who has done nothing but upset my sister?" he took a step towards Blake, but Katie quickly cut off his steps and placed her hand on his chest.

"That's not true, James." Ava spoke and was proud that her voice didn't shake. "He's loved me." she continued, taking a step toward her brother. Katie moved to the side, clasping his hand in hers. "I know he's your best friend, James, but I love him, too." her voice was gentle as she stopped in front of him.

James looked like she had slapped him. His green eyes narrowed into slits, his chest expanded in a deep inhale, and his hands clenched into fists.

"James, come on." Blake's voice was rough as he stared at his best friend. "I never planned for this to happen and you know that after Candice that I could never trust my heart with another." his words hit Ava and made her chest ache for him. "But Ava, she broke through and made me a happier, better person for it." he continued, his hands landing on Ava's shoulders as he pulled her back into his chest. "I won't ever apologise for the way Ava makes me feel, James, but I will apologise for lying to you these past six months." his voice held a determined, hard edge that had James stepping forward.

"You're the reason why I came home more times than not to find her crying." James spat the words like they tasted bitter on his tongue. "You're the reason she thought she wasn't good enough, and what? You just expect me to accept that you're the right choice for my sister?" his voice was low, dangerous and Ava could feel the panic welling within her.

"James, please." her words died on her tongue as James pinned her with a hard gaze.

"Don't even get me started on you." he spat with a twist of his lips. "You should have walked away from him the first time he fucked you over instead you kept going back for more, just like all the rest of them." the moment his words were out, she felt it like a slap to the face which made white, hot anger flow through her body.

"James, stop acting like this!" Ava blared at him, shocking Katie, who took a step back. "You're not my dad and you certainly aren't the brother I thought you was." she continued, her voice getting louder as she took a step towards him. She felt Blake's hand tighten on her, but she shrugged it off. "Let me tell you this, dear old big brother." she jabbed her finger in his chest. "It's okay for you to fuck around and knock up my best friend, but not me, huh? It's okay for you to get your happily ever after, but not me, huh? And it's certainly okay for you to pass judgement on my love life but nobody can with yours, huh?" she continued jabbing her finger in his chest with every word spoken. "Now James, I always loved that you took care of me, loved that you protected me and loved the fact that I had the best brother anyone could ask for; but if I'd have known this was how it would all turn out when I found someone that

I wanted to spend the rest of my life with, I'd have walked away from this house and you." she saw the hurt and betrayal on his face but she didn't care. "Just like I'm going to right now." with that, she turned on her heel and bolted for the stairs.

Blinking back the tears, Ava began throwing clothes haphazardly into her suitcase. Her mind was at war with the word vomit she had spewed at James. She knew that she'd hurt him, she saw it written all over his face but she was angry at him. Angry that he couldn't be happy for her and for his best friend who had been dealt the shittiest hand anyone could have.

She was also angry that with herself for accepting his relationship with Katie without a second thought. Angry that she was so happy for him to have his second chance at happiness when he couldn't bring himself to be the same for her, for Blake.

"Hey." Katie stood inside her bedroom door with her hand resting against her bump as Ava whirled around and pinned her with a death stare.

"If you're here to vouch for James, I don't want to hear it." the anger in her voice was palpable as Katie raised her hands in mock surrender.

"Oh, please." she huffed with a slight shake of her head. "He's one stubborn man, but he does love you and he cares about you." Katie walked further into the room as Ava shook her head. "He's just shocked at the moment, but he'll come around." Ava held her hand up to silence her best friend, tilting her head slightly as she listened to the deafening silence.

"You left Blake downstairs with James?" Ava asked, her eyes wide in fear as Katie nodded. "Alone! Are you kidding me!" she continued, quickly throwing her toiletries into the suitcase before zipping it closed.

"Ava, he's okay." Katie tried to reassure her, but she shook her head. "James won't do anything stupid." Ava cut her eyes to her.

"No, you didn't see what he did to Nathan when he got the wrong end of the stick." she hauled the suitcase from the bed. "There's a reason you know why Nathan won't speak to me." she continued, wheeling the suitcase across her bedroom. "And that reason is James and his stupid fists."

"I know, but he did try to force himself on you." Katie tried to defend James.

"Yeah, but Blake already saved me that day." Ava blew out a breath of frustration. "Look, I know you love James but I can't have you justifying his actions, right now." she sighed as she began thumping the suitcase downstairs with loud bangs. "I just need to leave." she finished the moment her eyes landed on Blake's dark ones, smiling up at her from the bottom of the stairs.

"Ready?" he cocked his head slightly towards the kitchen, making Ava furrow her eyebrows. "Go say bye to James." he took her suitcase from her and set it by the front door. "I'll be right here when you've finished."

Shaking her head, Ava stomped through the hallway and stopped short as her eyes landed on James, holding a bag of frozen peas to his cheek. Before she could turn around, his voice stopped her.

"I'm sorry." James gritted out, wincing as he placed the bag lower on his jaw. "I shouldn't have spoken to you like that." he continued, his eyes watching her as she slumped in the chair opposite him.

"What happened?" she asked, gesturing to his face.

"Blake." he chuckled as she gasped with her hand flying to her mouth, wincing as he shook his head. "He always did know how to deal with my temper." the laugh was bittersweet. "He didn't like the way I spoke to you either, and gave me a kind reminder." he moved the frozen bag from his face as he sucked in a deep breath. "Are you happy, squirt?" he asked, his eyes unwavering as he watched her.

"I am happy, just like you are." she gave him a sad smile. "Blake deserves to be happy, just like you do." her voice was gentle as her hand grasped his free one across the table.

"Then why have you been upset?" James asked, placing the frozen bag back on his cheek, which covered the swelling. Ava sighed, closing her eyes briefly.

"A miscommunication." she breathed out. "I thought his son was in my class." she sucked in a deep breath. "And that he was married."

"He finally told you about Candice and George?" the look of sadness filled his entire face as she nodded. "I'm glad he doesn't like anyone speaking about them, but I'm glad he's told you." James squeezed her hand. "I'm glad you're happy, just don't kiss him in front of me." James screwed his face up in distaste, making Ava laugh.

"I can't promise that, just like you can't promise me the same." "I definitely won't be kissing Blake." he barked out a laugh at her horrified expression. "Don't worry, I know what you mean." his lips pulled into a smile and her gaze softened. "So, you're moving out too?"

"Yeah, I want to be with him." her eyes cast down towards the table as her lips curved into a smile. "And I think you'll need the room once the baby is here."

"Hmm." he released her hand and rubbed the back of his neck. "Just don't take any of his bullshit, you're a strong woman and he needs that in his life. He needs someone who isn't afraid to go up against him every once in a while." he cocked his head to the side for a long moment. "Just don't tell him I told you."

"Promise." she whispered, standing and giving him a brief hug. "It'll be our secret." James wrapped his arms around her in a crushing hug.

"You best get going before Katie tries to make you stay for tea." she watched him quickly swipe his fingers over his eyes, dislodging the sting of tears that had gathered.

"See you later, James." she gave him one last squeeze before she turned on her heel and walked back to Blake.

Chapter Fifty-Three

Ava had spent the last hour unpacking her suitcase, smiling as she hung some of her clothes beside Blake's in the walk-in closet. She shook her head and wondered what his thoughts would be as she deposited her make-up and jewellery on the immaculate dresser. She looked across the expanse of the closet that looked like it was more lived in rather than the show house she'd come to love. The laugh bubbled out of her mouth before she could stop it.

"What's got you laughing?" Blake husked out as he wrapped his arms around her and resting his chin atop of her head. His bare chest pressed against her back.

"Nothing." she couldn't stop the giggle.

"Hmm." he moved his head until his stubble scraped against her ear. "Does it have something to do with us living together?" his voice was low as he asked, making her shiver.

"I don't think you're going to like how much I'll clutter your space up." her teeth sunk into her bottom lip as his lips pressed against her jaw.

"I hope you fill this house with everything that means something to you." his lips trailed towards her ear in a slow pass of flesh. "I want us to make this our home." he whispered, his words touching her in a way she never expected, before pressing a kiss beneath her ear. "Come, deserts ready."

The soft scrape of his sweatpants against her bare thigh had goosebumps prickling her skin as he sat beside her at the black granite dining table. Blake had placed a bowl of mixed fruit and melted chocolate between them, along with two glasses of wine.

"Here." his voice was low, holding a plump chocolate covered strawberry to her lips. Their eyes locked as she parted her lips and he carefully eased it into her mouth. His pupils dilated when her lips closed. The feel of the cold fruit sliding against her lips as his hand pulled back slowly caused her eyes to flutter.

"Hmm." she moaned as her tongue darted across her lips, removing the juice and chocolate with one swipe. His eyes flicking from her eyes to her mouth, watching every move she made.

"Those sounds make me so hard." he whispered, inching closer until they were a breath apart.

His finger dipped into the melted chocolate before slowly running his finger across her parted lips. Her heart hammered against her chest, her breath hitched in her throat, and her eyes fluttered closed. His tongue licked across her lips, a shudder took over her and a delicate moan escaped her parted lips. The corners of his mouth turned up in a devilish smile that had her stomach clenching and heat pooling in her core as he pulled away.

Ava gripped the glass of wine between both hands and brought it to her lips, tipping the wine into her mouth. Blake's long finger gently touched the side of her neck, slowly trailing over her throbbing pulse, making her gasp at the touch.

Blake quickly seized the glass from her, placing it back on the table. His large hand cupped the back of her head, his chest pressing against her arm as her head moved to the side. Blake's sinful tongue licked up the column of her throat.

"Blake." she groaned his name, her eyes closed as his tongue reached her lips. Swiping along the plump flesh once.

"You taste so fucking good." he breathed against her lips. "I can't get enough." his pupils were blown wide when he sat back and the predatory gleam she saw in their depths heightened her desire.

"Hmm." she hummed before her lips curved into a sultry smile. "My turn." she whispered.

Her finger dipping into the chocolate before slowly running her finger across his collarbone. She heard his breathing deepen as she inched closer and the first swipe of her tongue across his flesh had him groaning low in the back of his throat. The second swipe of her tongue had his hand fisting in her hair and the third had him crushing his lips to hers. Hard and demanding. His tongue was a solid muscle as he thrust it between her parted lips, sweeping, tasting, owning every inch of her mouth.

Ripping his mouth from hers, they were both panting harsh breaths and as he stood, his hands gripped her hips in a brutal hold before he hoisted her up onto the table. The coolness of the granite against the back of her thighs had her shivering. His eyes bore into hers as he slowly brushed the satin nightdress up her thighs. The fabric whispering against her flesh, causing goosebumps to erupt.

"Lay down, baby girl." he husked out and his gaze darkened as she complied. She heard him suck in a breath as wetness seeped from her. "So fucking wet." he groaned, and she watched him dip his fingers back into the chocolate before she felt the warmth of the liquid slithering across her folds.

The moment his tongue flicked against her clit, Ava bucked on a low moan. Blake's fingers curved around her thighs, pushing them further apart. His tongue licking a line directly to her opening, gathering the chocolate and her arousal on his tongue before he loomed over her. Pressing his lips to hers a moment before the burst of sweetness of the chocolate and the slight acidic taste of her arousal joined her taste buds. She swirled her tongue around his, sucking the taste of her from his tongue, and their combined groans of satisfaction filled the space between their lips as he pulled back.

Blake swirled his tongue once around her engorged clit. Ava moaned, her fingers tangling in his hair. Parting her folds with his tongue, he zig-zagged up her centre in slow, deliberate movements. His groan vibrated through her core, and her hips undulated against his mouth. His tongue circling her throbbing, engorged clit relentlessly, pulling moans of pleasure from her. The tight ball was building with every flick of his tongue against her clit, juices gathering at her opening. Her thighs shook, her breathing was hard pants.

Blake's tongue slithered down her centre, swirling around her opening before thrusting inside of her. His groan vibrated against her, which caused more wetness to seep from her. He continued to thrust his tongue inside of her. The wet slide of muscle against her inner folds had her grip on his hair tightening and her hips grinding down on his mouth.

"Blake." Ava moaned loudly as his tongue thrust into her pussy. "Oh!" she ground her hips against his tongue. "Fuck!" she hissed, his teeth nipping her tender pussy.

Blake grazed his teeth down the length of her pussy, slowly. His fingers digging into her thighs as he held her in place. Swirling his tongue around her clit before sucking it into his mouth, hard. A deep pressure building inside of her had her moaning louder.

Blake sucked her clit, his teeth grazing gently over the throbbing bundle. Juices gathering at her opening a mere moment before his tongue swept them into his mouth over and over. The ball of pure fire and heat was building faster, bigger, and it stole her breath.

Her hips moving of their own accord, her mouth open with moan after lustrous moan, her body arched, her fingers numb from the death grip on his hair. Deep inside her, the liquid fire and heat swelled tightly, the ball expanded, and she exploded on a loud scream.

Blake's primal growl rocked Ava to her very core as her orgasm splashed against his chin and chest. The long groan of pure satisfaction poured from him as he lapped up the copious amounts of liquid. Ava rode her orgasm until she collapsed against his legs. Tremors twitching through her muscles. Her breath ragged.

"I want to fuck you in the bath." he husked out, pulling her until she was sitting on the table.

He scooped her up in his arms, her shaking thighs wrapped around his waist and her arms around his neck. Powerful strides ate up the stairs and the expanse of the bedroom until they reached the bathroom. Carefully setting her down on her own two feet, she licked over her lips as her gaze travelled over the thick, long hard length of his cock outlined in the sweatpants.

Blake flicked the taps of the jacuzzi bathtub and poured soap into the water as it filled. He turned to face her with a wicked smile curved onto his lips.

"Nightgown off." his words were laced with command that had stoked embers of her desire.

He kept his dark gaze on her as she slowly inched the satin nightgown down her body and she watched him breathe deeply in slow, rhythmic breaths. His fingers hooked the waistband of his sweatpants, and she sucked in a sharp breath as he shoved them to the floor. Their eyes remained locked on one other and the minutes seemed endless until he turned his back to her and shut the taps off.

Ava watched him climb into the bathtub, his dark eyes snaring her as he held his hand out for her to take. The warmth of the water against her calves had her moaning slightly. His arms snaked around her waist as he gently sunk them both into the bath. The bubbles snaking around them and the slight groan as the water enveloped him made her shudder.

Blake eased her hips up and the cool air licked against her warm, wet breasts, she leant forward and felt the blunt, silky head of his cock rub against her entrance. Ava rocked her hips gently against the tip. His arm tightened around her waist, halting her movements. His cock slowly easing into her tight opening. His jaw clenched and the low guttural moan filled the room.

Inch by glorious inch, Ava was filled with Blake's cock until her ass touched his groin. She felt stretched and full to capacity, but that didn't stop her greedy pussy from pulsating. Blake's hands splayed across her stomach, slowly inching their way up until they captured her breasts.

His fingers pinched her nipples lightly before he smoothed his palm across the hardened peaks as her hips ground down on him.

Ava raised up on her knees, the thick column of his cock dragging exquisitely against her inner walls. A light moan fell from her parted lips. Her heart thundering against her chest, her nerve endings firing off more pleasure through her body as she slowly sank back down.

His tongue trailed the length of her neck, his fingers circled her nipples as she rose slowly. Her pussy fluttered, his cock throbbed, and his teeth grazed her shoulder. The tight grip on his cock was like a vise as she sunk back down hard.

"Fuck!" Blake hissed, his hands gripping her hips and raising her back up and thrusting his hips up to meet her descent. Their hips clashed deeper, and she cried out in ecstasy. Water sloshed over the edge of the bathtub with every thrust of their hips.

Slamming his cock deep inside of her. Her pussy contracted, juices leaked from her as she ground down before raising back up. Blake slammed her back down, over and over.

The room filled with combined moans and groans of pleasure, the sounds of their bodies meeting in wet slaps. Her body was careening towards another explosion. White hot waves overtook her body, her muscles clenched tightly, her head thrown forward and his teeth bit down on her neck as the dam broke and her orgasm crested in an arc of pure pleasure.

"Blake!" she screamed as her pussy gripped onto his cock tightly. Liquid rushed from her in hot splashes against his groin.

"I. Love. You." Blake bit out and punctuated each word with a slam of his hips and buried himself as deep as he could, spilling hot jets of cum inside her. The grip on her hips wouldn't leave a bruise as he stilled her movements and their harsh breaths filling the room.

Blake's arms banded around Ava's trembling body and without removing his cock, he sunk them lower into the warm, soapy water. His lips peppering kisses down her neck, his tongue soothing the bite marks on her shoulders.

"I love you too, Blake." she whispered, a smile on her lips and her fingers laced with his across her stomach.

"Hmm, not calling me Syn today?" he asked as his tongue flicked against her pulse.

"No, only when you're being a dirty boy." she husked out, making him groan in pure satisfaction.

"I don't know what I did to deserve you, Ava Asherton." he murmured against her ear. Her heart swelled with his words.

"You lived through hell to have a second chance." she whispered right back. "And I'm glad you let me love you, Blake Sinclair." his lips pressed against her temple as a certain peace washed over both of them.

Ava didn't know where the future was going to take them,

but she knew without doubt that she was never letting her *Delectable Syn* go.

Epilogue

Two Years Later

Blake was sat in the high-backed, black leather chair with his computer bleeping loudly, signalling that his next patient had arrived. His dark brown eyes glanced over the patient file but nothing determined the reason for an appointment, which made his eyebrows furrow as this appointment had been rushed through the system.

Sighing loudly into the sterile room, he brushed his fingers through his dark hair before pressing the 'call' button on the computer that will light up the television screens in the waiting room with the call to attend his office.

The soft knock on the door had him sitting straighter in his chair as he took a deep breath to settle his wayward thoughts.

"Come in." he called out over his shoulder, not bothering to look as the door swished open slowly.

He heard the delicate footfalls of heels against the tiled floor before the whoosh of air wafted that intoxicating scent towards him. His lips curved into a small smile as memories flooded through him. It felt like it was only yesterday that he'd first taken a lungful of the scent. Blackberries, wisteria, and jasmine filled his nostrils as he dragged a deep breath in. The scent almost stole his concentration. But he couldn't let that happen, he needed to stay focused, needed to listen to his patient and needed to diagnose as quickly as humanly possible before he lost his control.

Watching in his peripheral vision the tight black pencil skirt clinging to delicious, curvy hips as they swayed with each step before she sat on the plastic blue chair he knew was uncomfortable. The scent of her perfume was causing him to his hold on his control. He looked once more at the surname on his screen, and his lips twitched.

The moment he turned his chair to face his patient fully, he almost growled low in the back of his throat. The stunningly beautiful woman before him with her long brown hair cascading past her shoulders in waves, her green eyes framed with the longest lashes he'd ever seen, her pouty lips painted a faint pink colour accentuating her cupid's bow. The swell of her breasts tightly encased in the pale pink blouse but as his gaze roamed lower, his cock twitched at the sight of her generous thighs where her pencil skirt had ridden up exposing the thigh-highs and the delicate strap of the suspenders.

Fucking hell, this was going to be the hardest appointment he'd ever had.

Swiping his tongue over his lips, the edge of his stubble scraping against his tongue before his dark brown eyes stared into her green ones.

"What brings you here today?" he asked, trying to keep a tight hold on the thumping lust that was coursing through his body.

"I think." she began, her voice was a sultry lilt which made his heart beat a little faster and his cock began to swell in the confines of his tailored trousers. "I might have an ear infection." she finished, her eyes never leaving his.

"Alright." his voice was a little gruffer than usual as he tried to dampen down the desire he felt. "What makes you think you have an ear infection?" he asked, smiling slightly as he watched her delicate hand touch the side of her face. Her fingertips grazing over a tender spot, wincing slightly.

"It's painful here." she responded, before he tracked the movement of her fingertips moving lower until they reached her jaw. "The pain travels in a deep thrum and into my neck."

"Hmm." was all he could muster. His palms were sweating, his cock was inflating at an alarming rate and his pulse was beating wildly. Turning abruptly in his chair, he picked up the otoscope before standing to his full six foot three inches and made the few steps until he was standing beside her chair. "I'll look in your good ear first." he almost hissed out as his cock rubbed painfully against his zip.

He watched in rapt fascination as her delicate hands gathered her long waves and swished them over her left shoulder, making her scent cloak him. *Intoxicating.* The thought pulsed through him for the briefest of moments before he inserted the speculum into the ear canal. The light on the otoscope helping him see a perfect, healthy ear canal with no inflammation or buildup of wax. His heart rate had increased to dangerous levels as he watched her swish her hair back over her right shoulder. His large hand gently tilted her head a little more than necessary as his dark eyes landed on the small outline of a heart tattoo behind her ear. His thumb gently caressed the tattoo, before he could stop himself. He looked into her ear canal. Again, no inflammation or buildup of wax.

"Both ears are clear." he confirmed, placing the otoscope back inside the case. He strode across the office to the little sink and washed the sweat off of his hands. With his back to her, he asked. "What do you do for a living?"

"I'm a safeguarding officer." the sultry voice had fluid leaking from his cock.

"Sounds interesting and heartbreaking." he acknowledged, drying his hands, deliberately slowly as he willed his cock to deflate with no such luck.

"It can be heartbreaking, but it's rewarding." he turned at the precise moment her lips parted in the brightest smile he'd seen and it made his stomach tighten.

"Hmm, I bet." he murmured as he stood before her. His thighs pressed close so he fit between her parted thighs. "Look up." his voice still low as he looked down into her green eyes, his fingers lightly caressing the sides of her face and down into her jaw. He heard the sharp intake of breath and felt her stuttered pulse as he grazed the slender column of her throat. He watched her eyelids flutter for a fraction of a second before she caught herself. "Perfect, look straight ahead." his voice sounded strained even to his own ears. His cock pulsed against the zip, begging to be let free. Her mouth was in direct line to take his cock. All it would take was one small thrust, and he'd be buried in that succulent mouth of hers.

Shaking his head to dispel the thought, he continued the light caress of her neck, her jaw and up towards her ears. His dark gaze watching every flinch as he touched a painful spot on her left side.

"Is that painful?" he asked.

"Yes." the moment she spoke, he felt the jaw joint dislocate before snapping back into place with the movement of her mouth.

He was certain what the problem was, but he couldn't bring himself to remove his fingers, couldn't resist another slow exploration and certainly couldn't help watching her ample breasts straining against the buttons of her blouse with every rise and fall of her breaths.

"Well." he began, reluctantly removing his hands from her flesh. "You have Temporomandibular disorder." he watched as confusion settled on her beautiful face, her mouth twisting slightly. "Commonly known as TMD, inflammation of the jaw joints." he confirmed.

"Oh, what's that caused by?" she asked as she folded her hands in her lap.

"The joint in your jaw is dislocating every time you open your mouth, and it's clicking back into place, which has caused the inflammation." he explained. "You need to rest your mouth for a few days, nothing too strenuous." his eyes twinkled as he spoke, a sinful smile tugging his lips.

"Where's the fun in that Doctor Synclair?" the sultry voice had taken on a wicked edge as she smirked. The way she said doctor had desire sweeping through his entire being as he imagined her screaming that one word as he fucked her hard, fast and unrelenting.

"Take two ibuprofen for the pain." he tried to regain his professionalism before he acted on his primal instinct. "After a hearty meal." he smiled as his eyes devoured her luscious curves, slowly raking over every-fucking-inch of her body.

"Thank you." she breathed out, standing before him. Her tongue licked over her bottom lip. "Doctor Synclair."

Blake's hand shot out and cupped her jaw, his thumb caressing her cheek as he leaned closer. Dragging in a deep breath of her intoxicating scent as his nose trailed up her neck and his hand slowly moved to her nape until their lips were a breath apart.

"You make me so fucking hard." he growled against her lips. "You naughty, dirty, slutty, whore." he continued before swiping his tongue across her lips. The taste of her had him groaning. "We have five minutes left." he muttered as he quickly spun her until her back was against his front. "Bend over the chair, my dirty whore." he husked out, unbuttoning his pants and quickly freeing his aching cock.

Blake gently pulled her thighs apart, hooking his fingers around her red lace panties until they were in his fist as his gave them a quick, hard yank. The growl that vibrated through him as the fabric snapped sent a shudder down her spine. The heat from her pussy almost seared him, making his cock throb deep and hard in response.

"Open wide." he husked out before stuffing her mouth with her panties. "You can't be trusted to keep quiet." his words and husky tone had her moaning.

She whimpered as he sunk an inch into her tight heat. Her hips moving towards his, trying to gain more of him. She panted, grinding her hips again until he snapped his hips forward in a brutal thrust. His cock nestled deep inside of her slick heat.

A hiss leaving his mouth as her pussy tried to clamp around him. Tried to pull him ever deeper inside of her. His hands gripped her hips as he slammed into her, ripping a deep , muffled moan from her throat. Her pussy contracted, juices leaked from her before he slammed back in with a severity that had her hands gripping the chair. Blake slammed into her over and over again. Pulling muffled moans from her every time he bottomed out inside her.

The room filled with the sounds of their bodies meeting. He felt her muscles clench tightly around his cock as she threw her head back aching perfectly for him. His teeth bit down on her neck as the dam broke and her orgasm crested.

Her muffled scream and her pussy gripping onto his cock tightly had him burring himself as deep as he could, spilling hot jets of cum inside her. The grip on her hips wouldn't leave a bruise, as he stilled her movements and their harsh breaths filling the room. His lips peppering kisses down her neck, his tongue soothing the bite marks on her neck.

"I love you, Mrs Synclair." he whispered against her neck.

"Love you too, Mister Synclair." she breathed out as she pulled back, righting her skirt. "You haven't forgotten that we're babysitting for James and Katie tonight?" she asked, raising her eyebrows.

"No, I haven't." he assured her as he cupped her cheeks. "I just don't understand how we are looking after Amelia again. I was hoping to have you all to myself."

"It's their anniversary, Blake." she laughed as he pouted.

"I know, but still, we've only just come back from Argentina." he smiled at the memory of their honeymoon. "I'll be a little late tonight, I'm dropping the wedding pictures off at Maureen's as promised."

"Okay." the loud bleeping of his computer made her jump. "If she has any lemon drizzle cake." he watched her tongue flick over her lips.

"Yes, I'll bring some with me." he pressed his lips to hers briefly. "You better go, before I get in trouble." he winked at her before stepping back, away from his little temptress.

"Okay, bye." she smiled and yelped as his hand connected with her luscious ass. "Now I'm annoyed that we're babysitting." she pouted, which had him throwing his head back on a laugh.

"Love you, baby girl." he folded his arms across his chest to stop himself from grabbing his wife again.

"Love you too, Syn." she blew him a kiss before the door whooshed and swished shut.

Fuck, he loved Ava so much!

Printed in Great Britain
by Amazon